THE PICTISH PRINCESS

..and other stories from before
there was a Scotland

Dolan Cummings

Orual Press

ISBN
Paperback: 978-1-7394192-0-2
Ebook: 978-1-7394192-1-9

Cover illustration by the author, freely adapted from historical sources.

CONTENTS

PROLOGUE

Once upon a time, there was no Scotland. The people originally known as the Scots came from Ireland, or at least they spoke a form of Gaelic like the Irish, so we'll call them Gaels to avoid confusion. At first they lived only on the Western fringe of what we now call Scotland. That part of the country is as much water as it is land, so the Gaels of Dalriada were fine sailors. Much of the rest of the country was peopled by the Picts, who spoke their own language, lost to us now. The name Picts was given to them by the Roman invaders who fought them on and off for centuries before withdrawing from the British isles. The Romans said they painted their bodies with blue paint. Maybe they did, but they did not call themselves Picts. When they felt the need to call themselves anything, they sometimes called themselves the People of the Designs, because of the designs they carved on stones and maybe painted on themselves.

The Gaels and the Picts were not the only people living in what the Romans had called Caledonia, and would one day become Scotland. Long after the Romans left, the southeast corner of the country was settled by the Angles, who came from the northern European mainland, and whose British lands, known as Northumbria, also stretched into what is now England. Indeed, they would give that country its name, but before there was a Scotland, there was no Angle-land either. The Northumbrians did, however, speak a very old form of English. Finally, in the southwest of what is now Scotland, lived Britons whose ancestors had lived on the island that now bears their name since long before the Romans or the Gaels or the Angles, but probably not the Picts. Their language was a bit like Welsh, since the Welsh are descended from the same people, though by this time the lands of the Britons were separated by Angles and Saxons who had settled throughout much of what is now England.

So before there was a Scotland, there were four different nations in the land, speaking four different languages. Sometimes they fought, sometimes they formed alliances. And even within each of the four nations, there were different groupings and little kingdoms and constant struggles over power and land. One thing they all had in common – just about – was religion, a new religion. So new, in fact, that it was not accepted by everyone, and when people spoke in their various languages of 'the old gods', it was not always clear whether they meant the false gods they had once wrongly believed in, or real gods that might still somehow matter. And when they spoke of the new religion, the most educated people in each nation spoke Latin, the language of the Romans, which was now the language of the Christian church. A fifth language that did not belong to any of the four nations, but whose church said it belonged to them all. Or that they all belonged to it. One of those.

What follows is the story of some of the people who lived before there was a Scotland, and who sometimes fought and sometimes formed alliances, and who wondered about the gods and about God.

PART ONE

The Year of Our Lord Seven Hundred and Something

CHAPTER 1: MORGAN'S BABY

Morgan was gathering firewood when she noticed the basket floating on the White Water, a little river that ran close by her home in the boggy lowland woods. It was already dusk, and she was rushing to gather enough wood for the fire before the darkness took over, but her eye had been drawn to the last of the light playing on the water, and then to the mysterious patch of darkness made by the basket. She felt a tingle of anticipation before she could articulate why. Slowly it came to her that this could be the moment she had been waiting for. Waiting, with a combination of dread and excitement, since she had come of age as a woman. The basket was just the right size to contain a baby. By the time she had pulled it to the river bank with the help of a branch, it was no longer just to see what was in it, as if she had no idea. It was to see whether or not her baby was in it.

Morgan had been found as a baby by her own mother in similar circumstances, wrapped in a blanket under a bush. And her mother before her, the same kind of thing. As far as she knew, this was how all the women in her family became mothers. Other women did it differently, she knew. They took seed from their menfolk and grew their babies in their bellies like the animals. She did not envy them. It was a blessing to be given a baby as a virgin. Had not the Blessed Virgin Mary found her baby in a manger? The baby that was God. And there was an older story, too, about the prophet Moses being found as a baby in a basket in a river, just like this one. And yes, there it was: Morgan's baby.

Morgan's baby began to cry as she hauled the basket from the water, and was not comforted when she plonked her bundle of firewood on top of it, though she took care not to scratch its face, the only part of it that was not carefully wrapped up. It was that or take the baby out of the basket and add it to the bundle, and it was a good basket. She picked it up, heavy with its double cargo, and heaved it home. It was a short distance, but Morgan had to stop twice to rest. She might now be a mother, but she was not a big lass.

Her own mother was anxious when Morgan returned in pitch darkness, but she thought better of chiding the girl when she realised what she had brought home. Wordlessly, they removed the firewood from the basket and replenished the pile by the fireplace, and then turned to the baby. Morgan's mother picked it up, still crying, and brought it closer to the fire for a better look. 'A bonnie thing,' she said, and then handed it back to her daughter. 'Well?'

Morgan took the baby and sat on one of the two stools by the fire. Her mother sat on the other and watched as she carefully unwrapped the little package. Morgan took her time as she got used to the weight of the baby in her arms, fearful of dropping it as she unwound the fabric, which was unusually soft and fine. Finally, the baby was naked.

'It's a boy!' Morgan said, and her mother clapped happily, not so much because she preferred a boy to a girl as because every detail about her new grandchild was a joy.

'I'll call him Moses,' Morgan added, and explained where she'd found him.

'Very good,' said her mother. 'Moses it is.' She watched her grandson attentively. 'He must be hungry, and it will be many days before you can feed him.'

She spoke from experience, of course, and knew how to make animals' milk drinkable for a new-born. As she set about mixing some goat's milk with a concoction from her herb cabinet, spitting generously into the mixture, Morgan felt reassured to have her own mother's guidance and support. She felt no tingling in her breasts, but she knew something of the kind would not be far off.

Moses quietened when his mother held his naked body close to hers, though her clothes were rough. 'Look at this fabric,' she said, showing her mother the baby's fine swaddling clothes.

Her mother felt the material and made appreciative noises. Then she turned to the basket. 'Nice basket too.'

Mother and daughter exchanged looks, and then Morgan gestured that her mother could examine it further while she had her hands full. She was unnerved by the realisation that, despite her dependence on her mother's help with the baby, she had suddenly grown in authority as mother to Moses and, by extension, proprietor of the basket.

Morgan's mother picked up the basket and sat it on her lap to examine it, but its weight without the baby had already told her there was more to discover. She pushed aside some rougher fabric lining the bottom, and gasped. She reached in and withdrew a handful of metal fragments. 'Silver!' she whispered.

Morgan leaned in to examine the treasure in her mother's hand, causing Moses to grumble in annoyance. It really was silver: scraps of softly shining metal, some of them recognisable as bent-over fragments of old silverware, plates and spoons. There were even a few coins. Morgan had never seen anything like it. Her mother dropped it back in the basket and pulled out another handful from the haul.

'No wonder it was heavy,' Morgan said.

'What a lucky baby!' her mother said.

Morgan looked at Moses suspiciously, slightly afraid rather than elated. Still, this was good news, whatever it might portend. She and her baby were rich.

CHAPTER 2: CUTHBERT AND CWENBURH

Cuthbert and Cwenburh were born unlucky. Their mother died in childbirth, and their father was poor. Neither misfortune was especially unusual, but the way the twins were separated certainly was. They were still babies when their father had put them down at the edge of the field where he was working, a patch roughly hewn out of the thick forest that covered most of the land in those days. They were wrapped up against the cold, his precious little lambs. But the promise of fresh meat had been too much to resist for a passing eagle, which had swooped down and gripped Cwenburh in its talons, and carried her off, even as her poor father ran vainly after it, trying to scare it into dropping its prize. No chance. The child was gone.

After that, Cuthbert's luck did not much improve, unless you count not being abducted by a hungry eagle. He survived infancy and began working with his father. The work was hard. Life was hard. Their little part of Lothian, the land of the northern Northumbrians, was mercifully untouched by the wars and skirmishes that always seemed to be raging somewhere or other around them. But as Cuthbert grew into a young man, he began to wonder if war might not be so bad. He had no affection for the land, unlike his father, who had fought for it like his own father and grandfather before him. They had fought to take it from the people who had lived there before, and fought to keep it ever since. Maybe you had to fight for land to feel true affection for it.

Cuthbert was barely a man when his father died, and he had no other family. When a neighbouring farmer offered him a pittance to take over the working of his land, Cuthbert took the pittance and decided to seek his fortune on the battlefield. The only things he took with him from the squat hovel that had been his home all his life were the clothes he wore and the long, sharp dagger, or seax, that had been his father's and his grandfather's before him. The local thane had called for fighting men a year before, and Cuthbert supposed the offer might still stand. He knew that his great grandfather had been killed at the Battle of the Loch of the Herons, where the reckless King Ecgfrith had led his army in a bid to conquer the Picts. That had been a stupid notion, and the resulting defeat had been devastating to Northumbrian power in those parts. It was the Picts who were in the ascendant, and increasingly threatening all of their neighbours. Now the rumour was that the new king of the Northumbrians was preparing war on the Picts again, this time with the more limited aim of checking their power and consolidating his own. It seemed as noble a calling as any. And so Cuthbert found himself in a company of 30 or so men marching to the west to join more of their own countrymen as well as an army of Gaels, jointly to repel Pictish incursions.

Among the company, Cuthbert found two lads he'd known a little since childhood, Wilfrid and Alcuin. Wilfrid was a little older than Cuthbert and Alcuin, so he took it upon himself to look out for them and prepare them for the fighting to come. Not that he'd seen much action himself. They had little in the way of formal military training beyond sparring with one another or with a post set up for the purpose when they made camp. Alcuin was a fierce lad, however, and assured his new comrades that the secret of fighting was neither skill nor strength but sheer, bloody aggression. There's some truth in that, provided your opponent's lesser aggression is not supplemented by superior strength or skill. But the lads would learn that in due course.

The few days it took to march to the muster point passed in high spirits, despite the rough terrain, mostly through forest. For the first time in his life, Cuthbert was excited about what lay ahead. He had a feeling this campaign would be the making of him.

◆ ◆ ◆

Cwenburh's luck changed soon after she was taken by the eagle. Who knows how long it carried her or where it thought it was taking her, but it crossed the breadth of the country and was flying over the western sea when it finally lost its grip. Cwenburh plunged to her certain death, only she did not meet it. She landed in a fishing boat. Imagine the surprise of the boat's crew! This little bundle emerging from the sky, fluttering in the wind, before thwacking into the middle of their freshly landed catch. Cwenburh was rechristened that day: Lucky.

Lucky was taken to one of the littlest islands of Dalriada, where she was adopted into a fishing family. Like her long-lost brother, she too worked hard when she was old enough, but life was better for her than for Cuthbert, and she enjoyed a happy childhood. She grew into a real beauty and was widely admired, but she was a shy lass, and marriage was the last thing on her mind. Lucky spoke Gaelic, of course, like her adoptive people, never having learned the Northumbrian tongue spoken by her father and his people, so it was in Gaelic that she prayed every day. In Gaelic that she spoke to God.

In being adopted into a new family, Lucky had also been

adopted into a wider clan, and that was less unusual. The Chief often adopted new members into the clan, though they were usually young men of fighting age, or otherwise of use to him. Men like Cuthbert, in fact, seeking a better life and willing to pledge themselves to a powerful master who might give it to them. The Chief lived on another island, but when he visited theirs, he was lavished with hospitality and gifts quite beyond what the people could afford. Lucky prayed for him not to visit too often, and mostly it seemed to work.

God was less obliging when it came to fighting, which Lucky hated. The young men fought each other relentlessly, and it was often explained to Lucky that it was just as well, because they needed the practice. The men were regularly shipped off for a 'proper fight' with rival clans. In fact, Lucky was told she was lucky it was just the men. It was only within living memory that an Abbot of Iona had insisted on a Law of the Innocents throughout the Gaelic and even Pictish lands to protect women and children from the violence of war. But the name of the law was misleading. It was said that the real motivation was not so much to protect innocent women from violence as to prevent them from taking part in it. The Abbot's mother had witnessed a battle in Ireland with men and women on both sides, and been particularly shocked to see one woman thrust a reaping hook right through the ribcage of another. Some of the women on the island were pretty fierce too, but Lucky shied away from violence. She wondered why more people were not like the Abbot's mother.

Still, she had hope in her prayers. According to legend, Saint Columba himself had been a bloodthirsty warrior in Ireland, and had once single-handedly slaughtered three thousand men in battle. He had begun his mission to the Gaels over the sea as penance for his sins. Lucky prayed for others to repent like Saint Columba.

CHAPTER 3: THE BOY ON THE LOCH

The old man had lived all his life on the shore of this loch. Worked the land and fished the waters. Worked and loved and eaten and drunk and raised children and sung songs on the shore of this loch. It was his home and he knew the place better than anyone alive did, though it remained mysterious even to him. He had seen strange weather over the loch. Strange lights in the sky. He had seen strange men come and go, fought them or befriended them and gone on living on the shore of this loch. But he had never seen anything like what he had seen that morning.

It had been foggy, so at first he hadn't been able to make out what it was. But then it was unmistakeable: a boy. A boy, floating high above the water, seemingly sitting astride some kind of animal; the old man could not say what kind of animal, but the boy was plain and unmysterious except for the fact he was floating over the loch. He passed close enough to where the old man stood that he could see the expression on his face. The boy looked straight at him and laughed. The cheek of it. Then he had simply floated on, disappearing into the fog once more.

No one had believed the old man when he'd told them later that day. They said he was old and his eyesight could not be trusted. They said it had probably been a dream. People did not respect him as they once had. Oh, they were polite, even deferential to his years and experience, but they no longer took him seriously. Not the adults, at least. Actually, it was not that no one at all would believe him. There would be at least three exceptions: his young grandsons, Pyrdie and Pendrin and Peter. Most evenings, they gathered at his feet, often with the other children, and told them stories, some of them true stories. This evening he would tell them about the boy on the loch, and might or might not choose to embellish the story.

Some of the old man's stories were the same stories he had heard from his own grandfather when he was a boy. Others he had picked up since, either from first-hand experience or imbibed with drink round a fire. Sometimes he embellished those stories too. It depended what he felt like.

Often he told the children the story of how their people had been made from the very land they lived on. They were not like the foreigners to the south and west, who had come from across the sea nobody knew how long ago; it didn't matter. The foreigners were not *of* this land like their people. *Their* people had been here for as long as the mountains and the lochs, since God himself had forged the landscape and created them from the very same stuff to embellish it. To make it complete.

Their people continued God's work by carving on the stones he had left them, capturing the power and beauty of his animals and telling the stories of their own battles and other adventures, as well as carving abstract designs whose meanings were known only to themselves. That was why, when they had need to name themselves, their people called themselves not Picts but the People of the Designs. The old man had been a master carver in his time, but now his hands were old and withered and he no longer had the strength or steadiness for it. Now he carved stories with his tongue, so his children and grandchildren could put them in stone for their children and grandchildren.

It was true, though, that their people had not always

known God, had not always understood their origins and destiny as God's people. One stone on the mountainside told the story of how Saint Columba had come from the west, bringing the Gospel of Jesus Christ, and with it a wealth of other stories that made everything fall into place. So when Columba did battle with the druids to show that their old gods were no match for the one true God, the people could see that it was an echo of the contest between Moses and the magicians who had served Pharaoh.

The old man knew there was power of a kind in the old gods, and like Pharaoh's magicians, the druids had known how to harness it. Once upon a time, the druids had been the finest carvers among their people. They had used their skill in the service of the old gods until Columba came and showed them its proper purpose. A carving of a stag was still a carving of a stag, but it was no longer an idol to be revered, but an ornament to be enjoyed. Not a golden calf to be followed blindly in the wilderness, but a cherub on the Ark of the Covenant, a reminder of God's promises. Everything had fallen into place.

But the power of the old gods was no more than a distorted reflection of the glory of the true God. Worshipping the old gods made no more sense than trying to take venison from the carved image of a stag. There was no meat to be had there! The new religion made sense to the old man, and it comforted him to explain how everything fell into place. But the stories he carved with his tongue were not always as lifelike as those he had once carved with his hands. Not everyone was convinced by them. Some still craved the power of the old gods. But perhaps we'll meet them later. For now, the old man has a story to tell.

'I'll tell you what I saw this morning,' he began when the children had gathered round, though they had already heard the bare facts several times. 'I'll tell you what I *really* saw. Now, you've heard many tales about kelpies, haven't you?'

Pyrdie's ears perked up. He particularly liked kelpie

stories.

'You know how they appear as fine ponies, temping you to try and capture them so they can lure you towards the water. If you're foolish enough to touch them near the water, they'll take hold of you and drag you under to drown. But did you know that a man who captures a kelpie far enough away from the water becomes its master?'

This was indeed new to the children.

'And a kelpie master has more than a fine pony at his disposal.'

'He has a shapeshifter!' shouted Pyrdie.

'That's right,' said the old man. 'Nobody knows the kelpies' *true* shape, but they can appear not only as ponies, but as other beasts and even as men.'

'Yes, so they can seduce women!' said Pyrdie, but the other children shooshed him, because they found that kind of talk embarrassing, and the old man too said *those* tales were for when the children were older.

He continued: 'The kelpie master can command his kelpie to take any shape he chooses, and as long it's within its power to take that shape, it must obey. And that must include its true shape, which – apart from kelpie masters, as rare they are – no man has ever seen. Until this morning.'

The old man paused to let the children take it in. Pyrdie had gone quiet in contemplation, but Peter wanted clarification: 'The boy on the loch was a kelpie?'

'No,' said Pyrdie. 'He was *riding* a kelpie, wasn't he, grandfather?'

'I do believe he was,' said the old man. 'And I also believe I know who the boy was. The more I've thought about it over the course of the day, the more sure I am. That boy bore an uncanny resemblance to Prince Cargil.'

'Prince Cargil?' cried the children in unison..

'Prince Cargil,' the old man confirmed.

'But Prince Cargil has been gone for a hundred years,' said Pyrdie.

The old man laughed. 'Not quite that long,' he said, 'but it's true that it was a long time ago, when I was no more than a boy myself.'

'Then why isn't he an old man like you?' asked Peter.

'A good question,' said the old man, laughing again. 'And a puzzle, I will admit. But I have a theory, and it's a theory in the form of a story, which is the best kind.'

'Tell us the story,' said Peter.

'I will,' said the old man. 'Now, as you know, Prince Cargil was the son of King Uther, whose lands lay on the other side of the mountain,' he said, pointing across the loch at the big mountain. 'But when he died, his men refused to make Cargil king in his place, because they said a mere boy had not the strength to see off their enemies. So Cargil vowed to prove them wrong. He set off alone and vowed to return with a great prize to show his worthiness to be king. And, as you know, he was never seen again, and the mystery of what happened to him is the source of his fame to this day. Some say he was killed by a wolf or a bear. Some say he lacked courage after all, and ran off to live somewhere else where nobody knew he was supposed to be a king. And some say he was taken by a kelpie! Perhaps he saw a fine pony drinking from a loch or river, and thought that could be his prize, or the start of it, a fine pony to ride on his quest for glory. But perhaps that pony was a kelpie, and when he tried to capture it, the beast lured him into the water and drowned him. But there is *another* possibility.

'I realise now that Prince Cargil must indeed have encountered a kelpie, but the kelpie did not lure him into the water. The boy was too clever for that. Now, he couldn't have known what it was, but he had the sense to consider the possibility that the beast might not be what it seemed. So he lured the thing away from its watery home, and seized it there.'

'How did he do that?' demanded Pyrdie.

The old man hesitated, but only for a second 'He sang a song. He sang a beautiful song about a fair maiden, and the beast fell under his spell and followed him into a thick wood.

There, Cargil leapt onto the pony's back and clung on like a limpet to a rock. The beast would have reared up fearfully. It would have feinted this way and that trying to throw the boy. It would have brushed against trees to try to scrape him off. But Cargil clung fast and would not be shifted. Who knows how long boy and beast tussled in the wood? Perhaps the kelpie even changed its shape in an effort to unseat Cargil. That I can't say. But I do know that it failed. Eventually it gave up. It yielded to its new master. The boy triumphed. And then the kelpie will have given up its secrets. It will have shown Cargil its true shape, and more than that. Kelpies delight in bringing death to man. But they also have the power to offer life. *Eternal* life. That's why he looked no older when I saw him this morning than the day he left his people and disappeared.' The old man looked triumphant.

'That sounds like magic,' said Pendrin. 'I thought we didn't believe in that kind of thing.'

'We certainly do believe in everlasting life,' said the old man. 'And our Lord Jesus is more generous with it than any kelpie, as long as we end this life believing in him,' he added pointedly. Then he thought for a moment. 'I can't say how things stand between Prince Cargil and his maker, just that he's a kelpie master now.'

That seemed to satisfy Pendrin, and the old man went on to tell the story of what exactly Cargil and his kelpie had been up to on the loch that morning, but frankly it wasn't one of his best stories, so let's leave the old man and his grandsons for now, and see how Morgan is getting on.

CHAPTER 4: GOVAN

Within a couple of weeks of finding Moses, Morgan was able to feed him, and felt she was truly his mother. And, first things first, a Christian mother had to have her son baptised. That meant taking him to the holy town of Govan, at least a day's walk away. Morgan and her mother lived alone in the woods, and had few dealings with anyone else, but they visited Govan, or more often one of the local hamlets, once or twice a year to barter herbal concoctions for anything not furnished to them by the woods themselves. And it was only in Govan that Moses could be baptised by a priest. The church was not an ever-present part of life in those days and in those parts, even for folk less reclusive than Morgan and her mother. Larger settlements were sometimes visited by itinerant priests, but not the backwoods. Besides, Govan was a place of pilgrimage, and Morgan would enjoy the adventure. This time, as well as a few things to barter, Morgan took a couple of the humbler-looking scraps of silver. They would be useful in an emergency, but it would be dangerous to draw unnecessary attention to herself. She and her mother said a prayer together, and she set off at dawn.

The journey was uneventful. She stopped a few times to eat berries and cheese and to feed Moses. And she sang songs and chatted to herself until she came out of the woods and into open land where she felt less at home and did not want to be overheard by people or animals or anyone else.

Morgan arrived at the great church in Govan at nightfall, and asked to be taken in. She explained that she had come to have her baby baptised, and the churchwarden agreed to let her stay the night. She was taken to an outhouse where an older woman gave her a bowl of porridge and showed her a place for Moses and her to sleep. The woman also asked where Morgan was from, and why she had come alone. Morgan explained that she lived in the woods with just her mother, and they could not afford to leave the animals unattended. And in answer to the question that had only been implied, she explained that she had not given birth to the child, but adopted it – even though, she confirmed when asked, she had no husband. The woman went out briefly, apparently to convey all this to the churchwarden. Later Morgan heard the churchwarden talking to another man outside, but they spoke in Latin, so she could not understand. In the morning, she was given more porridge and then asked to wait in the church, where the priest would come and find her.

Now it was daylight, Morgan stopped to admire the church before going in, as she always did when visiting Govan. It was the biggest building she had ever seen, not that she had seen many, and those she had seen were mostly huts and hovels. But the modest wooden church loomed above the ordinary dwellings of Govan. It looked important, if not exactly beautiful. God's house. She said a prayer and went in, taking care to hush Moses as she did.

The church was empty except for two monks, who stood deep in conversation in a corner behind the altar, and the churchwarden, who was sitting in the opposite corner polishing some silver trinkets. Morgan thought of the silver she had about her, and wondered if she should make an offering, but before she could decide, one of the monks came over and said he was the priest who would baptise her baby. His name was Gawin, he said. Morgan introduced herself and Moses. The other monk had left the church but now returned with water for the baptism, which was performed in front of the altar. Gawin took Moses and spoke in Latin as he sprinkled the baby with water, and to Morgan in their own language as he explained the significance of the rite. He made her promise to do everything in her power to bring the boy up as a faithful Christian, and she did not hesitate to do so. He smiled, kissed Moses and handed him back to his mother. Then they all heard a great, deafening rumble from outside, followed by a palpable freshness in the air and the crashing sound of torrential rain.

The other monk rushed to the door and opened it to look out, clearly relishing the sudden storm. He and Gawin exchanged words in Latin and laughed. Morgan guessed they were joking about how he need not have bothered fetching water for the baptism, but for whatever reason they decided not to include her in the joke. The churchwarden went over and closed the door with a disapproving expression. He looked at Morgan and her baby: 'You'd better wait it out here,' he said.

Gawin motioned to her to sit down, which she did. The rain-loving monk opened the door again and slipped out, closing it behind him, and the churchwarden muttered and returned to his silver. Gawin sat down next to Morgan. He was not yet old, but not young either. He was clean shaven, both his face and tonsured head, and had kind eyes. Morgan decided she liked him.

'Perhaps it's a good sign,' he said, gesturing to the rain. 'Baptismal waters from Heaven itself.'

Morgan smiled, and kissed Moses.

Perhaps Gawin really suspected Morgan's being delayed by the storm was a divine nudge, because then he said, 'Tell me how you came to adopt your baby.'

Morgan had been prepared for the question; her mother had made sure of that. She explained how she had found Moses in his basket on the river; hence the name. Then she added solemnly, 'I assure you in God's name that I remain a virgin.'

Gawin nodded. 'Then I believe you,' he said conclusively.

The rain did not sound like it was about to relent.

'You know,' the monk said thoughtfully, 'people say Saint Mungo was born of a virgin. Mind you, even according to the legend, she did have to carry and give birth to the child, like Mother Mary herself. You've avoided even that trial.'

'It is the way in our family,' she told him.

He nodded, not quite registering what Morgan meant. 'It's not true, of course, about Saint Mungo's mother.'

'Not true that she carried the child? Did she find him like I found Moses?'

'No, no, my dear,' Gawin laughed. 'It's not true that she was a virgin. There's only been one virgin birth, and that was quite sufficient for the Lord's purposes.'

'So how did it happen?'

Gawin hesitated, in two minds about whether to continue, but then he smiled again. 'Make yourself comfortable,' he said. 'It's a long story.'

Morgan adjusted Moses, who was now fast asleep at her breast, and looked at the monk expectantly.

CHAPTER 5: THE STORY OF PRINCESS TENEU

'Her name was Teneu,' Gawin began, 'and she was a princess, the daughter of a pagan king. This was in the east of the land, but long before the Northumbrians settled there. She heard the Gospel from a wandering preacher, and immediately embraced it. Her father would not tolerate Christians, though, so she had to pray in secret. She prayed and prayed for the salvation of those she loved and of all mankind from the evil that surrounded them. And she was so taken by the story of the virgin birth, of the eternal light and justice of God bursting forth from a mere girl, that she wished to imitate the Mother Mary herself. Teneu prayed – with the presumption that comes of a certain kind of female rashness – that she might conceive and give birth to her own baby, have her own infant Jesus at her breast.'

Morgan was fascinated.

The monk went on: 'Well, soon enough, she found she was with child.'

'Inside her?'

'Inside her.'

'How did it get there?'

He hesitated again, wondering whether this girl were as innocent of the world as she seemed to be of nature. 'Nobody knows for sure, but whatever happened, the Lord spared her knowledge of it. I'm quite sure she was sincere when she said she had no idea where the baby had come from other than from the Lord, but there must have been a man involved one way or another. Those were dark days.'

Morgan looked puzzled, but he pushed on.

'Sadly, her father and his people were less charitable. Even among the pagans, it was a great disgrace for an unmarried woman to be with child. Their savage law decreed that Teneu should be taken to a high place and cast headlong downward to be broken into pieces on the rocks, torn limb from limb as she tumbled.'

Morgan gasped.

'The girl prayed for mercy, not to her father the king but to the Blessed Virgin. And she admitted her guilt, not for being with child but for imagining herself fit to imitate the Blessed Virgin. She prayed that God might forgive her foolishness and free her from her fate. She prayed that she might be saved in the name of Jesus, so that her heathen people would know that Jesus is the Saviour. And she promised to raise her offspring to be God's good and faithful servant all his life.

'There was no mercy from her Earthly father, who was at pains to show that he and his family were not above the law. All the people assembled at the high place to witness her fate. But Teneu kept calling out to Christ and his mother even as the king's men threw her down to die. Then came the miracle. The Lord must have put out his hand to break her fall, because she reached the bottom quite unscathed, not so much as striking her foot on a rock. It seemed to her that she glided down like a bird on the wing.' The monk stopped to savour the miracle.

'And then what?' Morgan demanded

'Well,' he said, 'Immediately, many of the people were won to Christ. They cried out for mercy and repented of their sins. They praised the name of God. And they said the girl must be innocent as she had claimed, that she must not be punished but set free with her honour quite restored.'

'Praise God,' said Morgan.

'Praise God indeed,' said the monk. 'But that was not the end of it. Not all of the people were convinced. The enemies of the faith said the girl's rescue was not a miracle but witchcraft. The said she was an evil magician and must be got rid of before she caused them harm. So the people were divided: some believed God had saved Princess Teneu, proving her faith was true; others insisted she had played a trick on them all and that as long as she lived among them they could not trust their senses. Out of the confusion, it was the stiff-necked pagans who prevailed, and called on the wicked king to devise another punishment for his daughter. If she could not be killed, she must be exiled. This witch, this evil magician, this harlot, must be put to sea in a little boat to suffer at the whim of the sea gods, they said.'

Morgan was rapt.

'So the king and his men took Princess Teneu and put to sea in a ship, taking along a little boat made of hide. When they had reached the deepest part of the sea, they set put the girl in the boat without oars or sail and set it adrift amid roaring waves that lifted it high and dropped it low from moment to moment. And by now it was getting dark. Teneu was not afraid, because the Lord had saved her once and she had no doubt that he could save her again if only it were his will. She prayed for the sake of the baby inside her that she would not be drowned. Well, presently, a current took hold of the little boat and propelled it away from her father's land and towards the opposite shore. The boat rushed over the water faster than if it had been under sail in strong winds or rowed by a team of strong men. The tradition doesn't tell us, but I like to think Teneu enjoyed the ride!

'The boat reached the shore just as the day dimmed finally into night. The princess got out and immediately felt the painful contractions of childbirth.'

The monk looked at Morgan, who was as ignorant as he of what that might be like.

'Desperate for somewhere to rest, she spied the embers of a fire at the treeline a little up the beach, perhaps left there by shepherds or fishermen. So she rushed over and managed to revive the fire with some dry wood that lay plentifully abound the place. Almost as if it had been left for her! So she endured the night by the fire, and finally gave birth just as the dawn broke.

'Soon enough, the smoke from Teneu's fire was spotted by some shepherds, who took pity on her and gave her food and water. They were Christians, thank God, and told her that a holy man lived nearby and taught boys who were destined to serve the church, so she agreed to be taken to him for shelter and ministration. Well, that holy man was holy indeed. He was Saint Serf, and that very morning he had heard an invisible choir of angels singing sweet praises to the Lord, and he had joined in, singing Te Deum. And, well, as soon as he saw Teneu and her baby, he knew what the angels had been so excited about. He cried out, "My dear, my dear!" and welcomed mother and child into his home. You see, he knew in his heart that this was a special child.'

'Saint Mungo himself,' said Morgan with satisfaction, since the name Mungo was the same as 'my dear' in their own language.

'That's right,' said Gawin. 'In fact Saint Serf gave him two names. After a few days he baptised the baby, and his mother too, as she had not yet been baptised. And he christened the child Kentigern. But as you will have guessed by now, Teneu and Kentigern stayed with Saint Serf, and the boy became his pupil. And he was such a good pupil, so attentive, so diligent and so pious in his study of the scriptures that Saint Serf grew to love him above all others, and called him by the nickname Mungo. And out of love and affection, that is how we know him today.'

Now Gawin was looking at Morgan's baby, as if having

for the first time seen a parallel between one baby of mysterious provenance arriving at the doorstep of a holy man, and another.

Morgan looked at the monk suspiciously. 'My son's name is Moses,' she said.

'It's a good name,' he said.

CHAPTER 6: FIRST BLOOD

Cuthbert had had enough of stories. The older men were full of them, every night around the camp fire. He wanted to see some action. Action of his own. Soon enough, he got his wish.

Out of nowhere, the Picts introduced themselves with a hail of arrows. Cuthbert felt one glance off his shoulder; luckily, it struck at an angle that did no damage, but as he reeled from the blow he stumbled and fell. The next thing he knew, men were rushing at them, cutting down anyone who could neither get out of their way nor offer resistance. That meant several dead or maimed before Cuthbert heard metal on metal. And it was only then that he really began to understand what was happening. He was alive, for now, having survived the first wave of an ambush. But he was down. It occurred to him to play dead and hope for the best. Maybe he could wait out the fighting and feign concussion when the Picts had been repelled. But fear of what might happen if the enemy prevailed combined with a sense of honour bubbling up within him. Better to fight and die than leave it to chance like a coward. He looked around him: beyond the dead and dying in his immediate vicinity, he saw that his comrades had formed a line to block the assault. His duty was clear: join them. Fight.

Less than an hour before the ambush, Cuthbert's company of Northumbrians had met their allies as arranged at the ruins of an ancient broch in what had once been Northumbrian territory and was now held by Gaels. But the Picts had known or guessed their enemies would muster there and had been waiting, hidden in the surrounding woods. Perhaps they had been watching them for some time, but they did not attack immediately. The Northumbrian and Gaelic captains had time to discuss their plans: another company of Northumbrians was expected soon, and when they arrived the plan was to march north into Pict country, with more Gaels to join them on the way. The captains had conversed with the help of one of the Gaels who spoke reasonably good Northumbrian and was able to translate; their own captain Beorhtred could manage pleasantries in Gaelic, but that was it. Fortunately, the language barrier did not seem to be a problem when it came to fighting. The more experienced Northumbrians and Gaels had rallied fast after the initial shock of the ambush and formed a line without words, or at least without words that conveyed much meaning. Indeed, nobody had to tell Cuthbert what to do.

The youngster pulled himself to his feet and drew his seax, first turning his back to the defensive line to check for attackers on his own side – none stood alive – before joining the nearest end of the line. Next to him stood a reassuringly fierce-looking Gael who acknowledged him with a grunt even as he swung his axe at an oncoming Pict, who swerved clear and thrust his weapon at Cuthbert instead. The debutant soldier parried the blow with his seax and then struggled to retain his footing as he tentatively dangled his weapon in his assailant's general direction. Fortunately, his Gaelic comrade struck more decisively, slicing into an arm and forcing the Pict to step back. As he did so, Cuthbert glanced along the line to see the carnage multiplied, with many telling blows on both sides. This was action. It was terrifying, but there was no time for fear until it was over.

Once it was clear that the defensive line was established and solid, the Picts withdrew and disappeared into the woods. They had done enough damage for now. The allies quickly regrouped and set sentries to look out for further attacks. The dead were counted: six of them, seven after a no-hoper was put out of his misery. Cuthbert and Alcuin were among those charged with burying them. Five more men were no longer any good for fighting and were told to make their own way home or to whatever shelter they could find to recover from their wounds while the combined company advanced as planned. There was some discussion about whether to continue to wait for the Northumbrian reinforcements, but that was resolved when one of the sentries announced men approaching. Here they were: fifty hardened soldiers, including a small company of Gaels who had joined them on their way. If they had been a couple of hours earlier, the enemy would not have dared attack. Still, someone pointed out, if there were bands of Picts looking for trouble this far south, it was better they knew about it.

Having helped bury the dead in a shallow grave, Cuthbert and Alcuin sat to rest against the wall of the ruined broch and wondered what it had been built for. It was a round construction of stone; most of what remained was no higher than waist height, but it was clear that the building had been much higher. People said it was hundreds of years old and must have been built by Picts before the other nations took the southern parts of their land, but it was also said that there were others in Pict country that were just as abandoned and ruined. If the Picts had built them, they'd forgotten why. Whether it was a fortification, a home or something to do with the old religion, the broch belonged to another age. The Picts they had just fought, including the couple they had just buried, were very much of their own age. They were not painted blue, but looked much like the Northumbrians and the Gaels.

That was not surprising. The noble families of the various nations often intermarried to seal alliances, though such marriages often outlasted the alliance. Mixed marriages were not unheard of among common folk either. In ever-shifting border country, there was often nothing more than language to keep the peoples apart, and languages could be learned. Cuthbert had already picked up the Gaelic words for blade, spade and corpse.

As the reinforced company set off, Cuthbert and Alcuin were joined once again by Wilfrid, who was on a high. While Alcuin had endured a similarly tentative introduction to action as Cuthbert's, Wilfrid had tasted his first blood, killing one of the attackers. (They later had it confirmed that this was true and not just talk.) He was a new man, he said. War was for him. Cuthbert felt a little jealous and a little disturbed. He was pleased to have survived his first contact and not disgraced himself. He could not say he had discovered his inner warrior.

CHAPTER 7: PANIC

After the christening and the storm, Morgan spent the afternoon in the market at Govan, exchanging what she had for some extra clothing for Moses as well as a trinket for her mother. She enjoyed the opportunity to talk to people when the chance arose, and to hear all the latest news, though much of it went over her head, as she knew little of the people and places of which the townsfolk spoke. Gawin had agreed to let her spend another night in the church outhouse, but she could not find him to thank him before setting off with Moses at first light. Anyway, she had promised to come back for more stories and, in due course, to begin Moses' education in the faith.

The return journey was as uneventful as the outward journey had been, but when they were almost home, Morgan felt an eerie unfamiliarity. Something was not right. Then a goat wandered into her path. It was Flossy. *Their* goat.

'Come here, Flossy,' she said to the animal. 'What are you doing out here?'

Flossy did not answer, but allowed herself to be nudged homeward by Morgan. When they arrived, Morgan had to put Moses down in his basket so she could round up another stray goat and a couple of hens and close the breached pen before going into the house with a sense of dread. Her mother was absent, as feared, and their things were in disarray. Morgan burst into tears.

When she had gathered herself, Morgan picked up Moses' basket and brought him into the house. She picked up an upended stool and tidied away a few bits and pieces strewn over the floor and then stopped suddenly when she remembered the silver. She rushed to the corner where she and her mother had stashed it. Gone. She quickly said a prayer: the silver did not matter, just as long as her mother was safe. Please, God, keep the silver and save mother from harm. Moses was crying; she picked him up and held him close. 'Don't worry, little one,' she said. 'Everything is going to be fine.'

Morgan put Moses back in his basket and set off with it for the nearest hamlet, praying that someone would know what had happened. She received a warm welcome from the mistress of the first house she came to, who congratulated her on her bonnie baby. Winnie had known Morgan since she was a baby herself, and had always been kind, often buying her mother's concoctions. She was duly shocked to hear she was missing, but it was indeed news to her. If anyone there had known anything, Winnie would have heard it. She advised Morgan to go to another hamlet, the one near the great road. This made sense. Whoever had taken her mother was most likely a stranger.

This time, Morgan was greeted by two lads working a patch of land outside the settlement. She knew the lads by sight, but not as well as Winnie. They too registered Morgan's new baby, but were less interested. They had seen her mother that morning, they told her, in the custody of a monk and three armed men. 'What monk?' she asked, bewildered, but they could not answer. They told her to ask in the hamlet: their own mother would know more. Indeed she did. She told Morgan her mother had been arrested for witchcraft and taken to the shrine of Saint Mirin. One of the men had told her so when they passed through the hamlet. Morgan was stunned, and the woman gently took Moses from her so she could sit down unburdened. 'Witchcraft?' she said, 'Mother a witch?' And then again, 'What monk?' It was natural that she thought first of the monk she had spoken to just yesterday, the only monk she had ever spoken to at length, but why would Gawin have raced home ahead of her to arrest her mother for witchcraft? Had she brought this on them by going to Govan?

'An old man,' the woman told her, and she was not young herself. So it was not Gawin? 'I've never seen him before,' she added.

'And did my mother say anything to you when you saw her?'

'No, dear. She was too upset. But I'm sure she'll be fine.

'Well, I must go to the shrine of Saint Mirin,' Morgan said, feeling the tears well up again within her at the thought of her mother in distress. 'Thank you for your help.'

'It will be dark soon,' the woman pointed out. 'You can stay here till morning.'

Morgan was reluctant, but realised she had little choice. If she set off in the dark, she'd soon get lost, and who knew what dangers lurked in the black of night?

Morgan settled at the hearth with Moses as their host got on with her chores, having waved away Morgan's offer of help. 'Please believe that my mother is no witch,' she said.

'Of course not,' the woman said kindly. 'Everyone knows you and your mother are harmless, but you know what must have happened. People in these parts swear by your mother's remedies. Word must have reached this monk and he's assumed the worst. That's my guess, dear.'

This did indeed seem the most likely explanation. Not that anyone had ever accused her mother of witchcraft before. Witchcraft was not something much spoken of in those days. Morgan knew some of her mother's concoctions had been used as part of the old religion, but her mother was a good Christian woman like her own mother before her and as far back as anyone could remember. Christians had not stopped feasting because their pagan forebears had feasted to the old gods. Why should they stop using tried and tested herbal remedies that worked perfectly well without any need for evil incantations or devilish rituals? It was nonsense. But why had this monk arrested an innocent woman over such nonsense? And how was Morgan going to convince him to let her go?

This kindly neighbour's response had been reassuring, and when her sons returned from the field for their evening meal and learned the news, they laughed off the charge of witchcraft. The silly old monk must be soft in the head, they said, though they had no particularly bright ideas as to what Morgan should do about it. They simply wished her luck pleading her mother's case. After dinner, Morgan was shown a corner where she and Moses could sleep, and everyone turned in. With the light blown out it was pitch black in the little hovel. Within minutes, the lads were snoring and Morgan relaxed a little. Still, soon she was the only one not asleep.

She kissed Moses, gently snuffling in her arms in the darkness, and allowed herself to confront another thought that had been bubbling below the surface of her consciousness. What if it were not just word of her mother's concoctions that had roused the monk's suspicions? She was an unmarried woman living alone with her daughter in the woods. A daughter who was also unmarried, and yet who had recently acquired a baby of her own. They were a strange little family, not even really part of such community as existed among the local hamlets. Otherwise, she would probably have been married to one of these lads by now. Their neighbours considered them benign, but they were outsiders, their ways little understood and easily misinterpreted. Morgan wondered how much she would help her mother's case by simply appearing in her wake, with a mysterious baby too. She wished they had a more convincing advocate, someone who at least knew her a little. She managed to fall asleep only once she had come to a resolution. She would not go to the shrine of Saint Mirin in the morning. She would go back to Govan. To Gawin.

CHAPTER 8: SAINT MIRIN

Morgan and Moses arrived at Govan well before nightfall, having made haste on a now familiar route. Gawin was not at the church, but the churchwarden recognised Morgan and directed her to the monastery on the edge of the town. Here she was recognised again by one of a group of monks working the land outside the rough buildings. It was the one who had helped with Moses' baptism and then run out into the rain. 'What's the matter?' he asked.

'I need to speak to Gawin,' Morgan said. 'He said he would be a spiritual guardian to my son,' she went on in words she had been rehearsing, 'and now our whole family is in grave danger.'

The monk looked thoughtful, surprised but not unfriendly. 'Come and sit,' he said, taking Morgan to a bench set against the wall of the main building. 'I'll get him for you.'

He went inside, and re-emerged with Gawin a few minutes later. 'I didn't think to see you again so soon,' said the latter, cautiously but not without warmth. He looked fondly at Moses, nestled in Morgan's arms, who gurgled happily.

'I'm sorry to trouble you,' she said. 'I didn't know where else to turn.' She told him what had happened.

He began to ask more questions, but when it became clear that Morgan knew no more than she had told him, he gave up. 'All right,' he said, 'There's nothing else for it but to go to the shrine of Saint Mirin and get to the bottom of this.'

Morgan felt almost elated with relief.

'We'll set off in the morning,' he said. 'Valentine will take you back to where you stayed before.'

'Valentine?'

'Valentine!'

The rain-loving monk, who had returned to his duties, came back over, and Gawin explained what was happening. Then he went back inside, and Valentine led Morgan back to the path. Moses cried all the way back to Govan.

When Valentine returned, he was not very happy either.

'You're going to the shrine of Saint Mirin?' he said to Gawin, 'Just like that?'

'I'm sure you can cope without me for a day or two,' he said

'Just don't expect a warm welcome.'

'Oh, I'm sure they'll have forgotten all about *that*!' Gawin said, laughing. *That* was a joke, but Valentine was in no mood for jokes.

'They're jealous of the pre-eminence of Govan, they don't like you and they won't appreciate you throwing your weight around. Besides, what if this girl's mother really is a diabolist of some kind? You'll be implicating yourself. And the rest of us!'

'I'll do no such thing. I'm going to get to find out what's going on, that's all. And, really, what hope is there for Christian love and fellowship if we let fear and suspicion reign in their stead?'

Valentine could not argue with that. 'I'll pray for you,' he said.

'You do that, my boy. And for us all.'

The following morning, Gawin came for Morgan just before dawn, and they set off together, taking turns to carry

Moses in his basket. As they walked, Gawin told the story of the saint after whom their destination was named.

'Now, Saint Mirin was an Irish monk and prior of Bangor Abbey at a time when the Christian faith was not yet accepted throughout the island of Ireland. So he sought out the High King of all Ireland to ask his permission to preach the gospel far and wide, but the pagan potentate refused. What could Mirin do? Well, he knew the High King's wife was pregnant, and close to giving birth. And you'll like this part, Morgan. He prayed to God to transfer the labour pains from wife to husband! So, when her time came, the High King was brought low by the terrible pangs of labour.' Gawin gave Morgan a knowing look, or rather a comically clueless look that made her laugh out loud.

'The terrible agony of childbirth!' she grimaced, making him laugh in turn.

'Yes, yes, for three days and three nights he writhed in agony,' he went on.

'Because of the horrible contractions,' Morgan added.

'Yes, the contractions. Terribly painful!'

They both had to stop to compose themselves, with Moses grumbling because he'd been left out of the joke.

'Anyway,' Gawin continued, 'After three days and three nights roaring with pain, the High King finally called for the holy man he had turned away. And of course Saint Mirin came and prayed to God to lift the pain, and in an instant it was gone, or I suppose it was returned to the king's wife, but her hitherto painless labour must have been nearly over by then. So Saint Mirin won the blessing of the High King of Ireland to preach the gospel far and wide, and that he did. And later he came over the water to these parts. This was a time when people here still remembered the Romans. Do you know about the Romans?'

Morgan did not.

'Well, that's a tale for another time, then. Suffice to say that the Christian religion was first practised here at the time of the Romans, but the history of the church is the history of backsliding and faithlessness as much as it is of repentance and faith, so by the time Mirin arrived, paganism was once again rife and the land was ruled by another pagan potentate, a great chieftain. This time, though, Mirin had no need to resort to strongarm tactics, because the chieftain's eyes were opened right away to Mirin's holiness, and he granted him the freedom to preach the gospel and the land to build a church. So for a time the gospel flourished once again. And when the holy man died, a shrine was established at that church, the shrine of Saint Mirin.'

'And that's where we're going,' Morgan said nervously.

'That's right. Today, there's a church and a small community of monks there, and it must have been one of those monks who took your mother. I'm sure she's quite safe.'

'Yes,' said Morgan, but now she realised she didn't want to talk about that. There was nothing to be said until they got there. 'Why do you say the gospel flourished for a while? Is it not flourishing now?'

Gawin was silent for a moment. 'Perhaps you never know at the time,' he said. Then, glancing down at Moses in his basket, he added, 'As long as there are little ones like this one to carry the flame, there is hope.'

They arrived at the shrine of Saint Mirin around noon. As Gawin had said, there was a church, though much smaller than the one in Govan, and a few simple huts, presumably home to the monks. As they approached, someone darted in from the outside one of the huts. By the time they got there, they had a welcoming party of two monks standing rather ceremoniously outside the church.

'Brother Gawin!' said one.

Gawin greeted first this and then the other monk each with a kiss on the cheek.

'And who is your companion?' the first monk asked, politely but too abruptly to avoid giving the impression that he had a very good idea who Morgan was. He was an old man, too, like the one who had taken Morgan's mother.

'This is Morgan, and her son Moses. I recently had the pleasure of baptising the child. Morgan, these are my brother monks Ninian and Alyn.'

Nods all round.

'Brothers,' Gawin continued coolly, 'we understand you can help us find Morgan's mother.'

Ninian and Alyn looked at one another cagily before Ninian, the old one, spoke up, addressing Morgan. 'Then I take it your mother lives in the woods a day's walk or so up the White Water?'

'That's right,' Morgan confirmed, 'we all live there.'

Gawin just looked expectantly at his brother monks.

'Well,' Ninian said, 'she's probably home by now.'

Morgan felt a surge of relief tempered by uncertainty. She looked at Gawin, who also seemed more relieved than anything else. He turned to her and suggested she go into the church to visit the shrine. Clearly, he wanted to speak to the other monks alone. Morgan agreed without complaint, though, and said she would thank God for keeping her mother safe, but she also planned a prayer of supplication to make sure.

With Morgan out of the way, Gawin put on his best diplomatic expression – making an effort to appear 'light' so he could not be accused of throwing his weight around – and asked what had happened. It transpired that the local strongman – perhaps a distant descendant of the potentate who had granted this very land to Saint Mirin for his church – had come to the monks with reports that an old woman who lived up the White Water was practising witchcraft. He had suggested they bring her to the shrine to examine her, and even provided three men to expedite the arrest. Ninian had gone with them to the old woman's home, and they had brought her back to the shrine. Well, she had given no appearance of being anything other than a harmless old woman with something of the woods about her that had presumably provoked the rumours. She was a herbalist, but a faithful Christian who had been able to recite the Lord's Prayer to the monks' satisfaction, which is to say without stuttering or catching fire. She had also been extremely anxious to go home to her daughter and grandson, so they had released her that morning.

'What's his name, this local strongman?' Gawin asked.

'Rhodri,' said Ninian.

'And did Rhodri the local strongman also examine the prisoner?'

'Well, yes he did, quite briefly.'

At that, Gawin knew there was no point probing his brother monks any further. They did not know why they had arrested Morgan's mother. They had merely been used by this Rhodri. He thanked them for their welcome and went into the church for Morgan. She and Moses both lay fast asleep at the foot of the shrine, smiling like angels. In fact, the scene was a little unnatural. Gawin knelt and said a prayer before gently waking Morgan. 'I think you should go home now. Your mother will be worried.'

She arrived home just before sunset, having followed the great road upriver till she found her bearings. Her mother had indeed been worried, and embraced Morgan and Moses so tightly she made the baby cry. Then she began crying, and sat down in despair. 'I'm so sorry,' she said, 'It's all my fault your silver is gone.'

Morgan had almost forgotten about that. 'The silver doesn't matter,' she said, 'but what do you mean it's your fault?'

'I spent one of the pieces, a week or two ago. It was just a little one. I gave it to a pedlar in one of the hamlets, for those knives I brought home, and I meant to tell you, I did, but I didn't think you'd mind.'

'I don't mind,' Morgan said, 'They're good knives, and look, they're still here at least. And there's the silver I took with me to Govan. We still have that.' Having convinced herself things were not so bad, however, Morgan was stung again by her loss. 'But those *monks* took the rest?'

'Soldiers,' her mother said. 'I don't think the silly monk knew much about it. The soldiers took your silver.' Before Morgan could respond, her mother added urgently, 'But promise me you'll not go back to that place. Let's put the whole thing behind us, bury what's left of the silver and say no more about it.'

Morgan sat next to her mother and held her close, bringing Moses' basket near so they could both admire him. 'All right, mother, we'll say no more about it.'

So, Morgan knew that soldiers had taken her silver, presumably having learned about it from the pedlar and tracked her mother down. And she knew the monks had been involved, thanks to an accusation of witchcraft that had probably been fabricated for the purpose of getting to the silver. But she did not know why such subterfuge had been necessary. They could easily have robbed her mother with impunity.

Morgan's mother did know that the man behind her arrest had been as interested in where the silver had come from as he was in the silver itself, and thus had wanted an opportunity to examine her, but she had also sensed he knew more than she did. The man, who was not a monk or a churchman of any kind, had insisted on interrogating her alone, and she had the wits to realise he was not seeking information so much as reassurance that she had none to share. All she could tell him was that she (not bringing Morgan into it) had found the silver in a basket on the White Water, and that apparently was all he wanted to hear. Morgan's mother did not even know who this man was, and he perhaps preferred it that way. So she did not mention him to Morgan at all, for fear that she would want to know more.

Of course, Gawin did know that the man's name was Rhodri, and that he was the local strongman, but he had not mentioned him to Morgan either. As he walked back to Govan, he prayed that Morgan and her mother would be left in peace from now on, and also that his brother monks would not be entangled in any further intrigue involving accusations of witchcraft or anything else of the kind.

CHAPTER 9: EUPHEMIA'S SONG

Euphemia sat in her favourite place to sit in the springtime, on the sturdy branch of an ancient yew tree by the side of the road that led in and out of the village. The branch was low enough for her to climb onto easily, but high enough to make her feel important. She was important, after all. Her father was the most powerful and respected noble in the glen. It was he who had raised an army to march south to fight the foreigners, and a successful campaign would only make him more powerful, and richer. He was not yet considered a ruler of their people, but these things were not set in stone. His victories would be carved in stone, like the stones that commemorated their people's past victories. And as his fame spread, he would be recognised as king of the glen, one of the six or seven nobles who claimed that title at any given time in different parts of their people's lands. She had heard him discuss it often enough with her uncle, who was already a bishop, and responsible for all three and a half churches in the glen. Her family's exalted status meant Euphemia was able to escape the more arduous chores the other village girls had to do, giving her time to spend on more important matters. Like sitting in her tree preparing to be a princess.

As she sat, she sang a song about the majestic beauty

of the fresh, fresh river that flowed through the glen and the green, green woods that graced its slopes and the blue, blue sky above. She did have a lovely singing voice, princess or not. She had just adapted her song to take account of the grey, grey clouds that in fact covered much of the sky that morning when she noticed she had an audience. A short distance up the road a young man had stopped to sit down and was listening to Euphemia's song. She did not recognise him, but she did not want to appear embarrassed or unsettled, so she continued singing. She sensed he knew she had noticed him, though, and sure enough, he soon got up and continued towards her.

'You've a lovely singing voice,' the young man said as he approached.

Euphemia came to a natural break in the song, smiled graciously and gave a very slight bow. Falling out of the tree would have given entirely the wrong impression. The young man returned her smile as he passed, but did not stop. Euphemia carelessly took up her song again as she watched him proceed into the village. She supposed she would learn soon enough who he was and what his business was.

When she returned to the village later that day, the young man was long gone. Well, she had hardly been standing sentry for him by the road. She had gone to the river to wash and then to the church, a mile outside the village, for a Latin lesson from her uncle. The young man must have left while she was doing that. Anyway, their serving boy Kenny confirmed that a young man had visited and spoken to a couple of the men who remained in the village because they were too old to join the war party. She would not stoop to asking the old men what the stranger had wanted, but she supposed her uncle would find out and might tell her in due course. If, of course, she did not see the young man again first.

The next morning, Euphemia sat again on her branch, singing this time about a brave soldier marching off to war to the beat of the drum, drum, drum. And this time, she noticed the young man as soon as he appeared on the horizon, and watched him approach. As he drew near, he nodded an acknowledgement and she paused her song. 'And why are *you* not off to war?'

The question was abrupt, but winsomely put. The young man smiled. 'My lady, I'm afraid I've no talent for fighting.'

'Then what is your lot?'

He smiled again. 'It's more fun if I let you guess,' he said, with a sparkle in his eye that made Euphemia smile despite herself. He was quite handsome, after all. Then the young man proceeded on his way, soon accompanied once more by the questioning beat and lovely melody of Euphemia's drum, drum, drum.

Later, Euphemia went to the river to wash and then to the church for a Latin lesson from her uncle. When they had finished, she asked him casually, 'Who's the stranger I saw going into the village yesterday and again this morning?'

'What stranger?'

So her uncle had not heard. 'I don't know,' Euphemia told him. 'A young man. Kenny said he spoke to the old ones yesterday.'

'Well, stay away from him,' her uncle said. 'A stranger who appears when the fighting men are away is not to be trusted.'

'Yes, uncle.'

Apparently this was not just an idle warning for a silly girl, because her uncle then summoned his assistant and whispered instructions. Then he fetched his sword from a fine wooden chest and gestured to the door. Euphemia and her uncle were going back to the village together.

The young man had been and gone once more, so Euphemia's uncle went to speak to the old men. Then he called in on Euphemia's mother and spoke to her privately. He told Euphemia there would be no lesson tomorrow, but he would see her in church on the Lord's Day as usual.

'Well?' she said to her mother as soon as her uncle had

gone.

'Well what?'

She gave her mother a beseeching look.

'Well, the stranger is Priten. Old Tarla's grandson. He grew up here, but left with his father when he was about your age now; you were too young to remember him. And well, apparently he and his father are hunting up on the mountain, and when the boy realised how close they were, he decided to visit old Tarla before it was too late.'

'So why did they leave all those years ago?'

Euphemia's mother sighed. 'Priten's father did not get on with your father. He was ambitious... He lost.'

'A political rival!' Euphemia said, more to herself than her mother.

'Anyway, your uncle's gone down the glen to speak to some friends. And if you see Priten again, you've to stay away, understand?'

'Yes, mother.'

The next morning, Euphemia sat again on her branch, singing once more about the majestic beauty of the fresh, fresh river that flowed through the glen and the green, green woods that graced its slopes and the grey, blue, grey, blue sky above. When Priten appeared, she was ready for him, and introduced an intrepid hunter into her song, watching with his keen, keen eyes for the swift, swift deer of the glen.

He smiled gratifyingly as he made out her words. 'A good guess, my lady. But I'm no hunter, either.'

She stopped singing. It hadn't been a guess at all. She had it on good authority that he was a hunter. He smiled his sparkling smile, but barely hesitated as he passed Euphemia's tree. 'Better luck next time!' he said.

She had to force herself to take up the song again as he continued on to the village, and she left the hunter out of it.

Next time, indeed. Euphemia wondered how many times the mysterious youth intended to visit his grandfather, and why his visits were so fleeting. She was sure her uncle was right to be suspicious that he had appeared when the fighting men were away. It was some coincidence that a hunting expedition should have brought her father's rival and his son back to these parts at such a time – especially if they were not hunters! And where was Priten's father anyway? It was all most suspicious. Most suspicious! Euphemia slipped skilfully from her perch and took a shortcut to the village.

Naturally, her father's house was the biggest in the village, and home to several retainers as well as the family. Old Tarla lived in one of the other, rougher dwellings. But he was more often to be found sitting by the kiln with two or three cronies. If Euphemia planted herself quietly in the nearby chicken shed, she should be able to hear any interesting conversation. And sure enough, having crept unnoticed into the village and taken up her position, it was with some satisfaction that she heard the familiar voices of the old men joined by the less familiar but no less gratifying voice of Priten. She could not hear everything over the incessant chatter of the chickens, but she could make out the gist. Priten was in fact talking about hunting. Apparently his father hunted with falcons, and the old men were impressed. But he did talk of hunting as something his father was doing rather than father and son together. When the conversation moved away from hunting, Euphemia struggled to keep up. They were using words she did not know, and there was something funny even about what she could make out. It was her own language but somehow different. It sounded old-fashioned, maybe, like some of the poems and songs she'd heard the old people sing and not taken much notice. Were they reciting ancient poetry? But then their speech returned to normal, and she heard Priten say he would return just once more before moving on with his father. She watched from the edge of the shed door as he departed. She knew the back of his head well by now.

The next morning, Euphemia sat again on her branch, singing this time about a great bard who composed sweet, sweet songs on his magic harp, on his magic harp sweet songs. Strum, strum, plucking airs from the air, from the air, airs, strum, she sang as Priten approached. And this time he stopped beneath her branch, smiling as ever.

'That's as close as you're likely to get,' he said. 'Especially as you'll not see me again.'

'Are you so sure of that?' she asked, breaking off from her song.

'Well, I'll not be back in these parts again. So you'd have to come and find me.'

'Maybe I will,' she said, making herself blush.

'Oh, I wouldn't recommend that,' he said, as if a shadow had come over him. But as he set off for the village, he turned again with that sparkle back in his eye. 'But if you do, maybe I'll show you my magic harp.'

Euphemia bowed graciously and resumed her song as she watched him stroll to the village for the last time.

It was also the last time she would sit on her branch.

CHAPTER 10: A FEAST

Lucky gazed at the statue of the Virgin Mary. If she half-shut her eyes, then at least for a second she could see it not as a statue, but as Mary herself, the Mother of God in the flesh. It was both intoxicating and terrifying. And it was becoming a habit.

Lucky spent every spare moment she could in the island's little chapel, communing with the Virgin. It was not exactly prayer. Lucky prayed all the time, not in the chapel, but as she went about her duties: cooking, cleaning, tending to the animals. She was in almost constant conversation with God. This was mostly one-sided, it was true, but she knew he was listening, because when she allowed herself to think wicked thoughts, he made his displeasure known. When she grew resentful of her duties, when she felt spite toward others or just downcast for no particular reason, God rebuked her in no uncertain terms. Not that it took much; there were no lectures, no angry tirades. He simply said her name, just like a parent telling off a child. And that was enough.

Just about the only time Lucky's conversation with God was suspended was when she came alone to the chapel and gazed at the statue of the Virgin Mary and saw it come alive. It was more visceral than prayer, a physical sensation rather than something comprehended. But it was no less holy for that. She felt herself in the presence of God. The God who had once walked the Earth, and not after being cast down in a thunderbolt from Heaven or even sprung miraculously from an apple seed, but instead grown in the belly of a mortal woman. The mortal woman Lucky saw before her now, shimmering with reality. It was a miracle in flesh and blood. Or in this case, wood, but still.

'Lucky!' came a voice that was not God's. It was Dervla, Lucky's sister, or technically her adoptive half-sister, or maybe adoptive cousin, in fact. It didn't matter; they shared a mother and a father now. Dervla had been sent to call Lucky back to her duties.

Lucky sighed and said a quick chapel-prayer – less conversational, more formulaic, but important for piety's sake – and called back, 'Coming!'

The Chief was expected on their island and there was to be a feast in his honour. Lucky stopped herself sighing again as she accompanied Dervla back to the village. 'Is it a big feast?'

'It must be,' Dervla said. 'Mother says they're bringing extra meat of their own!'

'Thank God for that,' said Lucky.

'Indeed,' said Dervla, 'I've never heard the like.'

And indeed, the feast was no ordinary feast. Lucky had no nose for politics, but when they got to the village and joined in with the preparations, even she could sense some kind of intrigue was afoot. As they worked, it transpired that the Chief who was expected was not the same Chief who had visited the last time, or every other time Lucky could remember. There was a new Chief. Only maybe the last Chief was not dead, and maybe the question of who was the rightful Chief was up in the air. So this new one was on his way with his men and a few fat pigs to slaughter, and another ship too was on its way full of more clansmen ready to feast on pig and pledge allegiance to the new Chief, and their island was blessed to be hosting this joyous occasion. Only maybe the old Chief would not feel that way about it. Maybe there would be other ships with other clansmen and other pigs who felt differently about the whole business. Ordinarily, Lucky was partial to a good roast, but as she listened to the mutterings of the islanders, she lost her appetite.

She confessed her fears to God and prayed that there would be no fighting. She prayed for the new Chief, and the old one, and for everyone else. That was all she could do, and so she prayed as earnestly as she could, expecting nothing, only believing that God was in charge, whatever happened.

When they had finished their part in the preparations for the feast, Lucky and Dervla went to the hillside over the harbour to watch the ships come in. There they were, not far now, converging on course for the harbour having come from different directions. On the beach below, the fishing boats had already been joined by the smaller boat that had brought the Chief's messenger, and men were preparing to receive the ships. The girls sat chatting idly as they watched, and before long they could make out the individual men on the ships, their bodies, their faces. Dervla waved excitedly, and Lucky joined in because it would have seemed rude not to. Some of the men even waved back.

'Which one do you think is the new Chief?' Dervla asked.

Lucky scanned the men on both boats, looking for someone with a chiefly bearing. 'I don't know,' she said. 'That one's very tall. Do chiefs have to be tall?' she asked, pointing to one man who towered above his comrades.

'The last one was.'

'Yes.' But aside from height, Lucky had no idea what to expect in a chief.

'And that one's quite handsome,' Dervla added mischievously, as she pointed to another.

'The last one wasn't!'

The girls giggled.

When the ships landed, the men disembarked in what looked like no particular order and greeted the islanders warmly as they worked together to secure the ships and unload various things, most notably and noisily pigs. Then there were more jovial greetings as the men from the two different ships embraced one another and bellowed to be heard over the pigs. Then, slowly, the whole company proceeded from the beach up the rough track that led to the village. Lucky and Dervla stood up and stretched before making their own way back to the village. The spring sun was just beginning to set.

There was no building nearly big enough to accommodate a feast of this size, so tables had been set up outside around a great fire over which two of the islanders' own pigs had been roasting since shortly after the Chief's messenger had arrived. They were soon joined by two more. The feasting would go on into the night. A gentle but persistent rain was not enough to douse the flames, or the spirits of the guests as they whetted their appetites with bread and fish and more, and as they drank.

As Lucky served the guests, she quickly sensed which was the new Chief. He was neither especially tall nor especially handsome, but things seemed to revolve around him, and the other men visibly deferred to him, including her father and her uncle, who was the head man on the island. The new Chief's name was Conall. In due course, Lucky's father introduced her and Chief Conall nodded graciously and thanked her for helping look after them all so well. He said her father and her uncle and the other islanders were good, solid people and she was a good lass. She introduced Dervla as she passed with a jug, and the Chief said she was a good lass too, and both sisters smiled modestly and excused themselves. There were many more exchanges of that kind as Chief Conall was introduced to all the islanders, however humble. There were not many of them, after all.

Later, with meat in their bellies, the leaders among the men made formal pledges of allegiance to the Chief. Lucky's uncle went first, followed by his brother, her father. Then various men who had come on the ships did the same, each naming the place he had come from and many adding long lists of their forefathers before acknowledging Conall as Chief and vowing to follow him in battle and to honour him in peacetime. After that, poems were recited and songs were sung, and with plenty of meat and drink on the table, the island women retired to eat and rest indoors. Having taken her fill, Lucky fell asleep to the sound of a favourite song, which sounded all the sweeter at a distance and filtered through the wall. She dreamt sweet, musical dreams.

When she woke in the night, the sound of the feast had diminished to a few gentle conversations. Most of the men were asleep. She pulled on her cloak and slipped out quietly to pass water behind the house. As she turned the corner, though, she found a group of men standing and whispering together. Her instinct was to turn back, but it was too late. They had seen her.

'Don't be shy,' one of them said.

They were all youngish men, five or six of them, strangers to Lucky. 'I was just...' She stopped herself; she was not about to announce her need for a pee.

'Just looking for some company, is it?' said another man. The others sniggered.

'No, sir. Don't let me interrupt you,' she said, and made to pass. An arm appeared in her way. She stepped back, properly afraid now, but the men didn't so much follow her as jostle among themselves to gawp at her while keeping their distance, uncomfortably close as it was.

'Don't be silly,' said the first man. 'Let's just have a little chat.'

Lucky felt panic rise within her as the men gazed at her in the moonlight. There was an urgency in their eyes that frightened her. They seemed hungry to take in everything about her appearance, irritated by anything in their way, from each other to Lucky's clothes. Still, she drew her cloak more fully around her, preferring to irritate the men than be eaten alive by their eyes. Then she felt a surge of courage and pushed on past the men. One of them reached out and grabbed her cloak. She span to face him and kicked as hard as she could between his legs. Her aim was true and he cried out as he folded over in pain. For a second the others seemed unsure what to do; then they fell about laughing. At that, an older man came over from where the remains of the fire were simmering in the distance to see what the commotion was. Lucky did not know him either.

'What is this foolishness?' he said, and the young men stiffened. Whoever he was, he had their respect. 'Get some sleep,' he said. 'You've had enough fun for one night.' Then he looked at Lucky, unsure what to make of her presence, so he simply nodded a good night and returned to the fire.

Lucky went straight back into the house. She no longer needed to pee.

CHAPTER 11: A PROPOSAL

Lucky's parents were worried. A proposal of marriage was supposed to be a cause for joy. But this felt less like a proposal than a demand. They did not know Chief Conall's son, and he did not know them. His first and only encounter with Lucky had been last night, when she had kicked him in the balls. It hardly seemed like a love match.

'Is he even serious?' Lucky's mother asked. 'Are we sure it's not some kind of joke?'

Lucky's father sighed. 'He's serious enough to have told his father it's what he wants. And his father's taken it seriously enough to bring the proposal to me. I don't know the man well enough to be sure, but no, I don't think it's a joke.'

Lucky's father had just pledged allegiance to Chief Conall, and a political marriage to seal the covenant would not have been unusual. But Conall had not said he wanted the match. He had said his son wanted Lucky. It was more whimsical than political, which made it insulting. Lucky's father would not have objected to a love match, not necessarily, but this was not that.

It did not occur to Lucky's parents to ask her what she thought of the matter. And look at it from their perspective: to do so would have been to shirk their responsibility for her.

Indeed, given that the proposal would certainly be unwelcome, it would have been cruel of them to present it to Lucky. They would have been making themselves complicit in the insulting whimsy of it – 'Would you like you to marry this oaf?' – as if they were indifferent. As if they didn't care. No, the question was not what to say to Lucky, but what to say to Chief Conall. Preferably something more diplomatic than, 'No, your oaf of a son can't have our daughter.'

'What if we said she's already betrothed?' Lucky's mother said.

'Then we'd have to produce a groom,' her father replied. 'We'd have to marry her off to one of the island lads. I don't think she'd like that.'

'You don't think she'd *like* that?' Lucky's mother answered. 'God alone knows what that girl would like.'

And now they were forced to confront the fact that Lucky was indeed quite odd. In a year or two, her sister Dervla would most likely marry one of the island lads, and she'd like that just fine. But Lucky was not like Dervla or any of the other girls on the island. They loved her no less for that. In fact, they loved her in a very particular way that accorded with her oddness. That girl.

'Then maybe we should give her back to God,' Lucky's father said.

Her mother tensed. The idea had come up before, not as a serious proposition, not as an idea to be acted on, but more as an observation of what Lucky was like. That unworldly girl who was always daydreaming when she wasn't actually praying in the chapel. 'That girl's destined for a convent,' they had said more than once.

'She came to us as a miracle from God,' her father went on. 'Plucked out of the air for us to look after, but perhaps only for a time. And maybe that time is over. Maybe the best way to save her from Conall's oaf of a son is to marry her to Christ.'

Lucky's mother was crying. She would miss that girl.

It was agreed that Lucky's brother Iain would take her

first to the mainland and to the priest who served the island. The priest visited only occasionally to perform mass in their little chapel, but he knew the girl and they were sure he would vouch for her and provide a letter of recommendation or whatever was required. Then brother and sister would seek passage to the holy island of Iona where Lucky would take holy orders and be sure to make a special prayer for them all before Iain returned alone. Lucky's brother was only 18, but he was more than capable as a seaman and generally smart enough to keep his sister and himself out of trouble. He was also excited about taking on the responsibility, so much so that he forgot to express his sorrow at losing his sister.

'I'm not losing a sister,' he said when his mother admonished him. 'We're all gaining a nun.'

The nun took the news surprisingly calmly. She told her parents that, yes, she did think she would quite like to go to Iona to serve God. She cried when her mother and sister embraced her to say goodbye, but that was because they were crying and it made her a bit emotional. When her father lifted her into the little boat that would take her to the mainland, she thought she saw a tear in his eye too, but she was too shocked by that to respond in kind. Iain did not cry, but then he was coming with her. Supplies were packed, and in what felt like no time at all, they were at sea. Lucky's adventure had begun.

CHAPTER 12: CONSTANTINE

Pyrdie, Pendrin and Peter watched from the hillside as the riders approached. Their people had spotted the riders some time ago emerging from the pass on the little mountain that sloped towards the homestead, and the boys had wanted to be the first to identify them. Now the riders were closer, Peter was the first to recognise one of them as Constantine, his older cousin, and indeed Pyrdie's brother.

'Is it?' said Pyrdie, squinting. 'He seems smaller.'

Peter and Pendrin looked at one another and rolled their eyes. 'Just watch as he gets bigger and bigger the closer they get,' Peter said.

'I didn't mean that,' Pyrdie scowled, but he was pleased to see his brother. He was back from war, then, and alive. He had set out many weeks ago with a war band led by Taran, an ambitious nobleman whose lands straddled the glen beyond the loch.

When he was close enough to recognise the boys, Constantine waved happily, and then galloped ahead of his comrades to greet them, dismounting and sweeping up Pyrdie in his arms almost in one motion. Peter and Pendrin had to steady his horse before embracing him in turn.

As the boys bombarded him with questions about

his adventure, Constantine looked down at their home with satisfaction. It was a humble place, comprising a modest longhouse and a sprinkling of huts dug into the ground. Between the settlement and where he stood lay first crop fields of oats and barley, and then pastures where the cattle grazed, though Constantine's thundering arrival had scared them into the distance. Beyond the homestead, the loch stretched majestically in both directions beneath the big mountain on the other side. It had been his first sight of the loch from the little mountain pass that had made Constantine feel he was home. But an enthusiastic welcome from the boys and now a close-up view of the homestead warmed his heart all the more.

'I'll tell you later,' he repeated in response to their questions, and turned to welcome his comrades who were now approaching.

'This is my brother Pyrdie,' he told them, 'and our cousins Pendrin and Peter. Boys, these fine warriors are Brude son of Taran and Donuel the Cunning!'

Brude son of Taran and Donuel the Cunning dismounted and ruffled the boys' hair.

'Come,' Constantine told them, 'you must be as tired and hungry as I am.'

After checking that the boys were in control of the horses, he led his comrades down the hillside, pausing to show them a standing stone marked with his grandfather's trademark design, their family's ancient claim to this land set in stone. The sun was just beginning to set, and the quality of light made the stone look all the more impressive.

They were greeted in the homestead by Constantine's mother and father, a couple of uncles and more curious children. When they were settled by a warm fire with food and drink, Constantine got down to business. 'I didn't intend to return so soon,' he said.

His family knew this, but had been making an effort not to seem too surprised to see him in case he felt less than welcome.

'During the campaign, word reached us from Taran's brother, the bishop, that something was amiss at home. Someone, indeed. Taran's daughter, Brude's sister, has disappeared. You remember Euphemia?' he asked his father, who had presented him as a warrior at Taran's court some years before.

'Of course,' his father replied. 'She's just a wee girl, is she not?'

'Oh, she's grown up a bit now,' said Constantine, trying to avoid eye contact either with Donuel, who was smirking, or with Brude, who was stony-faced. 'You haven't heard anything, then, about Euphemia's whereabouts?'

No one had heard a thing.

'Well, we said we'd search far and wide, so we'll be off again in the morning.'

Brude nudged him.

'But there is something else,' he went on. 'I don't suppose you've seen or heard of a strange hunting party around the loch? Or of a man who hunts with falcons?'

His family just looked at one another, shaking their heads.

'Do you think these hunters have taken the girl?' his father asked.

Constantine shrugged and looked at his comrades.

'It could just be a coincidence,' said Brude, 'but it seems they passed through our village around the same time my sister disappeared.'

'Well, good luck to you,' Constantine's mother said. 'I'll make sure you have plenty of provisions for the search.'

While his comrades rested, Constantine went to see his grandfather, who was sitting outside with the three boys and some other children.

'And how is our warrior?' asked the old man.

'Thriving, grandfather. Thank you.'

The old man waved the children away and bade Constantine sit next to him. 'You've seen battle now?'

Constantine nodded. 'Several skirmishes, a couple of more bloody affairs. I'm fortunate to have good comrades.' He did not add that he was fortunate to have been withdrawn from the campaign before having to face pitched battle, because he did not see it that way. His current mission was more urgent than attritional warfare against enemies who would always be there.

'I'll pray for you,' said the old man.

The warrior knew his grandfather did not approve of his vocation. Theirs was a farming family, if a relatively prosperous one; that was why his grandfather had been able to devote so much of his life to stone carving. As far as the old man was concerned, there was more than enough dignity in that without seeking glory in war. Fighting and politics were the business of the nobles. And as long as they protected the people from enemies while keeping the fighting away from the loch, they earned their tribute. A tribute of meat and grain, not men. But Constantine's mother was of noble birth; hence the fancy name, as his grandfather had always called it. And hence the notion that he might not become a farmer like his father and uncles, or even a stone carver like his grandfather. Constantine could be a warrior's name.

Constantine liked his name, but not because he harboured political ambition, not exactly. Constantine was certainly a name that sat nicely next to other fancy names, but there was one fancy name in particular that he had in mind: Euphemia. Constantine and Euphemia. It had a lovely ring to it. If they could only find her.

He told his grandfather about their quest, not mentioning his particular interest. He said they would ride around the loch to ask after the girl in the various hamlets and homesteads, and if necessary they would ride on over the mountain.

'I'll pray for the girl too,' his grandfather said. 'You know, just the other day I was telling the boys about Prince Cargil, who disappeared when I was a boy.'

'I remember the tale,' Constantine said. 'In fact, more than one version.'

The old man laughed. 'Well, there was a Prince Cargil, whose father reigned on the other side of that very mountain,' he said, pointing across the loch, though the big mountain was lost in the misty darkness. 'And, God willing, you won't need to search that far. But it's also true that he went missing and was never heard of again. Strange things happen in this world.'

'Yes, grandfather. I'll also pray for the girl's safety.'

'Do that, Constantine. Pray for us all. But look, those children are pining for a story. Why don't you step in for me? Just don't give them nightmares.'

So before bed, Constantine told the children about his adventures, which were quite exciting enough even if he left out the blood shed, the bones shattered and the lives destroyed. War was not for children.

CHAPTER 13: FEEDING THE CROWS

Wilfrid thrust his spear into the belly of the oncoming Pictish soldier, twisting up it upwards before withdrawing it and swinging to the left to meet the advance of his victim's comrade. These three were the first to make contact as the allies and the Picts ran at each other. Barely a second later, the Northumbrian captain Beorhtred joined the action, deftly using his spear to disarm the second advancing Pict by sending the latter's raised axe flying and giving Wilfrid an open target, which he did not miss. Two dead at first contact. Then the flying axe was seized mid-air by another Pict, who swung it at Beorhtred, who ducked just in time as the axe flew from the Pict's hand and into the chest of another advancing Northumbrian. Cuthbert hesitated as his comrade went down. He was unsure if the axe had maimed or merely winded the man, but he had no time to stop and see to him. By now, the two armies were fully engaged and he had to fighting to do. Meanwhile, the seemingly unstoppable Wilfrid had cut his way through the enemy throng and out the other side, and now turned to attack again, forcing the Pictish rear-guard to turn and face him.

An eagle flying overhead, if it cared to notice such things, would have seen the two bodies of men collide, a hundred or so on each side, and form a seething mass before a pattern emerged from the confusion. There was a steady rush round one edge of the chaos, as the Gaels, who had formed the right wing of the allied attack, slightly behind the Northumbrian vanguard, began to push round to attack the Picts from the side. This carefully orchestrated tactic, combined with Wilfrid's more spontaneous heroics at their rear, forced the Picts too to divide their efforts on different fronts. And there was carnage on all sides. Whatever the eagle might have felt about it, carrion crows were gathering in anticipation around the edges of the battle.

Cuthbert found himself in close combat with a Pictish warrior who had somehow clamped onto him from behind, disabling one arm, and was now trying to bring a blade to his neck. Unable to manoeuvre his free seax arm to use his weapon properly, all Cuthbert could do was punch his assailant repeatedly in the face over his shoulder; he was at least well positioned to do that, but from such an awkward angle, he could not apply the strength needed to do much more than annoy the Pict as the blade danced ever closer to his own neck. In desperation, Cuthbert bent suddenly forward, thrusting his backside sharply against his assailant. And indeed, his arse proved more effective than his fist: the move knocked his assailant off his feet, allowing Cuthbert to flip him over his own shoulders and onto his back, his flailing feet crashing into another combatant as he landed. Cuthbert quickly struck with his seax to finish the job, but as he span around to identify his next foe, he was aware of a stinging pain in his neck. The blade had done some damage even as its owner had been thrown. He put his hand to the wound, but had little time to assess its seriousness before he was once again locked in combat.

Wilfrid now met his match, or something approaching it, in a Pictish warrior who had been summoned to the task when the Pictish commander had realised Wilfrid's particular threat. The battle prodigy was now contained at least, and the fighting swirled around him as he and his opponent sized one another up with blows and parries. But the Gaels' flanking manoeuvre was beginning to tell. Caught in the allies' pincer movement, dozens of Pictish soldiers had either fallen or retreated. Beorhtred rallied his Northumbrian troops for what looked like being a decisive charge, while the Gaels prepared to sweep up what remained of the enemy. But then something uncanny happened.

There was a roar of thunder, and suddenly the sky darkened. At first, the fighting continued amid confused shouts and uncertain, conflicting commands in three languages, though it sounded like more. *Press on! Retreat! Hold the line! Who said that?* It was not just dark, but as black as night. It was mid-afternoon, and yet impossible to see your hand in front of your face. Those whose instincts told them to go on fighting could do no more than swing their weapons randomly in the dark, and they soon felt the folly of that, if not before maiming God knew whom. Then another roar, but this time unlike thunder any man there had ever heard before. Nobody knew where he was going, but every man fled.

When the day broke – whether it was the next morning or not he could not say – Cuthbert lay in a ditch. He sat up and looked around him, or tried to: as he moved his neck he felt a sharp pain. He touched the wound; it was nasty but no longer bleeding. His throat was intact. God willing, he would be fine. Unless the two Pictish soldiers he saw not twenty paces further along the ditch had other ideas. They were looking beyond him, though. He turned painfully to see a pair of Gaels rising from the ditch behind him. The foes regarded each other cautiously, with little appetite for more fighting. The Picts spoke between themselves in their own language as they surveyed the landscape, and then set off, backwards at first, but decisively. They seemed to know where they were going. The Gaels also conferred in their language and then looked at Cuthbert. Spontaneously, all three raised an arm to point in the opposite direction to that taken by the Picts. Cuthbert would have joined in with the Gaels' laughter if it hadn't hurt too much.

The allies had been fighting together long enough to know one another by sight, but as they walked, Cuthbert introduced himself properly in beginner's Gaelic. He also confirmed that, yes, he was a good friend of Wilfrid, who had been making a name for himself even before his latest heroics. (In fact, in the confusion of battle, few of those taking part had even seen those. And for all anyone knew, Wilfrid could be dead.) The Gaels were Domnall and Fergus. They were older than Cuthbert, but not much more than 20. Having exhausted Cuthbert's spoken Gaelic, the three soldiers traipsed in a dazed silence, broken intermittently when Domnall and Fergus spoke between themselves about the current campaign and about the politics of the Gaelic kingdom of Dalriada, and Cuthbert followed their conversation as best he could.

After walking for some time, they spotted another group in the distance. Cuthbert was pleased to recognise Beorhtred and Alcuin among the mixed company of Northumbrians and Gaels. It was as close to coming home as he was likely to get. Indeed, Beorhtred examined his wound almost paternally before pronouncing he would live. Few of their comrades had got away without injuries just as bad. Alcuin had a shining black eye and, more worryingly, a limp from a twisted ankle; hardly life threatening in the normal course of things, but any impediment to fighting – or running – could now prove deadly.

The weary allies made their way to the last hilltop muster point where they'd gathered and camped before the battle, and where much-needed supplies had been stashed. By the time the sun went down, there were about fifty of them. Half the number that had joined battle that afternoon.

Or the *previous* afternoon; no one was completely sure whether the sun had returned the same day or whether the darkness had stretched into night. Battle disturbed men's sense of time even in normal circumstances. And these were far from normal circumstances. Having found themselves hidden in ditches or copses or in the lee of boulders when the sun came up, the soldiers had little sense of how exactly they'd got there, or of how long they'd huddled there in the dark, or whether they'd slept or not, and they had no idea whether they had traipsed for a few hours or a whole day before finding the muster point. Yet, while there was some debate about what day it was, nobody seemed to want to talk explicitly about the mysterious darkness that had brought the battle to an end, let alone the terrifying roar that had sent them all flying. Despite his own burning curiosity, Cuthbert was not inclined to upset his elders by bringing it up. Instead, he and his comrades ate mostly in silence before setting shifts of sentries and going to sleep.

The morning brought a few stragglers, including Wilfrid, whose appearance cheered the men, but not as much as he would have liked. The lack of talk about the battle meant most still had no idea that he'd single-handedly opened a new front and slain a dozen of their enemies, including, just as darkness had descended, the champion sent to contain him. From his perspective, the battle had been all but won, no small thanks to himself. But for all the young man's heroics, the perspectives that mattered were those of the veteran warriors, and above all Beorhtred and his Gaelic counterpart. They were now deep in discussion, made still more ponderous by the need for interpreters. So while Wilfrid regaled the other younger Northumbrians with an account of said heroics, Cuthbert sidled up to the bilingual summit that would decide what happened next.

Domnall and Fergus sat within earshot of the allied leaders but at a respectful distance, so he quietly joined them. Fergus whispered that the Gaelic captain, whose name was Dougal, was keen to press home the allies' advantage by hunting down the company of Picts and finishing them off. After all, the whole point of the campaign was to deplete the Picts' capacity for aggression. Beorhtred seemed to agree, but was wary of risking another pitched battle in case the Picts had reinforcements. While they had slain many more of the enemy, the allies' own numbers were badly depleted, though not as badly as it had appeared last night; perhaps as many as 20 more soldiers appeared over the course of the morning. Emboldened by that, the captains agreed to send three small scouting parties to seek out the Picts and gauge their strength. They were to leave now and report back within hours, whether they found the enemy or not. If they did find them nursing their wounds in manageable numbers, the whole company would attack today.

The veteran warriors rose in good spirits and organised the scouts. Cuthbert was not among them, so he sat down and reflected on his experience of war so far. Yesterday, or the day before, had been his first pitched battle. Since the terror of his first contact with the enemy some weeks earlier, he had been involved in several skirmishes: two more hit-and-run ambushes and a few encounters while scouting away from the main company. That was how Wilfrid had distinguished himself, which was why he was among the scouts again. Cuthbert had barely held his own, but he was glad to have had the experience before facing battle. Even without the terrifying darkness and the unearthly roar – those things of which he would never speak – it had been unlike anything he had ever imagined. If he had not, before then, at least learned to keep his head as men were trying to kill him, he feared he would have died of shock the second he'd felt the malicious chaos of battle. He pawed his wound and felt quietly proud that he had survived.

And killed, of course. Cuthbert had landed some vicious blows in those previous skirmishes, but the man he'd thrown from his back and then stabbed through the chest was the first he was sure he had killed. There may have been one or two others after that too, but it didn't matter. Cuthbert had chosen war, and now he was a warrior.

Early that afternoon, when the scouts had been gone nearly two hours, the warrior sat chatting with his comrades.

The battle, and especially the subsequent scattering and reassembly of the company, had brought the Gaels and Northumbrians closer together, and rather than forming separate clusters, they now mingled more easily despite the language barrier. So when Cuthbert noticed something glinting in the woods just down the slope from their camp, he muttered first in his own language, 'Don't all look at once, but there's someone in those woods.' Then, in Gaelic, all he could manage was, 'Woods. Danger.'

In fact, the forewarned Northumbrians were not much better than the Gaels at resisting a concerted gawp, and more glinting in the woods was followed by furious rustling.

Domnall was the first on his feet, spear in hand, rushing down the slope. Cuthbert ran after him, as veteran warriors shouted commands to ensure sufficient men stayed behind to secure their position in case of a ruse. As Domnall plunged into the woods, Cuthbert instinctively hesitated at the edge. It was a good instinct. A Pictish soldier emerged from cover and lunged at Domnall from behind: Cuthbert was just in time to cut him down before he could do any damage, and then followed Domnall through the woods and out the other side; it was a small patch. But there was no sign of any more Picts. 'They could be in the grass,' Domnall said, frustrated – and pointing to be sure Cuthbert understood – and indeed there was plenty of tall grass about. But as they strode cautiously through it, jabbing with their weapons, there were shouts from behind, calling them back. It transpired that their comrades had killed two more Pictish scouts as they emerged from the side of the woods. One more had got away. But now the allies' own scouts had returned. There was news.

By the time everyone had made it back to the camp, word had already spread. The rump of the Pictish company had been found close by. The allies were going after them right now.

CHAPTER 14: MACCUTHBERT

An eagle flying over the clearing where the allies had fallen on their enemies would have seen just a handful of Pictish warriors escape with their lives into the hills as the victorious allied army marched back to their camp. And as darkness fell, it would have heard the same all-penetrating howl that spread outwards from the clearing to reach them all – vanquished and victors alike. Cuthbert fell a chill when he heard it. He knew Alcuin lay on the battlefield. He had found his fallen comrade with the battle all but finished, and seeing there was no hope for him, he had run him through with his seax, a final act of mercy for his friend. The knowledge that he had spared Alcuin unnecessary agony was a source of solace for Cuthbert, and after a shift on sentry duty, he slipped into a deep sleep.

In fact, while Cuthbert was a proven warrior now, he was not a skilful butcher. Alcuin lay alive on the battlefield. He abruptly returned to consciousness when a crow pecked at his face. At least his comrades had not *buried* him alive. There had not been time before darkness fell. But now he faced the indignity spared the dead in the ground. And worse than indignity. The crow at his face had backed off when he shuddered awake, but he felt sharp talons on his leg, and another beak battering painfully at his chest. He still had his axe by his side, and managed to wave it weakly in a bid to scare off his tormentors, but he could barely move his body. So he lay on his back, mortally wounded, he was sure, and prayed silently that he would die from his wounds before he could be eaten alive. But when the crows suddenly scattered, he knew it was not in answer to his prayers. It was too dark now to see them, but a second later he could smell the wolves. Hot, damp, Hellish. Another feeble wave of his axe persuaded the first of the beasts to pass him by in favour of a less animate meal, but he knew he would not be able to fend them off for long. The crows were also lingering. There were perhaps thirty bodies, mostly Pictish, strewn about the clearing. A feast for scavengers.

'Is anyone else alive?' Alcuin called out.

Someone answered in Pictish. Then there was another voice, but the sound it made was not like any language. Alcuin began to pray aloud, if for no other reason than to assert his humanity, to protest that he was not food. The Pictish voice also continued, perhaps in prayer, almost certainly for the same reason as Alcuin. The third voice wheezed and droned in solidarity. Their shared humanity was all they had left now. But the wolves and the crows were oblivious to it. The crows cawed cacophonously, drowning out the jabbering of their carrion, until a wolf began to howl. It was a howl that seemed to rise from the depths of Hell itself. And when other wolves joined in, it became a cry of triumph, an assertion of wolfdom. Whichever side had won or lost in the human battle here was of no interest to them. It meant nothing now. The humans that remained were food. And as the wolves' howl filled the clearing, all three survivors died instantly of terror.

When the howl reached Beorhtred and Dougal, they looked at one another grimly. They had agreed it had not been practical to bury the bodies, but they knew what that meant. And as Christians they took no more pleasure from the thought of their enemies ending up as carrion than their friends. Still, they had won the battle, finished the job. The scrappy, ill-defined war against the Picts was far from over, but the two captains and their men had done their bit for now, blunted the Picts' capacity to make war from here or hereabouts this year. They had done enough to justify going home.

Domnall and Fergus were excited when the much-anticipated news was confirmed. Not because they were going home, though. They had other plans. Domnall's uncle, who was also a distant cousin of Fergus, had asked them to run an errand as soon as they were free. Part of the reason for their excitement was that they knew so little about what this errand would involve, other than the handsome reward they had been promised. All they knew was they were to travel to Alt Clut, the mighty rock at the mouth of the Great Western River of the lowlands, which was the stronghold of the Britons and the ancestral home of Domnall's uncle's wife. There they would receive further instructions from her brother, whose name was Rhodri. They were to bring a third man, but someone they could trust not to talk about it, especially not to their fellow Gaels. And there was nobody in their own company who did not owe deeper loyalties to others among their countrymen. In other words, they would have to recruit one of the Northumbrians.

For Fergus, there was no debate to be had. 'Let's bring Wilfrid. The lad's a one-man army, a Northumbrian Cuhullin!'

Domnall shook his head. 'No, that lad'll be dead before he's seen two or three more fights. He takes too many risks and his luck'll run out. No, Cuthbert's our man. He's got a head on his shoulders and he likes it there. Besides, he's picking up the Gaelic.'

Fergus thought for a moment, a sceptical look crossing his face before departing in the face of Domnall's reasoning. 'All right, then. MacCuthbert it is.'

CHAPTER 15: OVER THE MOUNTAIN

Constantine and Brude and Donuel visited four settlements with no luck, taking them to the end of the loch and round the other side, before they found a farmer who said he had seen a man hunting with falcons. This had been a week or so ago, he said, so not long after Euphemia had gone missing, but the farmer had seen no sign of a girl, just a hunter with two birds. He'd been up on the mountain. A few of the locals had noticed the birds and watched them, wary for their own animals, but then they'd noticed something unusual about the birds' behaviour, flying here and there from a fixed point and back. Finally the farmers had spied the birds' master, the hunter, who had waved to them cheerfully, to reassure them they supposed. They had not seen him again since.

The lads rode on to the next homestead, where they were told a similar story. And the next, with the sighting at each a little more recent than the last. But then the trail came to an end. At the next place, the people had seen nothing. And between that one and the previous one lay a pass over the big mountain. It looked like their quest would take them over it after all. They made camp at the foot of the pass, built a fire and ate.

Then Donuel began to sing songs of valiant deeds on

the battlefield. Ancient songs. Songs passed down through the ages, from an otherwise long forgotten time of heroes and of magic. Donuel sang in particular of a feud between two sets of brothers who were cousins to one another. They raised vast armies to fight one another, as many on each side as there are stars in the sky. That was just as well, because the slaughter was also on a stellar scale. The heroes wielded terrible, magic weapons that could kill a thousand men with one blow. And yet since each set of cousins had an equally formidable army of heroes, neither side could gain a permanent advantage. The war often came down to wiles, which was why Donuel the Cunning loved this song in particular.

In one vital battle, the sons of Elphin had the upper hand over the sons of Ciniod, thanks to the hero Calcin, who seemed to be everywhere on the battlefield, bringing death and destruction like a plague for days and nights on end. The sons of Ciniod almost despaired, until their wisest counsellor pointed out that Calcin had a weakness, his attachment to his son Curetan, who was a valiant warrior in his own right. If Curetan could be slain, perhaps his father would lose heart. Only nobody knew where Curetan was or how to kill him. No matter, the counsellor went on. What mattered was only that Calcin *believed* his son was dead. Only, in those days, heroes did not lie. Better to lose the battle and face total destruction at the hands of the sons of Elphin than to speak a falsehood. The counsellor was undeterred. He pointed to a stout battle pony and announced that its name was Curetan. Taking his cue without hesitation, one of the sons of Ciniod, Drust, immediately slew the beast and set off into the midst of battle to announce he had slain Curetan.

Calcin heard the fateful news just as he was about to deploy the deadliest magic weapon known to man, which would surely have wiped out the army of the sons of Ciniod in a second. He hesitated. He roared in disbelief that it could not be true. But then he saw Drust himself, and believing the hero would never utter a lie, he asked him directly, 'Has Curetan really been slain?'

Drust answered back, 'Yes, Curetan has been slain by my own hand,' before adding in a soft whisper, '*but it is a pony called Curetan*'.

Hearing only the first part of Drust's utterance, Calcin despaired and lost heart. And his head. Because just then he was decapitated by another warrior of the sons of Ciniod, who thus took revenge for Calcin's humiliation of his own father decades before, but that is the subject of another song.

Constantine and Brude laughed uproariously at the conclusion of Donuel's song, though they had heard it many times before. They too loved these songs of a heroic age of magic and honour. And what was funnier about that whispered qualification to Drust's lie? The fact that it was whispered, or the fact that he'd felt the need to say it at all? They didn't know, but part of them yearned to live in a world where such things were felt to matter. Perhaps they dreamt that night about living in such a world.

They rose at dawn and set off up to the mountain pass. The going was tough, and at times they had to dismount and climb on foot alongside their horses. But the higher they climbed, the better the view of the glen and the loch behind them. Before they left the mountainside to follow the pass between two peaks, Constantine took several minutes to take in the view. He pointed out his home across the loch, and said a prayer for his family. He'd forgotten to do that before leaving for war, and had feared dying without ever seeing home again. If they found Euphemia on the other side of the mountain, they would return the same way – and he could introduce the girl to his family. If not, they would take another route back to Brude's glen in the hope of finding her that way. Either way, when they finally made it to Taran's house, they would probably be sent back to war.

As they rode through the pass, a steady drizzle turned to heavy rain, so when Donuel saw something on the hillside above them, the others were reluctant to investigate, preferring to push on. Donuel rode off anyway, cantering up the slope while the others waited grudgingly in the rain. What he found was a pile of stones that could only have been assembled deliberately, and on it the remains of two hares that had clearly been picked over by scavenging birds. He kicked at the stones probingly, but there didn't seem to be anything else to it. He rode back down to the others. 'It looks like a sacrifice,' he said. Constantine and Brude looked at one another uneasily, not sure what he meant. 'An animal sacrifice to the old gods,' Donuel continued. 'My own grandparents used to do it till the priest forbade them.' He shrugged. 'Let's push on.'

The rain stopped as they emerged from the pass onto the open mountain on the other side, and they were able to admire the glen beneath them, with a wide, sparkling river at its base. A large settlement lay on an island where the river split for a stretch before rejoining itself. Perhaps the men who had built it had diverted the river to suit their purposes. In any case it was an impressive-looking place. 'That must be King Gartnait's city,' Brude said, though 'city' was pushing it. They began a steady descent in the direction of what was at least the seat of a kingdom.

By the time they got there, their arrival was news to nobody: five armed horsemen forded the river to meet them. Brude introduced himself as Brude son of Taran, reluctantly adding a brief description of where this Taran held sway, since he knew that otherwise they would embarrass him by asking who his father was. He said he brought Taran's greetings and requested King Gartnait's hospitality and assistance. The leader of the five men announced that he was the king's son Prince Fidach. He said Brude and his companions were welcome and led them back across the river into the settlement. The locals looked up as they passed, interested but not surprised to see such visitors. Up close, the visitors could see the settlement's many wooden buildings included a church and several sizeable halls as well as smaller dwellings. They were taken first to the stables, where they dismounted and handed over their steeds to the horse master and his lads. Then they were led to the king's hall, where Gartnait awaited them.

Gartnait sat at the head of a table, flanked by courtiers, while numerous servants or hangers-on stood or sat around the hall. Gartnait was an old man now, but he had once been a legendary warrior, and had forcibly wrested his kingship here from the line of King Uther. After the mysterious disappearance of Prince Cargil, Uther had been succeeded by a nephew, whose own sons had then reigned until Gartnait had overthrown them. At the same time he had subjugated a number of neighbouring potentates – not quite kings, but their submission removed any doubt about his own claim to that title. When Brude was announced, King Gartnait was gracious enough to acknowledge that he knew of Taran and his campaign against the foreigners. 'What can I do for you?' he asked.

Brude explained that they were searching for his missing sister, and that their only lead was a man who hunted with falcons. At that, the king summoned an underling to his side and whispered instructions before sending him away. Food and drink were then brought for the guests and they sat at table as the king enquired politely about their journey until the underling returned with another man. 'I believe this is the man you are looking for,' said the king. Brude and Constantine and Donuel looked at the man, then at one another and then back at King Gartnait. 'Ask him whatever you wish.'

Brude stood up, faced the man and asked if he had been hunting with falcons on the other side of the mountain. 'Yes, I was,' said the man. 'What of it?'

Brude asked him if he'd also been hunting in their glen a week or so ago. 'I was. What of it?'

Brude shifted uncomfortably before telling the hunter they'd been following him in search of his sister Euphemia, who had disappeared around that time. He explained that he was Brude son of Taran, but he knew the hunter would have worked that much out by now and perhaps even recognised him from his boyhood. Brude had not told Constantine or Donuel that the hunter was his father's exiled political rival; it was a family secret, or had been. The hunter looked at King Gartnait. It was not clear what, if anything, they were to one another. It seemed to Donuel, observing without Brude's political discomfort, that the hunter was not looking to the king for permission to speak freely, but rather to gauge his mood. He had something to say, all right, and something not already known to the king.

The hunter looked back to Brude. 'I don't know anything about your sister,' he said, 'but nor have I seen my son since we passed through your glen. Perhaps they are together.'

A murmur of intrigue went round the hall. Brude did not know what to say.

'I did not know you had a son,' King Gartnait said.

'No, my lord,' said the hunter. 'He sometimes travels with me, but he is no hunter. And…' The hunter hesitated. 'I do not require him in order to provide my services.'

Donuel whispered to a still flummoxed Brude, who then managed, 'Might I ask what those services are?'

King Gartnait took control: 'This man is both a hunter and a seer. And he is not here because we are in need of hares for the pot.'

A ripple of laughter went round the hall. Brude did not know what to say.

The king now addressed the seer. 'Are you able to use your craft to help Brude son of Taran find his sister?'

Brude looked nervously at his companions. This was all happening too fast.

'If Brude son of Taran wishes it, I will,' said the hunter-seer.

CHAPTER 16: THE SEER

The seer sat cross-legged in front of the fire in King Gartnait's hall, gazing into the flames. Brude had reluctantly agreed to have him use his 'second sight' to search out Euphemia, and even more reluctantly to have this done in front of Gartnait's court. The king had assured him the seer worked best with an audience. All eyes were on the mysterious hunter, then, as he hunted for a vision of his one-time rival's daughter, the princess of the glen he had once sought to rule. 'I hold no grudge against your father,' he had whispered to Brude before taking up his position in front of the fire, 'and wish your sister only well.' Brude did not know what to believe, what to think, but merely stood impassively, flanked by Constantine and Donuel, watching the seer intently as King Gartnait and his court looked on more curiously.

After a while, the seer closed his eyes and breathed deeply for several minutes, muttering indecipherably to himself before giving any indication that he saw something by his second sight. Then he leant forward toward the fire, without opening his eyes. 'I see a girl sitting in an ancient yew tree,' he said.

Brude stiffened.

'I believe it is your sister Euphemia, Brude son of Taran.

But she is not at home in your glen.'

'Where is she?'

'I see water. And no mere river or loch, but the sea. She is close to the sea.'

'The sea?' said Brude. 'What sea? Where?'

'And now she is singing,' the seer continued, heedless of Brude's question, 'singing happily. She is singing of the sea and the sky and the sun. And of love.'

At that, Brude looked at Constantine and Donuel and detected disapproval and suspicion respectively. 'Who else is there?' he demanded.

Again, the seer continued regardless, 'She is singing of love and of joy and…' He hesitated.

'And what?' Brude demanded, impatient now.

'And she appears to be with child.'

Everyone gasped. When the initial shock had passed, Brude objected, 'She's been gone barely two weeks!'

Someone stifled laughter.

'And now she is falling from the tree,' the seer continued, 'And yet not from a tree. She is falling into darkness, into the black of night, falling, falling.'

Brude and his friends looked at one another nervously, suspiciously, thoughtfully.

'But now she rides the dragon. She is no longer falling but flying. She is the mistress of the dragon.'

'What is this rubbish?' muttered Constantine, but Brude hushed him.

The seer continued: 'She wears a crown, a crown of twelve stars, even as she rides the dragon. The dragon wants to devour her child, but she will not let it. She is the mistress of the dragon.'

Constantine and Donuel exchanged sceptical looks, but Brude was captivated, as were King Gartnait and his court, albeit with a more detached enjoyment. It seemed they had developed a taste for this stuff.

'There is a struggle,' the seer continued. 'Vast armies are

ranged on either side of a cosmic battle for dominion...'

Now Constantine smiled knowingly at Donuel the Storyteller.

'...one is led by the girl's child, and the other... But now all is dark again. The girl sits once more on the ancient yew tree. She sings of love, and of the sea and the sky and the sun. The sun is rising over the sea, all a-shimmering like fire.' He opened his eyes, returning to the actual fire in front of him. 'I see no more.'

'Well,' said Gartnait to Brude, 'these things are not all to be taken literally. But if the sun is rising over the sea, your sister is somewhere on the east coast.'

'Or will be,' added the seer. 'Not all that can be taken literally will already have come to pass.'

'And what of the rest?' Brude asked. 'This dragon and the crown and the battle? And a child?'

'My gift is second sight,' said the seer. 'Interpretation is best left to he who seeks the vision.'

Brude turned to his friends, who shrugged unhelpfully.

No more was said of the vision as the court dined that evening. King Gartnait was a generous host, and as his courtiers and guests ate and drank, they were entertained by more conventional means: musicians played on harp and pipes and drum, and a bard sang of Gartnait's legendary exploits. These were not quite a match for Donuel's song the previous night, but entertaining nonetheless. A particular favourite of all who heard it was the story of how Gartnait had conquered the kingdom of the elves.

The magical creatures had long held out against the conqueror, using their wiles to counter his superior might. Their armies had disappeared in the mist only to reappear at Gartnait's rear, they had conjured unnaturally large and vicious swarms of midges to torment his people, and their womenfolk had appeared at awkward moments to seduce his warriors. Gartnait had finally prevailed by tricking an elven ambassador into revealing his king's true and secret elven name, thereby robbing him of the magic that sustained his kingdom. As Gartnait and his army rode on the defenceless king's palace, it had disappeared into thin air, leaving Gartnait the undisputed ruler of the lands the elves had once called their own, where they had wrought mischief on any man who dared enter. This victory had added further to Gartnait's prestige as king of all he surveyed, adding the sprinkle of magic and myth on which true kingship depended.

At the song's chorus, the king joined in, holding aloft something he wore around his neck, as did all those present who had numbered among his finest warriors in those bygone days of yore. They were little stone arrowheads, left behind where the elven king's palace had once stood. Elves, it was said, cannot work metal like men do, relying as they do on magic rather than craft. So they made their weapons from stone, and now their conquerors wore them as charms as well as trophies. Since his victory, Gartnait's kingdom had never been bothered by elves or fairies of any kind. It was magically protected. Only the kingdom's bishop disapproved of this song, and he had been getting steadily drunker since the seer's performance.

Between songs, Brude spoke once more to the seer, since they were about to go their separate ways in the morning. The seer could not or would not shed any more light on his vision, but promised to send word to King Gartnait if he heard anything of Euphemia, whether from his son or anyone else. Gartnait would make sure word reached Taran. Brude was curious to know more about what had happened in the past between his father and this strange man, but the fact that his father had never mentioned it to him left him feeling uncomfortably exposed. As frustrating as it was to be left in the dark, he could hardly ask the seer to fill him in.

When everyone began retiring for the night, Brude, Constantine and Donuel settled down not too far from the fire and whispered among themselves. Donuel's mind was hard at work trying to interpret the seer's vision; Constantine was sure it was all rubbish. Brude did not know what to think. But in the morning they would continue on their quest, now heading east for the sea.

CHAPTER 17: SILVER

Cuthbert and Domnall and Fergus approached Alt Clut by boat, having sailed downriver from the Loch of the Elms, which straddled the lands of all four nations in those days. The fortress itself was less impressive than the mighty double-humped rock on which it stood, dominating the landscape for miles around, but up there it was intimidating enough. The Britons had seen off numerous Pictish attempts to take the Rock, and the adventurers were glad they came as friends. None of them spoke the language of the Britons, of course, but the boatman who took them assured them they would be able to make themselves understood by speaking Gaelic very slowly and gesturing with their hands. In any case, they'd been instructed to ask for a man by name: Rhodri, brother of Rhianwen of the Gaels (Domnall's aunt by marriage). He would surely speak Gaelic. They had their first opportunity to ask for him when they were greeted by two heavily armed horsemen patrolling the riverbank. And to their surprise one of them spoke reasonably good Gaelic. The patrolmen seemed satisfied if not particularly impressed by Rhodri's name, and told them to disembark and continue on foot to the strangers' gate at the base of the rock. The adventurers thanked the boatman and proceeded as instructed while the patrolmen continued upriver.

At the strangers' gate they were asked to wait while someone went to look for Rhodri. There was a small market in the vicinity of the gate, with plenty of bustle to keep them entertained while they waited, so they sat to eat the last of their provisions where they could watch the river they'd come down join the Great Western River and the latter spread out towards the sea and the lands of the Gaels and the setting sun.

After an hour or so, someone came over to get them. He was a young monk, which was both unexpected and oddly reassuring; monks were familiar figures to folk of all nations. 'You people foreigners visit Rhodri?' he asked in awkward Gaelic.

'We are,' said Domnall, and the monk led them through the gate and up a steep winding path to the fortress. At the top of the rock they passed through another gate and the monk ushered them into one of several small outbuildings by the side of the main fortress. He did not follow them in, but two men were waiting for them, sitting on stools at a large, bare table in the building's single room. One looked like a soldier. The other was obviously in charge. 'Rhodri?' Domnall asked.

'I am,' said the latter, motioning for the visitors to sit down on the remaining stools.

Domnall introduced himself, Fergus and Cuthbert. Rhodri did not introduce the soldier, but told them that the monk's name was Valentine and they were not to talk to him about anything they were about to discuss. Rhodri spoke Gaelic, but with a funny accent that made Fergus want to laugh; Domnall gave him a harsh look to keep him sober as Rhodri explained their mission. As he did so, Domnall and Fergus began exchanging looks, first bemused, then quizzical, but after some back and forth with Rhodri, they shrugged and seemed satisfied. Cuthbert could not follow a word Rhodri said, and could make little sense of what his friends said, so when Rhodri lifted a small chest from under his stool onto the table, he had no idea what to expect. When Rhodri opened the chest, Cuthbert gasped. It was full of silver.

Rhodri invited his guests to examine it more closely, and one at a time, they reached in to grab a handful before letting it slip between their fingers, clanging satisfyingly into the rest of the treasure. When Cuthbert took his turn, he saw that much of the silver was recognisable as table silver that had been cut up and bent over to serve as currency. He thought of Saint Oswald, the great Northumbrian king, martyr and saint who had died a century before. One Easter, it was said, Oswald had been about to dine with Saint Aidan, the Gaelic monk who had founded the monastery at Lindisfarne at Oswald's behest, when a great crowd of the poor came to beg alms. Well, Oswald not only gave them his and Aidan's own food to eat, but – lacking the Lord's own ability to make a modest repast feed multitudes – he also ordered the silver platter on which the food had been served to be broken up and distributed among the crowd. Overcome with loving admiration for this charitable gesture – and apparently not overcome with hunger – Saint Aidan had then grasped Oswald's right hand and exclaimed, "May this hand never perish!" And indeed it had not, even after the saint himself had died. To that day, it was preserved in the church at Bamburgh. Cuthbert looked at his own right hand, full of silver just like the stuff Saint Oswald had given to the poor, and shuddered.

'You can let it go now,' Domnall told him, laughing politely to reassure Rhodri. Cuthbert dropped the silver, not having noticed that he'd held onto it for longer than was expected or acceptable. He joined Domnall's laughter and smiled awkwardly at Rhodri, who was unperturbed. 'Relax,' he told Domnall. 'It's all counted, weighed and carefully documented!' He patted his tunic, where a document describing the hoard in minute detail was presumably secured. 'I don't have to *trust* you any more than you would trust me. Besides, I've already deducted your reward.'

With that, he handed them each three silver coins. Then he nodded to the soldier, and the two of them departed, leaving the adventurers alone with the rest of the silver.

'Well?' Cuthbert asked, alternating his incredulous gaze between the coins in his palm and the Gaels.

'Let's not tell him,' said Fergus. 'It'll be a funny surprise.'

Domnall was not in the mood for jokes. 'We've to take the silver back up the river,' he told Cuthbert in mercifully clear Gaelic. 'And we've to head towards Iona, but we won't get that far.'

Fergus was shaking his head and sniggering.

'Why?' Cuthbert demanded, annoyed to be left out.

'We're going to be robbed,' Domnall went on. 'By Picts.'

Cuthbert's basic Gaelic meant it took a while for Domnall to explain the plan fully. The mission to Iona was a ruse. Ostensibly the silver was a donation from Rhodri to the monastery at Iona, designed in part to enhance the prestige of the local saint's shrine of which he was patron. Perhaps it would have that effect anyway if the story got out as intended. In fact, the silver was meant for an ambitious Pictish strongman called Taran. Rhodri's brother in law, Domnall's uncle, had formed a secret alliance with him, one that involved both men usurping more powerful potentates on their own 'side'. Rhodri clearly had a stake in this alliance too, but he hadn't felt the need to explain it. Anyway, the silver was part of the deal, but the gift could hardly be made openly. The 'robbery' was both to save face and to create a bit of a stir that could be exploited all round. But there would be no actual violence. The adventurers merely had to go through the motions of putting up a fight, and then surrender the prize. Cuthbert shook his head in disbelief.

There was a knock on the door, and then the monk Valentine came in with food and drink. He pointed to some fresh straw in the corner for bedding and asked if they needed anything else. They did not, so he bade them good night and told them Rhodri would be back in the morning to see them off.

Valentine did not know why Rhodri had summoned these foreigners, and neither did he particularly want to know. He himself had been summoned from Govan to Alt Clut for his mother's wedding to Rhodri. She had been a widow for some years now, and while she had little wealth to speak of, their family name was prestigious, making her a fine catch for the ambitious Rhodri. But to be fair to her, she seemed ten years younger since she'd taken up with him. Having been sliding prematurely into old age, the widow had found a new lease of life with her new man, and her son could not begrudge her that.

Anyway, it was not that Rhodri lacked interesting ancestry. He claimed descent from a bastard child of legend. Centuries before, the legend went, a certain young woman had been seduced by a powerful nobleman. This had been in the early days of the church among their people, when Saint Ninian himself was engaged in the holy task of training priests to minister to the people, and travelling the land to encourage and support them. Well, the saint's spiritual mettle was certainly tested when the nobleman in question persuaded the pregnant woman to point the finger at her local priest. The whole community was outraged by the priest's alleged misuse of the girl, and the enemies of the church were quick to make use of the scandal. The reputation of the church and the very name of Jesus Christ were in peril among all those who heard the story. So, once the child had been born, Ninian called a meeting of the church and invited anyone who wanted to know the truth to come along. Everyone came along. And in front of the assembled people, Ninian reminded the woman that God himself was listening and hated lies, and asked her again who was the father of her baby. She stuck to her story, insisting that the priest had ravished her, and the assembled crowd was in uproar. But Ninian silenced them and declared that the baby itself would reveal the truth. And he spoke to the tiny infant at its mother's breast, 'Child, tell me who is your father!' And, amazing to relate, the baby spoke: 'That man is my father!' and pointed to the nobleman who was the real culprit. Thus Saint Ninian revealed the truth and preserved the good name of the church. But it was a strange tale for anyone to adopt as family history. Whether it was true or not that he was descended from the miraculous bastard, Rhodri, or whichever of his ancestors had first made the claim, clearly had an odd sense of humour.

Valentine's spiritual mentor Gawin knew about the marriage, of course, but he had not told Valentine that Rhodri had been responsible for the arrest of Morgan's mother. The matter was of no particular interest to Valentine. And of course Gawin had never learned of the missing silver, which, unknown to Valentine, partially explained the presence of the foreigners. If Gawin seemed suspicious of Rhodri, Valentine supposed, that was more than adequately explained by the fact that Rhodri was a worldly strongman, and the patron, probably for worldly reasons, of Govan's would-be rival monks at the shrine of Saint Mirin. Throw in that odd sense of humour, and who wouldn't be suspicious? Valentine had to remind himself that Rhodri made his old mother happy.

Cuthbert awoke in the night. He had an idea. What if he were to go on to Iona anyway? Make a little pilgrimage? He knew Domnall and Fergus were planning to return to their home in the islands once the job was over. Cuthbert had supposed he would return to Northumbria, but where was the rush? He was not someone who thought much about God or religion, but after the fake robbery he would be at a loose end. And having embarked on a career as a soldier – or soldier-cum-seax-for-hire, or pretend-seax-for-hire or whatever he'd be doing for the next few days – he felt he would benefit from some reflection, perhaps even some spiritual guidance.

He could at least now imagine a life for himself as a fighting man. He was no Wilfrid, but then Wilfrid was an exception. The veteran soldiers Cuthbert had got to know were more like himself. They were brave when they had to be, but conscious that a profession that called for bravery also called for caution. They were careful men who owned their fear even as they overcame it. He recognised the same quality in Domnall and Fergus, and supposed they'd also recognised it in him, which is why they'd asked him to join them. He doubted

Wilfrid would have seen the funny side of a mission with no actual fighting, little to no actual risk. There was no honour in it either. Just the silver that Cuthbert now found himself reaching for in the folds of his tunic and turning over in his fingers as he lay in the dark next to two Gaels on the rock of the Britons. Was this a good life? Or might he at least be on the path to a good life? What should he do next? He didn't know. Maybe God would tell him, if only he asked.

As a child, Cuthbert had been taken to Magilros, the monastery where his namesake Saint Cuthbert had been educated and trained to serve the church. It had just been a pilgrimage, but his father had joked about leaving him there to become a monk, and Cuthbert had cried, not sure that it was a joke. Now, the monastery at Magilros had been founded by the same Saint Aidan who had founded the monastery at Lindisfarne. Aidan in turn had been trained at the monastery on Iona. Indeed, it was there that he had befriended the future King Oswald of Northumbria, who had invited him to Lindisfarne. And now another thought occurred to Cuthbert. Perhaps when he got to Iona, he should donate his silver coins to the monks. The coins given to him by Rhodri were his share of the booty ostensibly meant for Iona anyway. Perhaps he should emulate not Rhodri, the ambitious and devious strongman, but Oswald, the king and saint who had shown that a man could be both.

Oswald's origin story was another Cuthbert knew well. The future king and saint had been taken to Iona as a child, along with his brothers and sister, but it was no pilgrimage and his staying there had been no joke. Oswald's father was Aethelfrith the Destroyer, the pagan king of Northumbria who had once slaughtered 1200 unarmed Welsh monks. Following their father's death in battle, the children had a price on their heads. The king's enemies and rivals wanted them dead or under their own control to serve as puppet rulers. There was nothing for it but to go into exile. Some said they chose Iona because an angel appeared to their mother and brought her to Christ, but Cuthbert preferred the thought that God in his providence got them there by purely worldly means. Iona was the heart of Dalriada, the land of their father's enemies, and the last place their own people would be able to reach them. Simple self-preservation had driven them there, and into the embrace of the church.

How different Oswald's life might have been had he inherited his father's kingdom as a pagan. How different might Cuthbert's life have been? Without Iona, without Aidan and those who had followed him to bring to gospel to the Northumbrians, his people might still be pagans like their forefathers. Devil worshippers. But Oswald had become a Christian in Iona, and when he had grown to manhood and reclaimed his throne, he had done so as a Christian king, fighting in the shadow of the cross, literally as well as figuratively, as his men carried a great wooden cross as a battle standard. Thank God for that. While Cuthbert did not spend much time thinking about God or religion, he knew he feared the alternative to the religion of God. He knew the old religion had been devilish to the core, that its practitioners had sought to summon dark powers, terrifying powers whose very potency lay in their opposition to God. He thought of the unearthly roar he had heard in the blackness of the battlefield, and felt a kind of vertigo wash over him and leave him coated in a cold sweat. He muttered the Lord's prayer and imagined himself on Iona and fell asleep.

CHAPTER 18: LUCKY'S ADVENTURE, PART ONE

Lucky and Iain arrived on the mainland before dusk, after a voyage that had been uneventful for Lucky but hard work for her brother, who had to worry about tides and difficult conditions. He left their boat in the care of the harbour master, explaining that he would be back for it in perhaps a week or two, depending on the journey. Then they made straight for the church through the modest harbour village. The priest welcomed them and offered them shelter for the night. He was very happy about Lucky's vocation and agreed to write a letter of recommendation.

They set off again at dawn. The next leg of their journey would take them north to Oban, a natural bay perfectly positioned for those sailing to Mull, the huge island that back in the mists of time had given birth on its far side to little Iona. The priest had said it would take at least two days to get to Oban, and as well as giving them advice about the best route, he'd provided an extra blanket for the journey since there could still be a nasty chill in the spring air. It was warm enough as Lucky and Iain tramped along the trail that hugged the coastline, though also quite rainy. After a few hours, they reached a fine vantage point, and Iain pointed to their own island far in the distance through the rain. Lucky had never seen it like that before, and strained to make out any recognisable features. She would miss her home, but she was already thinking about her new life in Iona. She was excited about the prospect of being surrounded by other people who wanted nothing more than to be close to God.

They did not encounter another soul that first day, until late in the afternoon, the trail took them deep inland so they lost sight of the sea, and they passed two men coming in the other direction. They stopped briefly and exchanged reports on the going either way. The men said there was a rough, muddy patch ahead of the siblings, but nothing dangerous. Iain told them the going was good from here to the harbour village he and his sister and set off from that morning.

'God bless you and speed your journey,' added Lucky. After that, the siblings continued in silence as the path continued along the beach. Only the silence was unlike the untroubled silence they had shared for most of the day. There was a sense of dissatisfaction, of something unsaid, until it was said.

'You're not a nun yet, you know,' Iain said.

'I know that,' said Lucky.

'It's not your business to bless passing strangers.'

'I didn't bless anyone. I asked God to bless them.'

'Why should He bless anyone because you say so?'

'It's not like that. Why are you so annoyed?'

'I'm not annoyed. I'm just saying.'

Back to silence, coloured now not by something unsaid but by something inexpressible.

When they reached the muddy patch in the path, they both struggled to keep their footing, now slipping and now squelching into the mud. Iain pushed ahead, while Lucky began to fall behind.

'Aren't you going to help me?' she said. 'I thought you were taking me to Iona, not making a pilgrimage of your own.'

He didn't answer, but pushed on through the mud, so Lucky did her best to keep up, growing increasingly frustrated and angry until she slipped and fell backwards, splat into the mud. Iain must have heard but did stop or even turn to see if his sister was all right. Not until he heard the quieter sound of Lucky sobbing. He turned to see her sitting upright but not even trying to stand. She sat with her arms round her knees and her face downcast. Her clothes and hair were now covered in mud and she was sobbing pathetically. As well she might; her brother and currently her only source of protection in this world was being horrible to her and he knew it. He squelched back and extended his hand.

Lucky fought the urge to refuse it. Part of her wanted to reject her horrible brother and stay here forever in the mud. Of course, she could not do that. Eventually she would have to give in and accept her brother's help. Even if she could stand up by herself, salvaging some degree of pride, she needed him to get her to Iona. She knew that. But it was not raw, practical necessity that overrode her childish urge to stay in the mud. She could have held on for hours before that kind of reality imposed itself on her. Lucky's childhood sulks had been legendary, and she had not so much grown out of them as reinvented them as spiritual experiences to be felt within rather than displayed without. But nor was there any spiritual self-indulgence in Lucky's heart when she reached out her muddy hand to take Iain's and smiled happily at him. There was only love. A boundless, inexplicable love that could only have come from God. And once her brother had helped her to her feet, that same love made her plant her other muddy hand squarely on his face, and to laugh wickedly at the resulting muddy handprint. Happily, Iain was equally infused with God's love, and laughed along with her and shook his head in resignation, before picking her up, throwing her over his shoulder, and carrying her through the rest of the muddy patch.

By the time they had returned to solider ground, it was almost dark, and they began looking for somewhere suitable to camp. A copse near the top of a hill looked suitably sheltered and afforded a reassuring view of the sea in the distance, so they laid out their blankets at its edge and Iain built a fire while Lucky drew drinking water from a burn that ran down the hill before washing the mud from herself as best she could. After that she was glad of the extra blanket the priest had provided, which she wrapped around herself while they waited for the fire to warm up. Iain said he was sorry for having been horrible to her, and she forgave him ungrudgingly. She did not know how to be a nun or even a nun-to-be, she said as they ate, and would probably make many mistakes. When they'd finished eating, he held her close as they watched the sun go down over the sea. Then they slept peacefully, Lucky dreaming of Iona and Iain dreaming of whatever he dreamt about.

They woke at dawn and pressed on until just after noon they reached a sea loch that stretched from the coast deep into the land. Walking round it would take hours, but they'd been told to look for a hamlet where they might find a boatman to ferry them across. In fact, it was a boat that alerted them to the whereabouts of the hamlet. Lucky spotted it bobbing about close to the shore and as they approached they saw it was moored by a collection of huts. Two small children began shouting when they saw the strangers coming, and a woman emerged from one of the huts. 'Are you wanting passage over the water?' she asked. 'My man's not here, but if you help me unload on the other side I'll take you myself.'

The boat was loaded with timber, and Lucky was afraid it would sink with three people on top, but Iain assured her they'd be fine and she trusted him. As they clambered aboard, the woman told the children to watch the pot inside, hitched up her skirts and joined them. The wind was not particularly favourable, but Iain helped the woman with the sail and they were on the other side in less than half an hour. Then they set about unloading the timber onto a waiting cart. Lucky did her bit, as did the boatwoman, but Iain did most of the work. 'You're a strong lad,' the woman said. 'I've another job for you if you want it, and can pay in silver.'

Iain looked at the cart suspiciously and the woman laughed. 'No, that's a job for our donkey when my man returns with her. I've a different cargo in mind for you.'

She pointed to a hut, just like those on the other shore, and led Iain over to it. Peering in through the entrance he saw it was piled full of boxes, baskets and bulging sacks. The woman and her husband were merchants of some kind, or perhaps every kind. She reached down to a pile of stuff close to the entrance, and drew back its rough fabric covering to reveal a dozen swords. Iain whistled in surprise.

'Think you can carry this lot?' she asked. 'They're for the fort at Dunadd, just a few hours from here on foot. You'd be there by nightfall and you and your wife would be welcome to spend the night.'

'My sister,' Iain interrupted, but as he did so, a glance at his sister should have told him she was not happy with this development. She was apparently trying to bore a message directly into his mind by means of a fearsome stare.

'Your sister. I beg your pardon,' the woman said.

'What do you think, Lucky?' Iain asked cluelessly.

'I think we have no need of silver, and no need of distractions, and no need...'

Before she could finish, Iain was standing in front of her, desperately trying to hush her. 'It's Dunadd, Lucky! The seat of the kings of all Dalriada! And if we take this little job we can see it up close and even spend the night there!'

Lucky could see that there was no arguing with her brother's enthusiasm. She turned to the loch and knelt down and began to pray.

'She's going to be a nun,' Iain told the merchant woman to explain his sister's odd behaviour. 'I'm taking her to Iona.'

'Oh, good for you,' she said. 'Dunadd is hardly out of

your way, and you may even find others making the same journey.'

Iain looked at Lucky, as if to say, 'See, it's a great idea,' but she still had her back to him.

He helped the merchant woman tie the swords into a bundle he could carry on his back, taking care to keep the blades from hurting him, though he noticed they were not all that sharp. Then she produced a small coin and handed it to him. 'I trust you, of course. The brother of a nun! But I'm sure you're not foolish enough to make an enemy of Dunadd anyway.'

She showed him the beginning of the trail, winding up a hillside from the loch, and explained the route and what to say to any soldiers they encountered on the way. When they arrived, they were to ask for the master of arms and request shelter for the night in the name of Mhairi of the Loch. 'That's me!' she added.

'Thank you, Mhairi. I'm Iain and my sister is Lucky. We're little islanders.'

'I can tell,' she said affectionately, and sent them on their way as soon as Lucky had risen from her prayers and taken up Iain's own baggage as well as hers. ('God bless you,' the girl said in response to the woman's good wishes.)

'Who is the king of all Dalriada?' Lucky asked after they had been walking a while.

Iain admitted he was not sure. Their father had once told him that kings were to common folk what chiefs were to livestock. Chief Conall would know who the king was, if indeed there was a king of all Dalriada at that time. Even piglike Iain knew it was not always as straightforward as that. But in Dunadd, perhaps they would find out for themselves how things stood.

After a few hours, there it was. The fort of Dunadd was by far the most imposing thing either of them had seen. Rising from the boggy plain, a natural hill had been transformed into a daunting military fortress, surrounded by a thick stone wall and capped by a huge stone roundhouse. On the slopes between the two were numerous stone and wooden buildings and fortifications. Most impressive of all, the whole thing seemed alive, with people in motion all over the fort. As Lucky and Iain drew nearer they could hear the fort too: a continuous mutter of voices, animal sounds and the thud and clatter of people at work. They approached by the only obvious route: a broad path through the bog, whose sides rose up almost to enclose them as they approached the great gate. Lucky felt as if they were being sucked into the fort as much as entering by choice. And of course, there were eyes on them every step of the way.

'State your business,' said a sentry standing on a parapet above the gate when they reached it.

'We were sent by Mhairi of the Loch,' Iain said boldly. 'I'm to ask for the master of arms.'

The sentry looked them both up and down and noted the great bundle on Iain's back. 'Open the gate,' he called to someone below, and the gate creaked open. In they went.

'Wait here,' said another sentry. 'I'll fetch the master of arms.'

He returned with the master of arms just a few minutes later. The latter seemed pleased to see them. 'Here they are, and ahead of schedule,' he said excitedly, motioning for Iain to unstrap his cargo, which of course was what he was really pleased to see. 'That woman is a marvel,' he added.

'She said we'd be able to spend the night,' Iain said, sensing it would be wise to raise the matter while the man's gratitude was fresh.

'Did she now?' He looked at the sky and saw that dusk was approaching. 'Yes, that's fine. This lad will show you to the common hall.' The master of arms gestured to a lad who was loitering by the gate, before picking up Iain's bundle. He was clearly surprised by its weight and had to heave it a second time to raise it to his shoulders.

'You're a strong lad,' he told Iain.

Iain smiled as he stretched his unburdened arms and shoulders. 'I feel like I could fly now!'

The master of arms laughed as he hauled his cargo away, and the lad led Iain and Lucky in another direction. Both looked around in awe at the end-of-day bustle of the fort, and as they were shown into a smoky and noisy wooden hall, Iain warned his sister to let him do the talking. 'And don't go around blessing people!'

'God bless you,' Lucky said to a man who was leaving the hall as they entered. She could not have known that his name was Dougall, and he had recently returned from captaining a campaign with the Northumbrians against the Picts.

CHAPTER 19: METALWORK

Dougall looked out at the setting sun and breathed deeply. He had been drinking in the common hall for most of the afternoon, sharing tales of the campaign with old friends and catching up on politics. He was glad of some fresh air, and the fading, shimmering but still brilliant light lifted his spirits even further. He turned to watch it play on the rocky outcrop far above him near the summit of Dunadd and the inner citadel. A footprint carved into that rock was the symbolic heart of Dalriada, where newly inaugurated kings placed their own foot to symbolise their dominion over the land and its people. As he watched, the light finally failed, leaving the rock in the shadow of dusk. Dougall wandered to a convenient midden and peed heavily. Then he stretched and shook his head vigorously to liven himself up. He had someone to see before turning in for the night.

The master of arms greeted him warmly, and invited him into his bothy. They were old friends. 'I hear you've a shipment of arms from over the water?' Dougall said. He meant Ireland, of course. The short haul up from the sea loch with Lucky and Iain had been the end of a much longer journey for their cargo.

'I have,' said the master of arms, handing one of the

swords to Dougall, and adding slightly apologetically, 'They're brand new,'

'Yes,' said Dougall, weighing the sword up, 'more's the pity. They don't make them like they used to.'

'Still,' the master of arms went on, 'They're better than anything we can make here.'

'And better than just about anything the Picts have,' Dougall added.

'And the Northumbrians?'

'Oh, they have some good stuff, but just like with us, the older the better. Their young lads fight with rubbish until they inherit something.'

'And I hear tell of a young hero in their ranks?'

'Ah, Wilfrid. Yes, he's a fierce one, but time will tell. I pray to God he won't secure his fame against a different foe.'

The master of arms laughed darkly. Both men were experienced enough to know it was only a matter of time before the allies were enemies once more. But that had as much to do with domestic politics as it did with the foreigners. The Northumbrian alliance had been forged by a man who called himself king of all Dalriada, but in reality he was hardly that. The truth was that Dunadd was in peril, having been menaced by the Picts for some years now, and its king could not rely on his fellow Gaels to defend it. That was why he had sought Northumbrian support. But he could rely on that only for as long as it suited the Northumbrians. Dougall swung the Irish sword this way and that before lunging at an imaginary foe. 'Ach, it's not bad,' he said, handing it back to the master of arms. 'Let's at least see if our smiths can match these.'

Dunadd was not renowned for its bladesmiths, but it was home to fine metalworkers of another kind. Lucky stood at the door of a workshop where two craftsmen were working intently on small pieces of what she assumed must be precious metals. She was momentarily hypnotised by their seemingly concerted concentration. It was infectious: even though she had no idea what they were actually doing, she felt for a moment as if she were part of it. And, since they were working by candlelight and it was dark outside now, it was a while before they noticed the stranger at their door. 'Hounds of Hell!' one exclaimed with a start when he saw her.

'I'm sorry,' said Lucky. 'I was just watching.'

'Then who are you?' he demanded, still recovering from his fright.

'My name is Lucky,' she said. 'God bless you.'

Now the other, less jittery craftsman spoke to her: 'And is there something we can do for you, Lucky?'

'Oh, no! I mean, no, thank you. My brother and I are on our way to Iona. He was carrying swords for the master of arms. From Mhairi of the Loch. But now he's asleep in the common hall. He's very tired. And I thought I'd have a look around, and when I saw…' She stopped talking, embarrassed to have found herself babbling.

'Well, come in and have a proper look if you like,' he said, causing the other to cast him a filthy look.

Lucky stepped inside the workshop, and the first craftsman sighed before rising. 'I can't concentrate now. I'm going for a drink,' he said, and quickly tidied away his things before pushing past Lucky on his way out.

'He was due for that drink anyway,' said the nicer man. He was also a young man, though much older than Lucky. And he had a benign smile that put her at ease. 'Have you seen such things before?' he asked, holding up a wonderfully intricate brooch.

'Nothing as beautiful as that,' she admitted.

'And these,' he said, showing her some buckles with figures carved into them. 'I'm especially pleased with these, because they tell the story of our people. I've been working on them day and night for weeks now.'

'Which is your favourite?' she asked.

The craftsman shrugged and blew out his lips. But then he picked one up decisively. 'This one depicts Scota,' he said, 'The Egyptian princess from whom our people are descended.'

'Egyptian? Like in the Bible?'

'Precisely. Scota was the daughter of the Pharaoh who oppressed the Hebrews, and who was drowned in the Red Sea when Moses led them to their freedom.'

'So we're descended from the wicked Pharaoh, not from the Hebrews?'

The craftsman laughed, 'I'm afraid so. But it's worse than that. Scota's husband was a descendant of the men who built the Tower of Babel. Do you know that story too?'

Lucky scratched her head. She felt that, as a nun to be, she should know all the Bible stories, but nothing was coming to mind.

'Never mind,' he went on, having put away what he'd been working on and begun polishing some bits and pieces more idly. 'Suffice it to say, tyranny ran in the family on both sides. So with the Pharaoh gone, and the long-suffering people having had enough of that sort of thing, Scota and her husband were driven out of Egypt and took to the sea with their hangers-on in search of new lands to conquer.'

He gestured for Lucky to pull over a stool from the corner and sit down, which she happily did.

'Well, first they settled in Spain, at the western edge of the known world. They fought the inhabitants and established a settlement of their own with a great tower which they called Brigantia, and over the years they swelled in number, but they could neither conquer the peoples around them nor live in peace with them. Many generations passed, but in time, Scota's descendants spied a distant island from their great tower. They sent three ships northwards to investigate, and they found the land empty, having been abandoned by giants. Of course, that island was Ireland.' The craftsman went on with the story for a while before he noticed that Lucky had fallen asleep on her stool.

Of course, he'd noticed from the moment she had appeared that she was a beautiful girl. He was not in the habit of explaining his work or telling stories to random strangers. But now Lucky's head was stooped wearily and she was dribbling from her open mouth. He laughed inwardly at himself for having thought of her as anything but a child. Then he put a blanket over her and finished his polishing before going to sleep in a corner.

Lucky dreamed of the Tower of Babel and the Tower of Brigantia and the Tower of Dunadd until she fell off the stool and woke in a panic. It was pitch dark now, but she quickly remembered where she was and calmed down. It would be hopeless trying to find the common hall in the dark, so she simply curled up in the blanket she found about her and went back to sleep until dawn.

She woke again at dawn, and immediately rose and stretched, keen to return to Iain before he had time to worry. The craftsman lay on his back in the still-dark corner and she could not tell if he were asleep or awake until he said, 'Is that you off, then?'

'Yes,' she said, 'thank you for the blanket.' She folded it and placed it on the stool. 'And for the story. Your work is very beautiful, sir.'

'Conall,' he said.

'Conall,' she repeated. 'That's our Chief's name.'

'Indeed? Well, I'm the Chief of this workshop. Just don't tell Aidan I said that. It was nice to meet you, Lucky.'

'You too, Conall. God bless you.' And with that she was off.

Iain was still asleep when she returned to the common hall, though most of the others who had slept there were getting up now. It was not the best place to sleep, more a place to crash when you had nowhere else to go. Only visitors spent the night there on purpose. The only Dunadd residents who slept there were those who had fallen asleep drunk. Like Aidan, Conall's fellow craftsman, who now staggered out of the common hall as grumpily as he had left his workshop the night before. Lucky resisted the temptation to say, 'God bless you'.

When Iain did wake, he struggled to get up. His back was stiff from carrying all those swords yesterday. He was a strong lad, but young enough that he could be oblivious to what was good for him beyond the moment, and Lucky just assumed he was superhuman, so there had been no one to counsel caution.

'Ooph!' he said, 'that hurts!' He made it to his feet and stretched painfully, baring his teeth.

Lucky patted his arm tenderly. 'Are you going to be all right?'

'Of course I am,' he said.

'You can walk?'

'*I can walk*,' he said sarcastically as he staggered back and forth to warm up. He motioned for Lucky to pick up his stuff, having wisely decided that stooping was beyond him for now.

Outside the common hall, a young girl was handing out bread from a large basket to anyone who wanted it.

'The king's hospitality!' Lucky said, before tearing hungrily into a chunk.

'My mother made it,' said the girl.

'Well, God bless your mother,' Lucky said, but indecipherably as her mouth was full.

Iain was also glad of breakfast, and was even given a piece of cheese to go with his bread, the girl having apparently taken a shine to him. Lucky did not allow herself to feel envious. 'Do you think we should pay our respects to the king before we go?' she asked her brother, half joking and half not sure.

'I don't think that'll be necessary,' said a familiar voice behind her. She whirled round to see Conall. 'He's a busy man.'

She blushed a little before introducing Conall the craftsman to her brother Iain and vice versa, and before the latter could ask how on Earth she knew this craftsman, Conall asked, 'Did you say you and your brother are going to Iona?'

'That's right.'

'Well, a party left for there about half an hour ago. If you'd like company you can probably catch them.'

The siblings looked at one another, shrugged and nodded. Lucky took leave of Conall a second time, Iain winked at the bread girl, and they were off.

CHAPTER 20: LUCKY'S ADVENTURE, PART TWO

Lucky and Iain managed a brisk pace once Iain's stiff back had warmed up, and by mid morning they caught sight of the pilgrims; Lucky had decided that was what they must be. There were half a dozen of them: two men and the rest women, it seemed at first, but as they drew nearer one of the women turned out to be a boy. He was the first to notice they were being followed, and soon they were all looking round, and then hesitating as they discussed what to do, before coming to a definite halt. They were waiting. Lucky and Iain sped up to keep from delaying them any longer than necessary. When they caught up, Iain addressed the men: 'We heard you're making for Iona. Can we join you?'

It was now clear that one of the men was a monk. 'You're welcome to,' he said.

Iain introduced himself and his sister, explaining that Lucky was to become a nun. There was a chorus of ahhs, and the monk explained that the boy was also a 'postulant', on his way to join the abbey at Iona. The future monk and future nun looked at one another awkwardly. He was a few years younger than her. Then the party set off again, sharing their stories as they walked. The women were the boy's mother and aunts, taking the opportunity to make an extra special pilgrimage. The second man was a warrior; in fact, it was Dougall. Lucky vaguely recognised him from the night before, but he looked at her so intently it made her uncomfortable. 'You remind me of someone,' he said smiling. 'Maybe a girl I used to know.'

She was relieved when it transpired that he was only going as far as Dunollie, the fort overlooking Oban. He would not be sailing with the pilgrims.

Still, Iain was glad to have an opportunity to speak to a warrior of Dunadd, and walked with him a little ahead of the others. In the fortress itself Iain had learned nothing of the king or the political situation. Dougall was happy to explain how things stood, telling him about the alliance with the Northumbrians and the complicated relations among the Gaels, including the one between Dunadd and Dunollie, but indeed it all sounded so complicated that Iain wondered if Dougall were deliberately trying to bamboozle him. To add further intrigue, Dougall mentioned in a whisper that the mother of the boy destined for Iona was the king's sister-in-law; the boy was the king's nephew. Then he asked Iain about his home. He claimed not to have heard of the new chief Conall, but he seemed to smile knowingly to himself at the mention of changing political arrangements in that corner of Dalriada. Occasionally their path afforded the travellers a view of the sea, and Iain wondered how things were with his family.

Meanwhile, Lucky walked mostly without speaking, half-listening to stories the monk told the boy and a quarter-listening to the women's conversation, though as they were all sisters they spoke mostly of personal things that meant nothing to Lucky. Her thoughts wandered and she remembered Conall's story about Scota and how their ancestors had travelled from Egypt to Spain to Ireland before settling in these lands. But in those days they had not been a

Christian people. Indeed, according to the story, they had been quite wicked, bent on conquest and domination. Lucky knew all too well that fighting was still rife both among the Gaels and between them and various groups of foreigners. Dougall's scars and warlike bearing were a reminder of that. But he was a Christian. They were all Christians, even the foreigners, she had been told. So there was hope. And now Lucky was going to the font of that hope: in Iona, Saint Columba had established his abbey, both as a base for his ministry to the whole land and as a shining beacon of Christian truth and Christian life. And Lucky was to be part of it. To live a life of prayer, to be with God, to embody his love. But she could not really imagine that life. Not yet. She looked out to sea when it appeared and prayed with all the might of her soul that she might be worthy of it.

As dusk approached, Dougall identified a good spot to camp for the night, and Iain helped him build a fire. The royal party had plenty of food to share with their new hangers-on, but, tired from walking, they ate mostly in silence. Then all slept soundly till morning, when they were woken by a rumbling sound in the distance.

'What is that?' asked the boy's mother, afraid.

'Horses,' Dougall answered. He listened intently as the sound faded. 'Not coming this way,' he added, 'and not that close to start with, but it was in the direction we're headed in.'

The company exchanged nervous looks as they rose. Horses meant armed men. They were unlikely to be a threat to pilgrims, and in these parts especially to Gaels, but you could never be sure. The monk took charge, leading them all in prayer. Lucky was strengthened by that, but Iain remained on edge, protective of his sister and watching Dougall for clues about what might be ahead of them and cues as to how to respond.

In time they descended into a small glen, where a shallow burn ran towards the sea. Their path crossed it, and on the far side lay a mess of hoofprints, which also sprawled upstream between trees along the shallower bank on that side.

Dougall ran stealthily up the slope, peering carefully over the horizon without standing tall against it. 'They're long gone, eastward,' he said when he returned, 'and our path follows the coast northward. Let's crack on.'

Iain could see that Dougall had also noticed human footprints amid the mess, though he'd chosen not to mention it. It seemed the horsemen had ridden into the glen and either dismounted or encountered men on foot before riding out again. There were no obvious footprints leading in or out of the glen, but then, away from the mess left by the horses in the immediate vicinity of the burn, the ground was too dry for footprints to show. He kept his thoughts to himself, then, though at least one of the three sisters also eyed the ground suspiciously as they passed through the glen. Lucky was blissfully unaware of any of this, and went on happily contemplating her new life all the while.

They made good progress for the rest of the day, and even as dusk began to fall, Dougall proposed pushing on to Oban. Nobody objected, and they finally reached it in time to see the sun set over the island that sheltered the harbour. They found shelter of their own in a large shed constructed for the benefit of travellers, who were looked after by the same locals who would ferry them to Mull in the morning, all being well. Their timing was providential. Several others had already settled in for the night. They included a merchant and his boy with goods for the abbey as well as several pilgrims and a pair of monks who turned out to be Picts. The monk from Dunadd conversed with them in Latin, and encouraged his postulant prince to do so too, without much success. It was not clear whether the boy's Latin was at fault or his temperament.

'What happened to the soldiers?' someone asked as a local woman distributed food to the travellers.

'They left in a hurry just before the new party arrived,' someone else answered. 'I don't think they were planning to sail with us anyway.'

'One of them was,' said the first person, 'the foreigner.

He told me so himself.'

'Another Pict?'

'No, a Northumbrian, I believe.'

Lucky listened with interest, but Dougall was out of earshot. Otherwise his ears might have pricked up at that.

The soldiers sat on the hillside. It had been a close-run thing. The three of them had been on the beach, enjoying the sunset and competing to skim stones on the water, when Fergus had spotted grouse on the hillside behind them and taken it upon himself to catch something for their hosts' pot. Well, he'd barely clambered up the hill when he caught sight of a party of travellers approaching in the distance. He'd instinctively edged into a thicket from where he could take a closer look without being seen, but almost gave himself away by laughing out loud in surprise when he recognised Dougall. The captain's imperious gait was unmistakeable. Fergus had rushed back down and called to Domnall and Cuthbert in a panicked whisper to get off the beach, where they'd shortly be seen from the road. And so they hid, taking cover in a copse on the hillside from where they could watch Dougall and Lucky and Iain and the others from Dunadd arrive into Oban and take shelter in the shed they'd been in themselves not two hours before.

It was not that they were doing anything wrong, or at least anything to which Dougall had the authority to object. But Domnall's uncle had been clear that they were to keep the operation secret. Dougall was a well-connected man, almost a politician as much as a soldier, and surely exactly the sort of person from whom the operation was to be kept secret. But then the secret part was the fact that the robbery had been fake. The 'news' that it had happened was actually supposed to get out, and precisely to men like Dougall. Domnall and Fergus argued between themselves about his for some time. But ultimately they were in agreement. The problem was that it was one thing for people to be told long after the fact, or rather fiction, that they'd been robbed while transporting the silver.

They'd agreed all along to vouch for Rhodri's fiction. But it was quite another to encounter someone like Dougall within hours of the alleged incident. What were they to say? 'Oh, Dougall, is it yourself? Good to see you, man! Now, you'll never believe what just happened to us! If only you'd been there, we could have fought them off together!' No, the young men didn't have it in them to pull off that kind of theatrics. They'd struggled to keep straight faces even as they were being 'robbed' by a handful of rather humourless Pictish horsemen. They decided there was no way they could face Dougall.

'There's nothing to stop *you* going back down,' Domnall told Cuthbert after explaining their position. 'The language barrier might even help. You can stutter and stammer all you want if you can just get the story out to Dougall.'

Fergus nodded in agreement. 'I think this might even be the best way to get it out. A lucky coincidence.'

'I don't know,' said Cuthbert. It had not occurred to him when he'd decided to go to Iona that he'd be doing so in character. None of them had put on an act for the other travellers in the shed. They'd all considered the matter pretty much over, Cuthbert even more than the others, since he was not related to any of the masterminds behind the ruse and could reasonably have expected never to hear of it again. And now this. 'Maybe it just wasn't to be,' he said.

Domnall and Fergus looked at one another and shrugged. They did not really mind either way.

The three spent the night in the copse, then, without a fire, for fear of drawing attention to themselves. Awake and sitting shivering early in the morning, they watched Dougall emerge from the shed alone, and march in his imperious gait across the beach, taking the path north. 'He's not sailing,' said Fergus. 'He'll be heading for the fort of Dunollie instead.'

'Of course,' said Domnall, 'no doubt on political business of some kind.' He winked at Fergus, 'We'd better give the place a wide berth on the way up the road.' Then he looked at Cuthbert. 'Well, maybe it's not too late, then. If you still want to go to Iona.'

Cuthbert was torn. His mind had been made up to go. And then not to go. He braced himself to rise and make for the shed, and then stopped short. He felt a bit embarrassed by his indecisiveness, and found himself swaying towards not going partly just to alleviate that embarrassment. But that was a silly reason. Maybe he should go. But maybe he'd be too late; maybe the boat was leaving this minute. He looked down towards the harbour, but the view was obscured by the landscape so he could not see the pier or any sign of the boat in the water. There was one way to find out for sure if he were too late or not. Once again, he braced himself, standing up this time. And once again he hesitated. 'No, I think wasn't to be,' he said, still looking down at the harbour.

'So you're going home?' Dougall asked, standing up.

'You can come home with us,' Fergus said, more because he felt awkward about the sudden prospect of parting so abruptly than because he thought Cuthbert would want to come along.

Cuthbert laughed. 'I appreciate the offer. But, yes, I'll go home now. This Iona thing wasn't to be.'

All three young men were standing up now. There was nothing to keep them in this chilly copse.

'Well,' Domnall said, 'let's pray to God that if we meet again, we're still on the same side.'

'Indeed,' said Cuthbert, taking each of his friends by the arm in turn. 'Farewell, and good luck.'

'Good luck, Cuthbert. And God bless you.'

With that, they parted, Domnall and Fergus setting off in the same direction taken by Dougall, though at a considerably more leisurely pace, and Cuthbert returning to the path that had brought them to Oban, to begin his long journey south and east.

When he reached a suitable vantage point, Cuthbert turned and sat looking out to sea. And after half an hour or so, there it was, the boat carrying pilgrims to Iona. If he felt a pang of regret, it did not last long. Since catching the boat was no longer an option, he felt a sense of repose, which reinforced his conviction that he'd made the right decision. It might be many days before another boat set off, and by then he'd be long gone. He watched the boat happily as the sun rose high into the sky behind him, making the sea shimmer beautifully as the boat disappeared round the island that sheltered the harbour. Little did he know what a near miss it had been, that the little boat on which he had almost taken passage carried his long-lost twin sister to yet another new life.

CHAPTER 21: NEW CLOTHES

Donuel the Cunning emerged from the mountain pass into Constantine's glen and dismounted from his horse so he and the beast could both drink from a burn that trickled down the mountainside. Brude had decided that he could not justify keeping the others on his quest for his sister, especially not on the strength of a dubious vision. Constantine had insisted for his own reasons on remaining with him, at least as far as the coast, where the vision had placed Euphemia. So Donuel had agreed to return alone and report back to Brude's father Taran. In fact, he was enjoying travelling alone, riding at his own pace and giving free rein to his thoughts.

Like Constantine, Donuel had been on only his first campaign when they'd been redeployed to help Brude search for his sister. In fact, he had volunteered; they didn't call him Donuel the Cunning for nothing. Unlike Constantine, Donuel was from a noble family and a long line of warriors, much more venerable indeed than Brude's. So he wore his ancestry lightly, feeling he had nothing to prove. There would always be more fighting to be done, but a quest to rescue a fair maiden did not come along every spring, so avoiding battle had not been his only motivation. Not that he had designs on Euphemia as Constantine did. It had been the romance of the quest itself that appealed to him. That's why he had been intrigued, perhaps too intrigued, by the seer's vision. He had always been fascinated by tales of the old gods and the old ways: animal sacrifices, visions, a whiff of sex. He was sorry not to be continuing on the quest with the others, but it had given him plenty to think about, and if Taran sent him back on the campaign, that would bring adventure of another kind, albeit with greater risks.

Having remounted his steed, Donuel looked down into the glen, and through the mist he could see some of the settlements he and his friends had passed through in their search for Euphemia. He thought he recognised Constantine's homestead across the loch, at the foot of the little mountain, but he was not sure from so high up on the big mountain. He whispered gently to the horse, and they began a steady descent through the mountain mist and into the glen. With no need to stop and make enquiries as before, Donuel made it around the loch to the homestead before nightfall, and having assured the family that Constantine was well, he was warmly received.

Pyrdie and Pendrin and Peter had endless questions for the visitor, especially when he told them about the magnificent court of King Gartnait and the story of how he had conquered the kingdom of the elves. He did not mention the seer or his vision, but said simply that Brude and Constantine were following up a rumour that Euphemia had been seen heading east. They would probably be back this way before long, but if not there was nothing to worry about. Constantine would be home for the harvest anyway. Everyone was happy with that, though sad that the girl was still missing. After a hearty meal, Constantine's grandfather invited Donuel to come and sit with him by the fire, overlooking the blackness of the loch. He began recounting an old story, and Donuel listened with interest, though he struggled to follow it all because it seemed like parts of the story were missing. Gradually it dawned on him that perhaps the old man thought he was talking to Constantine. The missing parts of the story must have been well known to his grandson. Donuel looked intently at the old man, trying to gauge whether he was temporarily confused and simply assuming Donuel knew things Constantine knew, or more far gone, not even aware to whom he was talking. The ease and familiarity with which the old man spoke suggested the latter.

In fact, the old man had not even known he was an old man until a few years before, when his wife had told him so. 'Who is this old man?' she had demanded one morning, recoiling in horror. In her rapidly accelerating dotage, she had not recognised him as her husband, not remembered where her life had brought her. Presumably, she had imagined herself still the lovely youth the old man had fallen in love with. He too had been a youth at the time, and lovely enough to her, but he knew that had been a very long time ago. It only came as a shock to be told it had been long enough to turn him into an old man. It occurred to him then that the difference between them was that he retained the capacity to be shocked. As unpleasant as it was to realise that he was indeed an old man, this was at least something he could accept once confronted with it. His wife, confronted with the same fact in the form of her husband's face, simply rejected it, rejecting him in the process. She had not lived long after that, and people had said it was just as well.

Back then, the old man's delusion had been of a different order than his wife's. He had not believed himself to be a young man, just naively assured that however old he might be, he was not an *old* man. But now it seemed he was going the same way. He told Donuel about a new carving he was working on, despite the fact that he had not carved stone since before his wife had died. Donuel listened attentively, taking a genuine interest as well as taking pains to humour the old man by playing the part of Constantine. There was no point trying to correct him.

In the morning, Donuel thanked Constantine's parents

for their hospitality, which included generous supplies for the rest of his journey. He asked them to convey his respects to the old man, who was still sleeping, and it was clear from the resulting looks and nods that his confusion was well established. 'I just hope he doesn't give up the ghost before Constantine returns,' said Constantine's mother. Pyrdie and Pendrin and Peter ran after Donuel's horse for as long as they could before he waved them goodbye and began his ascent up the little mountain and out of the glen.

It was approaching noon the next day when Donuel arrived in the glen ruled by Brude's father Taran, and as he neared their village, he sensed something was amiss. His approach had been observed, and several men were waiting for him. He recognised most, and in particular Taran's brother, the bishop, who bade him dismount quickly and ushered him into Taran's house. 'Where is Brude?' the bishop demanded.

Before he could answer, Donuel's attention was distracted by the sight of a corpse laid out on the table that dominated the hall. (He barely noticed the small wooden chest at the corpse's feet, which had recently been delivered to their owner.) Taran was dead.

'Is he on his way or not?' the bishop pressed.

'He's not,' said Donuel. He explained the situation as best he could, all the while trying to process what Taran's death would mean for the men fighting under him, for Brude, for himself. In fact, he had no idea just how momentous an effect Taran's death was about to have on his own life.

'In the next couple of days, perhaps even before nightfall, we're expecting a delegation of Gaels,' the bishop told him. 'I'm going to tell them you are Brude. And they are going to hail you as King Brude of this glen and the surrounding lands. Do you understand?'

For once, Donuel the Cunning was speechless.

◆ ◆ ◆

Meanwhile on Iona, for the second time in her life, the girl first christened as Cwenburh was also given a new name. From now on, Lucky would be called Sister Mary Brigid. In fact, nearly all the nuns had Mary in their names, so she would mostly be known as Brigid, a name she shared with only half a dozen of her new sisters. It would be some time before she was fully accepted into the community, but taking her new name from the very beginning symbolised Mary Brigid's commitment to her new life. It had transpired when they arrived that the young prince from Dunadd was on a kind of trial, here to experience monastic life for a while and see if it was for him. Presented with a similar opportunity, Lucky had been adamant that the community could take as long as it needed to accept her, but as far as she was concerned she was here to be a nun and that was that.

So Mary Brigid was shown to a suitably modest cell, where she would sleep and pray when she was not praying elsewhere. She sat down to unpack her equally modest bundle of possessions. Some clothes, a thin blanket and a tightly folded patch of vellum on which were written several psalms. This had belonged to her mother's father; Lucky had never learned to read, but perhaps she would now, her mother had said, pressing it into her hand. And then, wrapped in a scarf, the girl had something that was not modest at all. An altogether unauthorised heirloom. It was the statue of the Virgin Mary, stolen from the chapel on the island that had been her home until now. The statue that seemed to come to life when she contemplated it. She had feared she would not be able to do without it. But now it struck her that this was the worst possible start to her life as a nun. She begged the thing for forgiveness.

PART TWO

About ten years later

CHAPTER 22: HARVEST

Peter and Pendrin and Pyrdie were hard at work bringing in the harvest. They were strong young men now, and did the bulk of the hard work as their fathers supervised and the women gathered what they reaped. And they did not stop when they saw a lone horseman appear from the pass on the mountainside above them. 'Here comes our warrior,' was all Peter said, and the others nodded and carried on. It was not that they were not pleased Constantine was home, but they had work to do, and were no longer in thrall to war stories and tales of adventure. Actually, Pyrdie did harbour dreams of following in his brother's footsteps, but he knew talk of such things annoyed his cousins.

When not working on the farm, Pyrdie instead put his energies into carving stones like his grandfather had done, though the old man had died before Pyrdie could master the art, and he sometimes feared that without his guidance he'd never be as skilful. Peter was a born farmer like his father before him; he loved the land and he loved working it, and could not understand how anyone who had grown up here could want to leave. Pendrin was also a hard worker with a feeling for the land, but he spent every spare hour he could hunting alone, or simply roaming on the mountain or in the woods. The one person who did stop work at sight of Constantine was Dyrael, his wife.

Dyrael ran up the hillside for a closer look at her returning husband. The other women did not begrudge her that. They all lived with the fear that one year Constantine would not return from the summer's campaigning, but it was worst for Dyrael, the mother of his children. She'd faced enough tragedy when she'd lost their first two babies, one in the womb and one shortly after birth. Then they'd been blessed with twins, two years old now, and happily playing tethered to a post by the side of the field. Dyrael stopped when she ran out of breath and stood with her hands on her hips, holding back tears of relief and joy. Constantine caught sight of her and waved, and she waved back, now sobbing aloud. The other women exchanged indulgent looks and began a song of welcome, and one at a time the men joined in until the glen resounded with it, and Constantine began galloping home.

The rest of the family held back as the lovers were reunited. When they'd had a moment, Constantine's mother approached with the twins. She prided herself on her ability to carry them both even though she was no longer young, but she was relieved when Constantine took them from her and held them in his warrior's arms. They were crying now, unsurprisingly, but the warrior kissed them gently and whispered lovingly until they settled. Only then did he pass them to Dyrael before greeting the rest of the family. Peter was also married now, with a first baby on the way. Constantine was delighted to see his cousin's wife's prodigious bump. 'A playmate for the twins,' he said, adding with a wink, 'Maybe two!'

'Oh, don't say that,' said Anya with a look of mock horror. 'One's quite enough for now.'

Then, after tending to his horse, Constantine joined his family bringing in the harvest for the rest of the day. It felt good to be back on the farm, not thinking of war.

So as they ate their evening meal, the warrior did not

regale his family with tales of war or of politics. As long as he could reassure them that war was not coming their way, they were not interested. And even if Constantine had felt like talking about it, there were things they would not understand. Complications and subtleties. Secrets and lies. He was a seasoned warrior now, and complicit in more secrets and lies than he cared to think about, before even coming to the blood shed, the bones shattered and the lives destroyed. He was happy to be caught up in simple domesticity with his family, and above all with his wife and their twins.

Having stolen a precious hour alone with Dyrael, Constantine lay by the fire playing with the twins, giving and taking a ball of twine, a game that was surprisingly complicated with three players rather than two. It was easier when Anya came over to join in. Constantine asked when she was due; no more than a few weeks.

'If it's a girl, we want to call her Euphemia,' she said suddenly.

Constantine's face gave little away, long trained by all those secrets and lies. His earlier romantic obsession with Euphemia was the stuff of legend in Constantine's extended family. Having come back without the girl the year she went missing, he had gone searching for her again and again. For years. And without her brother Brude, who had apparently given up on her after succeeding to his father's throne. Constantine had searched again to the east, then to the north, to the west and to the south, through mountain and glen, forest and moor, and he had never found her. He had finally given up only when the skeleton had been found not far from Euphemia's home. Not that he had accepted it straight away. It could have been anyone's skeleton, he had pointed out. Except that it was just the right size, in just the right place. No other girl had gone missing like that. And Constantine had never really believed the seer's vision that had placed her alive and mysteriously pregnant by the sea. Finally, then, he had mourned for Euphemia. A strange mourning, for someone he had never really known. Indeed, the Euphemia he mourned had little to do with Brude's sister; she was mostly his own invention, even in her foibles and imperfections. Perhaps that had made it harder to let her go, perhaps not. But having mourned her, he had been able to move on. Dyrael was a girl from down the loch, a real girl, real in ways Constantine had not previously been able to imagine. So she felt no jealously for Euphemia, the ghost who had once broken her husband's heart. Why should she? It was Anya who felt a particular fascination for the story, perhaps because she was a step further removed.

'It's a fine name,' Constantine said, unsure whether he was being asked for permission.

Anya smiled. 'It's a lovely name. And I know it's a funny name for a farmer's daughter, but Peter has agreed, on the condition that if it's a boy we call him Elphin, after your grandfather.'

'The old man would be pleased with that,' said Constantine, 'and may the boy live as long as his namesake.'

It did not occur to him that if the boy was a girl, this blessing would be a curse, and happily Anya did not seem to notice either. Now Dyrael joined them, and sympathetically rubbed the weary shoulders of her grateful kinswoman.

'We'll know soon enough,' she said, clearly having picked up the gist of the conversation. 'Maybe there's an Elphin *and* a Euphemia in there!'

'Don't you start!' said Anya, and even the oblivious twins joined in as everyone laughed. But when Anya gave birth a few weeks later, there was only one new playmate for the twins. Elphin.

CHAPTER 23: WILFRID

Wilfrid ducked to dodge a blade swinging at his head, and immediately rose again, as if bouncing off the ground. As he did so, with great economy of effort he thrust his sword through the underside of his would-be assailant's chin, then kicked his victim in the chest to release his weapon, before spinning around to see his remaining foes flee. They were not Picts, but Britons, Men of the Rock. They were no lesser warriors man for man than any others, but when Wilfrid was in the mood like this, he was unstoppable. He and his comrades made short work of the battle, and for once, it was a battle of some consequence. King Eadberht would hold the territory on which they had fought, taking the rich farmland of the plain of Coel from the Britons. The Northumbrians had launched an aggressive campaign to their west after their strategic alliance with the Gaels against the Picts had been rendered void by the Picts' subjugation of Dalriada. Despite this triumph, the Picts had not the strength to conquer all their neighbours, freeing the Northumbrians to pursue conquests of their own. Whether the plain would now be settled by his countrymen, or whether Eadberht's men would simply tax those already living and working on it, Wilfrid did not know or care. He was neither a farmer nor a taxman, but a warrior, and one of renown. To his youthful aggression and swagger – qualities some had predicted would get him killed before his time – he had added wits and guile, and the slow accretion of experience had made him as close to invincible as a mortal warrior could be. He would report now to the seat of King Eadberht himself, Bamburgh Castle. But first, he and his comrades would make camp, feast, revel in their victory.

Wilfrid certainly revelled that night, having formed a rapport with a pretty young camp follower. She was from a Northumbrian village close to the plain of Coel, and among a number of near-locals brought along to cook and tend to the soldiers' wounds. With the campaign decisively over, she and the others would return home the next day, and that would be that. Perhaps Wilfrid would forget her name by the time he got to Bamburgh. But Ethel knew exactly with whom she coupled that night. She knew that any issue from their fleeting union would have the blood of a hero in his veins.

After breaking camp, the soldiers mostly disbanded. A small company was to remain as a garrison, having identified some ruins that could be made to serve as a fortification. The rest were free to go home. Just two were to accompany Wilfrid to Bamburgh. One was Edwin, a young relative of the king's who had been sent along to experience his first serious battle. The other was his mentor, and Wilfrid's former captain, Beorhtred. As they set off, Wilfrid detected an atmosphere between them, and surmised that the young man had not acquitted himself well. Not wishing to get involved, he tried to engage Beorhtred in conversation about something else as they walked, but given their shared vocation and similar temperaments, conversations between Wilfrid and Beorhtred never stayed away from the subject of war for long.

'Take heed of Wilfrid, young lad,' Beorhtred kept telling Edwin when he'd got the hero onto the subject. 'Here's a man who never turned his back on an enemy unless it was to kill him with a lethal fart!' It was a favourite joke of Beorhtred's, but rehearsed now without a hint of mirth or indeed any intention to amuse.

A moment later, though, Wilfrid obligingly let rip.

'There goes another fairy champion!' Beorhtred announced, looking back in mock horror at the hero's invisible victim.

Edwin just looked ahead sullenly as he trudged on, and eventually Beorhtred let the lad drift ahead to sulk alone as he talked to Wilfrid. There was also fighting to the south of Northumbria, against the Mercians. Beorhtred suspected they were in league with the Picts. They had begun raiding when King Eadberht had been occupied to his north, and continued after the conflict with the Picts had abated, as if taking their turn to keep Northumbria under pressure. There was no chance of Beorhtred and Wilfrid being redeployed to support their southern compatriots, though. The king had business for them at Bamburgh. 'Dynastic business,' Beorhtred added wryly.

Wilfrid nodded. He knew that meant disposing of a rival to the ever-disputed throne. Fighting an insurgent faction among their own people. But really it was all the same to him. Picts, Britons, fellow Northumbrians. Fairies for that matter. He was good at what he did and took pride in it. He was not without honour, either. He was a warrior, not a murderer, and would not kill a man without a fair fight. In his experience, men were equally reluctant to die without a fair fight, or at least a fight, so it was all good.

After a couple of days' hard trekking, they reached Magilros Abbey and the growing settlement next to it, where they were able to obtain horses for the rest of the journey. By then, amity had been restored between Edwin and Beorhtred. It transpired that Edwin had not disgraced himself in battle, but had objected when Beorhtred had punched another lad as punishment for cowardice. Sometimes there was a thin line between tactical retreat and running away, so there was often room for disagreement. The real issue was who had the authority to decide what was cowardice and what was not. In this case, that was Beorhtred, and Edwin just had to get used to it. Having emerged from his sulk, he was much more talkative as they rode to Bamburgh, and keen after all to take heed of Wilfrid. The hero was no storyteller, but he was a font of practical wisdom when it came to the use of different weapons – from seax to longsword to axe and spear – as well as tactics and manoeuvres, whether in single combat or full-scale battle. It was agreed that he would spar with Edwin if there was time when they got to Bamburgh.

In the event, there was not time. When they arrived, the castle was abuzz with the news that the pretender to the throne had had the temerity to seek asylum at Lindisfarne Priory. Having been pursued up and down the country since making his claim, and evidently having found less support than he had hoped for, Offa son of Aldfrith now thought to resist the king's authority under his own nose, on the Holy Island visible from the castle itself! Beorhtred and Wilfrid joined a company of men charged with arresting him. Edwin was to stay with his mother this time.

Meanwhile, not far from the plain of Coel, Ethel was thinking about her own son, the son she was sure was growing in her belly. After all, she had sacrificed a young goat to make sure of its sex. In doing so, she had promised Thunor, the mightiest of the old gods, that she would bring up her son to honour him if only he would watch over him and make him a famous warrior like his father. More famous even, and more mighty, because he would be blessed by the famous and mighty Thunor.

CHAPTER 24: ILLUMINATIONS

Mary Brigid looked at the new manuscript in awe. It was the most beautiful thing she had ever seen. More beautiful than any beautiful object she had seen in Iona or even in Dunadd, where she had once seen such beautiful things in their maker's workshop. The manuscript was more beautiful even than the sun setting over the ocean, than the stars in the night sky, than gloriously coloured birds in flight, than flowers miraculously blooming into God's Creation. Was it blasphemous to say so? Well, the manuscript too was part of God's Creation, and a reflection of his speaking it into being. She was looking at Genesis, the beginning of everything. Or at least the beginning of everything a human being could know.

Still, she could not afford to linger for long in the scriptorium, admiring manuscripts and contemplating such things. She had been there to read a new copy of a more mundane manuscript, checking for any errors before it was passed on to be copied again. An eagle eye for such things was her modest gift. Much as she would have preferred to be able to glorify God by working on the illuminations, she was happy to play a more humble role, grateful indeed. But now she was needed in the nuns' kitchen, or rather in the yard outside the kitchen, to butcher seals. The monks of Iona had special rights to the seals that congregated on the beaches of Mull, and usually it fell to the nuns to process the carcasses, taking meat as well as blubber for oil and sundry other purposes. It was hard work and not exactly pleasant, but Brigid did not object. A nun's life was one of quiet obedience as well as contemplation, and the two were not mutually exclusive. She could ponder the mysteries of Creation as readily when butchering its dumb animals as when admiring the beautiful works of men.

As Mary Brigid worked alongside her sisters Mary Caitlin and Mary Fidelma, they were watched over by the Virgin Mary herself, in the form of the statue young Lucky had brought with her to Iona all those years before. She had confessed to stealing it almost as soon as she'd arrived, and agreed to perform extra chores as penance, but it had been decided to keep the statue on Iona, and it now stood in a nook above the door to the nuns' kitchen and refectory, overlooking the yard. Brigid was no longer in the habit of gazing at the statue until it seemed to come alive, but occasionally she caught sight of it from the corner of her eye, and it was not an it but the Lady herself. This was a source of great comfort to Brigid, not only because she felt divine love radiating from the Lady, but because the experience connected her with Lucky, with her former self. She liked the feeling that her life was a story, with a beginning, a middle and – when the Lord willed it – an end.

Her beginning was a mystery: she knew she had been dropped from the sky into a fishing boat, a particularly dramatic instance of the miracle of new life, but really no more or less mysterious than the ordinary business of human birth, which she'd presumably experienced not long before. Then she'd no less miraculously learned to speak and to pray and to think and had a mostly happy childhood on her adoptive island. And then, as a young woman, she had been sent on a journey, experienced the adventure that had brought her to Iona. Here, in the middle of her life, she was learning the true meaning of obedience in the strict setting of a religious community. She had learned to butcher seals and many other useful worldly skills, and she had learned to read and write both Gaelic and Latin, having shown an aptitude for scholarly things. The nuns mostly lived separate lives from the monks. Speculation on this matter was the stuff of vulgar jokes in the world beyond Iona, but Brigid was oblivious to all that. She was allowed to spend time in the monks' scriptorium because she was useful there, and she was never alone with any one monk in that chilly place where no one's mind strayed for long from the tasks at hand. Living in community meant never really being alone, even in the relative privacy of one's cell. Recently, Brigid had begun teaching some of the younger nuns to read and write. So her life had a shape even in the absence of the things that ordinarily give shape to a woman's life. In time, she would grow old and die, embarking on another great adventure into mystery. She would see the Lady no longer fleetingly but for eternity, in the company of the saints and of the Father, the Son and the Holy Ghost.

Brigid's gaze was drawn now from the Lady to a monk who had appeared in the yard, almost as if the Lady's own distracted gaze was leading hers. It was Brother Paul. 'Good morning, sisters,' he said brightly.

The three sisters smiled warmly, but only Mary Caitlin, the eldest, spoke: 'Good morning, Brother Paul. How may we serve you?'

Paul explained that he and a couple of other monks were to travel to one of the monasteries of the Picts. He was packing their supplies, and asked for some dried seal meat and any other victuals suitable for such a journey. Mary Caitlin put down the carcass she was working on and asked Paul to wait while she went into the kitchen to gather the supplies. As she did so, Paul spoke to Brigid. 'I saw you admiring Brother Augustine's latest illuminations earlier.'

'Yes,' she said, tearing at a piece of cartilage, 'so very beautiful. You're not taking it away with you, are you?'

'Certainly not! A copy is to be sent to Ireland, God willing, but the original is to stay with us.'

'That's good,' said Brigid. 'We'll pray for your safe return.'

'Thank you, sister.'

Presently Mary Caitlin returned with a bulging sack, which she handed to Paul.

'Thank you, sister,' he said, making a show of struggling to lift it. 'We'll grow fat on this journey!'

'We'll pray for your safe return,' Mary Caitlin said, taking up her carcass.

'Thank you sisters, and good morning.'

It had occurred to Brigid that Caitlin, and perhaps some of the other nuns, resented her time in the scriptorium, and her familiarity with the scholarly brothers. She was not the only nun to have enjoyed those privileges; her own teacher Sister Agatha had been renowned for her scholarship, and that was not so unusual. But Brigid was the only nun currently employed in any capacity in the scriptorium, so she did stand out. Any sister prone to petty jealously would have been in danger of letting it get to her. Not that anyone said anything; not that what seemed to Brigid to be disapproving looks were certainly that. She knew only that the Devil wanted her to think so. Indeed, if any her sisters struggled with petty jealousies, that was between them and God. Brigid's burden was to resist getting involved. Tutting at the resentments of others was a roundabout form of pride, and one not to be indulged. She hoped her sisters could forgive her ambiguous facial expressions as she forgave theirs, and she prayed to God to focus her mind on more worthy things.

Paul thought more than he should of Sister Mary Brigid. He was troubled not so much by lust, the Devil's milk, which was easily digested and expelled. What unsettled him was a whimsy that came to him now and again. What if he had never become a monk, and Brigid had never become a nun? What if God had brought them together in quite different circumstances, and they could have lived as man and wife? That was solid food, and it gave Paul indigestion. He did not suppose it would go away just because he was leaving Iona for a time. The thing about whimsy, about fantasy, was that it was no respecter of distance either in space or time. It was always there in an eternal present. At least for the living moment, though, Paul had work to get on with, practical stuff to occupy his mind. He got on with it.

'The sisters must like you!' said Brother Aidan, innocently enough, as he examined the contents of Paul's sack, having heaved it into the boat.

'That's why we sent him,' said Brother Gregory, with a little more mischief.

Paul shook his head dismissively. 'Do you have the letters?' he asked Gregory, who patted his satchel in the affirmative. 'Then what are we waiting for?' He nodded to the boatmen to make ready, and as they did so the brothers knelt on the beach to pray together. They had received the blessing of the Abbot first thing that morning. The tide coincided with the monks' midday meal, which waited for no man, so they had to see themselves off. As the little boat put out to sea, Paul noticed the seagulls scatter as a large eagle soared overhead. He marvelled to think that the dumb beast could make their journey in a fraction of the time it would take them. For a moment, he wondered what it would be like to be an eagle, soaring like that above the concerns of men. But soon he was distracted by just those concerns. His brothers wanted to talk about their mission.

CHAPTER 25: THE WOMAN OF THE WOOD

Pendrin awoke suddenly. His dream had scared him awake. He had been dreaming about the woman of the wood, as he often did now.

He had first encountered her nearly a year before, while hunting in the wood above the farm. He had been looking in her direction for some time before realising she was in front of him, no further than twenty paces away. But she was staring right back at him, and she certainly knew he was there, though he was as absolutely still as she. Then he was distracted by a deer, which was what he had been there for after all, and when he glanced back in the woman's direction, he found she was no longer there. And then nor was the deer.

The next time he had seen the woman, or been allowed to see her, had been when he was simply wandering in the wood, muttering to himself about this and that. And there she was, quite naked, by the bank of a stream. He was convinced in that instant that she was a kelpie. Why? Precisely because he was captivated by her beauty, overcome with desire. Desire to approach her, to touch her, and then? Fear had followed hard and fast, even before she had suddenly vanished without a trace.

He had been afraid of the woman ever since. Afraid and intrigued. He had caught occasional glimpses of her throughout the year, some more certain than others. Sometimes it was hard to know whether he was imagining it. Other times, there was no doubt: she wandered brazenly into his path, only to disappear just as suddenly. On one occasion, he heard a dart whistle past his ear and into a tree just behind him, followed by a woman's laughter. He had retrieved the dart and had it still, a strange and strangely beautiful little thing. He was sure it had been made by elves, and held who knew what magical properties. Perhaps he should have thrown it away, but he did not. He feared it as he feared the woman of the wood. With a gnawing fascination.

It was not yet dawn and everyone else was asleep, but Pendrin crawled out of bed and went outside. At this hour, he could both see the stars and hear birdsong, that magical combination. It was cold, but he did not mind. He looked out over the blackness of the loch, and then, hesitatingly, at the even blacker wood behind and above him. The loch reflected what little light came from the heavens to dance on its gently undulating waves. The wood just ate the light up, giving nothing back. Pendrin would sooner have dived into the freezing loch than wandered into the wood at this hour. Still, he imagined himself doing just that: walking slowly into the wood, feeling its blackness close around him as he absorbed its always strange sounds and smells, and was himself absorbed into the blackness, the terrifying blackness where the woman of the wood waited.

He jumped with fright when his thoughts were interrupted by the sound of someone else emerging from the house. Almost as if he had been doing something wrong.

'You're up early,' Constantine said, ambling round to the side of the building to pee.

'Yes.'

'It's a lovely clear sky.'

'Yes.'

'Ahhh.'

A minute later, Constantine went back inside, back inside to his wife, leaving Pendrin alone with his thoughts once more.

Pendrin had not mentioned the woman of the wood to anyone. She was his secret. He no longer believed she was a kelpie, not really. He had entertained various theories about who or what she might be. If not a kelpie then an elf or some other magical creature. But increasingly he was sure she was a human woman. Indeed, it was her humanity that fascinated him. As strange and exotic as she was, there was nothing mysterious or unnatural about Pendrin's attraction to her. She was a beautiful woman: that had struck him again each time he had seen her, whether in her full glory or more fleetingly. So he was attracted to her in the same way he had been attracted to ordinary girls, only more so. She was perhaps a little older than him, and older than the girls he had admired before. But there was something else. The girls Pendrin knew and had flirted with were always associated with a familiar context: Dyrael's sister Pandra who lived with her family across the loch, Mary from the next farm but one, the little red-haired girl who served at the church. The woman of the wood was not part of Pendrin's own world in that way. She was a human being who somehow existed independently of that world. How? He was captivated by that question as much as by her beauty, and also frightened by it. Because surely to be a person was to be part of a community? To belong to a village, a hamlet, at least a family. He did not see how the woman of the wood could have a family in there with her. So, of what did her life consist? Perhaps she was a huntress, taking game with her elven darts. But, apart from the fact that he had never heard of a hunt-*ress*, even the most solitary and itinerant hunters made themselves known to other people, if only to trade with them. The woman of the wood was something else.

The sun came up and soon enough Pendrin was caught

up in his own world once more. The harvest was nearly over, but there was still work to be done. The whole family pulled together from dawn till dusk. Even Anya did what she could when she was not tending to the new baby. Elphin was the jewel of the harvest, his proud father Peter had said, and everyone was lifted by this addition to the family, even as he bawled at them. In a few years, he would be working hard along with the twins and everyone else, as his father had done when he had come of age, and his father's father, and his father's father's father from whom he had his name. The cycle of family life echoed that of the farm itself. Here was nature; here was life.

Perhaps Elphin would also follow his namesake by becoming a carver of stones. For now, that legacy had fallen to his uncle Pyrdie. There was little time for carving during the harvest, but Pyrdie was in the habit of absent-mindedly drawing patterns in the dirt with a stick as he rested. Sometimes he carved animals, sometimes abstract designs whose meanings were secret – indeed, there were many layers of secrecy – and sometimes human figures. Sometimes the figure of a woman, an image that played constantly in his mind. It was not only Pendrin who saw a mysterious woman in his dreams, you see, but also his cousin.

A word about those abstract patterns, then. The first layer of secrecy was the layer of secrecy that conceals all meaningful things from those without minds to comprehend them; oblivious animals and the like. The second concealed the particular kind of meaning of the carvings from those creatures capable of registering that something was going on but unable to distinguish between abstract and figurative designs. Those who could tell the designs were abstract were excluded by a third layer and perhaps a fourth: even if they guessed the designs had meanings, they had no way of knowing what they were. Then, for those who encountered the patterns as puzzles, perhaps because they were familiar with something similar in another culture, the solution to those puzzles remained elusive unless they were let into the secret, or rather secrets. Some symbols were known to everyone who belonged to the People of the Designs, others limited to particular groups in a particular place and time; some, in fact, were lost to time, at least as far as anyone knew. And some were known only to the men who carved them, and to anyone to whom they chose to reveal the secret. Pyrdie would have liked to think the woman he drew belonged to that last category. To anyone else, it would just be a carving of a woman, and not in itself particularly expressive of what it was about this particular woman that had so captivated its carver. Except that when Pendrin noticed it, he looked distinctly put out. He said nothing, though, but just stood up.

'About time to get back to it then.'

Pyrdie had seen the woman in the flesh nearly a year before. And again, quite literally. He had been carving on a large boulder not far from the wood, putting the finishing touches to a series of designs he had carved that summer, and had just packed up his tools and set off for home when it occurred to him to make a subtle change. He turned back, and there she was, admiring his work. She made no attempt to hide or flee as he approached, so he smiled warmly. 'Do you like it?'

'Very much,' she said. 'Would you like to see mine?'

'Your carving?' he asked in bafflement.

She smiled, and loosened her tunic, before pulling it down to bare her chest. Pyrdie was stunned, and not just for the obvious reason. The woman's chest was adorned with a beautifully ornate design, curling in from each shoulder to above her breasts. Pyrdie was astonished as a craftsman almost as much as he was inflamed as a mere man, and he was certainly that. But the woman quickly covered herself again, and left him speechless as she disappeared into the wood.

Just looking at his own rough approximation in the dirt of the female form took Pyrdie back to the thrill of that moment, if he let it. He scratched it away before rising to join Pendrin and the others going back to the harvest.

His work this summer on the boulder near the wood would not be so easily erased. There, on the side facing the wood itself, he had reproduced as faithfully as his memory and skill allowed the design on the mysterious woman's chest. It was not quite like anything Pyrdie's grandfather had ever taught him; perhaps a little more like one or two stones on the mountain, those whose meanings were lost. If his muse had seen his tribute, she had done nothing to acknowledge it. For nearly a year, Pyrdie had seen her only in his dreams.

CHAPTER 26: HARVEST FESTIVAL

Rumour had already reached the farm that a troupe of bards was touring the glens and performing for the locals as they celebrated the end of the harvest. So it was no surprise when a lad arrived from the next farm but one to invite everyone to join them and other neighbours from the surrounding area for some entertainment that afternoon and evening. It was not a long walk, the weather was clear and the moon would be near to full, so it was agreed that the whole family would go, with the exception of Peter and Anya, who would stay at home to look after baby Elphin as well as the twins. Pyrdie and Pendrin loaded up a small wagon with some food and drink, helped their older relatives climb on top, and set off with the rest of the family on foot. Constantine and Dyrael trailed behind, arm in arm, enjoying one another's company with the harvest behind them and the twins at home. It was a happy moment for everyone. When they arrived at their hosts' homestead, the neighbours greeted one another warmly. Improvised tables had been set out between the farmhouse and the loch. Young Mary took Pendrin by the arm and led him off to see her kittens. The red-haired girl who served at the church observed this and then acknowledged Pyrdie with a smile, but she kept her distance. The parish priest was also in attendance and took care to greet everyone individually. It was rare for so many of his flock to be gathered in one place that was not the church, and given the distances involved, they gathered there only a few times a year. Everyone was curious about the bards, who had pitched a tent on a newly bare field just up from the farmhouse but far enough to add to their mystique.

The priest led everyone in a thanksgiving prayer before the celebrations began in earnest. Then the food was laid out and the drink began flowing as old friendships were renewed, news shared and future plans discussed. A great fire was lit to keep the revellers warm as the evening cooled. Spirits were already high when the bards emerged from their tent and the drummer began rolling his drum. Then he led them in a column down towards the farmhouse. In addition to the drummer, there were two harpers, who began strumming as they walked, and a fourth musician who carried two horns, one long – which he blasted as they walked – and one short, as well as a kind of flute or whistle fastened around his neck. They took up position on a grassy verge that formed a convenient stage in front of the assembled revellers, and close was enough for the fire to cast its flickering light on them as the sun began to set, and one of the harpers began to sing. But it was the other who drew the attention of both Pendrin and Pyrdie. What was it about the slight young man that caught their attention? A certain familiarity, a mysterious atmosphere about him. And then – of course! – the realisation that he was not a young man at all, but a woman. The woman of the wood.

The rest of the revellers did not notice that the young man was a woman. They had neither familiarity with this particular woman's appearance nor sensitivity to her atmosphere to guide them. And anyway, they were too taken up by the song, which the bards brought to life through dance as well as music.

The song told the story of a kelpie who had tricked its

master, an ancient king, into ordering it to take the form of a demon with the power to turn anything to ashes simply by touching it with its right hand. The kelpie promised to use that power to slay the king's enemies and help him rule by fear, but as soon as the king had given the order, he realised his mistake: the kelpie-demon reached out its right hand to touch the king himself.

'Turn into a squirrel!' the king commanded, thinking he could quickly rectify his mistake. But he was wrong. The kelpie had not told him that, having taken the form of an ash demon, it no longer had the power to change to another living form, and so could not follow the king's order. The king fled in terror, and the kelpie-demon pursued him until his daughter the princess rushed to put herself between her father and his would-be nemesis.

The princess was beautiful, of course – as princesses in songs are obliged to be – so of course the kelpie-demon was immediately besotted. And when she asked it to dance, it could hardly resist. 'It's easy,' she said, 'just follow me'. And she stretched out her arms and raised one leg, and the kelpie-demon did the same. Then she shuffled to her left and took a bow, and the kelpie-demon did the same. Then she took a step back and jumped up twice, and the kelpie-demon did the same. Then she raised both arms and jigged on the spot, and the kelpie-demon did the same. Then she placed her right hand on top of her head, and the kelpie-demon did the same. Then she turned to her father and took another bow, and the kelpie-demon could do no such thing, because it had turned the ash the instant it had put its right hand on its head.

Everyone enjoyed that song. The children, and quite a few who were no longer children, even joined in the dance, but nobody turned to ash. And there were many more songs, but the princess featured in only one of them. It told a strange tale, also from a time of legend, and clearly long before Christianity came to the land. The people were blighted by pestilence, and to bring relief, the king ordered a priest of the old gods to build a shrine at a special spot between a sacred grove and a magical loch. The priest set to work, but every morning he woke to find his previous day's work had been dismantled. Eventually a mermaid appeared from the loch – as often happens in such tales – and explained that a human sacrifice would be required as a foundation for the shrine. In fact, the victim was to be buried alive under the shrine. So the priest appealed to the people for a volunteer, who had to be a young man in good health and of good character. Well, a young man of that description showed his good character by stepping forward and agreeing without a fuss to die for his people. He was a lowly commoner, but before he made such a momentous sacrifice he did have one condition. He did not want to die unmarried, inexperienced and unlamented. He agreed to be buried alive the next day on the condition that this very day, he would be 'wedded and bedded' so when he was gone he would be mourned by a beautiful and heartbroken bride. But who wants to marry a man today who will be sacrificed tomorrow? Nobody, it seemed, and certainly not one of the young, nubile women who would have appealed to our hero. With one remarkable exception: you see, this is where our princess came in again. The last person anyone would have expected, a beautiful virgin who surely would have been destined to marry a rich and handsome foreign prince, instead volunteered herself for instant widowhood to a commoner. And not grudgingly either. She married the doomed man happily, and then treated him to a night of passion many a man might have been willing to die for if only he'd known. And the following day, when he was buried alive, she wept and wailed and tore her clothes, mourning him as no woman had ever mourned her husband before or since.

The next and final part of the song was almost whispered. You see, it was just a rumour. What if, the very next night, the young man had crept from his premature grave, perhaps with a little help from the outside. And what if that mermaid had not really been a mermaid at all? And what if the princess did not want to marry a rich and handsome foreign prince? And who had been dismantling the shrine every night anyway? And what if the princess also disappeared that second night, never to be seen or heard of again? Nobody knew, so there the song ended – and the audience roared with approval. Even Pendrin and Pyrdie were swept away by the performance, though their attention had of course been focused on one player in particular, the harper who had twice broken off from playing the harp to dance the part of the princess. How anyone could not have seen that this was a woman was beyond them, but then they were already under her spell. And perhaps they were not alone.

'I noticed at least a couple,' said Gwy, as the four young women lounged in their tent early the next morning, reviewing their performance.

'Oh, come on, there were three or four,' countered Peg.

Fay shook her head with a wry smile. 'Try six,' she said.

'Six young men under your spell just here! I must admit I'm impressed,' said Gwy.

'Oh, can't you tell just by looking at me?' Fay said. 'Am I not radiant?'

'You are, you are,' chimed in Tes, 'but then you're always radiant, so it's hard to tell.'

'That's true. But look who else is radiant today. I do believe I lost one of my young men in the night. And now I can tell Gwy is the culprit!'

Gwy was certainly radiant now. 'Well, you can't have them all to yourself,' she said through her blushes. 'Especially since you don't even enjoy them.'

'Oh, if you only knew how much I enjoy them,' Fay retorted. 'You can keep your filthy animal antics. Will he dream of you a year from now? Or will he forget you as soon as he's found another bitch in heat?'

Gwy's response was more catlike than bitchy, a swipe of her claw that stopped just short of Fay's face. There was no real animus in it, any more than there had been in Fay's verbal swipe. The bards often expressed their mutual affection in the form of insults. Mutual respect was shown only on ceremonial occasions. Then the Sacred Virgin was given due reverence, as were the Daughters of the Sun and the Moon and the Avatar of the Dragon. Then it did not matter if the Daughter of the Moon had enjoyed a roll in the newly harvested hay with one of the Sacred Virgin's admirers.

CHAPTER 27: LINDISFARNE

Cuthbert was praying alone when the commotion began. At first, he tried not to be distracted. When it became clear that the disturbance was not about to die down, he took a breath in frustration before launching himself back into prayer with still greater resolve: 'Lord Jesus Christ, Son of God, have mercy on me, a sinner. Lord Jesus Christ, Son of God, have mercy on me, a sinner. Lord Jesus Christ, Son of God...'

'Cuthbert, come quick!' came a voice that was not the Lord Jesus Christ's. It was Ewald, a young novice monk who had become a particular friend to Cuthbert since they had arrived at Lindisfarne within days of one another around six months earlier.

'Can't you see...' Cuthbert broke off when he saw that Ewald was in a genuine panic.

'Soldiers,' the boy said breathlessly, 'The king's men. They're here for the pretender.'

Cuthbert sighed. He'd seen this coming as soon as Offa had scurried onto the Holy Island two days before.

'The bishop has gone out to speak to them,' Ewald continued. 'I think it would help if someone like you went out too.'

'Someone like me, huh?' A sinner. The kind of sinner

whose sins had sent other men to their maker.

Ewald grimaced awkwardly.

'All right,' Cuthbert said, rising from his knees and following Ewald, though he was not convinced the appearance of someone like him would help matters at all.

When he recognised Wilfrid and Beorhtred, Cuthbert sent up a silent prayer just to avoid saying something irreverent. He'd come to Lindisfarne to find peace, and God had sent him this. Well, the Lord certainly had a sense of humour. When they recognised him, his old comrades were less restrained.

'Well, if it isn't Cuthbert the Gael!' bellowed Beorhtred.

'What the holy Hell are *you* doing here?' Wilfrid demanded in delighted surprise.

'I was enjoying some peace and quiet till you came along,' Cuthbert said wryly, aware that their friendly greetings were at odds with the prevailing atmosphere, which was pregnant with violence. He did not cross the invisible line that divided his 'side' from that of his old friends. The bishop stood with several monks outside the church that stood at the heart of the monastery, forming a barrier of sorts against the company from Bamburgh. The soldiers had clearly decided not to breach that barrier, for now.

Beorhtred took it upon himself to bring Cuthbert up to speed: 'We've just been explaining to the bishop here that this is a political matter. We have no intention of entering the church under arms. We only ask that the brothers bring out Offa son of Aldfrith so we can escort him to the king.'

'And I have just been explaining to these men,' the bishop added, without looking at Cuthbert, 'that Offa son of Aldfrith has come here to seek sanctuary, and I cannot turn him over to those who would do him harm.'

Cuthbert was already regretting coming out into the midst of this. But then young Ewald was the only person who had expected him to be able to do anything about it. It pained him to see the look of expectation in the boy's face when all he could do in response was shrug. To everyone else, Cuthbert was a mere bystander, however grizzled by battle, and he had no intention of proving them wrong.

Beorhtred made it clear that unless the monks produced Offa, his orders were to arrest the bishop himself and take him to the dungeon in Bamburgh Castle until he relented. The monks were outraged, but the bishop agreed to go peacefully. That was that, then. Beorhtred and a couple of others took the bishop away, wasting no time as the tide was coming in and would soon cover the path over the mud flats to the mainland, which only appeared at low tide. The other soldiers remained to make sure Offa did not go anywhere on foot or by boat unless it was with them. Wilfrid sent a couple of men around the church to check for alternative exits. When one of the monks made to go back in the front door, Wilfrid stopped him. 'I'm afraid none of you can go in there till Offa comes out.'

More outrage, but Wilfrid was unmoved by protests, pleas or spiritual threats, and nobody had anything else to offer, Cuthbert included.

'You hear that, Offa?' Wilfrid shouted into the church. 'No one is coming in there till you come out. That means no food or water. You'll save everyone a lot of time and trouble if you just come out now.'

At that, a couple of monks appeared at the entrance from inside. 'Are we allowed out?' asked one, but he and his friend were quickly shooed back in by another monk who had more thought for decorum. For now, the monks were putting up a united front with their charge. Wilfrid laughed dismissively and set his men to building a fire.

With the tension at least dampened by the bishop's removal, Cuthbert felt able to go over and greet Wilfrid properly, much to the dismay of Ewald, who threw up his hands and wandered over to join his brothers standing idly by the church. Wilfrid took Cuthbert's arm warmly. 'Don't tell me you're a monk now?'

'No, just a visitor,' Cuthbert told him. 'I've been here six months now, making myself useful as best I can. It really has been very peaceful. Until now.'

Wilfrid laughed. 'Well, I can only apologise! But I suppose the situation speaks for itself.'

'I suppose it does.'

'Any chance your friends will see sense and give him up?'

Cuthbert shrugged. 'Monks are a pretty stubborn lot. They're loyal to the bishop and now the bishop's not here to give them new instructions.'

'That man would sooner die than change his mind anyway. I know the type.'

'True enough.' Cuthbert shifted uncomfortably. 'So what are your orders?'

'To wait the bugger out. We're all God-fearing men, old friend, and we won't violate the sanctity of a church. If the monks won't give him up, we'll wait till he cracks on his own.'

'So why bother taking the bishop?' Cuthbert asked, and immediately withdrew the question by answering it. 'Politics. And none of my business.'

'Nor mine, Cuthbert. Nor mine!'

Cuthbert took his leave and returned to the monks, who quickly surrounded him, demanding to know how he knew the soldiers and what he intended to do to get the bishop released. Eventually he convinced them there was nothing he could do. They knew he had been a soldier, so it was hardly shocking that he knew other soldiers, and it hardly implied any sway on his part. He reassured them that the soldiers had orders to respect the sanctity of the church. They would simply wait until Offa gave himself up.

'Oh, so they won't actually march into the church and murder the man at the altar,' said one monk. 'They'll just wait outside until he's forced out by starvation. Is that what you call respecting the sanctity of the church? It rather puts the letter of the law ahead of its spirit.'

'Soldiers are very literal men,' Cuthbert told him.

When things had calmed down, Cuthbert went to sit alone under a lonely tree by the side of the church. He was soon joined by Ewald. 'I understand that there was nothing you could have done,' the boy said. 'I just can't believe we stood there and watched him being led off like Christ from Gethsemane.'

The comparison had also occurred to Cuthbert, but by now he'd had time to think it over and get his defence in. 'If the bishop was like Christ, then we did well to learn from Saint Peter's mistake. We did not make fools of ourselves trying to resist his arrest. And nor will we deny knowing him should anyone ask. Not that there's much doubt, especially in your case, my tonsured friend.'

'Why did they call you Cuthbert the Gael?' Ewald asked suddenly.

'It's a long story,' Cuthbert answered.

Ewald looked around him at his fellow monks, sitting or standing around, bereft of their leader, amid the handful of bare buildings that made up the monastery. And at the soldiers camped there to keep anyone from coming or going from this barren island on the edge of the world, which had seemingly just been abandoned by God himself. 'Do you have an urgent appointment somewhere?'

In fact, the name had stuck after Cuthbert's first brief adventure with his Gaelic friends Domnall and Fergus. His own people, not least his old friend Wilfrid, had been impressed by his spirit of adventure, to go off with the foreigners like that, and by his ability to speak the Gaelic language a little, which proved useful on many later occasions. Over the years, Cuthbert the Gael had made himself useful for commercial as well as political purposes. But he had only become more or less fluent some time after that first adventure, when he had married a Gaelic woman, Eithne. That was a different kind of adventure, which had ended in great sadness when she had died in childbirth, taking the child with her. Cuthbert excused himself. The wave of grief had somehow taken him by surprise, as if he had not known where his story was going. He walked the short distance to the beach and looked out to sea, the spray from the rocks masking his tears.

CHAPTER 28: MURDER

The siege had gone on for two days and two nights when things became even more tense. Monks and soldiers stood, sat or sprawled in two indistinct but antagonistic clusters outside the church, staring at one another malignantly. Offa was stubbornly refusing to come out. The monks admitted he had started with a small amount of food and water in the church, but said he was certainly starving now. They had of course been forbidden to take him anything, and protested angrily when they were searched before being allowed in to see him. But now there was a more urgent question. The monks themselves were running out of certain essential provisions that had to be brought in from the mainland, having been due for a resupply before the siege began. The soldiers, growing impatient, were adamant that nobody would enter or leave Lindisfarne until the monks gave up Offa. But it was not obvious that they could stop the monks resupplying themselves without resorting to force, and the monks knew that was a line the soldiers were reluctant to cross. Surely could not cross. Wilfrid was not above using intimidation, however, and had the physical presence to frighten men of peace without so much as drawing his weapon. But the trick was losing potency with overuse.

Observing even more powerlessly from under his tree, Cuthbert was wondering what would happen when Offa finally did come out. He would be taken to Bamburgh, of course, but then what? The king would have him killed as a traitor. There would be a trial of some kind, perhaps, but would that satisfy the bishop? For all that he had professed simply to have been sheltering Offa from injustice, it was clear to Cuthbert that there was more to it than that. Why had Offa chosen Lindisfarne of all places to seek asylum? Why had the king's men had orders to arrest the bishop? Cuthbert knew little of politics, but it was obvious that discord between the king and his bishop was not new. The church and its princes did not always manage to stand above earthly dynastic politics, any more than the secular powers kept out of the church's business. Maybe the bishop really was for the pretender. This was a mess, and whatever happened next would be unlikely to resolve the discord for long.

'Can we not just go and get him?' one of the soldiers pleaded for the hundredth time. 'I'm not saying kill him in the sanctuary – just go in, drag him out and take him back to Bamburgh?'

'No, we can't,' Wilfrid answered for the hundredth time, shouting now. 'Our orders are clear. The king's men will not enter that church.'

Cuthbert sighed, stood up and ambled over to the soldiers. 'I'm not one of the king's men,' he said. He picked up a seax one of the soldiers had left on the ground with some other kit, and marched into the church. A moment later, he came out again, dragging Offa behind him on his knees. And there and then, outside the church at the heart of the monastery of Lindisfarne, he slew the pretender by driving the seax through the nape of his neck and deep down into his chest. Offa spluttered blood from his mouth and crashed forward, more blood gushing from the wound to stain the ground. There was no question that he was dead.

The monks were stunned. The soldiers too. The deed

done, Cuthbert walked back to his tree, sat down and began to pray for forgiveness. 'Lord Jesus Christ, Son of God, have mercy on me, a sinner. Lord Jesus Christ, Son of God, have mercy on me, a sinner. Lord Jesus Christ, Son of God...'

Wilfrid was the first observer to get over his shock and act. He had his men roll Offa's body up in a blanket and assigned four of them to carry it on their shoulders. 'What's done is done,' he told the monks. 'I suppose you can expect the bishop back shortly after we get this to Bamburgh.' But the monks were no longer looking at Wilfrid and his men. They were looking at Cuthbert. He had never been one of them, but he had lived among them for six months. They had always known he had a dark past, but they had thought they knew him, that he was as good a Christian man as one can expect to know in this fallen world. And now this. So sudden, so brutal, so unexpected. And the bishop was not here to show them how to react, let alone what to do next.

Even as he prayed, Cuthbert knew he could not stay on Lindisfarne. Not now. He would ask for forgiveness, of course, but he would not be doing so as even an associate member of the community. He was just another sinner now, an unwelcome intrusion from the sinful world outside the monastery. Given the politics of the situation, he did not suppose the secular powers would punish him for murder. He had done the king a favour. But neither did he expect thanks. Thanks would have defeated the purpose of his intervention, which was only effective because it had been gratuitous. The king could not be held responsible for the murder, because Cuthbert was not accountable to him, not for this at least. It could hardly be argued that Cuthbert had simply acted as a loyal subject doing his duty by removing the king's enemy. Not when the king's own men were right there with orders not to do what he had done. He had just done it, as if on a whim, as if he had taken an irrational dislike to this Offa and decided to kill him for no better reason than that. The murder only benefited the king as long Cuthbert was a renegade, a lone murderer, a madman. For that reason, there could be no question of his going with Wilfrid and the king's men either. Wilfrid knew that too, and did not even look at his old friend, much less bid him farewell, before packing up and setting off on the road back to Bamburgh with his men. Cuthbert decided to wait for the tide to come and go, washing away the soldiers' footsteps, before setting off himself, to where he knew not. In the meantime he would have to contend with the monks.

One monk had witnessed the murder with particular horror. It was not only the unexpected nature of this brutal killing, but the fact that it had befallen a pretender to the throne. The observer knew very well that the difference between a pretender and a rightful king was often no more than a matter of who murdered whom. Offa had been fool enough to announce his intentions to a king in a position to have him killed. If, instead, he had made sure of his own support first, he could have had the pretender-on-the-throne killed and taken his own rightful place. And even if his support had fallen short of that, perhaps if he'd made enough of a nuisance of himself while staying out of harm's way, he'd have had the good fortune of someone like Cuthbert stepping in and sparing everyone the embarrassment of having to choose between two rival kings. Even then, though, his reward would have been living and ruling with a target on his back. The monk shook his head at the ways of the world, of principalities and powers, and thanked God for sparing him all that.

CHAPTER 29: BONIFACE

King Brude rode majestically up the glen, followed by his bishop and a dozen men, and then a handful of ladies and servants. He had spent the previous night as the honoured guest of one large homestead, and this evening he would be the honoured guest of another. Then another, and another. Thus he was making his way through all the major settlements of the glen and of his wider lands. At each settlement, he formally requested fighting men to join him in the spring, when he would ride south on another campaign, and at each settlement he was promised many great warriors. Often this pledge was cemented by the recitation of a poem or song commemorating the heroic deeds of the warriors' ancestors. Then, more quietly, the bishop would speak to the leading nobles of each place and agree a particular number or men, great warriors or otherwise. This was how it had been throughout Brude's kingship: it was no secret that Bishop Boniface was the power behind the throne. How could it have been otherwise? It had often been said that the bishop was the brains behind King Taran's rise to power, and when the late king had died unexpectedly, his young son could not possibly have been prepared to wield that power. He'd had a ready-made puppeteer, who had been in charge ever since.

King Brude knew as well as anyone what people said about him. There was a lingering sense that he was not a 'genuine' king, but he did not let that get to him. He knew that the secret of kingship – the secret of occupying any role – was not to give credence to other people's doubts. He had learned that from Bishop Boniface, who was not really a bishop and whose name was not really Boniface. Or at least that was one way of looking at it.

Boniface had once had an argument with a pious monk who had pointed out that there were no bishops in the scriptures. That may be so, he had told the monk, but there are certainly bishops in Rome. He had been to Rome, or so he told people. In fact, there was a wild rumour that he'd served as Pope for some years, but even he denied that. He did claim to have been ordained as a bishop by another Bishop Boniface, also known as Saint Curetan, who had been a direct descendant of the sister of Saint Peter and Saint Andrew (the former of whom, lest we forget, was known to his mother as plain old Simon). So there was nothing particularly unusual about the fact that Boniface had taken a new name, but the bishop thing was more ambiguous. Whether or not he'd been ordained by a saint of the church, the institutional church had known nothing of his bishopric until he had inveigled his way into its good graces *as* a bishop. It was in that sense that he was not really a bishop. On the other hand, there he was.

And there he had been just a decade or so ago, after the fall of Dunadd, lending religious authority to its conquest by Onuist, the now undisputed High King of their people, and effectively of the Gaels too; King Onuist also claimed ancestry among the Gaels, so his kingship was not only bought with blood spilled. The conquest had come shortly after the coronation of Brude, who had been more than content to be recognised as an underking of the new imperator. In the years since, Brude had consolidated that position with Boniface's help, supplementing military victories over the enemies of Onuist with strategic alliances with suitable parties both locally and further afield, some of whom were also enemies of Onuist. There is neither Jew nor Greek in Christ, as Boniface was fond of saying. And this evening, the bishop would sanctify another alliance, a holy union indeed. This evening's was to be no ordinary royal visitation. Their host was the wealthiest man in Brude's kingdom, not excluding the king himself, and for that reason he had been chosen for the honour of hosting a royal wedding.

King Brude was to marry an exiled Gaelic princess, formerly of Dunadd no less. Bronagh had been a mere girl when her father had lost his kingdom, and was sent to Ireland for safekeeping. Now she was a fine, educated and indeed beautiful young woman, or so Boniface had assured Brude, though neither had yet set eyes on her. In importing a bride for his king from abroad, Boniface was deliberately breaking with the tradition among their people that favoured the heirs of royal mothers. Not that the tradition had ever been honoured religiously, especially when internecine conflict led to dynastic uncertainty, as it so often did. But while foreign princes had often been brought into a royal line to sire heirs through native princesses, the introduction of a foreign princess was much less common. It signalled Brude's status as a modern king like those in other parts of Christendom, and perhaps compensated somewhat for the relative novelty of his royal line.

King Brude was also excited about his wedding. He could not help but be excited. The politics of the matter were exciting enough. Various factions of defeated Dalriada were keen to form alliances with influential houses under Onuist, and he had secured the most important, or at least the one that had been dominant in the old order; Boniface would ensure this was not their only iron in the fire. But Brude was also excited as a man. In that capacity, he would have only one iron in the fire, so to speak. He and Bronagh would become one flesh. While he had yet to see his bride in the flesh, they had exchanged letters. Her Latin was excellent. He was sure he was going to like her.

Before they reached their destination, the king's party encountered a group of monks on the path. The bishop trotted ahead with one of the king's guards and greeted them in Latin. It turned out they were from Iona, and were travelling to the monastery in the next glen. But two of them belonged to the People of the Designs – Brothers Gregory and Paul – and presumably they had been chosen for the mission because they spoke the language. They had been planning to ask for shelter for the night at the next settlement. Well, now they were invited to a royal wedding. Having accepted gratefully, they held back while the king and his men rode ahead, and then continued on foot.

'Have you heard of this King Brude?' Aidan asked the others. They explained that there were lots of lesser kings under Onuist, and a good few Brudes wielding power to some degree or another. This one seemed to be grander than most, but Gregory admitted he had not heard of him till now, and Paul nodded his assent. Still, these were interesting times, especially here in their homeland, which was partly why they were all here. Maybe this Brude would prove to be an important king and it would do no harm to have his patronage in some form.

The abbey on Iona had never been under serious threat from the Picts, but the subjugation of Dalriada had obviously affected the church that claimed jurisdiction over both peoples, and indeed everyone else. That its most important centre in the wider region also belonged to a particular nation whose fortunes were on the wane was hardly insignificant. Different religious communities had a way of rising and falling in importance along with secular power bases. On the other hand, Iona had never belonged solely to the Gaels. It was not only a centre of the universal church, but had long been cosmopolitan in its actual composition, home to monks of many nations. Indeed, it had been under the influence of the Pictish church – and ultimately the Northumbrian church

– that Iona had accepted the so-called Roman reforms a generation earlier.

The monks agreed that the wedding could an opportunity to cultivate friendly relations with secular powers among the Picts as well the church. And it was in the course of this discussion that Gregory realised something. 'Did the clergyman who greeted us say his name was Boniface?'

'He did,' said Aidan.

'Well, I may not have heard of his king, but I have certainly heard of Bishop Boniface.'

'Aha!' exclaimed Paul, who seemed even more astonished than Gregory. He stared ahead at the company on horse just still visible on the path ahead of them. 'Do you think *that* is our Bishop Boniface?'

Gregory explained to Aidan that Bishop Boniface had been corresponding with the Abbot of Iona for some time, not failing to mention more than once that he had been with King Onuist when he had taken Dunadd, despite (which he did not mention, but they had subsequently learned) having nothing to do with the regular court; he had simply got there first, when Onuist's favoured bishops remained at a safe distance. Boniface wrote to assure the Abbot of his and his people's desire for Christian peace and love between their nations, and of the special regard in which he and his countrymen would always hold Iona as the font of the gospel in the corner of the world they shared. He asked for guidance on certain liturgical matters, just as his namesake (the one he claimed had ordained him) had once written for guidance to Lindisfarne. The Abbot had shown these letters to some of his Pictish monks, including Gregory and Paul, and all had agreed they reeked of worldly politics. The Abbot had sent polite replies, but this obscure bishop had certainly not been deemed worthy of a visit from the Iona monks during their visit to his country. And yet, there he was.

CHAPTER 30: THE ROYAL WEDDING

As Paul watched Bishop Boniface perform the marriage rites between King Brude and Princess Bronagh, he could not help imagining it was actually himself and Brigid being joined as man and wife. It was all he could do to stop himself muttering along with the vows. Of course, the king could keep his crown and his princess bride. Paul envied him only his freedom to marry, to live in that sense an ordinary life. He did repent that envy, repent his frankly outrageous desire for an ordinary life. After all, he had vowed to live only for God. He repented the fact that he desired anything more than God. Repented. He did not just regret it: he pictured himself fleeing headlong back towards Christ, his only desire, his only comfort. And yet he knew it was only a matter of time before he would unrepent, wander off again, go on indulging his sinful desires, if not by succumbing to them, worse, by cherishing them. He prayed to God to free him from this absurd dance of his conscience, of his imagination, of his soul. Then he forced himself to attend to what was happening around him.

The ceremony had been short and to the point. All religious if not romantic pieties observed, there was no attempt to disguise the political nature of the marriage. The guests were here to witness a political union, and one that unmistakably enhanced the status of King Brude. It was much less a family affair. The king's mother had died shortly after his father. His sister had also died around the same time. (There were rumours about those untimely deaths, of course, but no one version of events had been widely enough believed to stick.) Brude's only remaining close relative was his uncle, the bishop. His real family now was his steadily growing court. And it was an impressive court for a still quite obscure underking. The men who travelled with Brude were skilled warriors from noble families. At the wedding, they were joined by many more nobles, several of whom were recent 'acquisitions', having previously been attached to other royal houses. And now a royal bride.

Princess Bronagh's bridal party consisted of her brother, her mother and a handful of retainers, her father too having died, shortly after losing Dunadd. Despite their small numbers, they carried themselves well, preferring to let natural aristocratic bearing speak for itself than to labour the point with finery and showy manners. That said, they wore some exquisite jewellery; evidently the treasures of Dunadd had not all fallen to Onuist.

As for the princess herself, she was beautiful in the way all brides are beautiful, if no more than that. In any case, her appearance clearly did not disappoint King Brude, nor his her. More importantly, she had greeted him with a smile as familiar and affectionate as any smile between two people who know one another only from letters. And she blushed. Brude seemed to like that, and his face shone back into hers. And, after all, why should a political union not also involve genuine affection between the two parties?

Other prominent guests included Prince Fidach, who brought greetings and gifts from the neighbouring King Gartnait, not Fidach's legendary father but the late king's nephew of the same name, Fidach's cousin, who had succeeded the old king on his death less than a year ago. It was whispered in some corners that if the young Gartnait had come in person, he'd have had his throat cut. His kingdom was ripe for the taking by the tumescent King Brude. But that was an exaggeration at best. Brude and his counsellor-puppet master sought influence before lands. Greetings and gifts were good enough for now, even if they were borne by the soon-to-be underking's cousin.

Then there was the Briton, Prince Rhodri, and his wife. In fact, he did not call himself a prince, but when it came to wealthy foreigners, it was best to err on the side of too extravagant honours. It did no harm. Rhodri had travelled at least some of the way with the bridal party, but of course he had come much further, bringing blessings from the shrine of Saint Mirin, wherever that was. His wife spent much of the evening deep in conversation with a Northumbrian lady, a relative of King Eadberht no less, who had brought her son Edwin to experience his first visit to a foreign court. The young man seemed to enjoy himself, and while the other foreigners made do with dog Latin and a few hybrid phrases to communicate with the locals, he made everyone laugh with his attempts at their own language.

Further entertainment was to be provided by a troupe of bards, whose reputation preceded them and whose appearance was therefore much anticipated. It was not for monks to enjoy a wedding feast long into the night, however, so having eaten and drunk enough, the brothers took their leave. They were shown to a temporary shelter that had been erected outside the longhouse, where they could sleep in relative peace, at least until merrier guests were ready to join them. There was just one person already asleep in the shelter, an old man. Paul noticed that his blanket had fallen away, and went over to tuck him in. Gregory and Aidan were a little surprised to see Paul seem to whisper an old song or poem to the sleeping man, and to come away with a tear in his eye, but then Paul was notoriously sentimental.

Paul dreamt that night of his wedding, but now the

bride was not Brigid, or indeed Princess Bronagh, but someone else entirely. A woman he had known long ago. In another life, really. Before he had given his life to Christ, or at least vowed to do so. Half-waking, he rebuked himself, and restored Brigid to her rightful place at his imaginary side, before remembering that too was wrong. There were too many layers of wrong. He prayed to God to free him from dreams and daydreams, from the incessant fantasising that cluttered his consciousness. But no.

'Hush, my darling,' Brigid said, gently stroking his hair. Then she put her warm mouth on his, her hot body on his, and in an instant Paul was far from that makeshift shelter by the side of the longhouse where his countryman had married Brigid's countrywoman. He and his love were far from all this, and just as far from Iona. And as ever, there was so much more to the dream than warm mouths and hot bodies. They lived far away, on their own island somewhere, with a fresh spring that trickled down to a sheltered beach, a few goats grazing on verdant pastures, a garden to tend. And, yes, the gentle tinkle of a child's laughter. Now Brigid was walking towards him along the beach, their toddler on her hip, and she was laughing at something he had said, as she used her free hand to brush her hair from her face, fighting a losing battle against the breeze. Paul reached out and pushed it back for her and then took her supple, womanly body in his arms, the toddler now conveniently out of the way as the dream returned to warm mouths and hot bodies, albeit on a beach now.

In the morning, the brothers prayed together, and as they did so, Paul tried to use the part of his mind that would otherwise have been wandering to apologise for just that, to plea for forgiveness and relief. Brigid knelt at his side to aid the effort.

The monastery they were to visit was less than a day's journey now. They accepted only a fraction of the generous provisions they were offered, left over from the wedding feast. The servants who offered them this food were not up early like the monks, but had not been to bed. A few guests were still celebrating in the longhouse; the servants blamed the bards for keeping them in the mood all night. Gregory wondered if it had been their music that had given him strange dreams. Paul said nothing. By now, no music could be heard from the longhouse, just indistinct chatter and occasional laughter. It was time for the monks to go.

CHAPTER 31: FAY

The bards had finally finished playing in the early hours of the morning, retiring to their tent to sleep, though one or two of them may have slipped out at some point for more private performances, arranged over the course of the evening with winks and whispers addressed to first baffled and then delighted young men. In the morning, they reviewed the previous night's public performance as usual, though it had been no ordinary night. A royal wedding had been a new experience for them all. There had even been foreigners. All very exciting.

'Did you see the bishop's pendant?' Tes asked the others. 'A huge thing, and solid gold by the look of it, depicting their murdered god on his cross. Very gruesome.'

'Oh, yes,' said Gwy, 'I've seen them before, but never that big. I've never understood why they worship the cross. I mean, they say he came back to life. Why not show that instead?'

Fay laughed. 'It would certainly be more cheerful. But people need sacrifices. The Christians deprive themselves of real sacrifices, here and now, to propitiate the real gods. So they've no choice but to put all their faith in a legendary human sacrifice to the great sky god of their imagination. Sheer superstition. And you're right, gruesome. Douse me in the fresh blood and guts of a lamb or a kid and it'll wash off. They drape themselves with these awful images all the time. It's perverse.'

'Unnatural,' agreed Gwy.

'And yet remarkably popular,' added Peg. 'We'll greet the harvest moon alone this year. Again.'

The harvest moon would soon be upon them. Once upon a time it would have been a magical night for communities up and down the glens. The Daughter of the Moon would have been garlanded with leaves and flowers and the people would have sung sacred songs, forgotten now, except by such as the bards. This year, like the last and the last before that, the bards would hold hands and sing to the harvest moon, but they would do so alone. They were priestesses without a people. And thus not really priestesses at all. It had been like this since the Master had abandoned them. Even before that, though, they had observed the sacred rituals with a dwindling congregation of outcasts and misfits scattered far and wide, a few of them old enough to remember when the old gods had seemed to be holding strong against the god of the Christians, the rest desperate for a taste of the magic they had heard of only in stories.

'Do you think he'll come back?' Gwy asked, trying to sound idly curious rather than pathetic.

'No,' said Fay. 'He's not coming back.'

As the bards set off with their little wagon late that morning, Pyrdie arrived from the other direction, oblivious to the fact that he had just missed the woman of his dreams. He told the servants he'd been informed that King Brude's court was here, and he'd come to offer his services for the winter months as a stone carver. He was told to wait until Bishop Boniface was ready to see him, and as he waited he watched the furious preparations being made for the court to move on. Not only the king's entourage, but several exotic guests were preparing to depart to the far corners of the land. Pyrdie had never seen so much human activity in one place and at one moment. He was spellbound by it all. Before long, the bishop emerged from the longhouse: 'Stone carver?' he shouted.

Pyrdie waved his arms: 'Here, sir!'

'Well?'

'My brother Constantine is one of the king's trusted warriors. He told me the king requires stone carvers, and I learned from one of the best, our grandfather.'

'Is that so? And how is our Constantine?'

'Well, sir. He asked me to send our family's congratulations on the king's wedding.'

'Well, you can tell him that yourself,' said the bishop, nodding to Brude, who had emerged after him. 'Majesty, this is our friend Constantine's brother. A stone carver.'

'Is he now? Which one are you, then?' Brude asked.

'I'm Pyrdie, Majesty,' he answered with an awkward bow.

'You probably won't remember the time I visited your farm, will you?'

'I do, Majesty. You were searching for… Yes, I remember,' he said abruptly, now remembering Constantine had told him to keep his mouth shut around the king. So he certainly didn't add, 'But silly me, I thought the other one was Brude.' Maybe Constantine had thought his little brother wouldn't notice after all these years. Or maybe Pyrdie really had been mistaken about who was who. Eyes open, mouth shut.

'Well, young man,' the bishop said, 'you will have the honour of carving stones to adorn the first ever stone church in the kingdom.'

'Very good, sir.'

The bishop summoned a steward and bade him introduce Pyrdie to the other assorted tradesmen and servants who would follow the king on foot to his seat, and the site of the first ever stone church in the kingdom.

There were two more stone carvers in the company, so Pyrdie naturally gravitated to them as they walked, though one of them, an older man, was a Northumbrian who understood their language only a little and could not speak a word. The other, a lad about Pyrdie's age, explained the foreigner was to be their master, and teach them the latest styles from his country. Pyrdie was quietly appalled, but he did not dwell on this, because the whole company was abuzz with something else: the amazing performance of the bards at the wedding party.

From what people were saying, it did not take Pyrdie long to deduce that these were indeed the very bards he and his family and seen perform for the harvest festival barely a week before. But, amazingly, it seemed nobody even in the sophisticated audience of a royal wedding had noticed that one of the bards was a woman. In the case of his own people, Pyrdie had put it down to the fact that they barely ever encountered anyone from beyond their own community, and were thus inclined simply to take people as they seemed to be. Certainly, Pyrdie's mysterious woman had been dressed as a man like the others; and of course bards were expected to be men. But surely it was obvious to anyone with eyes to see, and experience of men and women beyond their immediate kin, that one of these bards was a woman, and not even a mannish one. A beautiful woman. It was true that Pyrdie had seen more of her than most when he had encountered her previously, but surely one did not have to see a woman's breasts to know she was a woman!

Pyrdie did not know his cousin Pendrin had seen even more than that, however fleetingly, when walking in the wood. They had never discussed it, not when each had cherished the mysterious woman as his own deep and precious secret, nor after they had each watched in private amazement having recognised her as one of the bards. So neither knew what the other knew. And even if they had discussed it, they could not have known that they were not the only young men to have been amazed that night, as the object of private dreams had played and danced in the guise of a young man in front of everyone in their mostly oblivious world. But Pendrin knew something none of the others knew, Pyrdie included. He knew that not just one, but two of the bards were in fact women! Because Pendrin had been summoned with a wink and a whisper to an assignation with the enigmatic horn player who had turned out to be another beautiful young woman. Gwy had instantly supplanted Fay's place in his imagination, and taken a place in his heart he had not even known was there. But more of that much later. For his part, Pyrdie remained devoted to Fay and her magical breasts.

An eagle with an interest in our cast of characters might have watched them branch out in different directions from the homestead of the no-longer-quite-as-wealthy nobleman who had hosted the royal wedding. The monks, who had left first, were now well on their way to the monastery they were to visit. The priestess-bards, who had left next, were making for a sacred grove where they could greet the harvest moon with due reverence. And now the king's entourage was back on the road, heading home to the seat of the king, where Pyrdie was to carve stones to adorn the first ever stone church in the kingdom. Meanwhile, the wedding guests too set off in all directions, those with the furthest to go riding south, as the king himself would do with his warriors in the spring. To make war in the name of King Onuist. Though surely not against his own wedding guests. We shall see.

CHAPTER 32: MOSES

'Moses is a bastard! Moses is a bastard!' the boys chanted with malicious glee, having jostled their victim into a corner of the yard. Moses glared back at them, his eyes burning with hatred. Then he lashed out, catching the side of one boy's head with his fist and kicking another's shin. For a second, it felt good to fight back, but inevitably, escalating to violence resulted in many more blows raining down on Moses himself. Malicious fun turned to fury, as Moses' assailants were infected by his own rage.

'Stop that right now!' shouted Gawin, grabbing a boy in each hand and pulling them away from Moses. The others also withdrew, just as if Gawin had five hands rather than two. He then did his best to clatter all five of them about the head – though, in the confusion of boys' heads, at least one escaped its punishment – before making them line up against a wall. Then he clattered Moses' head for good measure, and had him join the others. 'I will not tolerate fighting,' he said. He glared at them for a few moments until everyone had calmed down. 'Now, come inside and we'll begin your lesson.'

The lesson consisted mostly of Latin, though as usual Gawin also took time to expound on the Bible passages the boys were reading. Moses was if anything a little slower than the others when it came to Latin, but he loved to hear Gawin preach, and preaching was really what the monk did. Today, he selected a passage from the Sermon on the Mount, and paid special attention to Jesus' injunction not to resist evil, but to respond to a slap on one cheek by inviting one's attacker to slap the other. The relevance of the passage was not lost on the boys, which was more than could be said of its wisdom. Gawin had to stop one boy slapping another there and then just to test his piety. To Moses' classmates, it was simply natural to respond to violence with more violence, just as they had done when Moses had struck out at them in the yard; they did not trouble themselves with the question of whether they had deserved it according to their own standards. Those standards they had from nature, true enough: an eye for an eye, a tooth for a tooth, like Jesus himself had said when he was still talking worldly sense. And they had them from their fathers, who taught them to fight back when they were attacked; and again, there was no need to complicate matters by bringing their own provocation into it. But Moses did not have a father. He was indeed a bastard; everyone said so. The closest thing he had to a father was Gawin. Everyone knew that too, which was why Gawin had clattered his head like the others': to show there were no favourites, to return the boy into the pack. And because Gawin expected better of Moses.

Moses had come to Govan to spend the late summer with the local boys for lessons each evening from Gawin or one of the other monks. He stayed in the monastery itself, and during the day he was put to work with chores while the other boys worked with their fathers: blacksmiths and other tradesmen of the town who wanted their sons to be able to read and write. The monks taught them to read and write in their own language as well as Latin, and there was a rich poetic tradition for those who cared to study it, but it was Latin that especially appealed to the more ambitious men of the town. It was not only the language of the church, but also the language of power.

Gawin knew perfectly well that the other boys had been bullying Moses. The fact that he had no father gave the boys an easy insult to use, but if not for that, they would have found something else. Because Moses was an outsider, and in more ways than one. He was not from Govan, of course, but sometimes he gave the impression of being not quite of this world. In that way, he was very much his mother's son. Not just any mother's boy, but Morgan's.

Moses' mother was a strange woman from a long line of strange women, and there was no point pretending her son was not also a strange boy, whether by nature or nurture. Gawin had never fully understood how Morgan had come by her son. She seemed to think finding him floating on the river as a baby had been an accident, but of a kind that ran in the family, which made no sense. But she was a sincere Christian woman, and Gawin had decided it was not for him to delve into a mystery that did not concern him. He had promised to oversee the boy's education and spiritual development, and that was just what he was doing. After the lesson, he sat alone with Moses, and asked him to explain what he understood by Jesus' words in the Sermon on the Mount.

'That morality is never enough,' Moses said.

'Elaborate.'

'I mean, every time Jesus brings up a precept of morality, he asks us to exceed it.'

'Like an eye for an eye?

'Yes. Because the point is not that you *must* take an eye for an eye, but that you can only take *one* eye for one eye. You exceed the moral precept by taking not even that.'

'Are you so sure? Don't you think that when the other boys hit you back they thought they were in the right? That it would have been cowardly to walk away?'

Moses smiled. 'I don't think they thought about it at all. If you asked them about it now, I suppose they would say something like that.'

'And would they not have a point? Even if they were *also* driven by unworthy passions, did they not have *some* justice on their side?'

'I suppose they think I was wrong to respond to words

with blows, and they were righting that wrong by hitting back.'

'Do you disagree?'

'Not entirely. But it is disingenuous to pretend that words do not hurt. And wrong to imagine that blows cannot serve in place of words.'

'Is that so?'

'Well if the words are insults, then blows can convey the same sentiment quite eloquently. I had no intention of maiming anyone,' Moses said, before adding from behind hooded eyelids, 'any more than you intended to harm me by clattering my head. You were making a point, weren't you?'

Gawin stopped himself from smiling. 'Yes, I suppose I was.'

'Of course, I understand that I should not have struck out, or even responded with insults. That would have been just as wrong. And you would have been just as right to punish me by clattering my head.'

'I'm glad you see it that way. By natural standards, you had the right to respond in kind. But you're quite right: Jesus asks us to exceed those standards. Not to live by our own rights.'

'To love not just our neighbour but our enemy.'

'That's right. And do you think you can do that?'

'No,' Moses answered confidently. 'Not without supernatural help.'

'Then never stop asking for it,' Gawin told him, his expression reminding the boy that knowing the right answer was not enough.

The next evening, Moses did not rise to the other boys' provocation, but simply smiled beguilingly from behind those hooded eyelids. By the time Gawin arrived to let them into their classroom, they had tired of that game and begun tossing pebbles at the foot of a wall. Moses could not make sense of the new game, and almost resented the mental effort of trying to do so. He was glad when it was time to go back to struggling with Latin instead.

CHAPTER 33: PRECIPICE

Valentine was not involved in the boys' lessons. He could have been a good teacher, but his evenings were taken up with other matters. Thanks to his family connection to Rhodri, and thus to the court at Alt Clut, he had become a kind of ambassador between Govan and the Rock. He was not directly responsible for raising taxes; as a churchman, that was hardly his place. But like all Christians, he owed loyalty to the governing authorities, which for his people meant the rulers of the Rock. And it was therefore his duty to warn the people of Govan that the Rock was in peril, and their support was needed to ensure its defence and prevent the Picts from taking it and then crushing the Britons as they had crushed Dalriada. It was likely that the Picts were now in league with the Northumbrians, who had recently annexed the plain of Coel, depleting the Britons' fighting capacity in the process. So Valentine had already appealed to the townsfolk for gold and silver, for grain and other supplies, above all for young men to join the war effort. Now he had been authorised to visit a handful of Govan's richest men and to promise them land and title in return for their support.

He returned to the monastery after a successful visit in time to see the boys leaving after their lesson, and recognised one lad as the youngest son of the man he had just been to see. Too young to fight, for now, as his older brothers would. The boys paid Valentine no notice as they shuffled out, but two of his brother monks stiffened as they saw him approach, and then greeted him deferentially. This was not good, but what was he supposed to do about it? You can hardly scold someone for treating you with too much respect, not at least without reinforcing the very deference you mean to dispel. So he just smiled as warmly as he could, and no doubt looked like an idiot. At least there would be no deference from Gawin, who was setting young Moses to some task or other before bed. Sure enough, when he saw Valentine, he greeting him wryly: 'How go the affairs of state?'

'Govan will play its part,' Valentine told him.

With Moses out of the way, Gawin approached Valentine in a more confidential tone. 'Are they really going to attack Alt Clut again? Haven't they learned the Rock is invincible?'

'Your confidence may be misplaced,' Valentine told him in a whisper.

'I see,' Gawin said, chastened.

The truth was that his confidence in the Rock was based on sheer ignorance. The Picts had attacked it before in recent years and got nowhere. Most Britons who even bothered themselves with such things took for granted that the Rock was invincible. The Men of the Rock, however, those who had defended it before and would defend it again, were less sure. And of course they were right. Indeed, if you had asked Gawin as a churchman if anything of this world were really invincible, he would have emphatically denied it. The church itself was the only invincible thing in the world, and only as long as she stood on the true rock that was Christ and proclaimed a kingdom not of this world. Everything else was straw. Gawin knew that, regardless of his ignorance of military affairs. But it was a hard thing to know. If Alt Clut fell, anything might happen. The Picts were Christians, but then so were the

Gaels they had harrowed, so were the Northumbrians who had taken the plain of Coel. War between Christian peoples was sadly a perennial feature of this fallen world.

'Let's pray.'

The brothers prayed together – just the two of them, who now shared the unwelcome knowledge that the world as they knew it stood at a precipice – before they joined the other brothers for the night prayer. The other brothers who knew and yet did not know.

In the morning, Gawin found Moses struggling to light a fire in the kitchen, and showed where a pile of hazel twigs was kept. 'We use these for kindling,' he said, 'in memory of Saint Mungo.' And he showed Moses how it was done, and how the twigs, though almost green, took flame like dry wood to start the fire. 'Do you know the story of Saint Mungo and the fire? Then I'll tell you.'

As Gawin began the story, he remembered telling the story of Mungo's birth to Moses' mother all those years ago. He remembered how it had occurred to him when he'd finished that the baby Mungo's arrival at the doorstep of Saint Serf was strangely echoed by Moses being brought to him to be christened. And now here was another partial echo.

'When he was a boy, Mungo lived in the monastery governed by Saint Serf, along with several other boys who were instructed by the saint, but to tell the truth, Mungo was his favourite pupil.' Gawin avoided Moses' eye as at this point. 'Now, the boys were responsible for tending to the lamps for the divine service, and each night it was one boy's job to bank the fire in the kitchen for that purpose, carefully shielding the coals from drafts so they'd retain their heat till the morning. One night this task fell to Mungo, and he discharged his duty diligently. But the other boys resented Mungo's virtue and excellence of character, and secretly extinguished the coals along with every remaining flame in the monastery. So when Mungo woke at cock crow to light the lamps, he found no fire with which to do so. He realised immediately that his rivals had done this out of malice, and decided to run away. Was that the right thing to do?'

'No,' Moses answered. 'He should have put the matter in God's hands. Or at least Saint Serf's.'

'Well, before Mungo got far, that's what he decided. The monastery was surrounded by a hedge, and when he came to it he stopped and recovered himself. He decided it would be better to suffer the slander and persecution of his peers and trust in God than to flee as if guilty. And then his simple faith took him further still. He reached into the hedge and broke off a branch of greening hazel. Then he held it aloft and prayed to the God who spoke all light into being to provide for now for the lamps. Well, sure enough the branch burst into flames as if Mungo had breathed fire onto it like a dragon.'

'But he had not, had he?' Moses interrupted.

'No. God did it.'

'Good.'

'Right. And the flame burned so bright that all shadows fled from the surrounding area. And Mungo walked with it back into the monastery and into the church at its heart. And all of a sudden, all the lamps of the monastery began to be lit, one by one, and even the coals in the kitchen fireplace were reignited without Mungo even having to touch his flame to them. So everyone awoke and came to the church to see what was happening, not only the monks and the boys, but even lay people who lived around the monastery. And they marvelled, because they saw that Mungo's torch burned without consuming the branch, just like the burning bush that had appeared to Moses.' Gawin stopped abruptly when this new kind of echo caught him unawares.

'Now, that story I know,' said the little boy.

'I should hope so,' Gawin said, recovering himself. He smiled and continued, 'Well, just as God chose your namesake to be the lawgiver to his people, it was clear that he had chosen Mungo for a great purpose. We know now that he was to preach the gospel to his own people, and now we are part of his legacy.'

'But what happened next? Did the flame speak? Did Mungo have to take off his sandals?'

'Ah, good question. No, the flame did not speak, and I can't account for Mungo's footwear. But once all the lamps of the church were aflame, the torch went out as suddenly as it had been ignited, leaving Mungo holding the untarnished branch of greening hazel as if nothing had happened. And yes,' Gawin added, remembering why he had started. 'That is why we use hazel twigs for kindling even now, despite their unsuitability for the purpose.'

'It seems to work,' Moses noted, looking at the fire they had made.

'By the grace of God it does,' Gawin agreed. And then: 'In fact, there's something else. The law Moses gave to the Israelites was all good and all holy. But we don't follow it in every detail today.'

'Because we are sinners.'

'No... Well, yes, that's true, we are sinners, and we struggle even to follow the ten commandments. But we still avow those. There are other laws Moses gave his people, about sacrifices and about what kinds of food to eat, that don't apply to God's people today. You see, God in his goodness never stops acting in the world. And it is our duty to pay attention.'

'I see.'

'In the monastery of Saint Serf, the order was that a fire was to be kept through the night for use the next day.'

'And we don't do that here, now.'

'No, because we must have faith that each morning God will renew the gift of fire, even if we use hazel twigs for kindling!'

'I see,' Moses said thoughtfully. 'Thank you for the story. I must see to my other chores now.'

Gawin shook his head as he watched the boy scuttle off. It was time for him to join his brothers for morning prayers anyway.

CHAPTER 34: A NEW START

Having left Lindisfarne, Cuthbert wandered aimlessly for many weeks, offering his services as a labourer to anyone who would feed him. He spent the winter working for a blacksmith, and when spring came, so too did word of a new campaign against the Britons. It seemed King Eadberht had formed an alliance with his old enemy King Onuist. The Picts and Northumbrians were friends now, and determined to crush the Men of the Rock together. Cuthbert had nothing against the Britons, but he was not a blacksmith any more than he was a monk. He was a soldier. He set off to find the nearest thane recruiting men for the campaign, and soon found himself marching northwest with a small company.

After a couple of days, they made camp by a good-sized settlement where arrangements had been made to supply them for the campaign. Cuthbert helped lift the supplies into two wagons, and as he did so he noticed a merchantwoman who was heavily pregnant. Indeed, he noticed not only because of her swollen belly, but because she was in obvious discomfort, and soon began staggering for balance until she was helped to the ground where she lay groaning. Perhaps the excitement of the soldiers' arrival had brought on her labour.

In any case, a lad was sent to summon a midwife, who duly arrived and asked for help taking her inside. Cuthbert was the first to volunteer, perhaps because he was older than most of the other soldiers and less intimidated by the female body in its horrible glory. He had reasons of his own to want nothing to do with childbirth, but he was not thinking of that now, just offering help where it was needed. The woman did not seem to have a husband, but one of the other merchants said her name was Ethel. 'Stay calm, Ethel,' the midwife said. 'You're going to be fine.'

When they got her inside, Cuthbert asked if there was anything else he could do. There was not, so he excused himself and returned to his comrades. Before they set off in the morning, though, he returned to see how the labour was proceeding. He was just in time to hear the child let out its first cries on entering the world. She was a girl. Her mother was strangely distraught, but Cuthbert had no time to puzzle why. He was on his way.

Once he was on his way again with the company, though, Cuthbert's thoughts did turn to his own child. He'd never learned whether it was a boy or a girl. And for the first time in many years, he thought of his long-lost sister. Only now did it occur to him that he had lost two babies in the course of his life, perhaps two baby girls. He remembered the first time his father had told him he was a twin, and at how at first he had thought it was a joke. It was not a joke, but had something of the quality of a cruel one. His father had wanted to remind Cuthbert that he knew things about him he did not know about himself. This was a good one, not something the boy could have seen coming. A twin? A sister? An eagle? And you never told me till now? He wondered if his mother would have told him sooner. Less cruelly. Yes, he'd lost a mother too, come to think of it. And a wife, for that matter. Eithne, dear Eithne. Both in childbirth. So what if he had taken a few lives, and only the one in cold blood? In fact, he had not killed even Offa in cold blood, not really. It had been a heated situation.

He'd felt suffocated. Granted, nobody had been looking to him to resolve the situation. It had been none of his business one way or the other, but that was precisely what had given him uniquely the ability to lance the boil. Or so it had felt at the time. It did weigh on him still, but yes, he had sorrows enough of his own. He tried to forget all that. He hoped Ethel's daughter would live to grow up strong. For a moment he imagined being her father, holding her in his arms, loving her. Maybe he would die in the fight to come. Maybe it would be no bad thing.

The baby girl's actual father was at Bamburgh. He would play no part in the campaign against Alt Clut. Wilfrid was married now, and his wife bore another child, one surely unlikely ever to learn of its illegitimate half-sister, through a cruel joke or otherwise. But that was not why he remained at Bamburgh. The murder of Offa, while convenient for the king, had not put an end to dynastic politics. Experienced muscle – and iron – was required at the court in case of unspecified threats. So Wilfrid found himself sparring with young Edwin after all. He did not particularly mind, especially as it meant he could also spend time with his wife. Seaxburh was the lady-in-waiting of a noblewoman from the south, who was in exile on account of dynastic politics in her own country, but their marriage meant she would stay at Bamburgh even when her mistress returned. Perhaps one day, husband and wife would retire to the country, but for now, Wilfrid served Eadberht and his wife served the exiled noblewoman and they enjoyed what time they had together. Seaxburh was very lovely, and she made Wilfrid laugh because she was cleverer than him, but respected him no less for that. Instead, she teased him with a rare warmth that made others envy their relationship. And as she watched him spar with Edwin, she did not disguise her admiration for his physical prowess.

Edwin would never be Wilfrid's equal when it came to fighting, but he was a keen student and shaping up to be competent at least. He had other masters when it came to hunting and to books and other noble pursuits. His mother had taken him to the court of one of the underkings of the Picts for a taste of international politics – yes, that was him at Brude's wedding – and he'd come back full of stories and of enthusiasm, so people reckoned one day he'd serve the king as a diplomat, assuming the king kept his crown, of course.

Edwin certainly had a nose for politics. His brother was Ewald – the monk who had befriended Cuthbert at Lindisfarne – and from him he had extracted every detail of the story of what had happened to Offa there. Edwin had been intrigued by this 'Cuthbert the Gael' and especially the fact that he had once been a kind of diplomat. He also knew Wilfrid had known the slayer of Offa well, but he never broached the subject directly with his sparring partner. He did ask him about what it was like to fight alongside one neighbouring people against another one year and with the latter against the former the next. It was a natural enough question for a young man interested in relations between peoples, and Wilfrid was happy enough to share his easy-come, easy-go philosophy, such as it was. He even told the story of his first campaign, joining the Gaels to fight the Picts, and of his friend who had gone on to Dalriada for an adventure of his own. If he withheld that friend's name deliberately, or even registered the connection with recent events, Edwin could not see it on his face. Since then, as Edwin knew very well, Wilfrid had fought both with and against Gaels, Picts, Britons and his own countrymen. It was all the same to him.

Edwin would have liked to meet Cuthbert even if he had not interpolated himself so dramatically into the dynastic politics of Northumbria. He would have loved to know what he'd been thinking when he slew Offa. But more than that, he would have liked to ask Cuthbert what it had been like to live in and between Northumbria and Dalriada, in and between two languages. To be married to a woman of another nation. He knew the latter was common practice among royals and would-be royals, but Cuthbert's story fascinated him because there had been none of the politics that motivated such unions. From what Ewald had told him, it seemed to have been a love story.

Cuthbert never got as far as Alt Clut. The plan had been for Northumbrian forces to support the Pictish assault on the Rock by attacking from the other side, and cutting off any supplies or men coming from the river. But news reached Cuthbert's company well before they arrived that their support was no longer required. The battle for Alt Clut was over.

CHAPTER 35: TWO SURPRISES

The messenger was already in a state of agitation when he reached the monastery, and when he was told Brother Valentine was at prayer and could not be disturbed, he was incredulous. Clearly, he was not used to the ways of monks. 'Is it a matter of life and death?' the warden asked, just as incredulous about the messenger's impatience.

'Yes!' he answered emphatically, but then added before he'd had time to think about it, 'Or it least it *was* a matter of life and death.'

'So is it or isn't it? the warden demanded, now sharing the messenger's impatience.

'Oh, oh, oh,' the messenger stuttered in frustration, 'Oh, believe me, Brother Valentine is going to want to hear this news. Now!'

'Oh, I'm sure he will want your news,' the warden said, 'but in this place we have a different way of thinking about "now"'. He looked at the sky, perhaps trying to estimate the time, perhaps just contemplating the Heavens. 'Calm yourself, man. Brother Valentine will see you before long. There's a bench here if you want to sit down.' And with that, he went back inside, closing the door after him. Now it was the messenger to looked to the Heavens, and demurring to sit down, paced impatiently back and forth in front of the door that still stood between him and the recipient of his message.

Soon enough, though, perhaps having been disturbed by the commotion, Brother Valentine emerged.

'Well?' he demanded pensively. He clearly did not have to be told what the news was about. He'd been waiting for it right enough.

Gawin watched from a distance. He could not hear what was said, but its importance was clear from the two men's body language. After just a few words back and forth, Valentine clasped the messenger by the arms and looked to the same Heavens. 'Praise God! Praise God!' he said loud enough for all his brothers to hear. It was good news. Having dismissed the messenger, he turned to Gawin and the other monks now clustered in the corridor. 'The Men of the Rock have routed the Picts,' he said. 'They marched out to surprise them before they even got near the Rock itself, and it's an overwhelming victory. King Onuist himself has been slain!'

Gasps all round. Gawin blew out his cheeks and sighed. Praise God indeed.

When Morgan arrived in Govan, she detected a strange atmosphere, but it was unlike anything she had experienced before, so she found it impossible to name it. The people were friendly, smiling greetings as she walked through the town, but then the people of Govan were famously friendly. This was something else. There was a sense of relief, joy even. She recognised a woman gutting fish outside a hovel and asked her, 'What's going on? Is it a festival?'

The woman laughed. 'Better than that, hen. The Men of the Rock have seen off the Picts again. And killed their king this time.'

'Oh,' Morgan said, barely registering that this had something to do with war.

'Did you not know there was a war on?'

'Not really. I live in the woods, you know.'

'Well, it's good news, believe me. We were afraid of

being overrun, massacred, who knows?'

'Oh, that is good then. Thank you, hen.'

Morgan proceeded to the church, smiling at passers by now with more confidence since she knew what was going on. She recognised and was recognised by a few others on the way, and agreed to return the same way to dispense herbal concoctions when she was finished at the church. She was pleased to find Gawin there, since she had come to see him as much as to conduct business. He was just as pleased to see Morgan, and sat with her to pray for half an hour before they caught up on Earthly matters. It was the first time they had talked since she had come to collect Moses at the end of the summer.

'They tell me there's a war on,' she said.

'Well, yes, there is, or was, but thanks be to God it seems our side have won it.'

'Thanks be to God.'

'And how is young Moses?'

'He is well, thank you. He recites psalms to us from memory every day. And scratches his letters on the slate tile you gave him.'

'That's good to hear.'

'And he speaks of becoming a monk.'

'Ah.'

Valentine was pottering at the back of the church, and had been innocently overhearing the conversation until now. Now, he stood silently and listened.

Morgan struggled to read Gawin's face in the dark of the church. 'Did you speak of this in the summer?'

'Not exactly.'

'But you don't seem surprised.'

'Of all the boys, Moses is the most spiritually inclined. He is interested in subjects that bore the other boys.'

'Yes, he speaks often of things you taught him.'

'It's only natural, I suppose. He has no other father figure in his life.'

'Apart from God,' Morgan pointed out, almost teasingly. She hardly had to add, 'Is God not enough?' So she did not.

Gawin was unrattled anyway. 'But there's something else, you see, pertaining to the fact that Moses has no Earthly father.'

'And what's that?' Morgan asked, concerned now.

'I'm afraid the other boys were tormenting him,' Gawin told her. 'They call him a bastard.'

Morgan sighed. 'I'm sorry for the boy. It is hard to explain to outsiders how things are in our family. But I will not lie to Moses. I resolved from the beginning I would never invent an imaginary father for him.'

'You're quite right, of course,' Gawin said, 'But there's something else you should know.' He paused, seeking divine help. 'It's not easy for me to say this. You see, there is a rumour that Moses is *my* son.'

Morgan laughed out loud. 'Oh, my. Oh, I don't know what to say.' And then, suddenly. 'Wait. *Is* Moses your son?'

If you could have seen the look on Valentine's face when he heard that, you would have laughed out loud yourself.

Valentine had heard the story, of course. He knew Moses was a foundling, or at least that his mother said so. He had never been entirely convinced. Would it have helped if Gawin had told him that this was apparently considered the normal way of acquiring children in Morgan's family? Possibly not. And naturally, Valentine had also heard the rumour that Gawin was the boy's father, but he had never for a second credited that. Morgan's comically bizarre question now brought the two possibilities together in a most unexpected way. Gawin was surely not Moses' natural father by Morgan or anyone else, but what if he had been involved somehow in arranging his adoption?

'I can assure you he is not my son,' Gawin told Morgan coolly. 'I mention the rumour only because it's natural for Moses to look to me as a father figure for the same reasons others draw more foolish conclusions. It's not terribly surprising if he thinks of following in my footsteps.'

'You think this is about you?'

Gawin was taken aback. 'Well, no, of course it's not about me. It's about Moses. And his relationship with God, of course...'

'It's just that he doesn't want to be a monk here in Govan like you.'

'Oh?'

'He says he wants to go and be a monk in Iona.'

'Iona!' Gawin almost spat. (The eavesdropping Valentine was equally scandalised.) 'Why would he want to go to Iona?'

'Isn't Iona the most important abbey there is, and famous throughout the world?'

Gawin took a deep breath. 'Famous, certainly. But really no more important than any other place of Christian prayer.' And despite himself, he went on, becoming quite heated. 'You know, sometimes it's as if those upstarts on Iona think they invented Christianity, as if the Gaels graciously took it upon themselves to bring the Word of God to the nations. Well, the Gospel might have been news to those island savages, but this monastery was founded by a disciple of Saint Ninian, who was practically a Roman.' Gawin stopped suddenly and shook his head with a half-smile, as if having just spotted a ruse of the Devil. 'I'm sorry, Morgan. I shouldn't have said that. It was proud and un-Christian and unkind. And not entirely true either.' He paused and smiled, checking himself again. 'The Gaels are a fine people. As fine as any of us, that is.'

Valentine too was vicariously chastened. He shared Gawin's sinful but simmering resentment of Iona's fame, but – unlike Gawin – he also knew the Gaels had played an important part in saving Alt Clut from the Picts.

CHAPTER 36: THE COMBAT OF CUHULLIN AND FERDIAD

Not all who celebrated in the camp of the victorious Men of the Rock on the evening after the battle were native Britons. The Rock's commanders had appealed far and wide for support, and while the Northumbrians were now siding with the Picts, there were many warriors of defeated Dalriada who either had no chiefs of which to speak or whose chiefs were not yet bound by oaths of allegiance to King Onuist or any other Pictish overlord. For them, this fight had been an opportunity for revenge. Among them were a certain Domnall and a certain Fergus, veteran Pict-fighters who had been biding their time with non-military affairs till now. They had brought their professional and unflashy fighting skills to what had been a professional and unflashy victory. Marching out to meet their would be conquerors, the Men of the Rock had wielded the element of surprise devastatingly, so there had been little in the way of ebb and flow to the battle. It had been a rout right enough.

And now, in celebration of their great victory, Domnall

and Fergus decided to entertain their new friends by enacting one of their own favourite episodes from the Gaelic legends. One or two polyglot soldiers tried valiantly to translate Fergus' commentary into the language of the Britons, but for most, the sheer spectacle and the music of the poetry was entertaining enough. All present were fluent in the poetry of combat, and in the universal language of male bravado.

'For complicated reasons we needn't go into,' Fergus began, 'the great hero Cuhullin was the only man standing to defend Ulster against the armies of the rest of Ireland combined.'

He pointed to Domnall, who took up a heroic stance with his hands on his hips.

'But he was such a formidable warrior they could not get the better of him.'

Domnall raised his arms triumphantly and slowly twirled to acknowledge his audience.

'Day after day, he stood at the ford of battle and saw off so many armies of men that it was decided it would be better to send a single champion against him than to waste more lives by the score. But after a few brave souls had tried and perished, champions were not exactly queuing up for the job. Part of the problem was that Cuhullin had a unique and mighty weapon, the Spear of Agonising Death, which had been given to him by the legendary warrior woman Scathach of Skye. Indeed, it killed men with such cruelty it could only have been designed by a woman.'

Domnall illustrated this fact with a mysterious jig involving both hands and feet and culminating in a disgustingly lewd facial expression.

Fergus went on: 'Having debated the matter at length, the men of Ireland decided to send Cuhullin's own foster brother against him, since the mighty Ferdiad had a skin of horn that no blade had ever pierced, and according to prophecy no fatal blow would ever breach that defence. So they sent messengers to Ferdiad, but the messengers returned without him. Why should he fight his own foster brother? So they sent poets and bards to mock and ridicule him in verse, threatening to shame him so badly he'd never be able to show his face among men of honour. That he could not tolerate, so this time he answered the summons. And now they turned on the charm. If he did agree to take on Cuhullin, he would be given lands and chariots. And limitless wine and freedom from taxes. And a gigantic leaf-shaped golden brooch belonging to Queen Mebd of Connacht herself. And – why not? – even Mebd's daughter Princess Finnabair of Connacht as his consort. But still, Ferdiad was reluctant to fight his own foster brother, until Queen Medb pulled on the same strings that had brought Ferdiad before them.

"It sounds like Cuhullin was right," she said to the men of Ireland.

"Right about what?" Ferdiad demanded.

"Right to say that slaying you would go down as one of his lesser triumphs."

'And, at that, the deal was struck.'

The narrator now stepped forward to inhabit the role of Ferdiad, nodding assuredly at the audience.

'Now, Ferdiad's own charioteer warned him that no good would come of this fight, but Ferdiad was not to be put off, and having mounted his chariot, he had his charioteer turn the horses and chariot round three times as a salute to the men of Ireland, before driving out of the camp.'

Fergus did the same in his invisible chariot.

'It was dark when they reached the ford of battle, and they could not see if Cuhullin was in the vicinity or not, so Ferdiad asked his charioteer to keep watch while he slept. Then shortly before dawn, Cuhullin was up and ready and approached the ford in his own chariot. Ferdiad's charioteer woke him and warned him again that this was a bad idea, observing how magnificent a warrior Cuhullin was. But Ferdiad told him to keep his opinions to himself, since it was enough to have one foe to contend with. Then the two warriors squared up in their chariots, Ferdiad on the south side of the ford and Cuhullin on the north.'

And now, squaring up in their invisible chariots, Domnall and Fergus began to inhabit their roles with such conviction that their audience no longer saw two players acting out the story, but instead witnessed, as if at first hand, the legendary combat of Cuhullin and Ferdiad. And it began, like all the truly great battles, with poetry.

In elaborately beautiful verse that sadly is not reproduced here, Ferdiad welcomed Cuhullin to the ford, only to be told it was not his place to do the welcoming, as this was territory held by Cuhullin. Then Ferdiad reminded his foster brother that when they had trained together under Scathach of Skye, Cuhullin had been his kit boy, looking after Ferdiad's spears rather than presuming to wield one against him. Cuhullin answered that things were different now, as Ferdiad was about to discover. With that, they renounced their friendship, and went on to exchange extravagant threats and insults for several hours. A key theme on Cuhullin's side was that, had their positions been reversed, he would never have agreed to fight Ferdiad, and least of all for a girl who'd no doubt already been sworn to fifty other men who'd failed in their mission because he had killed them. Eventually, Ferdiad announced he'd had enough of threats and insults and they were going round in circles. 'What weapons shall we use?' he said.

'You were first to the ford, so you choose,' answered Cuhullin.

Ferdiad suggested they use the weapons with which they'd trained with Scathach of Skye. So their respective charioteers each produced an arsenal of throwing discs, knives and darts of various sizes, which they began throwing at one another, each fending the other's weapons off with a special shield. This also went on for hours, until the sun was high in the sky.

'This is getting us nowhere,' Ferdiad observed again.

'Let's try spears.'

So from noon till evening, they threw their spears at one another. This time they did occasionally draw blood, but nothing decisive, so they decided to pack it in for the day. And having exhausted themselves of animus, they embraced warmly before retiring. Even their horses grazed together and their charioteers shared a fire as they slept.

Early the next day they met again at the ford of battle, and this time it was Cuhullin's turn to choose their weapons. He woke the charioteers and bade them hitch up the horses: today they would fight chariot to chariot with their favourite broad stabbing spears, Cuhullin said, since they might finish the matter today by stabbing rather than throwing like yesterday. And all day they rode at one another, stabbing and jabbing one another as they passed and leaving puncture wounds so wide and deep a bird could have flown through them and out the other side. Yes, even Ferdiad's legendary skin of horn was breached at last, and not just once but repeatedly. But both warriors were so tough they kept at it hour after hour till their charioteers complained *they* were exhausted, and out of sympathy for their loyal assistants, the warriors agreed to lay off for the day. They embraced warmly before retiring. Even their horses grazed together and their charioteers shared a fire as they slept.

The next morning as they met at the ford of battle, Cuhullin noted that Ferdiad looked awful. 'There's a dullness in your eyes, and your hair's lost all its shine,' he said.

'Well, don't think it's from fear of you,' Ferdiad replied. 'There's not a warrior in Ireland I can't best.'

And, at that, they were off again with the poetry. This time, the dominant theme came from Ferdiad, and the gist was that he had indeed been wrong to agree to fight Cuhullin for a woman, but he could hardly back down now. The fight was a matter of honour, and who happened to be in the right or in the wrong was of no consequence.

Cuhullin told Ferdiad it was his turn to choose their

weapons.

'How about broadswords, then?' he said. 'Maybe we'll finish the matter today by hacking rather than stabbing like yesterday.'

'You're on,' said Cuhullin.

So the two picked up their broadswords and their giant, full-length shields, and they hacked and hewed and sliced at one another for hours, sometimes cutting lumps of flesh out of one another the size of a baby's head. But neither warrior fell. And when evening fell instead, they agreed to suspend hostilities. They were sad now as well as hurt and exhausted. Their horses did not graze together that night and their charioteers did not share a fire as they slept.

Ferdiad rose early and went to the ford of battle to prepare for what he knew would be the final day of combat. He put on a silk apron next to his horny skin, then a leather apron, then one made of solid rock, and finally – dreading the Spear of Agonising Death – a double-thick apron of double-smelted iron. On his head, he put a tried and tested helmet, ornately decorated with exotic jewels from the East, and as impenetrable as it was beautiful. Over his back, he threw a gigantic shield with fifty knobs and bosses, then in his right hand he took his most lethal spear, and in his left a curved sword with a hilt of red gold. Thus arrayed, Ferdiad began running through his repertoire of battle moves, a terrifying dance of death demonstrating his mastery of his weapons and indeed of his own heavily armoured body. And as he warmed up, he was inspired by the prospect of facing Cuhullin once more to invent ever more amazing moves. Nobody had taught him such moves; not even Scathach of Skye had imagined such moves before that morning when Ferdiad invented them.

Cuhullin arrived at the ford of battle and saw Ferdiad's amazing moves, knowing they would soon be deployed against him. He told his charioteer to watch their combat closely, and if at any point it looked like he was facing defeat, to heckle and badmouth him to get his temper up; and conversely, if at any point it looked like he was about to clinch the fight, to egg him on and roar him to victory. Then he put on his own battle garb, and as Ferdiad watched he began his own warm-up, with his own amazing moves, which, like Ferdiad's, soon surpassed anything he had been taught by Scathach of Skye or anyone else. This fight was set to be the greatest contest the north-west corner of world had ever seen.

And then it was on. From the half-light of dawn till high noon they went at each other, each using all his strength and skills to seek advantage over the other, and raising a clamour that echoed in the heavens. Then, with the battle at fever pitch, Cuhullin launched himself into the air and landed feet first on Ferdiad's gigantic shield, hoping to strike at his head over the rim of the shield. Before he could strike, Ferdiad simply nudged his shield with his left elbow, throwing Cuhullin aside easily into the mud of the ford. Cuhullin launched himself again, landing again on Ferdiad's shield, but this time, before he could strike, Ferdiad nudged his shield with his left knee, throwing Cuhullin again to sprawl on the muddy brink of the ford.

Cuhullin's charioteer did as he'd been told. 'Call yourself a warrior?' he shouted to his master. 'You're more like a bad tempered toddler trying to wrestle a cow! The lad's making a joke of you, you useless imp!'

This seemed to have the desired effect, and Cuhullin rose again in a rage and launched himself furiously onto Ferdiad's shield. But Ferdiad gave his shield the slightest of shakes, and threw the bad tempered toddler once again into the mud.

Now Cuhullin rose again in a frenzy unlike anything seen before. As he rose, he twisted his body quite against nature, spinning like a whirlwind even as his feet remained planted in the mud. With each turn, he seemed to grow in size, till, having torqued himself a hundredfold, he loomed over Ferdiad like a monstrous, furious rainbow. Ferdiad was not cowed, but went at Cuhullin all the harder. So closely and so fiercely did they fight that their shields burst into pieces and their spears split into shreds. The river itself was thrown off its course by the violence of the struggle, hovering mid air, fish and all, before carving a new bed for itself at least fifty paces away and leaving the fighters in the mud. The sound of their clashing weapons so unsettled the goblins and other supernatural creatures that lurked by the ford that they began screeching and squalling to drown it out. And their cries reached the armies of Ireland camped miles away, sending their horses mad and their camp followers fleeing far from Ulster. But still neither warrior could gain the advantage.

They had been fighting with swords alone for some time when Cuhullin let his guard drop and Ferdiad seized the opportunity to sink his blade deep into Cuhullin's chest, unleashing a flood of blood that almost replenished the displaced river. With the tide turning against him, Cuhullin called to his charioteer to prepare the Spear of Agonising Death. Ferdiad heard the command, and knowing the Spear of Agonising Death was launched from the attacker's foot, he lowered his shield to protect himself. But Cuhullin then threw a javelin over the top of Ferdiad's shield, which pierced his chest and made him fall back, exposing his underside just as Cuhullin's charioteer hurled the terrible weapon to his master. Cuhullin caught the thing in the fork of his foot and in the same motion directed it towards his enemy. In an instant, the Spear of Agonising Death burst through Ferdiad's double thick apron of double-smelted iron, through the apron of solid rock, through leather and silk as if they weren't there at all, and it entered Ferdiad's rear portal as if by invitation, whereupon it opened up into thirty barbs to ensnare the man completely from within.

'That's the end of me,' Ferdiad said. 'And the prophecy was right, for the fatal blow did not breach my own skin of horn, after all.' And, then, having recited several lines of valedictory poetry, he died. Cuhullin plucked Queen Medb's golden brooch from his foster brother's body and looked at it sadly before responding with many more lines of verse. Then he sliced Ferdiad open to retrieve his weapon.

As Fergus completed his narration, lying prone on the ground as the dead Ferdiad, Domnall as Cuhullin mimed the painstaking process of packing away the Spear of Agonising Death. Then, as Domnall helped his friend to his feet, the two laughed louder than anyone in their loudly appreciative audience. The end.

CHAPTER 37: POLITICS

Brude and his men missed the battle by several hours. It was not their fault. They were ambushed by Gaels before they could meet up with the main body of Onuist's army. It was a fierce skirmish, as bloody and deadly as that of Domnall and Fergus, if not that of Cuhullin and Ferdiad. It was of course another performance orchestrated by Rhodri and Boniface, put on to keep Brude's army back from the real action. And by the time Brude's muddied but victorious warriors met up with their countrymen, the latter were in full retreat, so they simply joined them trudging north, not making too much of the fact they had won their own battle; there was no place for score-keeping or recriminations among comrades.

Constantine thought only of getting home to Dyrael and the twins. Perhaps this would be his last campaign; he was growing tired of the tragedy of war and the comedy of war alike, and feared leaving his wife widowed and his children fatherless for either. He thought also of his brother Pyrdie, and wondered if it had been a mistake to introduce him to Brude's court. Pyrdie would be back on the farm now, but he'd spent the winter carving stones for Bishop Boniface. Possibly carving the not so bonnie face of Bishop Boniface on said stones. When the brothers had spoken briefly before Constantine set off on the campaign, Pyrdie had been full of the excitement of the court: foreigners, politics, women maybe. Constantine decided to have a word when he got home, make sure the lad was not getting carried away with silly ideas.

Back at Alt Clut, Rhodri was in danger of getting carried away with the thrill of victory. He was ecstatic. His plan had come together perfectly. The only blemish was that he would not be publicly credited with the victory. The chronicles would give that honour to his rival Teudebur, who had the allegiance of nearly enough important men now to call himself king. But the people who mattered on the Rock knew Rhodri's role had been crucial in their victory over the Picts. That included his part in bringing Gaels to the fight, of course, but also his contacts among the Picts. Few knew of the sneakier manoeuvres he had orchestrated, like the one involving Brude, but it was widely known that he'd obtained the vital intelligence about the timing and route of the Picts march on Alt Clut, and about the whereabouts of King Onuist. The boldness of cutting off the head of the snake matched the audacity of the offensive itself, which would not have been possible without Rhodri's contribution. He had enhanced his reputation as a man of influence, and thus made himself even more influential. He sipped his Burgundian wine and enjoyed a warm glow as his wife and primary admirer looked on indulgently. Sadly for Rhodri, this did not last. A messenger was announced and rushed in breathless: 'King Onuist lives!' he exclaimed.

'What?' demanded Rhodri, but did not wait for an answer. 'Rubbish! I saw him slain with my own eyes!'

'Sir, the word is it was the king's brother Talorgan who was slain. He was to lead the assault on the Rock.'

'No, no, no,' Rhodri said, furious. He happened to know for a fact that Talorgan had been nowhere near the battle. He was in a monastery in his own country. If the Picts were claiming Onuist lived and Talorgan was dead, it was because

Talorgan had simply taken his brother's name along with his crown. 'The devious bastard!'

In fact, it took a Pictish messenger many days' hard riding to reach Talorgan and inform him of his brother's fate and his own transformation. It had been Onuist's devious idea, the original one, to secure his legacy this way, and his closest aides had put the plan into action immediately after his death, which was how word had reached the Rock and other politically important centres throughout the land before arriving, almost as an afterthought, at the monastery where the new Onuist had been secured.

'What's going on?' Aidan asked his brothers, having just been woken by the commotion.

'A messenger,' said Gregory, who'd woken a minute before. 'It sounds like important news. Paul's gone to find out more.'

Paul had been lying awake when the messenger arrived. He'd heard horses, then gates being opened and closed, urgent voices, feet dashing about. By the time Gregory awoke, Paul was on his own feet and off to see what was happening. Now he returned. 'Brother Marcus won't tell me anything,' he whispered, 'but it's obvious the news is for the prince first and foremost. And presumably concerning the campaign.'

'Let's pray,' said Gregory, and the brothers knelt together in prayer, at first a prayer of pure supplication without any particular object. As monks, they wanted nothing but to do God's will. Indeed they exulted in their powerlessness to affect the world around them. All was in God's hands. In particular, the campaign was no concern of theirs, except inasmuch as it involved fellow Christians, fellow sons of Adam for that matter, on both sides. So next they prayed for the souls of victors and vanquished alike. But of course God had called each of the brothers to Iona, so while they were not exactly political envoys, they did have a duty to consider the flourishing of their community to the glory of God. That was why they were here, so far from home. So finally they prayed that God would guide them in discharging their duty. If there were anything they needed to know, they prayed that God would make it known to them in his own way, and grant them the wisdom to act on it according to his will. And no sooner had they finished their private prayers than they were called to join their Pictish brothers for corporate prayer. The three of them exchanged encouraging glances and nods, and off they went.

Over the course of the day, it became clear that the news had been bad news for the Picts. Their campaign against Alt Clut had failed. But there was more. Intrigue of some kind. There was much rushing about and whispering on paths and in shadows. And discord, perhaps, among the Pictish monks, simmering all day and bubbling up whenever the rhythms of the monastic day gave it time and space to do so. Eventually, the brothers from Iona were summoned by the Abbot.

'I believe you're due to return to Iona the day after tomorrow. When you get there,' he told them, 'it is likely that word will already have reached your brothers that Prince Talorgan has been slain at Alt Clut.'

'The Prince Talorgan currently residing at this very monastery?' Gregory asked, smiling as if this must be a joke.

'Yes, that's the one.'

'I see.'

'Only Prince Talorgan is no longer residing at this monastery. King Onuist is.'

The Iona brothers looked at one another nervously.

'I would not lie to you, even if to do so were not also to insult your intelligence,' the Abbot continued. 'You understand the situation as well as I do. My people are ruled by a king who chooses to call himself Onuist. I will not argue with that, and neither will the men who stood by a king called Onuist when he was slain near Alt Clut some days ago. There will be rumours, but I have instructed the brothers here to have nothing to do with them. We submit to the Earthly authorities on Earthly matters, and that is the end of it. Is something funny?' This was addressed to Paul, who had apparently allowed himself to smile.

'Not at all, Brother Abbot,' Paul said, embarrassed. 'I'm sure I speak for us all when I say we understand completely. We have no more desire than you to meddle in politics. I merely smile at the folly of the world.'

'Good,' said the Abbot. 'The world is not my concern. And I am not asking you to lie to anyone, simply to understand how things stand.'

'Indeed.'

The Iona brothers were dismissed.

When they next had time alone together, they agreed to share this information with their own Abbot in due course, but otherwise to accept the brute fact that King Onuist was King Onuist. When Aidan referred to the monarch as 'King of Picts', however, Gregory pointed out that no such title existed, since, as we know, the Picts did not refer to themselves as Picts at all. This took some explaining.

'So it's *insulting* to refer to your people as Picts?' Aidan asked eventually.

'Many consider it so,' Gregory confirmed.

'But you never said anything, all the years I've known you.'

Gregory and Paul looked at one another and shrugged. 'It really doesn't matter, Brother Aidan,' said Gregory. 'We've lived among foreigners long enough not to take it the wrong way. We know there's no malice in it, and we even say it ourselves.'

'But all the weeks and months we've been here, I've been merrily insulting our brothers in their own country, in...' He stopped himself from saying 'Pictland,' as he had been merrily doing all along. 'And now, when we're about to leave, you tell me... Well, what are you supposed to call yourselves?'

Gregory and Paul spoke in unison: 'The People of the Designs'. It was no less clumsy-sounding in their own language than when they translated it into Gaelic for Aidan.

Nor did it roll off the tongue in Latin. The People of the Designs were an old people, it had always been said, who for most of their history had felt no need to distinguish themselves from any *other* people, because there *were* no other people in the land. 'Or at least,' Gregory added, 'not sons of Adam.'

'Then what?' asked Aidan, intrigued by this sudden qualification.

'Oh, stop it,' Paul told his countryman. 'You'll frighten the poor foreigner with your foolishness.'

End of conversation.

Paul had lain awake these past two nights, silently muttering verse after verse of scripture. He had most of the Psalms and several of his namesake's epistles committed to memory. Muttering the words was not the same as meditating on their meaning, but it was better than letting his thoughts wander, his fantasies run riot. Tonight, though, he could stay awake no more. He succumbed to sleep, and with it to Brigid.

'Darling, where have you been?' she demanded teasingly. 'Don't you know how much I miss you when you're gone? How much *we* miss you?' And suddenly they were on the beach on their little island, their toddler demanding to be lifted into Daddy's arms.

'I missed you too, my love,' Paul said, heaving the infant up, 'both of you.'

'Hmm.'

'Oh, tell me you're not cross with me.'

Brigid pouted and narrowed her gaze before relenting: 'You know I can never stay cross with you for long.'

'I'm so lucky to have you. And you, my lucky charm,' he said, kissing the toddler. Then he took Brigid's hand and they walked along the beach a while, talking gently about nothing in particular until he stopped and gazed into the sky. 'It looks like rain. Let's go inside.'

They went inside, and as usual the toddler did not make a nuisance of himself.

Before long, Paul slept and dreamt within his dream,

and Brigid was not Brigid but someone else, and there were no words.

CHAPTER 38: LETTERS

Far to the south, at the double monastery of Wearmouth-Jarrow, another monk fought off sleep. He was deep in the works of the late Bede, a writer of histories who would later be revered as the Venerable Bede. At that time, though, Bede was still fondly remembered at Wearmouth-Jarrow by many brothers who had known him personally. Our monk had arrived from Lindisfarne only months ago, but by now had read almost everything the great man had written. And tonight, he was rereading Bede's treatment of the history of his own (our monk's, not Bede's) people, which is to say the People of the Designs, or as Bede called them, the Picts.

According to Bede, the Picts had come from Scythia, far to the east of the Greeks who had written the much older histories on which Bede ultimately drew. Indeed – and this was not lost on our monk – to the Greeks, the Scythians were alien, exotic, barbaric even. Perhaps just as the People of the Designs seemed to the Northumbrians. In Bede's account, our monk's forefathers had wandered in search of a new homeland, and first tried to settle in Ireland, home to yet more barbarians, not even Christian at the time. The Irish had urged them to wander on, to the northern part of the island of Britain, and even encouraged them by providing them with supplies, and indeed – seeing that they had no wives – with Irish women with whom to found their new nation. This was on the understanding that, in the case of any doubt about the succession of kings, preference would be given to the female – and thus Irish – royal line rather than the male. This was apparently the origin of that custom among the Picts, which persists to this day, Bede had written. Our monk smiled. It was as good an explanation as any, though he knew the custom was not much observed in his own day, if it ever had been.

Our monk still took an interest in the affairs of his homeland, as much as one could at such a distance. He had occasionally been consulted as an authority on Pictish affairs, both here at Wearmouth-Jarrow and at Lindisfarne, where he had made his life until the unfortunate incident involving the pretender and the renegade soldier had caused such turmoil, leading to numerous comings and goings. He liked Northumbria and the Northumbrians. Not more than his own land and people, but just fine. The monasteries here were advanced seats of learning, and that suited our monk's scholarly bent, though he had not known he had it until he got here. So he preferred to think of his relocation all those years ago as a vocation, a quest even, rather than an exile, though that was certainly how it had started.

Since arriving at Wearmouth-Jarrow, though, our monk had begun in earnest something he had only toyed with at Lindisfarne, his own history of the People of the Designs. It was a history that would supplement the speculative myth-history of Bede and others, with more reliable information about the developments, events and personalities that had shaped his homeland and its people in recent centuries. He had written to the monasteries there requesting confirmation of half-remembered stories and genealogies and any further detail or documentation the brothers could provide. He hoped one day to visit those monasteries, and perhaps to survey some of the important historical sites. Perhaps he would even visit his own former home, but that was certainly not possible under current circumstances. The reasons for his original exile from his homeland had not changed. This was also the reason his letters were signed in his monastic name, and did not mention his nationality, let alone his previous identity.

'Brother Martin!' came a voice from beyond the vellum page. It was Brother Ewald, who had been sent to summon Martin for night prayers. This personal reminder service was an indulgence that reflected the esteem in which the scholar was held.

'Is it that time already?' Martin said in the heavily-accented Northumbrian for which he was also known and affectionately teased.

'I'm afraid so.'

He closed his eyes for a few seconds, silently transitioning from his scholarship to his more quotidian monastic duty, before rising and accompanying Ewald to join their brothers.

By this time, most of Martin's letters had got no further than the monastery at Magilros, where they would languish until someone was sent from there into Pictland, or more likely a traveller stopped at the monastery on his way there. Imagine travelling monks in those days as ants, slowly traversing the country from monastery to monastery, largely heedless of national frontiers, and imagine how their paths must have crossed. They rarely crossed literally – at the same time, that is – but since letters could be deposited at monasteries, it was only a matter of time before another traveller came along who could pick them up – if someone remembered – and take them a little further towards their intended destination. Unless the matter were important enough to warrant a dedicated courier, this was how monks and monasteries communicated with one another. This, for example, was how Bishop Boniface's letters had reached Iona. And as luck would have it, the slow, antlike paths of monks had aligned in such a way that one of Martin's letters had now fallen into the hands of the very same Bishop Boniface. He was not the intended recipient, but the letter was not exactly private anyway. Martin had intended his letters to be read, copied even, and passed on to anyone who might be able to help with his enquiries. Boniface was in the habit of copying letters that came his way whether their senders intended it or not. He was quite conscientious about that. Having copied this one and sent it on his way to the monastery for which it was intended, he began composing his own reply. He had little to say about the Scythian nonsense, but he did have much to contribute when it came to the much more recent dynastic politics of the People of the Designs, though as a modern man with an international outlook, Boniface did not demur to refer to his people as Picts, as the rest of the world did. In particular, he made sure to let the historian know about the exploits of an important Pictish underking by the name of Brude. No doubt this would indeed be of interest to Martin, but – again, as luck would have it – it would be several years before Boniface's letter made its way to Wearmouth-Jarrow.

Far to the west, however, a letter now arrived in Govan. Unusually, it was not for Valentine but for Gawin. And it came not from any of the lands central to our story, but from the Brittonic kingdom of Gwynedd in what is now Wales. It was from Gawin's former teacher, Emrys.

Gawin read it several times. At first, he thought the old man must have lost his mind. It was certainly no ordinary letter. There was no, 'Dear Gawin, I do hope this letter finds you well,' nor even, 'Greetings in Christ, peace and grace be multiplied upon you'. There was no acknowledgement of the nearly twenty years since they had last seen one another at Whithorn before Emrys had set sail for Gwynedd, nor any anticipation of a future meeting. Instead the letter began by telling the story of how Saint Ninian and his holy brother Plebia had once sat together reading Psalms on a remote hillside when it had begun to rain heavily. They should have been quickly soaked and unable to read, except that an invisible vault formed over their heads, keeping them perfectly dry. This supernatural shelter held out until Ninian's thoughts began to drift from God's Word, and the rain broke through, but surmising what had happened, Plebia simply nudged his brother, bringing him back to what they were reading, and the invisible vault was immediately restored.

Naturally, Gawin knew this story well. It had always reminded him of a famous Pictish legend, according to which a great warrior had once shielded his comrades from a sea of elvish arrows raining down on them by leaping into the air and spinning his spear at great speed to form an impenetrable barrier. But he did not linger on the parallel now, because the letter itself was telling him not to let his attention stray. He read on. The rest of the letter was written in a bewildering blend of their own language and Latin, and partly in verse. There were numerous allusions to the Bible, and especially to the books of Isaiah and Daniel. But most of the letter was given to lauding great heroes from the history of their own people, indeed from a time when the Britons had dominated the island that now bears their name, when you could have walked from Gwynedd to Alt Clut, or indeed to what was now Edinburgh, without passing through any land inhabited by foreigners. In those days, Edinburgh had been Din Eidyn, the capital of the Brittonic kingdom of Gododdin. And Emrys' letter included praise for the warriors who had died avenging an attack on Din Eidyn by foreign invaders who had settled to the south, the forebears of the Northumbrians. Emrys reminded Gawin that Mynyddawg Mwynvawr had hosted the assembled warriors for a whole year of feasting before the warband rode south full of mead to meet their foes. Then these three hundred warriors, each adorned with a golden torc, had taken on thousands of the foreigners, slaying them by the score so the crows would be able feast for a year in imitation of those who now fed them. But, one by one, the champions of Gododdin also fell – Cynon son of Clydno, Caradawg and Madawg, Pyll and Ieuan, Gwgawn and Gwiawn, Gwyn and Cynvan, Peredur with the arms of steel, Aeddanand and that one-man palisade Gwawrddur, who fought as bravely as Arthur himself, though lacking his might and skill. Even as their numbers dwindled, they continued to slaughter their enemies, until the whole warband from Gododdin lay dead, saving only Aneirin, who lived to tell the tale.

Having read Emrys' letter through from start to finish several times, Gawin reluctantly came to the conclusion that the old man had indeed lost his mind. There was no indication of what Gawin was supposed to make of all this, no context by which to make sense of it. He shook his head. But then Emrys was the most learned man Gawin had ever known. He owed his teacher his attention, even if he had gone mad. He wondered when the letter had been sent. It was unlikely that word had reached Gwynedd even by now of the Men of the Rock's victory over the Picts, but Emrys would have known war was imminent, even if the war he knew to be imminent was the last one or the one before that. So perhaps his letter was meant as a warning for Alt Clut. Perhaps this was the context in which the references to Gododdin were to be understood.

Gododdin too had had a rock for its stronghold, a rock near where river met sea on the other side of the land. The rock of Gododdin lay to the south of a river flowing east, while Alt Clut lay to the north of a river flowing west. Gododdin had eventually been conquered from the south, while Alt Clut was menaced from the north. Gawin had an image of the sun rising in the east, sweeping the Britons of Gododdin away, before arcing round to sweep away Alt Clut as it set in the west. It was not – as once might have seemed likely – that the Northumbrians had gone on to conquer the Picts before continuing on their own arc of conquest, but perhaps the spirit of conquest had been transmitted through wars of attrition to the Picts themselves and then continued its bloody passage through Dalriada and now to Alt Clut.

The Men of the Rock had triumphed, for now – even killed the Picts' king, or his brother (amounting to both and neither) – but despite the scale of their victory, they were in no position to conquer anyone. Not the Picts, not the Northumbrians, who it was said had backed their failed campaign. Their enemies would gather strength. Attack again, as the Northumbrians had attacked Gododdin again, and conquered it, barely a generation after the heroic warband had marched south to slaughter and be slaughtered. The Britons' martial culture venerated men who feasted for a year on end before riding drunk into battle and their doom. Perhaps it was not surprising they had never conquered the foreign invaders. And perhaps Emrys' letter was not so much a warning as a prophecy. Gawin put it away carefully in a leather folder where he kept his most valued correspondence. Later, though, while dining with his brothers, he thought again of its contents, and in particular of the elliptical reference to Arthur.

Emrys had always been fond of the stories of King Arthur, who it was said had once ruled the whole island of Britain. In some of the stories, he was a ruler of unparalleled virtue, a pious man and a champion of the poor and the oppressed. In others, he was fatally flawed, the Britons' own King David, whose virtues and greatness only served to make more tragic his fall into sin and weakness. Because, after all, what had become of his great kingdom? Like Israel it was divided, invaded, much of it conquered. And unlike King David, Arthur had no promise from God that his people would prevail regardless of his own failures. Gawin thanked God for sending Jesus Christ to fulfil that promise and to extend it to all who believed in Him. He knew Christ's church would prevail, but not as one nation conquering others. Nations would continue to rise and fall till Christ's own kingdom came. How long, oh Lord, how long? Perhaps in the meantime Alt Clut would fall, and the Britons would be overrun. Because instead of a promise from God, the Britons' great King Arthur had put his trust in the counsel of a wizard, an avatar of the Dragon. Thank God Jesus had redeemed souls and not nations, freeing them one by one from dependence on mighty warriors and mortal kings, in the next life if not this one.

CHAPTER 39: IONA

Brigid had just finished reading De Locis Sanctis, a great work by the late Abbot Adomnan, who was just as important to the Abbey of Iona as Bede was to Wearmouth-Jarrow. The book was a detailed description of the Holy Land, so detailed that Brigid had been able to imagine herself there. Part of her wished she could actually go on a pilgrimage to Jerusalem, walk on the very ground where Jesus and his disciples had walked, where the early church had first flowered. She knew it was hot there, hotter than she had ever experienced – and a summer's day on Iona could be pretty scorching, at least if the climate of Dalriada was all you had ever known. And she knew that many strange languages were spoken there, by strange looking people, no doubt amid strange smells. But more than the exoticism of the location, it was of course the significance of what had happened there that fascinated Brigid. She did not dare to imagine what it must have been like to see the Lord Jesus in the flesh, to sit at his feet on the mount, or to jostle for position amid the crowds who gathered to hear him as he spoke from a humble fishing boat. And she could not bear to think of him suffering on the cross for her sins; she made herself acknowledge the fact, but she felt horribly ambivalent about whether it was right to contemplate the spectacle. Whether from pious humility or impious squeamishness, Brigid only felt comfortable imagining herself in the Holy Land after the Resurrection and Ascension of her

Saviour.

She had often wondered what it must have been like to be there on the first Pentecost, when the people of Jerusalem heard a great whooshing sound from the sky, and converged on the place where the disciples were gathered, to find them crowned with fire and speaking in tongues. And they were amazed because although there were Jews there from 'every nation under Heaven', each heard these simple, uneducated Galileans speak in their own tongue. There were Parthians and Medes and Elamites and others from even more places Brigid had never heard of except in the pages of the Bible. Were there Gaels too? Brigid had never heard of Jews living in Dalriada, but the Bible said, 'every nation under Heaven,' so there must have been Jewish Gaels, or at least Gaelic proselytes, there too. Adomnan had based his book on the testimony of a Gaulish bishop called Arculf, who had been blown off course and ended up on Iona on his way home from the Holy Land. So who was to say that Jewish merchants had not done the same before him? The hand of God had surely steered the boat in both cases.

Then Brigid remembered the story Conall the craftsman had told her in Dunadd, about how their people were descended from Scota, the daughter of the Pharaoh. That was a legend, of course, and not be relied on like Scripture. Perhaps it was not true, and even if it were true, perhaps Scota was not the same Pharaoh's daughter who had adopted the infant Moses, though Conall had mentioned the parting of the Red Sea, which suggested she was. And if Scota were indeed the mother of Dalriada and also the adoptive mother of Moses, and thus in a sense of the Jewish people, then the Gaels and the Jews were siblings.

It was a pleasant whimsy, but Brigid knew perfectly well there was nothing special about the Gaels, or any other of the nations. It was only through Christ that anyone, Jew or gentile, was counted an heir of Abraham and a child of God. So the nations were supposed to be united in Christ. On Iona it was easy to imagine they were indeed. Most of the brothers and all the sisters were natives of Dalriada, of course, but they also rubbed shoulders with Irishmen, Picts, Britons and Northumbrians, as well as occasional visitors from other parts of Christendom – and not all there by accident like Arculf the Gaul. Beyond Iona, Brigid knew, things were less harmonious. Even at the abbey, they heard often of wars and rumours of wars. Every day she prayed for Brothers Paul, Aidan and Gregory, who – God willing – would soon return from their sojourn in the land of the Picts, her people's conquerors. Some spoke of the Picts as Philistines waging war on God's people, and perhaps allowed to do so as a punishment for Dalriada's sins. Brigid knew that was to make the same mistake she entertained only as whimsy. God's people were not any nation, but the church, and the church straddled the nations and kingdoms of men. That was the reason her brothers could safely sojourn with the Picts, the reason indeed that two of those brothers could be Picts. The people of the church could say shibboleth or sibboleth; Jesus, Yeshua, the Son of Man did not care.

As Brigid left the library with these thoughts, it began to rain heavily, but she did not rush back inside. She had a little precious time of her own before she was expected with her sisters for prayers, and she did not want to spend it alone in her cell. Not when she could enjoy the rain, and gaze up at the glorious sky stretching over the sea, not when she could listen to the swirling of the waves and the cries of the gulls. She walked to one of the tall, stone crosses that stood in the grounds of the abbey, and placed her hand on the wet stone as she breathed in the freshness of the wet air. She could feel the presence of God all around her, and began to weep with joy.

When Brigid recovered herself, she turned her attention to the stone cross itself, and noticed that her hand was tracing the carvings on its surface. The stone was ornately carved with various designs: serpents wrapped themselves around one another at the edges of the stone, but these were tame serpents, serving as ornamentation. They were not like the serpent in the Garden of Eden, who had tempted Eve and provided the opportunity for Adam to fall by watching it happen. And here was the second Adam, Jesus Christ, in the form of a baby in arms of the Virgin. Things had gone better when man came out of a woman rather than the other way round. Poor Adam had not had the benefit of a mother; no wonder he was a terrible husband. Brigid thanked God for Jesus and Mary. God could have come to Earth as an orphan, or even as a fully grown man, perfect in every way and all at once. But he chose to come as a son, not just the Son of God, but the son of Mary, Daughter of Israel, and thus in a sense a brother to all humanity, Jews and Gaels alike; Picts for that matter. He lived a mortal life, his perfection all the more astonishing for being revealed in real time and on a human scale. A child who never lied nor sulked nor bullied, a man who never coveted nor envied nor resented nor even felt proud of his own excellences. What must it have been like to have Jesus Christ as a brother, as a friend? As a son? And yet it was only because Jesus Christ was all of those things that he could suffer and die on our behalf, as one of us, for his brothers and sisters and friends, for his church. Brigid could not contain her gratitude, and nor could she express it. And so she wept again, in joy and in sorrow, until it was as if the very rain that fell from Heaven fell in sympathy. All Creation wept in joy and in sorrow for Jesus Christ, son of God.

The carvings on the cross also depicted other stories. Brigid especially liked the picture of Daniel in the lions' den, where he stood flanked by a lion on either side. Brigid had never seen a lion, of course, but these seemed to her more like big dogs, affectionately jumping up to greet their master, though it was true that the craftsman had given Daniel a rather nervous expression. The Bible did not say Daniel had not been afraid, though he surely knew that God would preserve him. It was King Darius, who loved Daniel but had been tricked into consigning him to his apparent doom, who was beside himself with fear and anguish. He had not known any better. Brigid felt sorry for kings, mere men who lived with the illusion that they were the masters of the Earth and responsible for all that happened on it. No wonder they too were notoriously terrible husbands.

Brigid thanked God that she would never have to suffer the disappointment of a terrible husband. It was not that her celibacy was not a sacrifice. She wanted desperately to be married, to love and be loved. She felt the loss of it every day. And it was not that her celibacy was merely a means of avoiding disappointment, as if that were all that could be expected of marriage. She had little doubt that men and women could taste real joy together amid the anguish and misery of mortal life. Indeed, she was not far from the intuition that joy as experienced in and of this world is inextricable from anguish and misery. But that was precisely why she had foresworn all such feelings. Every day, every hour, she made a conscious effort to set her mind on the things above, on the things eternal. The things against which her sacrifice in this life was like chaff in the wind. Now she could almost smell those things, taste them, and once more she wept for joy.

CHAPTER 40: TRANSFIGURATION

The Daughter of the Moon and the Avatar of the Dragon held hands and raised both arms in the air before beginning their prayer. It was dusk, and already the moon was visible: the full moon, the Dragon Moon. The Daughter of the Sun and the Sacred Virgin had prepared the sacrifice, a young lamb, but the honour of killing it would fall to the Avatar of the Dragon. This was her festival, just as the Harvest Moon belonged to the Daughter of the Moon, and the Summer Solstice belonged to the Daughter of the Sun. At the Winter Solstice, the Sacred Virgin was symbolically married to the Dragon himself, but that was a different kind of rite, altogether more sombre, and without any sacrifice save that of the Sacred Virgin herself, pledged for another year to remain untouched by man. Thus, each priestess had her season, but all were interconnected, related. So in each festival the priestess of honour was served by one of her sisters. Tonight the Avatar of the Dragon was served by the Daughter of the Moon as she greeted the Dragon Moon. At the Winter Solstice, the Sacred Virgin was served by the Avatar of the Dragon because she was marrying the Dragon. At the Harvest Moon, the Daughter of the Moon was served by the Daughter of the Sun to celebrate the sun's bounty. And at the Summer Solstice, the Daughter of the Sun was served by the Sacred Virgin because it was the renewal of the Virgin's sacrifice each winter that made the sun rise and linger through the summer.

When the Daughter of the Moon and her servant the Avatar of the Dragon had finished their prayer, the Sacred Virgin and the Daughter of the Sun held hands and raised both arms to sing their humble tribute. This would go on all night, culminating in the sacrifice itself and the invocation of the Dragon. And as tedious as it all might have seemed to a less interested observer, Pendrin watched in fascination. He was one of several onlookers, not all young men, who had been drawn to the ritual. More indeed than the priestesses had been able to count at any of their rituals for some years.

Of course, Pendrin would not have been there had he not caught a glimpse of the Sacred Virgin in the woods nearly a year and a half ago, and come under her spell. And he probably would not have been there had he not had that more lingering encounter with the Daughter of the Moon at the harvest festival last year. But he was not here to greet the Dragon Moon just because he'd become infatuated with a handsome young woman or two. He had not, after all, attended the priestesses' Harvest Moon ceremony shortly after the festival. Hardly anyone had. But this time, like the other observers, he had felt something in the air. You see, unlike that assignation at the Harvest festival, orchestrated with winks and whispers, Pendrin was not here by any kind of arrangement. Nobody was. The priestesses did not organise and publicise their rituals as the bards did their performances. They simply performed the rituals as they had been taught. People either came or did not come.

Pendrin had been dreaming of Gwy since the last full moon, and more intensely than ever. In fact, he had never stopped dreaming of her since their encounter, but not like this. Sometimes he dreamed also of Fay, his first infatuation; he could not help that and did not try. But this past month, his dreams of Gwy had been more real almost than the encounter itself. And the closer the Dragon Moon had come, the more real his dreams had felt. For the past few days, he had found himself daydreaming about his nocturnal dreams, his mind wandering incessantly as he worked on the farm. Even as he tended the cattle he could not stop lusting after Gwy. And even as he gathered dung for the fields, he seemed to smell something else in the air. He breathed it in, and found that he was yearning for something that was in Gwy but beyond Gwy. It was only when someone else had mentioned that the moon would be full that night that Pendrin made the connection. A month of ever more frenzied fantasy, day and night now that the full moon approached. He was being driven mad by the moon.

But no amount of knowledge of the natural world and its cycles could have told him where to go that night. He would never have guessed the location of the sacred grove deep in the wood on the other side of the little mountain from the homestead, where the priestesses had come to greet the Dragon Moon. Somehow, he had simply known, or not known, but felt his way there. Late in the afternoon, he had told his brother Peter he was going to see to his traps, and then simply set off – bringing more food than he could possibly need – and trudging for hours through the heavily wooded slopes until he had found himself at the edge of the grove, the moon now clearly visible and illuminating the priestesses: Gwy, Fay, and only now did it occur to Pendrin that he knew the others too, that all the bards had been women. The moon also shed light on the other onlookers, who stood about the edges of the grove. He thought he knew two or three of them, but he could not be sure. They were not like a Christian congregation, recognising and greeting one another as they assembled for worship. Each had arrived alone, bringing an offering of food, and each was focused solely on the priestesses and their ritual.

When the Dragon Moon was at its fullest, the Sacred Virgin and the Daughter of the Sun held the lamb they had prepared in place on a large rock that served as an altar. The

Daughter of the Moon produced a long knife and held it aloft so it caught the light of the Dragon Moon, before handing it to the Avatar of the Dragon, who knelt and pointed it north, south, east and west before rising to her feet and skilfully wielding the blade in a circular motion that ended by cutting the animal's throat. Blood spurted forth. The onlookers gasped, not because they were impressed by the slaying of a goat, but because of the effect the sacrifice had on the priestesses. The Avatar of the Dragon held the bloodied knife aloft and beamed exultantly. The others stood about her, their faces to the moon, their arms dramatically straight at their sides. All four were like torches blazing into the night sky, as if their faces were illuminating the moon rather than the other way round. Then the Avatar of the Moon touched the bloodied knife to the cheeks of each of her sister-priestesses in turn, and it was as if in doing so she extinguished the torches one by one. But still the Dragon Moon flooded the sacred grove with its light. Now the Daughter of the Moon took the sacrificial goat and held it as high as she could above the head of the Avatar of the Dragon, who plunged the knife into its body to bring forth another stream of blood over herself. Then the Daughter of the Moon returned the goat to the altar, and the Daughter of the Sun and the Sacred Virgin joined her in a chant as they walked slowly around the blood-drenched Avatar of the Dragon. Pendrin could just about make out the words they chanted, but could make no sense of them. Perhaps the meaning of the chant was not in the words. As the three priestesses walked and chanted, the Avatar of the Dragon began to laugh heartily, gazing into the sky. A spilt second before he followed her gaze, Pendrin fancied she seemed to levitate, but follow her gaze he did, and when he saw what she saw, he could not look away from the stars even to see a levitating priestess.

The constellations swirled and throbbed in the sky, their old shapes dissolving and new ones half-forming before dissolving again, dispersing and reassembling and spiralling this way and that. It was breath-taking. Beautiful. Unnerving.

And then, there it was in the sky above them. The Dragon. The stars aligned in the unmistakeable shape of the Dragon, a great winged worm in the sky, as if come to claim his sacrifice. Pendrin gasped in amazement. He wanted to look around him to see if the other onlookers saw what he saw, but he could not take his eyes off the spectacle itself, the fire-breathing monster made of stars. So he did not take his eyes off it. The Dragon flew about the sky, now seeming to rise ever higher, now seeming to plunge towards the Earth, before fixing on the moon, the Dragon Moon, and breathing his fire on it, making it glow even brighter. Then, three times, the Dragon circled the Dragon Moon, and three times the priestesses let out an unnaturally deep wail of approval. At least, Pendrin had to assume the sound came from the priestesses. His eyes remained fixed on the Dragon. Three times it circled the Dragon Moon. Three times a great wail went up. And then, blackness. Silence.

The next thing Pendrin knew, it was morning. And he was stuck high in a tree.

Pendrin's cousin Pyrdie was not there to witness the ritual, to greet the Dragon Moon. He was asleep in bed through all of this, perhaps dreaming of the mysterious woman he could not know was the Sacred Virgin. Like Pendrin, he still dreamt often of Fay, but there had been no particular intensity since the last full moon, and no mysterious urge to forsake his bed and seek out a sacred grove tonight. In the months since Pendrin's encounter with Gwy, Pyrdie had discovered a new world of his own, not a world of magic and ritual and priestesses and monsters, but the world of the court of King Brude and his formidable Bishop Boniface. A world of foreigners, politics, women maybe.

At first, Pyrdie had resented being asked to learn foreign carving techniques and designs, but he had quickly begun to master them, and they had duly come to feel less like an imposition and more like an expansion of his own repertoire. Vine scrolls, for example: most versatile. His Northumbrian master Old Bert treated him well and respected his craftsmanship. Pyrdie got on with the other court hangers-on and kept a respectful distance from his betters, while keeping his eyes and ears open enough to learn about things he had never imagined. He looked forward to returning next winter to see what progress had been made on Bishop Boniface's stone church, to work on further ornamentations and to catch up on the gossip of the court. For now, though, Pyrdie was at home in the only world he had ever known before the court. Working on the farm, sharing life with his family, it was easy to forget there was a world beyond the homestead. Even when he sat alone on the hillside, working on his own designs and thinking his own thoughts, it was almost as if he had never been away.

Pyrdie was retrieving a stray calf from the wrong side of the burn when he noticed Pendrin ambling down from the wood. 'Where have you been?' he shouted, leaving the calf for a moment.

Pendrin did not answer.

As he came closer, Pyrdie could see he was in a daze. 'Pendrin? Are you all right?' he asked. Now Pendrin looked at him, and stopped when he reached him. 'Are you all right?' Pyrdie asked again.

'Something happened,' Pendrin said.

'What happened? Something bad?'

'No, I don't think so. Not something bad.'

'Then, what? Something good? Have you been with a girl?' Pyrdie added with a smile.

A look Pyrdie could not identify passed across Pendrin's face. Then Pendrin pointed to the calf, which was wandering off again. 'I'll help you,' he said, and the two of them ran to catch up with it before ushering it back over the burn. This intrusion of normality seemed to dispel the odd atmosphere, so Pyrdie tried again. 'Are you going to tell me what happened?'

'"What happened"?' Pendrin said, as if he'd spent the night in his bed, woken as normal and had breakfast with his family before coming out with Pyrdie to see to the cattle. Then, as he remembered he'd done none of that, he said, 'Oh, "what happened". Yes, I spent the night in the wood.'

'Well, you're a braver man than I. But is that all that happened? It sounded like you had a story to tell.'

By now, Pendrin was returning to himself. 'Oh, well maybe I do. But it's a story for another time.'

'Fair enough,' Pyrdie said, as they walked with the calf back to the herd. 'I do hope it's a love story.'

◆ ◆ ◆

Paul and Gregory and Aidan had been travelling homeward for a couple of days when they discovered that most of the meal they had brought for the journey was rotten. Beneath the good meal near the top of the little sack was a mess of soggy mush, not fit for a donkey to eat. 'Well, that's rotten luck,' said Aidan, dumping it at the side of the path. 'Perhaps we'll pass a farm or settlement where we can seek mendication.'

'God willing, we shall,' said Gregory.

But God's will put something else in their way. A troupe of bards heading north.

'Well met,' said Gregory. 'And God bless you.'

The bards returned his greeting warmly enough.

Gregory went on: 'I don't suppose we could trouble you for a little food? I'm afraid our supplies have gone bad.'

As it happened, the bards had a plentiful supply, thanks to Pendrin and others like him who had brought offerings to the Dragon Moon ceremony. They whispered among themselves, debating half-seriously whether it was sacrilegious to allow these holy offerings to be eaten by godless Christians. Before this went on long enough to embarrass all concerned, however, they came to a consensus that it did not matter. Better to feed godless Christians than let the food go to waste.

As Peg plundered their little wagon for disposable but not insulting provisions to hand over, though, Fay noticed something and felt a jolt in her stomach. Suddenly, her breathing was laboured. One of the monks looked like someone Fay had once known. A man who had been very important to her. Indeed, it was not the first time she had mistaken a stranger for this man. Many times over the years she had felt that jolt in her stomach at the moment of misrecognition before realising it was not him at all. Only this time the shock had barely passed before it returned. She was not mistaken. This was him. This monk. Paul, in fact.

'You're a monk!' she exclaimed, with contemptuous amazement. 'A Christian monk!'

Paul duly recognised her in return: 'Euphemia?'

Fay's expression changed to one of half-ironic wistfulness. 'Euphemia. Now, that's a name I've not heard in a *long* time.'

CHAPTER 41: LOVE STORY

Fay had her gaze fixed steadily on Paul. Through that gaze, he could still recognise the Euphemia he had known, but she lurked in new depths. And apparently she no longer went by the name Euphemia. She was someone else now. Well, that was something they both had in common. Something else, in addition to the love story they shared.

'It's also a long time since I heard the name Priten,' he told her.

'If I'd been about to call you something,' she said, 'it wasn't that'.

Gregory and Aidan looked at one another nervously. Even to a couple of monks without interesting pasts, the chemistry in the air was unmistakeable. Apparently Paul had an interesting past. One involving this young man. The other 'young men' looked at one another just as nervously. Peg gestured to Tes: do I hand over this spare food or not? Tes shrugged. Gwy moved next to Fay, put her hand on her shoulder in a gesture of support. Fay just glared at the monk, who, despite his carefully measured response to being confronted with Euphemia, had the look of a deer caught unawares and frozen in place. Peg gave the food to Gregory, the one who had asked for it, getting the matter out of the way.

Gregory took it in the same spirit, thanked the young man. Then he looked at Paul: well?

'God bless you,' Paul said to Fay suddenly, then extended the blessing with a glance to the other bards. 'And thank you for the food.' With that, he strode on past the bards, prompting his brothers to bow in gratitude and follow him. Fay did not turn to watch him, but stared ahead of her at where he had been standing. Gwy did look round, bewildered and intensely curious, as did the others, but they soon realised they would learn nothing from watching three monks' backs disappear into the distance, and turned back to look at Fay. Well? Fay appeared to wipe a tear from her face before striding on in the same direction as before, away from the monks. Her sisters simply followed with their now slightly lighter wagon.

That evening, there was a story to be told in both camps. Or perhaps that should be a story in each camp.

'Could you really not see she was a woman?' Paul asked his brothers in disbelief. 'They all were!'

Aidan and Gregory looked at one another. 'They looked like lads to me,' said Aidan, and Gregory nodded.

'Did they have beards?' asked Paul.

'No,' Aidan conceded, 'but then neither do we.'

Paul sighed. 'All right, but were they as tall as we are. As broad of shoulder?'

They paused to consider this. 'I can't say I noticed,' Gregory said. 'Certainly they were not especially big lads.'

'No,' agreed Aidan, 'I'd have described them as slight of build.'

'Right,' Paul said, 'and did you not look at their features at all?'

'Their features?'

Paul hesitated in frustration. He could hardly ask his brother monks if they had not seen how lovely these 'lads' had been to look at. How gorgeous their faces, how even their modest, men's clothing had not concealed their feminine shapes. True, after all these years, Euphemia still had a slim or even slightly boyish figure, but a woman's figure nevertheless. And, even as preoccupied as he had been with her, he had not been able to help noticing the others, at least one of whom had the bust and hips to remove all doubt. Was he uniquely sinful, to have taken all that in almost at a single glance? Perhaps he was.

Gregory realised this was going nowhere, and asked Paul instead. 'Your former name was Priten? Both my grandfathers were Pritens.'

'Indeed? Yes, that's right,' Paul said. 'It feels like another life altogether.'

'I understand,' Gregory said, 'and there's no need to speak of it, if you'd prefer not to.'

Paul sighed. Perhaps speaking of it would keep it out of his dreams. Perhaps it would make them worse. He sent up a silent prayer, waited a moment and then decided to tell the story. But before he could tell the story of Priten and Euphemia, he had to explain who Priten had been, who he had been.

'I was not born into a Christian family,' he said. 'My mother was a believer, but my father's people had never embraced the faith, and though they did not speak of the old gods, neither was I christened or catechised as a child. But later my father had political ambitions, and... This is something I should have mentioned before now...'

Aidan and Gregory looked at one another, then back at Paul.

'Bishop Boniface, this so-called King Brude, I know them. I grew up in their village.'

'You did what?' Gregory asked, visibly thrown by this fresh revelation.

'How did they not recognise you?' added Aidan.

'I barely recognised them. The bishop was rarely at home when I was growing up. And he wasn't a bishop and he wasn't called Boniface. As for Brude, well, he was a bit younger than me, but he is not as I remember him.'

Aidan hesitated before asking the obvious question: 'You're sure we're not talking about a different bishop and another Brude altogether?'

Paul smiled. 'Yes, I'm sure. I grew up in the glen where we attended the wedding. Our village was very close. And the old man who was asleep in the shelter... that was my grandfather.'

'Ah,' his brothers said in unison, remembering how Paul had sung to the sleeping old man.

'Well, my father was politically out-manoeuvred by the bishop's brother, and Brude's father, Taran, so we left when I was 14 or 15 and my father became an itinerant huntsman. He taught me to hunt with falcons, but my heart was never in it, so I took to walking in the mountains while he hunted, disappearing for days at a time, foraging in the woods and rivers, communing with nature. That kind of thing.'

'That kind of thing is dangerous for a young man who does not know Christ,' Gregory said.

'Indeed. As you've guessed by now, I began to feel drawn to the old religion. I was alone out there, but I never felt alone. I felt I was part of nature, at one with it, and I learned to talk to the animals. Or at least they got used to me talking to them and I imagined they understood me. But the animals did not talk back to me. Others did.'

Aidan shuddered.

'Remember that I was innocent of such things,' Paul told him. 'Easy prey, if you will. But it's a strange thing: someone who communes directly with such beings is in less danger than one who encounters them through mortal men and women. In the first case it is simply an encounter with the supernatural. In the second it quickly becomes false religion.'

Gregory nodded sagely.

'What kind of beings?' Aidan pressed.

'Oh, elves, fairies, call them what you will. They are not like natural creatures that can be studied and put into categories. And of course most of the stories you hear about such creatures are sheer superstition. But it's as wrong to disbelieve their existence altogether as it is to indulge in such superstition.'

'Are we talking of demons?' Aidan asked as Gregory listened more cautiously.

'Yes and no,' Paul answered. 'I later grew to suspect that depends less on the thing itself than on how men relate to it. You must understand that not all paganism is alike. There is, I won't call it *innocent*, but at least a *natural* reverence for God's Creation that comes from an intuition of God himself. There could be no agriculture without it. And it naturally gives rise to all kinds of relatively harmless folk customs, like the harvest festival, for example, to mark the rhythms of nature and give thanks for its bounty. And without knowledge of true religion, we have a tendency to attach all kinds of other beliefs to such folk customs, some of them harmless, others...

'Well, the supernatural beings I spoke to did not catechise me in those beliefs. How could they, being their objects and not their authors? I began to seek out those beliefs for myself. I asked my father what he remembered, but he had little interest in such matters, at least at that time. My grandfather knew much more, though, and I visited him whenever I could. While the memory of my father and his conflict with Taran remained fresh, I could not show my face in the village, where my grandfather was allowed to live out his days, but I would meet him by arrangement in the wild places, and he told of a time when everyone had worshipped the old gods. I was fascinated. For him, though, those memories held none of the romance they did for me. He knew nothing of communion with nature as I did, or of magic as I would.'

A nervous glance passed between Aidan and Gregory.

'For my grandfather, and for much of his generation, the worship of the old gods had been ordinary, something taken for granted. Boring even. For me it became something quite different.' Paul broke off now and prayed silently. His brothers joined him.

The bards sat about their own fire. Fay had been silent all day since their encounter with the monks. They had all eaten largely in silence. Now, Fay signalled to Gwy that she could remove the arm that had been around Fay's shoulder almost constantly since their encounter with the monks, and which, until now, had been much needed. But now she was ready to tell her story.

'You remember the royal wedding last autumn,' she began, 'I didn't mention it because, well you know we don't talk about our old lives. And besides, I did not really think about it. It did not get to me.'

'Think about what?' demanded Tes.

'What didn't get to you? added Peg.

'Let her get on with it,' said Gwy.

'Well, that was my family,' Fay revealed, 'the groom was my brother.'

'King Brude?'

'Your brother is a king?'

'Let her get on with it!'

'Well, that's the strange part,' Fay replied. 'He *wasn't* my brother.'

Gwy put her hands to the mouths of Tes and Peg to pre-empt any further interruptions.

Fay went on. 'My father was a nobleman called Taran, who always aspired to be a king, and evidently died many years ago. His brother, my uncle, was the bishop who presided over the wedding. The groom, the man they called Brude son of Taran, King Brude indeed, well he was not my brother. I believe he was my brother's friend Donuel. Donuel the Cunning, they called him.'

'Cunning indeed to make himself king in another man's name,' Peg said, having freed herself from Gwy's muzzle.

'So what happened to the real Brude?' Tes asked, doing the same.

'I have no idea. I don't believe he was at the wedding at

all. Perhaps he's dead or in exile. No doubt there's quite a story there, but it is not my story to tell. It was a strange experience finding myself at a family wedding like that, but it's no longer my family, even if the groom had been my brother. That's what I meant when I said it did not get to me.'

'Not like that monk,' Gwy observed coyly.

'No, indeed,' said Fay. 'And that brings me to the beginning of my own story, when I gave up the life of an almost-princess for something else.'

Now, the others stayed silent, in rapt anticipation.

In the other camp, Paul came to the same matter, having described how he had grown in knowledge of magic over the years, and even trained his own father in the art of second sight, a residue from the old religion that was sufficiently valued to be quietly tolerated among nominally Christian communities, if not by the church herself.

'My father and I were hunting in the glen where I'd grown up when we heard that Taran was away at war, and I decided to take advantage by visiting my grandfather, who had been too frail to leave the village for some time now. My father was not interested, so I went alone. And as I approached the village, I heard a lovely song coming from a yew tree. Only it was not a bird but a girl, and one even more beautiful to look at than to listen to. That was Euphemia. I liked the look and sound of her and the feeling seemed to be mutual. I say this on the basis of a few words exchanged on my way in and out of the village two or three times, but it felt real enough. She put me in her songs and that put me under her spell, so to speak. But she was barely a woman and I had no intention of lingering in those parts more than a few days, so it seemed a harmless flirtation. It never occurred to me that she would come after me when I moved on. How would she even know where to look?'

'And yet she did come after you,' said Gregory.

'How did she know where to look?' asked Aidan.

'A little bird told me,' Fay explained to her friends, who

looked suitably intrigued. 'Or so it seemed, at least. I often chatted to the little birds who shared my tree, but this was the first time someone had spoken to me up there. The voice spoke neither in human language nor in birdsong, but as soon as it had spoken I knew where to go.'

'I can't believe you've never told us this story before,' said Gwy, almost crossly.

'Shhh!' said the others.

Fay continued: 'I don't think I thought of anything else all day. But nor did I think I would actually go there. I was not so naive that I did not know better than to run around after a strange man like that, exposing myself to who knew what kind of danger. After all I was practically a princess. Indeed, it was only that evening, when my mother scolded me for something or other – I can't even remember what – that I resolved to seek Priten out. If my own mother would not treat me with the respect I felt I deserved, perhaps he would. And after all, if his father had happened to come out on top of that dispute with my father, Priten would have been practically a prince.'

'So just like that you decided to run away with him,' asked Peg.

'Oh, no. Nothing as certain as that. But my pride was just enough to overcome my fear, or my good sense, if you prefer, and at least seek him out. After all, I had another incentive. When a little bird suggests a particular course of action, it's hard not to be intrigued.'

The others were also sufficiently intrigued not to interrupt now.

'So the very next morning, just before dawn, I crept out of the village and set off. As I passed my yew tree in the dark, I whispered an acknowledgement to my guide, and fancied I heard a murmur of approval. Then I skipped over the river on the stepping stones I knew so well, and made for the wood as directed. I arrived just as the sun was coming up, and its light now dappled the darkness of the wood. I don't know how many hours I stumbled through that wood, somehow just knowing which direction to take so that while there was never anything quite like a path, I never found myself hemmed in or forced to struggle over obstacles of any kind. Then I saw it, almost like remembering a dream. At the base of a steep bank, almost obscured by the gnarled roots of an old tree, there was a wooden door, round like a great battle shield, but instead of a boss in the middle, it had a metal ring to one side for a handle.' Fay hesitated now, shocked by the vividness of the memory.

'And you opened it?' Peg asked excitedly.

'I tried, but it was so heavy. I was able to pull it open just enough to peek inside, but no further, and it was pitch black. I thought I could just about have climbed in through the gap, but that would have meant plunging into the blackness with no idea what was inside and no guarantee I'd be able to climb out again.'

'So what did you do?' asked Tes.

'I did what I was best at. I climbed a tree and sat in it to wait. Only I did not sing. I listened. I listened for anyone approaching through the wood, for any voices that might come to me. I listened, but for a long time I heard nothing but the natural sounds of the wood. Birdsong that was no more than birdsong, the occasional animal in the undergrowth. Nothing else.'

'And then,' Gwy pressed.

'And then the door opened.'

'Almost as soon as I emerged,' Paul told his brothers, 'I heard laughter, seemingly all around me, emanating from the very trees. At first I thought it was fairies, and maybe it was, but then I detected something different, a more particular laugh that was at once more innocent and less so. It was stifled laughter bursting forth and then continuing like a torrent. Then I realised it was a girl's laughter, but I looked all around me, and at first I could not see any girl.'

'I think I know who it was and where she was sitting,' Aidan said.

'What was she laughing at?' Gregory asked.

'Why? Why could you not stop laughing?' all three of Fay's friends demanded.

Instead of answering, Fay began laughing at the very memory, laughing uncontrollably. And her laughter was so charming the others could not help but join in, which made her laugh all the more.

'But *why*?' managed Gwy between shakes of laughter.

Fay managed to calm herself for long enough to get out: 'Because he was stark naked... and erect!'

Well, that set them all off again.

'I've no idea,' Paul said. 'You see I went back inside to get dressed, and when I came out again the laughter had stopped.'

'You were not dressed?' Aidan asked, slightly incredulously. And for the very first time, it dawned on Paul why Euphemia had been laughing that day.

PART THREE

Another ten years later,
more or less

CHAPTER 42: SHONAGH

Shonagh took off her clothes and folded them neatly on the rock before standing and peering down into the sea below her. She had made this dive countless times, but the anticipation always made her heart beat faster. The drop was more than twice her own height. She took a moment to steel herself, and then she was gone. The slightest of springs carried her clear of the rock as she stretched her body forwards, her arms reaching out in front of her, and let her momentum drive her head-first towards the water. It was freezing. That and that only she registered with her whole body before a flick of her wrists began her ascent and with a few kicks of her legs she was breathing again. Or rather gasping, joyfully.

She treaded water for a few seconds before kicking her legs to push herself backwards in the water as she gazed up at the sky. She wished she could bathe here for hours, but it was far too cold. She knew from experience that if she stayed in too long, it would be hard to climb out, let alone warm up afterwards. She said a quick prayer of thanksgiving and then reached forwards, lifting her legs behind her in the water to propel herself on her belly back to the rock. She barely used her arms to swim, except for balance, but it took all the strength in her arms to lift her high enough on the lower rocks to gain a foothold and climb out. On one occasion, she'd been unable to do it because her muscles were seizing up from cold, and had to swim across the bay to where there was a sandy beach. And then walk and clamber, freezing and naked, all the way back round. That was why she did not let herself stay in the sea too long.

Once safely on the lower rocks, she climbed back up, every hand and foothold familiar enough that she did not have to think about it. When she reached the top, her skin was mostly dry from the breeze. She shook and wrang her hair before slipping her clothes back on and jumping up and down on the spot to warm up. The sun would soon be setting, so she took a last deep breath of salty spray and began ambling home.

Shonagh was the only person she knew who went anywhere near the sea for fun. For her fellow islanders, the sea was a source of food and other useful supplies, mostly from seals. It was a means of transport, at least if you chose to think of it as that rather than a barrier in need of traversing. And it was deadly dangerous, threatening to drown anyone who fell into it, if they didn't die of cold first. Or worse. Beneath the waves lurked terrifying monsters; God's playthings, man's doom. But Shonagh had special dispensation to do strange things for fun, even as the other women span yarn or churned butter or did other normal womanly things. Shonagh was a princess, formerly of Dunadd no less. She was the twin sister of the Princess Bronagh who had married King Brude. She had not attended the wedding only because she had been heavily pregnant at the time. And unmarried.

'Ma, ma!' the twin girls shouted in unison from the yard as she approached home. Twins ran in the family. 'Have you been in the sea again, you mad cow?' A love of swimming did not run in the family.

'I've told you before not to call me that!' Shonagh said dutifully, but she enjoyed her daughter's insults. That was how they showed affection.

'How's my lovely mermaid?' asked Diarmait, as ever more conventional in expressing his affection as he greeted Shonagh at the threshold. Then he embraced her and drew her inside with the same motion. 'You chickens keep playing out here till dark, all right?'

Diarmait was both Shonagh's husband and the father of the twins, though their own wedding had only just preceded the girls' birth. He had been a retainer at the Irish court where the twin princesses had been taken with their mother after the fall of Dunadd, but he had been close enough to his own boyhood to have taken a shine to the not-quite-womanly girl and to enjoy her obvious admiration of him. The few years that separated them were less significant than the social chasm between the princess and the retainer, but that had only provided oxygen for their slow-burning romance in the otherwise suffocatingly familiar environment of the court. So why Shonagh and not her identical twin? Why Diarmait and not another strapping lad? Who is to say? But it took years of stolen glances and awkward encounters, which slowly became lingering and orchestrated, before they even spoke properly. And years more before rapport evolved into romance. And nor was their romance conducted recklessly, until it was, around the same time Shonagh's twin's more respectable pairing was being arranged. When the unbetrothed sister's pregnancy was discovered, the net of suspicion was not cast wide. Diarmait had to flee.

Afterwards, Shonagh lay by Diarmait's side, her head on his right shoulder and her right leg over his middle, as she traced the line of the scar on his chest with her fingertips. A scar of love, inflicted all those years ago by a young Irish nobleman in the name of the lady's honour, but more likely motivated by jealousy, whether born of desire for Shonagh or the sensitivities of status. A little deeper and the wound would have finished their romance altogether. She craned her neck to kiss the scar, and he stroked her hair, before gently guiding her face upwards, drawing her mouth to his. Limbs were also adjusted.

Diarmait had flown first to a monastery, and thence into Dalriada, a reversal of his beloved's exile. Then, with a marriage sealed between Bronagh and King Brude that brought wealth and influence to her family, cooler heads had decided that Shonagh's premature motherhood might in fact be considered less a loss to the family than an investment in its future. Especially when she gave birth to healthy twins. If her 'marriage' could be made good, two more princesses, quietly raised on an island out of the way, might one day – with the political status of Dalriada more settled – prove to be worth their weight in gold. Diarmait's family, though humble, had always been loyal to its rulers. Its status could be massaged into something approaching gentility, giving the twins a respectable Irish heritage on their father's side that would not diminish their status as royalty of Dalriada. A messenger was dispatched to find their father, who had already secreted himself on a suitably remote and sparsely populated island of his soon-to-be wife's country. And thus their romance had been allowed to resume, domesticated, in the fresh sea air of that island. There, a princess was free to strip naked and dive into the sea when she felt like it. There, a little family was free to live modestly, peacefully, happily.

When the little princesses came in somewhat after dark, their father was stoking the fire and their mother stirring a cauldron of pottage as it cooled. The little family ate together, and then Diarmait told a story, one of the good old stories from his homeland, and a favourite of the girls. It was a story about a very special dog and a very special pig.

'King MacDatho of Leinster had a hound called Ailbe, who was so strong and fierce that he was like a guard dog for all Leinster, and became famous throughout all Ireland. In fact, MacDatho's neighbours wanted him to make a gift of the hound: messengers were sent from King Aillil and Queen Medb of Connacht and from King Conchobar of Ulster, each offering great riches, cows and chariots and everlasting friendship in exchange for the animal. MacDatho was resigned to giving Ailbe away, but to whom should he give him?'

'To King Aillil and Queen Medb of Connacht!' said the first twin.

'To King Conchobar of Ulster!' said the second. They knew their father had relatives from both parts of Ireland, so he could not be offended by their choice either way.

'Well, King MacDatho could not decide so easily, and he neither ate nor drank and nor could he sleep while the messengers feasted in his hall awaiting an answer. And nor would he talk to his wife, who tried repeatedly to offer comfort and counsel. He just paced back and forth fretting over the matter and muttering to himself. So, eventually, his wife spoke up anyway, and said, "Why don't you offer the hound to both parties, and let them fight it out?"'

At this stage, the twins joined in, chanting MacDatho's well-worn words: '"Shush, woman! Can't you see I'm trying to think?"'

Diarmait resumed alone: 'And he paced some more and muttered some more, and suddenly he exclaimed…' He waited for the girls, then all three sang at once: '"I've had an idea!"'

Shonagh did not join in, but laughed heartily, enjoying Diarmait's favourite joke at the expense of his own sex. And he continued: '"Why don't I offer the hound to *both* parties, and let them fight it out?"' He acted the part with such ingenuousness that the girls could not join in because they were falling about laughing.

'Well, MacDatho was energised by his brilliant idea, and summoned the messengers from Connacht, telling them that having struggled with great perplexity and doubt, he had decided at last to give Ailbe to King Ailill and Queen Medb, and they were cordially invited to come with their retinue of warriors to enjoy his hospitality as they collected the hound. The messengers from Connacht were well pleased, and set off to deliver the good news. Then he summoned the messengers from Ulster and told them that having struggled with great perplexity and doubt, he had decided at last to give Ailbe to King Conchobar, who was cordially invited to come with his retinue of warriors to enjoy MacDatho's hospitality as he collected the hound. The messengers from Ulster were well pleased, and set off to deliver the good news.

'Before long, the day came when the warriors of Connacht and the warriors of Ulster both arrived at King MacDatho's hall, and the king slaughtered his fatted pig. No ordinary fatted pig indeed. For seven years the beast had been fed on the milk from sixty cows. It was a ginormous pig. So big, in fact, that it came with forty oxen just as a garnish, as well as all the usual trimmings. Yes, cabbage too, darling. MacDatho himself brought in the roast pig with all the rest, and all agreed that it would make an excellent dinner. But with so many honoured guests present, who was to carve the monster? Surely it was the Devil himself who whispered that the honour should go to the bravest warrior in attendance. Soon the word went round that with so many great heroes of all Ireland in attendance, who between them had performed so many brave deeds and won so many great trophies, the pig must surely be carved by whoever could be reckoned the bravest of them all. King Ailill and Queen Medb agreed. King Conchobar agreed. What they could not agree on was who that warrior might be. Before a great squabble could begin however, one champion of Connacht, namely Cet MacMatach, seized the great carving knife and declared that any man more worthy than himself must prove it by defeating him in battle.

'One after another, the heroes of Ulster stood up to challenge Cet MacMatach. And one after another, before they could lay a hand on him, Cet dismissed each of them with a withering put-down that made him sit down in shame. One was reminded that the last time the two warriors had met, he had run away leaving his chariot and horses. Another was warned that his father before him had attempted to defeat Cet, only to lose his hand to his own spear. A one-eyed warrior was cautioned that his handicap made his challenge unwise, all the more so because it was the very man he challenged who had taken his other eye. Many more warriors of Ulster were reminded of relatives, body parts or both they had already lost to Cet MacMatach, and one after another, they sat down in shame. But just as Cet was sharpening the great carving knife and about to plunge into the roast pig, the door to the hall flew open and in strutted Conall Cernach, to great cheers from his Ulster countrymen.'

The twins now chanted another favourite line: 'Just in time for dinner!'

Diarmait continued: 'Then he addressed himself to King Conchobar, "Who is this about to carve for us?"

"It is Cet MacMatach," Conchobar told him, "to whom the honour has been granted".

So Conall turned to Cet and greeted him in verse, great verse of the heroic age that sadly is lost to us now, and Cet responded in kind. All we do know is that, for once, Cet was outboasted and outmenaced by a rival, and Conall triumphed in the war of words, so Cet was forced to yield, only salvaging a little pride by insisting that if his brother Anluan had been there, it would have been a different story.'

'Oh, but Anluan is here!' chanted the girls with bloodthirsty glee.

Diarmait continued: 'And with that, Conall produced the severed head of Anluan from his belt, and threw it hard at the second greatest slayer of relatives and taker of body parts in the hall. Cet was thoroughly defeated, and left the pig to its new carver.

Conall began carving the great beast, taking huge mouthfuls as he did so, before distributing the best parts to his Ulster countrymen, and leaving only the two front legs for the men of Connacht. They were not very happy with that, and leapt up in anger. The men of Ulster leapt up too and the two sides squared off. And so, before they could even fill their bellies, they joined battle, which soon burst from the hall into the courtyard outside, and after someone pulled up a great oak to use as a weapon, the violent throng spilled even out of the courtyard into the surrounding countryside, where there was after all more room to fight with chariots as the Irish did in those days.

It was unclear which side had the upper hand, so King MacDatho decided to let the hound Ailbe decide who should be its new master. Let loose into the general melee, Ailbe chose Ulster, and joined in with the rout of Connacht as King Ailill and Queen Medb fled with their warriors. After a lengthy pursuit, the hound leapt at the royal couple's chariot, and caught the axle between its teeth. Well, their charioteer Ferloga cleverly manoeuvred the chariot so Ailbe was dislodged, or at least most of him was, as his head remained clamped to the axle, severed from his body. And Ferloga's heroics did not stop there. With King Conchobar's chariot bearing down on his enemies, their charioteer handed over the reins and slipped from their chariot to lie hidden in the heather, and when Conchobar's chariot passed over him he leapt into it and seized him by the head. So Conchobar offered Ferloga any reward he chose not to break his neck. "I don't ask much," said the charioteer. "Just take me home with you and have the women of Ulster and their daughters sing to me every night that I'm their darling".'

And now Diarmait looked at Shonagh and the girls and said, 'What do you think of that ladies? Would you sing to Ferloga to save my neck?'

For the umpteenth time, the ladies looked at one another and then back to Diarmait, before chanting nonchalantly: 'Ach, he can break your neck'.

Diarmait guffawed.

CHAPTER 43: MORTALITY

When Fay dreamt, it was often as Euphemia. She was, after all, still the same person, possessing the same memories until the Euphemia memories ran out and Fay's took over. That line was a very blurry one. Now she dreamt she, Euphemia, was inside Priten's lair, the door closing behind her just as she had feared when she had first found it. Euphemia was trapped in the darkness. Terrified.

That scenario had never actually occurred, but nor had it faded from her consciousness, even after the fully clothed Priten had invited her in, leaving the door open, and coyly kicked his bedding to one side before inviting her to sit on a low stool while he sat on the floor. It was a cosy little hovel, a man-made cave lined with stone slabs that stretched into the darkness. She asked Priten if he had built it himself and he laughed at her. It was an ancient dwelling, he told her, possibly not even human in origin. There were others, scattered about the country if you knew where to look, and he knew where to look, so he made use of them in his wanderings. How had Euphemia known where to look, he wanted to know.

In her dream, though, Priten was not present. Someone or something else certainly was. Lurking in the blackness. Something not known but only dreaded. Someone calling to her. 'Euphemia! Euphemia! Euphemia!'

'Fay! Fay! Fay!' Only now it was Tes calling her, waking her with an insistent whisper, the arm that had found her in the pitch blackness resting urgently on Fay's chest, her breathy lips almost touching Fay's ear.

Slowly, Fay remembered where she was, when she was. Who she was. An ancient cave dwelling, but not Priten's, not at least the one of which she had been dreaming. It was another of the secret network of cave dwellings to which Priten had introduced her all those years ago. Or introduced Euphemia? Fay's slow inner recovery of herself took a split second of worldly time, and now here she was, in the urgent moment, Tes demanding her attention. 'Fay! Fay! Fay!'

'What is it?'

'There's someone outside! Someone trying to get in!'

Fay wriggled her elbows, shrugging Tes aside and propping herself up to attend to the disturbance. 'It's a deer,' she said after a few seconds. 'A young, clumsy one, but just a deer.'

'Are you sure?'

'Quite sure. Go back to sleep.'

Tes went back to sleep, but Fay could not. Now she was fully Fay again, and in the absence of urgent demands on her attention, her thoughts returned to Gwy. She and Tes had seen their old friend two days ago, and in her waking moments Fay had barely ceased thinking about it. Gwy was no longer the young woman they had known and loved. No longer the Daughter of the Moon, but instead the Wife of the Farmer, which is to say, a farmer's wife. They had known that already. It had been years since the priestess-bards had parted ways. But to see it was something else. They had watched Gwy in the glen below them, wandering among her new family's cows as they grazed, two small children in tow. 'Is that another one in her belly?' Tes had asked. And yes, it looked like it was. And then her husband. Fay would not have recognised Pendrin unless she had already known it was him. The youth she had once enchanted in these very woods was now a paunchy man. Gwy's husband. Fay had always assumed it would be a desperate mismatch, but – admittedly from a distance – the couple seemed to go naturally together. It was like watching a farmer and his wife who were both perfect strangers to her: of course they went naturally together.

Their lives had changed forever after two things happened almost at once. Peg had fallen ill and Gwy had fallen pregnant. The priestesses had remedies for both conditions, but then they also had charms that were supposed to prevent them in the first place. When charms failed, remedies had a tendency to do the same. Peg died within days. The others were grief-stricken, but for Gwy grief was supplemented by panic that seemed to grow in her belly along with the child. She fled to Pendrin, her sometime paramour, who could not have been the father of her child since they had not been near his family's glen for months, but who accepted her happily. This much she had told her sister-priestesses, having returned to bid them farewell. She had not said whether she had told Pendrin about her pregnancy or let him believe it was a product of their reunion. Nor did she say what his family had made of the matter. She was a stranger to them, and no longer very young. Perhaps her accidental pregnancy had come just in time for her to enjoy a normal life as a wife and mother.

Fay and Tes had not been so young either when Peg died and Gwy fell pregnant and got married. Now they were even older, well into their thirties. Still fertile, perhaps; Gwy's bump was testament to that. But marriageable? They were outsiders. Practitioners of the old religion, with no place or standing in any Christian community. And there were no communities of the old religion, not in these parts, not in the mountains and glens and woods and rivers and groves the priestesses knew, the land to which they belonged. To practise the old religion anywhere else would not be to practise it at all. They had won a following not so long ago, it was true. When young men like Pendrin were drawn to their rites, away from their farms and their churches to experience the magic of the old ways. But while not all who had felt the call of the old gods had been young men like Pendrin, it was hard to put away the suspicion that the lure of nubile women had been as important as whatever else the gods might have had to offer. As a matter of fact, when they were not bedazzling audiences in male guise, Fay and Tes were still beauties by any standard. But they would not always be so.

'At least we have each other,' Tes liked to say, and Fay would kiss her affectionately on both cheeks. But what kind of life could they have together? What becomes of ageing priestesses? What, in particular, becomes of a Sacred Virgin who is no longer young, but simply barren? Tes did not want to talk about that, but Fay kept coming back to the question like someone pushing her tongue at a loose tooth.

The Master who had instructed the young priestesses in the craft, given them their ceremonial names and roles, had never told them what would happen when their youth faded. And the Master had been gone some dozen years now. The Master who was their only connection with the old religion as it had been practised before their grandmothers and great grandmothers had been forced to accept the new religion, before the People of the Designs had lost touch with the old ways. Fay still thought of the Master often, asking him a thousand questions, though the memory of him could tell her nothing new.

The Master had claimed to be hundreds of years old. His priestesses were never sure whether or not they believed him. He was a habitual liar, and did not seem to care whether his lies were found out within days or never believed in the first place. But often, what seemed to be his most outrageous lies turned out to be true. Certainly, he had known things no one else knew, and showed the priestesses secrets that served them well long after he was gone. Like how to appear as men rather than women. Like how to perform the rites that might or might not attract onlookers bearing offerings. And how to reward those onlookers with a glimpse or more of the Dragon in the sky.

Sometimes it had been easy to believe he was hundreds of years old. And no doubt the old man had enjoyed having four nubile young women in his service, but he had never exploited them in that way; he could hardly have done so with the Sacred Virgin and kept his credibility. Because despite all the lies, in his own way, he was a man of integrity. If there was often doubt about the things he said, there was never any doubt about who he was. The Master. The keeper of the old ways. His priestesses believed in him even if no one else did. Even after he abandoned them, leaving them well enough trained in the craft to keep doing what they had been doing, but lacking the centuries-old wisdom or supernatural knowledge required to adapt to changing circumstances. Like their own transformation from ageless youths to mortal women.

Peg's death and Gwy's pregnancy had resolved matters for Peg and Gwy. Fay and Tes hung on, and hang on they could, perhaps well into their mortality. If youth and beauty had been unspoken requirements of the priestesses, no such qualifications were required of them as bards. They had always performed as men, and if handsome men, then at least handsomeness did not wither with age quite like prettiness. Fay and Tes continued to perform as a duo, and were considering taking on one or two apprentices. Perhaps that was one answer to the question of what becomes of ageing priestesses. They could devote themselves to their more mundane service as musicians and entertainers to the Christian communities of the land, who enjoyed songs and stories even if they cared little for the cycle of the moon and the unseen powers that animated the land even as they worshipped their murdered sky god. But could Fay and Tes really instruct young Christian men in the bardic craft, a craft that for them had always been bound up with both their religion and their sex? Or could they take on young women?

Might they even initiate young women as priestesses? Might they do so without a Master?

Fay must have fallen asleep as she wrestled with these thoughts, because the next thing she knew Tes awoke her again, this time by throwing open the door to their lair and letting the sun shine in. She had snuck outside to gather berries for breakfast, and she did not like to eat alone. 'The birds are calling for you,' she sang, 'and the sun is missing your lovely face!'

Fay made a not-so-lovely face, but she wriggled her toes to wake her sleep-stiffened body, and hauled herself up and outside to join Tes on the grassy slope just outside the door. At least it was a beautiful day. Fay looked up at the tree that sheltered the door, and though it was not the same door and not the same tree, she saw herself, some twenty years younger, sitting in the tree and looking down at the door. The door to her new life.

CHAPTER 44: FREIA

Freia arrived at Bamburgh Castle with trepidation. In fact, it might be more accurate to say she was delivered to the castle with trepidation, though the trepidation was very much hers rather than her delivery man's. The merchant simply dropped her off with the rest of the kitchen supplies, in the yard next to an outhouse, presumably the kitchen. He took only a little more care when lifting her down from his cart than he did with a sack of oats. 'This one's for the scullery,' he said roughly. As far as she could tell, he said everything roughly. After less than a day's acquaintance, she was glad to be rid of him, or for him to be rid of her.

'How old is she?' the steward asked, looking at her sceptically.

The merchant placed his hand roughly on Freia's head, indicating her height. 'This old,' he said, roughly.

The steward shrugged, and proceeded to ignore the girl completely while he went about his business of accounting for the less animate new supplies. Eventually he was satisfied and the merchant set off without a word to Freia. She at least had the good manners to stick out her tongue at his departing back.

'What's your name?' the steward asked at last.

'Freia,' said Freia.

'Right, well I'm Oswald, and I'm in charge of things around here.' He said this not self-aggrandizingly, but with the air of someone born to better things but now resigned to his fate. He was about the same age as Freia's mother, which is to say not yet 30. 'But all being well, you won't have much to do with me. I'm putting you in the charge of my wife Oswaldina.'

'Yes, sir,' said Freia.

'Oswaldina!'

Oswaldina appeared from inside. She was unexpectedly tall and thin, and the left side of her face was badly scarred, perhaps burnt or scalded, which made it hard for Freia to read her expression.

'This is the new scullery maid,' Oswald told her.

Oswaldina raised her good eyebrow. 'I suppose she'll grow.'

Oswald laughed. 'Name's Freia,' he added, and set about packing away the supplies without another word.

'You'd better come with me,' Oswaldina told her bluntly, but the hand she placed on Freia's shoulder transmitted more human affection than the girl had felt since leaving her mother.

Oswaldina showed Freia into the kitchen, which was dominated by a huge fireplace, huge at least by the standards of anything Freia had seen before. Two large tables were arrayed with pots, knives and other implements. Various vegetables hung from the ceiling. In one corner, steps led down into a pantry, which smelled of meat and damp, while Oswald was stacking dry goods in another corner. Oswaldina showed Freia to a door on the other side of the kitchen, which led to an outdoor area under a rough shelter, equipped with a barrel of water and a stack of other vessels of different sizes, as well as brushes and rags. 'Your own little empire,' Oswaldina said with a flourish. Freia looked about her and then curtsied awkwardly to acknowledge the joke. Oswaldina seemed pleased enough with that. 'Of course, you can sleep inside by the fire. And you'll have the place to yourself at night. There's another girl who helps here, but she sleeps in the castle itself.'

'Very good,' said Freia, though she had never slept on

her own before, and was a little afraid. 'Was there another girl before me?'

'No,' said Oswaldina, 'just me, but younger! Besides, there are more people in the castle than we've ever had before, so if anything we'll get even more help, God willing.'

'Oh, good,' Freia said, still thinking of a bedmate as much as a workmate. She had no idea what to expect of the work itself. That was to change soon enough. The king was hosting a feast.

That night, Freia slept better than she had expected. The kitchen was warm, if a little smelly, and she knew she would get used to that. The following morning, she was woken by Oswaldina and given breakfast. Oswaldina made sure Freia saw where her porridge came from and how it was made, and Freia was bright enough to realise she'd be expected to get it herself from now on. Then the other girl appeared at the door and Freia was introduced: she was Ethel.

'My mother's name is Ethel too,' Freia said.

'Is it? I don't know anyone else called Freia,' Ethel told her.

'No, it's quite old-fashioned.'

'I like it!'

Freia smiled. Ethel was a little older than her, but already seemed nice. She was the same height, but more squat, and her hair looked to be cropped under her bonnet. Ethel was more slender, with long, blonde hair of which her mother had always been proud, and which she kept in a bun under her own bonnet. She was prettier than Ethel too. These details were noticed but not discussed, as Ethel showed Freia her own duties, which were to be shared by both girls in preparation for the feast. First came the fire, then making dough for bread and batter for cakes. From the late morning onwards, Oswald appeared intermittently in the kitchen with fresh gannets, and then vegetables and finally fish, all of which Oswaldina set about preparing, drafting in the girls when she needed them. By mid afternoon, the kitchen was uncomfortably hot, and the girls stood outside in the scullery to cool down whenever they could; Oswaldina did not seem to mind the heat.

On one such break, they could see guests arrive for the feast in dribs and drabs. They all seemed very grand to Freia, but that was all she could have told you, having little sense of what to look for or notice about grand folk. The girls could also see a group of boys playing on the beach below the castle. Ethel pointed out two or three of her favourites, telling Freia their names and notable personality traits, before adding, as if it were necessary, 'I like boys. Do you like boys?'

Freia blushed and changed the subject. 'What happened to Oswaldina's face? Do you know?'

'Yes. It was a fire. Her village was burned down by Mercian soldiers. That was years ago, before she married Oswald. I think she was married to someone else, but he was killed.'

'Oh, how sad! And, tell me, was she already called Oswaldina when she married him?'

'No, I don't believe she was! I think she took his name to help forget about her old life.'

'I suppose that makes sense.'

'Look, there's Balther making a nuisance of himself as usual.'

Before Freia could observe Balther's mischief, Oswaldina called the girls back into the kitchen. Freia looked again at her scarred face and wondered if the fire had given her an unnatural tolerance for the heat of the kitchen.

The rest of the day passed in a blaze of hot toil and no little confusion, as Freia struggled with countless new and difficult tasks, but she was grateful that Oswaldina never lost her temper when even Ethel scowled in consternation at the new girl's clumsiness. It was dark when they finally finished their work, handing over to the gentler young ladies of the castle to serve the fruits of their labour – not to mention the breads and meats. All three of them sat in the scullery to cool down now, and Freia quickly fell asleep. When she awoke a few hours later, the others had returned to their quarters in the castle, and feeling a nip in the air, Freia went inside to sleep by the remains of the fire. In fact, she only half-slept, her head full of unwelcome cookery techniques and the resulting smells. She got up before dawn and found that fresh – which is to say freshly dirty – dishes had been added in the night to the pile of cooking vessels and implements they'd piled in the scullery before calling it a night. Very efficient. She had another busy day ahead of her.

Freia had been hard at work for an hour before Oswaldina appeared. 'Good girl,' she said. 'If I can spare Ethel later on I'll ask her to help you. There's a lot still to be done in the kitchen.'

Freia nodded. When Ethel did appear another hour later, though, it was to drop off yet more dirty dishes from the castle and then disappear into the kitchen. She did at least manage a sympathetic smile. So Freia laboured on. This was far from being the first hard work she'd had to do, but there was so much of it that her fingers began to blister. So when she noticed a boy of about her age watching her from the castle ramparts, she scowled moodily. He may have been one of the boys Ethel had pointed out on the beach the day before, but Freia could not remember and nor did she much care. When Ethel finally came out to help her, he disappeared. Ethel looked sympathetically at the blisters, but she was also tired from her work in the kitchen. Between them, they finished Freia's work before dark and sat down to rest.

As they rested, Ethel explained that although the feast was over, there were still more people in the castle to be fed, and she and Oswaldina had also been preparing provisions for the king and his men to take on the road. They were leaving tomorrow, with some of the guests, and riding to York. Ethel was afraid that meant there would be nearly as much washing up for Freia to do tomorrow as she had done today, but at least she would be able to help more. Freia thanked her, and said she was sure she would get better at washing up in time, so she could work faster and not need so much help.

'Where did you live before?' Ethel asked her.

'Oh, with my mother,' Freia told her. 'We live in the north, and my mother's a merchant woman. She says I'm not old enough to learn her trade yet, but now that I'm old enough for this kind of work, she decided I should earn my keep, so she sent me to work here for three years. It was a good piece of business, she said, and I suppose I'll understand about that sort of thing when I'm older and return to join her.'

'I see,' said Ethel.

'And what about you? Why do you sleep in the castle and not in the kitchen?'

'Oh, I'm an orphan,' Ethel told her. 'But my father served the king and it was decided that I belong here, so I'm allowed to sleep in the dormitory with the younger ladies of the court.'

'Is that nice?'

'It would be if they ever stopped talking!'

'Really? I think I'll have just the opposite problem. No one but mice to talk to.'

'Oh, I can't stand mice!'

'I suppose that's because you're a lady,' Freia said teasingly.

Ethel obligingly pushed her nose into the air. 'Don't worry, I'll still talk to you common folk as long as you know your place.'

'Yes, madam!'

In the weeks that followed, Freia did indeed get better at washing up, but while she needed little help from Ethel, her friend would often come to the scullery just to keep her company as she worked. And when they had time, they enjoyed walking together on the beach, sometimes watching the boys play. Occasionally, they even spoke to the boys. Ethel did not tell them Freia was the new scullery maid; she said she was a new lady at court. Freia did not know if this was intended as a joke, still less if it was taken that way. But she enjoyed it anyway. And Ethel was an outrageous flirt, so it was easy for Freia to benefit from the atmosphere of excitement she generated without having to do much more than smile and nod along.

CHAPTER 45: THE PROMISE OF MAGIC

The spider closed in on its prey in the darkness of the cave. It was a manmade cave, not that the spider knew or cared about that, and it was quite empty now. The manmade cave had been carved out hundreds of years ago, and occupied by men intermittently ever since, but it had only been home to the spider's kin for some twenty years. The spider's distant ancestor had been hiding in a fold of a girl's dress – an almost-princess's dress, not that the spider's distant ancestor had known or cared about that – when the girl had wandered into the cave at the invitation of its occupant. This occupant had once been an almost-prince, not that the spider's distant ancestor had known or cared about that either. The spider's distant ancestor had been too preoccupied with removing itself from its now worryingly turbulent hiding place, and finding a better place to hide. Our spider had no such concerns. She was intent on her food, an unfortunate insect whose ancestry need not trouble us here. So if first kisses leave an aura that lingers for decades in the place they take place, the spider was as incapable of detecting one here as she was indifferent to the romance of it. She sprang; she seized her prey. If such auras do exist, however, the one in this cave would have preserved the memory of the first kiss between a very young Euphemia and a not much older Priten.

Priten was no predator. He was thrilled to have Euphemia in his lair, but he was excited more by the fact that she had decided to track him down and shown up than by the fact she was physically within his grasp. He liked her, and wanted to find out all about her. Oh, he knew who her father was, but that did not interest him. He wanted to know about her, about what she was like, about what she thought. About why she was there. But she was the one asking the questions. What is this place? Did you build it yourself? What's down there in the dark? That kind of thing. He shifted to stand between her and the darkness, not between her and the door as a predator would have done. Still, she moved closer, curious about what was in the darkness, not minding proximity to its guardian. But suddenly she was not looking into the darkness. She was looking into Priten's eyes, and he into hers. An aura was born.

The kiss did not last long. It did not have to. Its work was done in an instant. The young lovers stood blushing at one another until Euphemia returned to the stool by the door where she had been sitting before she'd grown curious about the darkness. 'Do you have anything to eat?' she asked. 'I'm really quite hungry, you know.'

Priten produced a fine little breakfast of dried meat, nuts and berries, and as they ate, Priten sitting on the floor next to Euphemia's stool, they silently dared and double dared one another to hold the next glance a little longer. That was a happy little breakfast, which deserved a lasting aura as much as the kiss.

But nothing lasts forever. Not breakfast, not a kiss. Not the furry flesh that for a time clung to the bones of a dead lynx that would later be found in the vicinity of Euphemia's village, and, suitably rearranged, passed off as the bones of a young woman. Not very convincingly passed off, you might think, but the resemblance was enough to satisfy the cleverest man in the glen, a man of the world who also had the authority to speak for another world. Bishop Boniface gave the lucky animal a Christian burial, and with it buried the romantic rumours that were circulating about the missing princess, an unwelcome distraction from the good news of her brother's nascent kingship.

By then, Euphemia had left her family inwardly as well as outwardly, and gave little thought to her soon-to-be-late father, her soon-to-be-grieving mother or her soon-to-be-transformed brother. Taran and Brude were on the campaign against the Gaels and Northumbrians on which the former would lose his life. The latter, of course, would not see the battle in which his father died. He would be searching for his sister, and that search would take him to the court of King Gartnait, where he would encounter a seer who claimed to see Euphemia in a vision, both with child and engaged in a mysterious cosmic conflict. Which of these unlikelihoods would have seemed more far fetched to Euphemia is hard to say. And yet here she was with the seer's own son. The very son who had trained him in the art of second sight.

Euphemia had guessed Priten was a bard of some kind. Little did she know he was in fact a magician, though his lair had already given her a sense of his hidden depths. Soon enough, she would learn more, even as she fell from girlish infatuation into something more like love. As she did so, the excitement of that happy little breakfast faded and matured into a more particular but notoriously treacherous promise. The promise of magic.

Some twenty years later, in the cave now empty of human beings if not their auras, the spider carefully, lovingly, cocooned her prey.

CHAPTER 46: MARRIAGE?

After some months at Bamburgh Castle, Freia was allowed a few days' leave to visit her mother. She was to travel most of the way with a party riding to Edinburgh. It consisted of Edwin, a nobleman who was apparently close to the king, his wife Edith and his brother Ewald, a monk who had recently arrived at Bamburgh from Wearmouth-Jarrow, as well as a couple of soldiers. Edith was kind enough to let Freia ride with her; the girl had not yet grown enough to trouble the lady's horse. Freia made herself useful by cooking for the party when they stopped to camp, and endeared herself to all when she stepped in to take over when one of the soldiers was struggling to start their fire. As they ate, the brothers spoke of politics, which meant nothing to Freia, except that it was clear Edwin had important business at Edinburgh involving foreign visitors. Edith seemed unhappy about this, and kept asking 'What if this? and 'What if that?' The soldiers just played dice.

About noon on their second day of riding, Edwin asked Freia if she knew where she was. She looked about her. She was not sure, but did not want to seem helpless. 'I think so,' she said awkwardly.

Edwin pointed to some hills in the distance: 'Do you see

the gap between the rounded one and the flatter one?'

'Yes, I see.'

'Your village is just below the gap. If I'm not mistaken you'll pick up a path soon enough if you just head in that direction.'

'Yes, I remember the path,' she said, and with Edith's help she climbed down from the horse.

'Good luck,' said Edith, 'and safe journey back to Bamburgh'.

Freia curtsied her thanks and was on her way, stopping only once to look back and see the party on its own way. A nervous hour or so later, there was the path. She was home.

Freia's mother was not there when she got to their small but jolly dwelling with its distinctively colourful thatched roof, but she greeted a couple of neighbours who were working outside their own homes.

'Back from Bamburgh, lass?' asked their closest neighbour Hilda, who sat weaving in the space between their two homes.

'Just for a visit.'

'What's it like there? Did you meet the king?'

'It's very nice. I've seen the king many times, but he doesn't talk to scullery maids!'

'Not even our Freia!'

Freia blushed with embarrassment. She did not like being teased about that kind of thing. 'I did travel most of the way home with a nobleman and his party on their way to Edinburgh if that'll do.'

'Very fancy, Freia!'

'Do you know where my mother is today?'

'She was here this morning. Probably just on business locally, I should think. Do tell more while you wait.'

Freia obliged, then, taking a stool and chatting to Hilda and a couple of other neighbours who caught wind of her arrival and came to say hello. It was a couple of hours before her mother duly appeared.

When Ethel first saw her daughter waiting for her, she panicked. 'What are you doing here? Is something wrong?'

'No, Mam, nothing is wrong. I've just come home to see you!'

'They haven't sacked you, then?' Ethel asked more sarcastically, realising her daughter had not been dismissed and no one would be demanding a refund.

'No, Mam. Oswaldina says I'm a good girl, and they're pleased to have me. I'm to go back in a few days.

'Good, that's good. Then it's lovely to see you.'

'She's grown,' chimed in Hilda. 'Don't you think she's grown?'

'Stand up, lass,' said Ethel.

Freia stood up.

'I think she has,' Ethel agreed, and then said to Freia, 'They're treating you well then?'

'Yes, Mam.'

'And have you learnt useful new skills?'

'Certainly.'

'Well that's good then,' Ethel said, taking a stool of her own. She looked from Freia to Hilda and back again. 'And have I missed any news?'

'Oh, I was saving the best part.'

'Oh, yes?' the two women said as one.

'I've fallen in love,' Freia announced, and then paused for effect.

'In love?' Ethel responded, gratifyingly imbuing her voice with just the desired level of intrigue. 'Is that so?'

'Yes, I've met a boy called Alcuin, and fallen in love. And we're going to be married.'

Ethel clapped her hands together and exchanged indulgent looks with Hilda. 'Well, you'd better tell me all about it!'

'Well,' began Freia, 'Alcuin is very handsome, and very strong. And the fastest runner and the strongest wrestler of all the boys at Bamburgh.'

'That's very impressive,' Ethel said, before adding a note of caution. 'And is this Alcuin in love you with too?'

'Oh, yes,' Freia said. 'He says I'm the prettiest girl not only at Bamburgh, but in all Northumbria. Maybe the world. He says he's not sure because he's only seen Northumbria, but certainly Northumbria.'

'Well, that's a fine thing,' Ethel said, nodding along with Hilda.

'And that's not all,' Freia went on. 'He says I'm the *cleverest* girl he's ever known. Apart from his mother, and she's a grown-up, so that hardly counts.'

'No indeed,' agreed Ethel, 'and that's quite a compliment. I wonder who the boy's mother is, to be giving the boy such unusual expectations in a woman.'

'His mother is a noblewoman from the south,' Freia said with pride, though this news caused Ethel and Hilda to exchange anxious looks. The sons of noblewomen did not generally marry scullery maids. 'And his father is a famous warrior,' she added, eliciting more of the same. 'His name is Wilfrid the Mighty,' she went on, and Ethel's expression became something else entirely.

'Wilfrid the Mighty?' exclaimed Hilda. 'There's a name to conjure with!'

Ethel shot her a look.

'They say he's the greatest warrior our Lothian has ever produced,' Hilda went on. 'He used to win battles single-handed, they said. Punisher of the Picts, Basher of the Britons... Grinder of the Gaels...'

'All right, that's enough,' Ethel said impatiently. 'Freia, are you quite sure this boy is Wilfrid's son?'

'Dead sure, Mam.'

'It's time we went inside. You must be hungry, no?'

'Famished!'

As her mother prepared her broth, Freia heard her mutter to herself, as if having forgotten she was not alone. Ethel could not help it. She was in fact notorious among the villagers, and among those she traded with as a merchantwoman, for muttering to herself all day long. Perhaps Freia had not really noticed before because having been raised by a mutterer she had not thought of it as unusual – and only now, having spent time away from her mother for the first time, did it strike her as odd.

Or perhaps it was because, in the company of her young daughter, Ethel had always woven her muttering into chatter with the child – and now, having got used to being properly alone again, it would take some adjusting. After all, Freia had gone away not seeming that different to Ethel from the infant who had barely been able to talk back to her. And now she was back, not more than a few months older, but with a new confidence, a little personality of her own, a love interest. All that, in any case, was the subject of Ethel's muttering as she prepared her daughter's broth, without a thought for the fact that Freia was in the room with her. Not that Freia could make out the particulars. As she waited for her dinner, she fiddled awkwardly with a stray curl that had escaped her bonnet.

"Let's see it, then,' Ethel said as she set the food in front of her daughter.

Freia obliged by removing her bonnet and letting down her long, blonde tresses.

Her mother tutted as she pulled at some slightly matted locks. 'I'll comb it while you eat,' she said, handing the girl a wooden spoon before fetching the ornate whalebone comb she had always kept just for Freia, but not trusted her to take to Bamburgh with her. The two activities were not at all compatible, though, and Freia spilled her broth several times as her mother tugged at her hair.

'Aren't you eating?' Freia asked, hoping to distract her tormentor for long enough to eat her dinner.

'I'll eat later,' she said. But at least she had stopped muttering, even if only to chide Freia for her poor hair care.

That night, Freia was woken by her mother's muttering. Again, perhaps Ethel had always muttered in her sleep, and

Freia was only disturbed by it now because she had grown used to its absence. But perhaps her mother did not normally mutter in her sleep, but did so now because much was on her mind.

Ethel had not thought about Wilfrid for many years. Nor had she known he would be at Bamburgh when she had sent her daughter there. While the old songs were still sung, there had been no recent exploits to place Wilfrid anywhere in particular in the world of mere mortals. He was in danger of fading altogether into legend. And in any case, Ethel's particular interest in Wilfrid had rested on a certain assumption. When she had given birth to a girl rather than a boy, it had been easy to forget her promise to Thunor, that she would bring up her son to be a mighty warrior worthy of the mightiest of the old gods. That had been a youthful, foolish promise after all.

'A youthful, foolish promise,' Ethel muttered clearly enough for Freia to make out. 'What would you want with a mere girl anyway?'

Freia rolled over so her mother was behind her, and tried to go back to sleep.

In the morning, Ethel announced that she would accompany Freia when she returned to Bamburgh, and that tomorrow was as good a time as any. She had business there anyway, she said, and it was only right that she should see the place her daughter would be seeing out her childhood.

'What do you mean by that?' Freia asked.

'Well, at the end of the three years we agreed you'd work in the kitchens, you'll be a young woman.'

'I suppose so,' said Freia, blushing with discomfort.

'And if you're going to be in love and you want to get married, that's something you should look forward to.'

Freia had not really thought of it like that. 'I suppose so,' she said again, as her childish dream of marrying Alcuin and living happily ever after was transformed into something quite different. She had not expected her mother to take it at all seriously. She had expected to be indulged, or teased. She still did not really believe she would ever be a young woman, and nor did she particularly want to be one. At least, it was not something she wanted all the time, and definitely not right now. She wanted to be herself. She was happy as a little girl fantasising about love, and did not want to be a young woman forced to reckon with its realities, whatever those might be. Panic rose within her as she considered the matter, before gradually subsiding as she remembered that three years was a very long time – unimaginable, really. There would be plenty of time to get used to the idea of being a woman before it became a reality, and perhaps by then she'd find it was something she wanted more than not.

'It's not been easy for me to raise you without a father,' Ethel told her. 'It's important that we find you a suitable match in good time, so you don't end up like me. If your Alcuin is the right boy, so much the better.'

'Yes, Mam,' said Freia. She was far from being the only child she knew of with a missing parent, but she had always detected a bitterness in her mother's voice on the rare occasions that she spoke about Freia's 'father'. She had learned not to raise the matter, contenting herself with the knowledge that he had come from somewhere else and gone away again. For as long as the girl could remember, she and her mother had lived in this village, and maintained friendly relations with Hilda and the other neighbours, but her mother had never spoken warmly of them in private. She did not consider herself one of them. As a merchant woman, Ethel lived on the fringes of numerous communities rather than in the heart of any one in particular. And as worshipper of Thunor, albeit a secret one, she was an outsider in a more profound sense. Freia knew little of her mother's religion. Her various superstitions were not so different from those of the Christian villagers, and she was not above praying to the Christian saints too.

Indeed, as Ethel began the day's muttering in earnest, prayers were dispatched in all directions. She had never had

Freia christened, worrying that might be a provocation too far for the old gods. But if the girl was to marry, it would have to be a Christian marriage. And if her groom were also to be her half-brother, no one need know but Ethel and Thunor himself, who would now have two doses of warrior's blood to conjure with. It had been vain of Ethel, she now realised, to imagine it had been up to her to raise up a great warrior in Thunor's honour. Freia, too, would be no more than a vessel, Alcuin a conduit. Perhaps their issue would be the great warrior Ethel had promised and been promised. He would be christened as a matter of course, but no matter. Ethel would not try to interfere, or to whisper secrets in the babe's ear. If it was destined, then one day, somehow, he would discover his true identity.

CHAPTER 47: THEY GROW UP SO FAST

'They grow up so fast,' Mary Brigid said to Mary Caitlin, who smiled in agreement. They were watching two younger nuns instruct a new novice. Remembering themselves first as novices, then as young nuns growing in responsibility, in holiness. By the grace of the same God who now welcomed the novice into their fold, and gave their younger sisters the grace and patience to nurture her. Not that much grace was involved in the butchering of seals, though patience was certainly required of beginners. While bent over a seal carcass and pulling at a not quite severed flipper, the novice suddenly slipped and skidded into one of the young nuns by her side, causing the latter to cut herself badly with her fearsome butcher's knife.

Brigid was first to respond, rushing to her sister's aid as the novice sat where she had fallen with her hands over her mouth. 'I'm so sorry! I'm so sorry!' she squealed.

Caitlin went to her and reassured her as she helped her to her feet. The other young nun was less forgiving, scowling at the novice's carelessness until Caitlin checked her with a glare. 'Accidents happen,' she said, even as she glanced over her shoulder to gauge the seriousness of the injury.

'Aggi, help me get Mary Hilda inside,' Brigid told the

uninjured nun. Her patient had fainted. The two of them heaved her into the kitchen, Brigid taking care to keep the bandage she had improvised from her own shawl tight around the girl's hand. 'Bring me that lamp,' she told Aggi, 'and then some water.'

The injury was not as bad as Brigid had feared. It had looked like the thumb might be in a similar state to the seal's flipper, but it was mostly secured as God intended, just badly cut. Brigid washed the wound and rebandaged it with the cleanest rag Aggi could find in the kitchen. The rest of the healing process was up to God himself, but they could pray, and Brigid cuddled the now fully conscious Mary Hilda and sang her a little song, which helped return the pinkness to her hitherto rather green face.

Later, Brigid discussed the matter with Caitlin. The latter was worried about the novice, whose complexion had not yet recovered from the incident. 'There's a shadow over that girl,' Caitlin said. 'You know how fierce Aggi can be. I think that look shocked the girl more than the injury.'

'I can believe it,' said Brigid. 'Aggi and Mary Hilda are still like natural sisters.'

Brigid spoke as someone who remembered with fondness her own natural sister (actually adoptive, but that had never mattered) but had not seen her for two decades. And Caitlin was no closer to her own natural sisters, if she had any. They were all nuns together; 'natural sisters' was simply the most convenient way to describe the particular bond between these two younger nuns, who had arrived together at Iona from the same remote island and had even shared the same name. They had been given such different religious names in part to dissolve their natural bond, the better to integrate them into their new community, but they remained as close as ever. Sister Aggi loved Sister Mary Hilda in a way that had made her hate her other sister, the clumsy novice who had caused her injury, but who deserved Aggi's love and sympathy no less. Even as Brigid and Caitlin spoke, Aggi was praying in penitence. Caitlin's worry was that the novice was doing the same.

'False penitence is a terrible thing,' Brigid agreed, 'and in this case a species of pride.'

'I told her that,' Caitlin said, 'and she begged forgiveness for that too, but I don't believe she sees the difference'.

'What's the girl's name?' Brigid asked, suddenly aware that she did not know.

'You know, I don't know either,' Caitlin admitted. 'I don't believe she has yet taken a religious name and I could not tell you her given name. She came here alone in the winter, so she has no contemporaries to be distinguished from, so we just call her "lass" or "girl" or "pet"'.

'The poor thing.'

'Indeed. We must remedy this.'

But then the business of the Abbey took over, and the novice remained nameless until both Mary Caitlin and Mary Brigid had forgotten she was nameless.

◆ ◆ ◆

Morgan watched Moses chopping wood. It was a marvellous sight. It had been several years since the boy had outgrown his mother in height, but since then he had grown in all sorts of ways that did not merely surpass Morgan's slight physique, but bypassed it completely. He was like a different species. Of course, Morgan knew what a grown man looked like even if she had never known a grown man, in particular not known the prototype from whom Moses took his particular shape, Moses' father. She could only suppose he would once have looked like Moses. The way the boy wielded the axe was not the way Morgan had tried to teach him, the way her mother had taught her to do it. His body seemed to know how to do it as his father would have done it. How to chop wood like a man.

When Moses smiled or frowned, sometimes Morgan

saw herself in him, could feel what it was like to make a particular expression. In particular there was the glowering smile from behind hooded eyelids. That had come from Morgan's mother, who had helped raise him and lived to see him chop wood like a man before she had died. But at other times, Moses made faces all of his own. She wondered if those were from his father. She did occasionally see a look on Moses' face that reminded her of Gawin, but no, those were mannerisms rather than glimpses of anything deeper. Moses had literally learned them from Gawin along with his letters. For the past few years, Moses had been apprenticed to a blacksmith in Govan. From him he had learned the basics of the craft, and no doubt some choice language he knew better than to use in front of his mother. He was a young man now, and not so impressionable as he had once been. Morgan wondered if that should make it easier to discern the original influence, the one that had shaped him before the world, before Gawin, before their family. But when she looked at him, she saw only her Moses, a young man now, but no less hers for that.

Morgan had always been honest with Moses about his origins, about how things were in their family, so she had always been clear that she did not know his father. His father's identity was a mystery. But she did at least acknowledge that he had a father. Every child had a mother and a father: Morgan was Moses' mother and his father was missing, unknown. It had actually never occurred to Morgan that Moses would also have a mother who was missing, unknown. Because it had never occurred to her that Moses had been conceived in the animal way before being delivered to her. The mechanics of the family tradition were mysterious and never discussed. As far as Morgan was concerned, she was Moses' mother, and that was that. As Moses had spent more time in Govan and been introduced to the ways of the world, he had begun to question all this. Not out loud, not to Morgan. Moses loved his one and only mother and would not say anything that might hurt her feelings. But he did wonder if he had another, missing mother as well as a missing father. He wondered if he had more than one original influence, a second source that was not so much a prototype like his father, from which his male body had taken its shape, but one that had perhaps contributed to his face, his expressions, to who he was even.

Moses enjoyed the work at the forge. It was hard work, but he found it satisfying, just like chopping wood. It was hot, but he did not mind that either. You could always stand outside for a few minutes to cool down, and in the shadow of the awning on those rare days when the sun made Govan its anvil. And on some days, if you were lucky, when you stood outside for a few minutes to cool down, you could exchange pleasantries with the blacksmith's daughter, a small, dark girl with bulging eyes and a keen sense of humour. Moses was hopelessly in love with Martha.

Inconveniently, Martha was betrothed to Ieuan, one of Moses' former classmates and a great nephew of Rhodri. Moses did not dislike Ieuan, but the two young men were very different. Moses was physically strong, of course; a blacksmith had to be that. But there was a gentleness about him too. While he had not fulfilled his childhood ambition of becoming a monk, he remained as pious and indeed as unworldly as ever. Part of what he liked about working in the forge was that there was not much talking. The blacksmith occasionally bellowed over the din to instruct his apprentice, but for the most part the two men bashed away wordlessly, and Moses set his mind on the things above, distracted only by occasional thoughts of Martha, or thoughts about his thoughts of Martha, or about this and that. Ieuan was much more of a talker, a charmer indeed, who made men laugh as easily as he made girls giggle. And he was handsome, attractive to women where Moses was merely sweet. And, to cap it all, he was valiant. As was befitting a young man of a wealthy and influential family – more wealthy and more influential than ever thanks to his Great Uncle Rhodri – he had been apprenticed not to a forge, but to the Rock. He was a warrior, and had proved himself in battle more than once. He was just the kind of young man girls wanted to marry. Moses knew this, of course, but he could not let go of the hope that perhaps Martha loved him and not Ieuan, and that somehow they would be married instead. He told no one of this, least of all Martha.

'What's on your mind?' she asked him now as he rested now outside the forge. 'I often wonder what you're thinking about when you look into the distance all dreamily like that.'

He did not answer, 'I'm dreaming of you, my beloved. I'm dreaming that one day you'll be mine, and perhaps your father will ask me to take over the forge and I can ask my old mother to come and live with us so I can look after her. But mostly I'm just thinking of you, of your beauty, of the way you laugh like a little waterfall and how much I want to kiss you.' Instead, he gave her a detailed description of the job he was currently doing for her father, making metal supports for the new doors of the church.

'Oh,' said Martha, 'that's interesting.'

Ieuan had rather more interesting things to say to Martha. Ieuan was much enamoured of the legends of King Arthur and his knights. That was natural enough for a young warrior of the Rock, but he also had a gift for storytelling. He regaled Martha with tales of derring do, of brave knights and fair ladies and noble quests, and when he talked like that she could not help but giggle and enjoy it despite herself. Despite herself because she did not really love Ieuan. Not the way she loved Moses, or at least the version of Moses who had taken hold of her imagination. When he stood looking dreamily into the distance, he was surely thinking of something other than metal door supports. But then perhaps not. Perhaps she was fooling herself that there was something else going on in there. She knew for a fact that Moses was more pious than Ieuan and she liked that. She thought it right that a man should be devoted to God, if only because it would make him a better husband. Moses did not join in with the rude jokes of the other young men. The rude jokes that admittedly made Martha laugh when Ieuan told them, but of which she nevertheless thoroughly disapproved. She almost felt sorry for the other young men who saw Ieuan charming the ladies with such vulgarity, and imagined they could do the same. When they told the same jokes, it made Martha's skin crawl. Ieuan had the charm to get away with it. But best of all was Moses, who did not make such jokes at all. Moses, who looked at her like that from behind those hooded eyelids. Moses, the infant foundling with the strange mother and utterly mysterious father. Moses who was not quite of Govan, not quite of anything Martha had ever known. Yes, it was Moses she loved.

CHAPTER 48: EDINBURGH

Constantine and his men arrived at Edinburgh just before nightfall. They were expected, but their welcome was not warm. A party of soldiers rode out to meet them and escort them up the hillside to the fortress that sat atop the rock of the east, the rock that had lost its capital status when Gododdin had been conquered and it had become the northern stronghold of the Northumbrians. They were here to discuss the Rock of the west, which held out still against the People of the Designs, who sought it as their southern stronghold. Their Northumbrian hosts had agreed to help them and take their own share of the spoils, on the understanding that the new frontier would be permanent. 'Pictish expansion' would stop with Alt Clut. Perhaps that was why they made sure their guests felt like anything but conquerors here in Edinburgh. The outriders brashly pointed weapons, grunted warnings, spoke among themselves with no regard for the dignity of their guests. They clearly wanted Constantine and his men to feel like vassals, admitted grudgingly to plea for help, and as likely to be flogged and dismissed as offered hospitality, agreement or not. Constantine swore under his breath.

An hour later, he and his lieutenant-cum-interpreter

Agron were greeted in the castle's great hall by Lord Edwin, representative of King Eadberht. Angered by the attitude of their escort, Constantine had prepared a speech to the effect that he was not here to negotiate. He was no diplomat and he did not speak for King Onuist (nor even King Brude). His understanding was that an alliance had already been agreed, and his orders were simply to discuss logistics. That he could do.

Edwin immediately disarmed him by greeting him warmly in his own language. 'You are most welcome,' he said, 'and I trust you and your men will be comfortable here. To that end, I am at your service.'

Constantine thanked him and said he hoped they would not trouble their hosts for long. Then, worrying this sounded ungracious, he added, 'It's nice to be here'.

Edwin smiled and then threw Constantine even more by making a pun on his language's words for 'rock' and 'nice'. 'But if you'll forgive me,' he went on, 'I must switch to my own language for the benefit of our friends.' He looked around, drawing attention to the assembled Northumbrian captains. Constantine nodded his assent, and nodded again to acknowledge the others, who did likewise. Edwin continued, 'And this way, your comrade's presence will not be in vain,' and only then began speaking in the Northumbrian tongue.

Agron translated: 'I suggest we get down to business.'

'Good.'

Ewald watched the proceedings keenly from the edge of the hall, keeping a respectful distance as a someone without military knowledge or authority. Their party had arrived at Edinburgh only a matter of hours before their Pictish guests, having been delayed on the way. And the last of the captains who had been summoned had arrived shortly after the Picts, so Ewald had not yet had an opportunity to greet his old friend, if old friend was what he was. That captain, of course, was none other than Cuthbert.

Cuthbert eyed up Constantine as he spoke. He had the

look of a veteran soldier, a certain world-weariness tempered by the deep, existential patience that comes with few activities other than military campaigning. Which is to say Cuthbert saw himself in Constantine. The latter was too much on guard to see himself in Cuthbert or anyone else. He did notice Ewald lurking in the shadows, registering with suspicion the presence of a churchman. Cuthbert and the other captains were at least soldiers like him, but not necessarily men like him.

The basic plan he proposed was little different from the last time a concerted attack had been attempted. Of course, Constantine had not been with his people's main attacking force that time. He had been with King Brude, tangling with stray Gaels while the main force was routed by the remarkably well-informed Men of the Rock. And of course, Cuthbert had also missed out on that attempt on the Rock. Indeed, no Northumbrian had seen action that day, so nobody minded if the plan lacked novelty. It was more or less dictated by geography anyway. Northumbrian forces were neither needed nor wanted to support the main body of the Pictish army attacking from the north. They were to attack from the south and the east and to seize control of the river. Cuthbert wondered if he would at least get that far this time. Constantine did not react when one of the other Northumbrians made a crack about having to show up early this time so as not to miss out again. Not even when the same captain referred to 'King Talorgan… Sorry, King Onuist'. That matter was settled now, regardless of what anyone suspected or indeed knew pretty certainly to be a fact. And Constantine had a thick skin when it came to things that were none of his business. Edwin did react to that, though, shooting his compatriot an angry glance. But the plan was agreed, and did not require the People of the Designs and the Northumbrians to pledge to be bosom friends forever.

When Edwin announced the meeting was over, servants came in to prepare the hall for supper to be served, and the ladies of the court also began to drift in from the anteroom where they had been entertaining themselves. Ewald stepped out of the shadows and made straight for Cuthbert. He thought it better to get the awkwardness over with. And indeed, if anyone had a right to be less than friendly, it was he. The one who had witnessed the unexpected murder all those years ago, not the one who had committed it. Cuthbert was surprised to see him, but not startled: 'Ewald,' he said, 'it's been a long time.'

'Indeed. It's good to know you're still alive.'

Cuthbert smiled enigmatically. He had come close to death many times, and could hardly say he did not deserve it. 'How are things at Lindisfarne?' he asked.

'Oh, it's also been a long time since I was part of that community, though all was well when I visited on the way here from Jarrow, where I've been since… Well, since not long after we last spoke.'

'I see,' said Cuthbert, surmising that Ewald's relocation around that time may not have been a coincidence, but demurring to enquire further.

'My brother Edwin resides at Bamburgh,' Ewald added, gesturing to where Edwin stood deep in conversation with Constantine.

'Ah! Now that you mention it, I see the resemblance.'

'He mentioned that you would be here, that you'll command a company in the campaign.'

'Indeed. If you stay in any line of work for long enough, you get good enough to instruct others. Including the church, I suppose?'

'Yes, I suppose so. I wondered if you'd go back to soldiering, or… Well, I didn't know.'

'I've tried my hand at many trades, but this one won't seem to let me go. ..And now here's my commander, your brother.'

Edwin had indeed mingled his way over. 'Oh, I won't be commanding anyone when it matters,' he said, taking

Cuthbert's arm in greeting, 'but I'm happy to meet you. It's always good to be able to put a face to a name one has heard so much about.' Cuthbert and Ewald both looked somewhere between awkward and mortified by this apparent lapse in Edwin's diplomatic guile, but the lord continued without seeming to notice. 'And I can assure you that your name is well known to me from the good report of those who have been worthy to command you in recent years. I do not pretend to be ignorant of other matters, but they need not concern us now.'

Cuthbert nodded gratefully. He was not in fact widely known as the slayer of Offa son of Aldfrith, but – having discovered Lord Edwin was Ewald's brother – he did feel better knowing he knew of the incident rather that being left in doubt. Maybe Edwin was a decent diplomat after all.

Ewald excused himself.

'I understand you are proficient in the Gaelic tongue,' Edwin told Cuthbert.

Cuthbert confirmed this in Gaelic, having been impressed by Edwin's evident grasp of Pictish and curious to know just how multilingual the diplomat was.

'Oh, I merely dabble,' Edwin said, also in Gaelic. 'It's good to know we have a captain who is fluent, given the role played by our Gaelic friends in the last attempt on the Rock. This time, though, we are hopeful that a substantial faction of Gaels will join our assault.'

'I'll be happy to help any way I can,' Cuthbert said in their own tongue, having had his fun. Edwin would never be taken for a Gael, but nor was he likely to struggle to be understood by one.

'I'd like to introduce you to our guest,' Edwin said, and coaxed a slightly reluctant Cuthbert over to where Constantine and his interpreter stood awkwardly with the most senior Northumbrian captains. They had already exhausted the conversation by asking Constantine if he had fought at the fateful battle when Prince Talorgan (no mistake this time) had been slain. He had simply lied, telling them that, yes, he had been in the thick of it that terrible day, and looked forward to having his revenge by seizing the Rock from the Britons once and for all.

Cuthbert noticed the brooch that fastened Constantine's cloak, an impressive thing of unmistakeably Gaelic design. He complimented its owner via his interpreter and asked its provenance, assuming it would be war booty. Constantine explained that his king had married a princess of Dunadd, and she had given it to him as a mark of gratitude after he had saved the royal couple's favourite hunting dog from a wild boar. (This was true.)

'How funny,' Lord Edwin said. 'My men and I ran into a wild boar on the road today. Quite literally. One of my soldiers rode over it and came off his horse. God alone knows what drove the animal into our path like that.'

'Is the man all right?' asked one of the senior captains.

'Badly bruised,' Edwin answered, 'and it was some time before he quite recovered his senses, which is why we were delayed, but nothing broken it seems. He'll live.'

'And the horse?' Constantine asked. Through his interpreter, it was hard to tell whether he asked from compassion or out of mischief.

'Happily, the horse is unscathed,' Edwin answered in a tone appropriate to either, 'which is more than can be said for the boar.' With providential timing, the roast boar was now brought in on a great platter. 'Shall we?'

CHAPTER 49: SISTER LUCKY

After evening prayers, and her light duties discharged, something made Brigid wander towards the bay on the ocean side of the island. Being summer, it was still light, but the sun was beginning to set, and it was indeed beautiful, but that was not why she was there. Brigid's eyes were drawn not to the light playing on the ocean, but to the sea itself, to a figure in the sea, not far from the shoreline but moving steadily away from it. Brigid sped up, clambering down the hillside that led to the ocean, until she could identify the figure.

It was the troubled young novice, the one who had been under a shadow since the accident in the seal yard. She was walking, slowly but determinedly, deeper and deeper into the ocean, the waves lapping about her so their watery darkness climbed ever higher up her light brown robe. Brigid did not hesitate, but ran as fast as she could down the beach and into the water. 'Sister, no!' she shouted as she splashed through the shallows, 'sister, no!' Then she slipped and lost her footing, falling face first into the freezing water, and when she recovered herself she saw that the novice was almost out of her depth. Brigid had never swum before, but now she found herself powering towards the novice with great bounding strokes of her arms and legs that lifted her over the surface of the water. She reached the novice just as the latter was struggling to keep her head from going under. Or at least part of her was. As Brigid had been swimming towards her, the novice had kicked away hard from the last solid ground beneath her in a bid to put the matter out of her own control, and her animal will to live had begun to assert itself, testing whether her conscious will had done enough. But the battle was not over.

Any sea creature with the wits to read a woman's face would have seen the novice's contorted with ultimate conflict as she forced herself face-first into the water, gurning for death, only to crane suddenly upwards, her eyes rolling desperately as she reached splutteringly for the surface. And again. And again. Until, on her fourth ascent, she collided with the shadow of an angel. Her body was no longer her own, but was swept up into the angel's, whose legs arced elegantly through the water, taking the novice's with them until both bodies were flat on the surface of the water and the angel's legs powered them back to the shore. Back to life.

Brigid laid the now compliant novice face down on the beach, and encouraged her to cough up the sea water that had begun to drown her. As she did so, Brigid took a moment to recover from her own exertions, if indeed the exertions had been her own, but now was not the time to contemplate that. She saw a figure in the distance, walking along the top of the beach, and called for help. The figure was soon at their side. It was Brother Paul.

'Please fetch a blanket,' Brigid asked him, 'she's frozen'.

'You must be too,' he said, and made as if to remove his own robe to warm her, before thinking better of it. Instead, he ran off with the swiftness of an angel, a land angel this time, returning a few minutes later with blankets, fresh water and Sister Mary Caitlin, with two more nuns in tow.

Brigid now lay all but on top of the novice to conserve what warmth remained in her, stroking her hair and singing to her as she had sung to Mary Hilda, the young nun for whose injury the novice blamed herself. The young nun whose wound had become infected, and who had died just two days before.

The nuns wrapped the exhausted novice in one of the blankets, and Paul lifted her onto his shoulder and began carrying her back to the nunnery. They put the second blanket around Brigid, who drank thirstily before gesturing that she was ready to follow Paul, and the nuns began trudging up the beach. Two more monks had appeared, having heard the commotion, but Paul declined their offer of help and continued with the novice as far as the nuns' refectory. By now the other two nuns had caught up with him as instructed by Mary Caitlin, and took their sister from him and over the threshold. Paul waited by the door to satisfy himself that Brigid was all right, before taking his leave and joining his brothers to return to their more mundane evening duties.

Once inside, the nuns took the wet clothes from Brigid and the novice. Brigid was given a dry robe, the shivering novice simply wrapped in more blankets to warm her up and laid on a bench near the fire. 'I'll stay with her,' Brigid told Caitlin.

'You've done well enough so far,' Caitlin said by way of agreement, and genuflected solemnly as she muttered a prayer for the novice and her nurse, before going back to her own more immediate business.

Brigid pulled up a stool so she could sit by her patient and make her drink a little water. Then, for the first time since pulling her from the sea, she looked her in the eye, demanding her full, conscious attention. 'You have committed the gravest of sins, sister! The gravest of sins!'

The novice began to cry, and Brigid wiped the tears from her face even as she held her gaze. 'Even if you had killed Mary Hilda with your own hands, which you did not, you belong to Christ, and you must lay your sins on him! Including this one! This gravest of sins that you have committed because you lack faith, because you insist on storing up your own sins, real and imagined, as if you could be expected to atone for them apart from Christ and his church. Pray with me, sister, pray for the faith that you lack!'

Suddenly the novice responded, crying out: *'Credo! Adiuva incredulitatem meam!* I believe, Lord! Help my unbelief!'

'Good girl,' said Brigid, taking to her knees and leading the girl in prayer. This went on for several hours, until zeal gave way to exhaustion and Brigid told the girl to go to sleep, waiting only to see that she did so with a look of peace not seen since the accident, before curling up on the floor next to her patient's bench and going to sleep herself. As she slept, Brigid dreamt she was the one Paul had taken in his strong, manly arms and carried on his shoulders. Carried who knew where? Somewhere warm and happy. But even within the dream, she knew it was a harmless whimsy and it did not trouble her. Soon she was dreaming she was a dolphin, frolicking merrily on the waves to celebrate God's Creation.

After dawn prayers, the novice was seen by the Abbess, and it was agreed that, in addition to other remedial measures, she would continue to receive spiritual counsel from Sister Mary Brigid.

'Then why did she have to die?' the novice demanded at last, having skirted around the question for some time.

'God said, "I will have mercy on whom I have mercy, and I will have compassion on whom I have compassion." It is not for us to puzzle over such things. You must know, sister, that I cannot swim in water any more than you can swim in water. And yet here I am, and here you are. Is that not a miracle for which we must be grateful?'

'I am grateful,' the novice insisted, 'but if God wants me to live, does he not also want me to ask why?'

'Perhaps he does, but I don't believe he wants you to ask me, because I don't know what to tell you other than that God loves you, and I know that will not satisfy you coming from me. You must pray, girl, pray…' Brigid stopped, realising what she still did not know. 'What is your name, girl?'

'My name?'

'You have a name, don't you?'

'I've not yet taken a religious name,' the girl said sheepishly.

'Yes, that much I knew, dear,' Brigid said, 'but what did your people call you?'

The girl looked at Brigid as if relieved that someone had finally asked, but Brigid could not be sure that was not her imagination. 'Shonagh,' she said at last. 'Actually, they called me Little Shonagh, because when I was really little, another Shonagh came to live on our island, and she was a princess. And pregnant with twins at the time.'

'So she was Big Shonagh?'

'Yes,' Little Shonagh said, laughing, 'she certainly was.'

'Well, Little Shonagh, I think you have a lot of praying to do.'

'Yes, Sister Mary Brigid.'

The two sisters prayed together for several hours, then, alternating between psalms and silent supplication. When she sensed the novice was flagging, Brigid brought their prayers gradually to a close and announced they would rejoin the other sisters in the day's monastic routine, which of course included many more prayers. They followed the same pattern for several more days, until at the end of their time together one morning, Little Shonagh announced she was ready to affirm her vocation once and for all take by taking a religious name.

'Have you considered a name you might like?' Brigid asked her. 'Is there a saint with whom you can strongly identify?'

'No, none in particular,' the novice said. 'I think you should name me.'

Brigid thought for a moment, remembering how she had somehow found it in herself to pluck this girl from the sea, just as she herself had once been plucked from the sky, before pronouncing, 'I shall call you Sister Lucky.'

'Very good, sister. I like it.'

CHAPTER 50: DONUEL THE CUNNING

Ewald arrived back at Jarrow late at night. The following day he reported to the Abbot with news from Edinburgh, as well as Magilros and Lindisfarne, having visited both abbeys on his return journey. In addition to the impending war, there were various items of church business to discuss, so Ewald almost forgot that he also had a letter for Brother Martin. And though he was reminded when he saw the scholar during lunch, the monks remained silent as they ate, so with various other distractions getting in the way, it was only on the third day after his return that Ewald finally found a suitable opportunity to hand over the letter.

'It makes no difference,' Martin said, dismissing Ewald's apologies. 'When you spend your days reading about things that happened hundreds of years ago, you develop a different perspective on time. This letter itself has probably been in transit for months if not longer. Another few days will do no harm.' Absently, he placed the letter on top of a pile of documents on his desk, as if indeed he might not read it for many more days or even weeks. He was a scholar, after all, and not a soldier awaiting orders or a merchant fulfilling them.

Nor even a monk like Ewald with worldly responsibilities. Martin spent those hours not taken up by monastic routine immersed in the past, communing across the centuries and across Christendom with scholars who had lived much like himself, doubly removed from worldly concerns. There's was a vocation within a vocation, a retreat within a retreat. The light from the narrow window of Martin's little study was fading now, but it would be back. Time was not of the essence.

When Ewald had left, however, it was not long before Martin picked up the letter and broke its seal, perhaps less from any worldly urgency than precisely from a desire to escape into the ages. Ewald's visit, however welcome, had been an interruption, leaving him distracted. He put the letter down again and lit a candle slowly and carefully, relishing the ritual, the smell of the ages, before setting the candle in its holder and picking up the letter. But as he began to read, his consciousness was snatched from the ages and thrust into the here and now, or at least into a very particular there and then. The then being some ten years ago when the letter had been written, shortly after a royal wedding. And then, almost immediately, Martin's consciousness drifted back another decade to when he himself had left the there. The there being his homeland. Or rather, not Martin's homeland, but the homeland his former self had left behind, some twenty years ago, with his former name. It was less familiar name, however, that got his attention. 'King Brude,' he said out loud, weighing each word deliberately. He glanced out of the narrow window, where stars were now visible in the deep blue sky, as if he wanted to share the joke with the divine comedian who had made it. 'King Brude.'

◆ ◆ ◆

Dyrael watched the twins scrubbing down their father's horse. They worked well together, not squabbling or bickering like many siblings, but in harmony, with unity of purpose, however mundane. Dyrael was proud of that. Proud of her son and daughter, who remained in harmony even as they grew into a young man and a young woman, no longer just 'the twins', but Talorgan and Mary. They were the eldest of their generation, and beloved of their younger cousins, much as their father had been beloved of their cousins' fathers. Dyrael could see Constantine in both of them. His easy bearing belied by his quiet watchfulness. Mary would be fine, but Dyrael worried about Talorgan. She did not want him to follow in his father's footsteps by becoming a warrior. Until now the possibility had been mentioned only in jest. She did not know what her husband really thought about it. But watching her son groom his father's horse, now tall enough to do so comfortably, made Dyrael uncomfortable.

Constantine had returned for just a couple of days. It would have made more sense to ride straight from the Northumbrian border garrison along the great eastern river to where the main body of King Onuist's forces was assembling. Instead Constantine had sent his men ahead while he himself crossed the river as soon as was practicable, and headed north to see his family. To be with his wife, however fleetingly. Dyrael was glad of that, but part of her worried it was bad luck, too much like goodbye. She had searched Constantine's expression for signs of a premonition, but she saw only his desire for her, a desire without worry or foreboding. She had sent him to wash and rest himself while the twins saw to his horse and she turned things over in her mind. She knew her kinswoman Gwy had once dabbled in the old religion. She thought of asking her to divine the future, but that was a wicked thought. She tried instead to put her faith in God.

When Constantine was not being comforted by his wife, he was too haunted by the past to worry about the future. No particular trauma, just year after year of bloodshed, bones shattered, secrets and lies. His dreams were mostly nightmares, but only vaguely nightmarish, and more like memories of summers past than of any particular summer, an atmosphere of dread grown too familiar to generate fear.

Only now, having dozed off, Constantine was taken back to one particular day some twenty years ago. The day he and Brude had set off from this very farm for Brude's own home, only to be intercepted at the top of the little mountain by Brude's family serving boy Kenny, who had been waiting for them for days. He warned Brude that his father was dead and his uncle planned to kill him. There was nothing to do but to flee. For Brude, that is, there was no decision to make. Constantine still remembered the look of horror on young Kenny's face when he realised his master's friend was going to abandon him. That, in fact, was almost the whole substance of the dream. A boy of ten or eleven, aghast that his own unquestioning and unwavering loyalty was not shared by his master's comrade in arms, a noble warrior now revealed to be without honour. In the dream, the boy's face was Constantine's own, contorted by sudden disillusionment.

There had been no such emotion from Brude. After all, they had just left Constantine's family, who owed fealty to whomever succeeded Taran as the local strongman. If that were his brother rather than his son, who were they to question it? Who was Constantine, noble warrior or otherwise? The two friends shook hands, and Brude lifted Kenny onto his horse and rode south. That had been that. And that had been the unembellished substance of Constantine's report to Brude's uncle on arrival at the village. For once, there had been no need for secrets or lies. Of course, Boniface also had news for Constantine, news of a secret and a lie he now had no choice but to make his own. King Brude.

Constantine still owed fealty to the old friend who bore the name of the third friend they had both abandoned, but he now spent more time in the service of the High King to whom Brude in turn owed fealty. Or at least to the king who bore the name Onuist, even if he had once been Talorgan, like Constantine's son. And, no, Constantine did not want his son to follow in his footsteps, on that tangled path through treacherous bogland, at the end of which you would be lucky if you remembered your own name.

◆ ◆ ◆

When King Brude dreamt, sometimes he was King Brude, and sometimes he was Donuel the Cunning. Not the young Donuel the Cunning who had been a friend to Brude and Constantine before taking on his new identity, but another Donuel the Cunning. One who had actually been cunning enough to get out of Boniface's absurd masquerade and gone on to live a life of his own. In fact, those dreams more often came to him as daydreams. Which is to say they did not come to him at all: he sought them out, preferring his imaginary life as carefree Donuel to his actual life as king, or rather king in name only, and not even his own name.

In theory, Brude was underking to King Onuist, and in fact he had more lands than most of his peers, which yielded healthy tribute, but while he was free to enjoy his wealth, in political terms, his real master was Bishop Boniface. Brude's kingship was useful to his bishop, whose own ambitions had always been to the fore, even if there were largely inscrutable to his king. It was Boniface who managed relations with King Onuist and with his other underkings, as well as the various foreigners with whom he corresponded, ostensibly on behalf of his king, and whom he occasionally presented to Brude, who was expected to nod politely and keep his mouth shut. Half the time, the silent king would be away in his happy place anyway, his backside on the throne of King Brude, his mind roaming the mountains on horseback as Donuel the Cunning, valiant warrior, protector of fair maidens and scorner of bishops and their ungodly schemes. Indeed, the only time Brude actually felt close to God was when he was far from the bishop, galloping through the glens on his actual, flesh-and-blood horse. Naturally enough, the bishop also managed his king's relationship with the church, but he could not stand between the man and his maker when he and his beast filled their nostrils with the rushing air they'd been created to enjoy.

At first, the newly anointed King Brude had imagined things would change over time. That he would gradually learn to assert himself, become king in more than name. Then perhaps it would not matter that it was not his own name. After all, he was not yet 20 for the first few years of his kingship. There was no disgrace in having a mentor. And it was not that Boniface was a bad mentor. He treated his king with respect, never talking down to him in front of others, and condescending only constructively and in private. So King Brude did learn from his bishop-mentor. He learned about politics, at least in the sense of protocol, but that is to say what he learned was really how to perform the role Boniface had ordained for him. He never had any idea what Boniface himself was up to. When the bishop's schemes and the king's own wishes came into alignment, it was purely by coincidence.

The high point of Brude's kingship, the happiest coincidence, had been his marriage to Princess Bronagh ten years into his reign. It was a political match, of course, but there was nothing forced about the smiles, blushes and lingering looks witnessed by their wedding guests. They were indeed happy together, bonding over mutual language lessons, and by a shared love of riding and hunting with dogs, until Bronagh was forced to give that up when she became pregnant. They were both thrilled about the baby. But there was to be no baby. Bronagh died in childbirth, and her baby with her. And something in her husband died too.

Perhaps it would have been a blessing if that something had been King Brude, liberating Donuel to run away, hide under a rock and grieve the one thing that had made his life as Brude worthwhile, and then gone off to live that life of his own. It might even have been a blessing if the bereavement had finished off what was left of Donuel, what might have been of Donuel, and left Brude to take ownership of his situation, with a harder heart, perhaps, but also with some kind of resolve. Instead, Donuel-Brude sank into double despair.

So, after nearly twenty years on the throne, half of them spent waiting for his kingship to become real somehow and half pining for what might have been, whether as king or free man, King Brude was not afraid to die. And maybe he would die in battle, like a proper king. For battle loomed. He had insisted on leading his own contingent of men to join King Onuist's forces preparing to attack Alt Clut, and for real this time. 'Insisted' at least in the sense that he had made it clear this was his intention, and Boniface had agreed after only a mild show of resistance. Clearly, it was also Boniface's intention, but still. There would be no foolish schemes, no sideshows, no pretence. King Brude would lead his men into battle, seeking death or glory. As he rode south, for once the king did not feel the need to fantasise about being someone else. Not even his true self. He fully inhabited his role.

CHAPTER 51: BAMBURGH

Ethel and Freia arrived at Bamburgh at a good time. A splendid-looking company of soldiers was about to leave for Alt Clut, as much to dignify the campaign with King Eadberht's own royal seal as to reinforce the already substantial Northumbrian force closing on the Rock of the west. The king himself was inspecting his men as mother and daughter were admitted through the castle gates, and Freia nonchalantly pointed him out on their way to the kitchens. Ethel pretended not to be impressed, but he was the king, after all, and his height and looks did not disappoint.

This was more than could be said for the shabby figure who had arrived at the castle almost at the same time, but humbly stepped aside to let the ladies go first – a gesture befitting a monk, which was what he was. He had then presented his credentials and shuffled in without drawing much attention at all. Nor, surely, would he stay for long, Freia had told her mother. Bamburgh was a convenient final stop for monks travelling from the south up to Lindisfarne; the food was better here, but that would be where he was headed. The monk was now standing and admiring the king's soldiers, no doubt in awe of their splendour; this was not a sight a mere monk saw every day.

'You chose a fine day to return,' said Oswaldina, greeting Freia outside the kitchen from where she too was enjoying the spectacle, 'though we could have used you yesterday and the day before, with an army to feed!'

'I'm sorry to have missed the action,' Freia said briskly. 'This is my mother.'

Oswaldina and Ethel bowed politely to one another, but neither said anything. Freia realised Ethel was uncomfortably out of place, and for the first time ever she felt protective of her mother, which in turn made her feel both proud and a little guilty for enjoying it.

'If it's all right with you,' she said to Oswaldina, 'I'll just give my mother a quick tour. She'll have to leave first thing in the morning, so there's not much time.'

'Of course,' Oswaldina said.

Ethel was surprised to find herself impressed by her daughter's palpable feeling of ownership of Bamburgh, albeit from a lowly vantage point. Her tour began with the kitchens, where the highlights included the temporarily depleted larder – Oswald was in there taking inventory – and the fireplace where they would spend their final night together before Ethel departed. Then they circled the yard so Freia could point out various other parts of the castle. The soldiers had by now trooped out of the gates for a final meal before setting off, and the king was back in his hall or his chamber or wherever; the tour would not intrude on him, but no matter.

'And that's the sea,' Freia said finally, as if she she'd had it installed. 'Lindisfarne is over there.' Scullery maid she might be, but if she knew her place, she was not bounded by it. She was at home here. Ethel felt the same sense of relief she had felt when she had decided to place the fate of her grandchild in the hands of his divine sponsor Thunor. Freia was mature enough now to play her own part in that drama. Ethel would leave her to it, pray for the best, and perhaps retire one day with her daughter and Freia's own family, which might or might not comprise the girl's half-brother and their heroic offspring.

Meanwhile, Freia's maybe future in-laws conversed in one of the rooms she had airily pointed to, naturally quite unaware that their son featured so prominently in the thoughts of the little scullery maid and her peculiar mother. They had more urgent business on their minds. 'Is it really necessary for you to go?' Seaxburh demanded, not for the first time.

'I serve at the pleasure of the king. The king has asked me to go, so go I shall,' Wilfrid replied just as wearily.

'But it's been so long since you saw battle. You are out of practice,' Seaxburh added more tentatively.

'Indeed, and people say I am living on past glories. I won't have that,' Wilfrid countered.

'The people who say that, my dear, have no past glories on which to live. There are no songs about them. They are jealous. That is all.'

'No doubt they are, my dear, and so they should be. I am a fine warrior. And a fine warrior fights for his king. Unless you also think I am ready to be put out to pasture? I'm not yet 40 in God's name!'

'There's no need to bring God into it, Wilfrid. I'm only suggesting that your talents might be better used to train other men. Men with fresher legs and faster reflexes.'

'Oh, I'll show you fresh legs and fast reflexes,' Wilfrid said laughing. Then he took hold of his wife, and decisively ended the conversation.

The matter had never really been in doubt, of course. And having left his wife in no doubt about his affectionate devotion to her, Wilfrid took his leave and strode out of the castle gates to rejoin the king's men as they finally began their long march to Alt Clut. Seaxburh watched from the castle ramparts till she could no longer make her husband out in the throng of soldiers. Maybe she would never see him again.

Also among the throng of soldiers was a man of similar years to Wilfrid, but this was no veteran. This man had not handled a weapon since taking holy orders many, many years before. He was the monk who had arrived at Bamburgh at the same time as Ethel and Freia, barely a couple of hours ago. And he was clearly a monk on a mission.

In the morning, Ethel set off early as planned. She had business at Berwick, she said. She embraced Freia warmly and made her promise to look after herself. And her daughter watched from the castle gates as she took to the road and slowly but steadily made her way northwards, and back to her own business. So maybe this was the moment Freia's own life really began, but that's another story.

CHAPTER 52: THE HAMMER BEAT OF WAR

Moses was busier than ever at the forge. War was in the air once more: word was the Picts and Northumbrians were preparing another concerted attack on the Rock. From dawn till dusk and sometimes after dusk, he and the master blacksmith worked the bellows, pounded metal, and wrought skilfully. They produced dozens of spearheads and other weapons, armour and metal parts for countless purposes, all of them military. All the other forges in and around Govan and beyond were doing the same. The birds and animals and even the fish in the river heard the beat of war, grew used to it. And the monks in the monastery too prayed over the almost unending din, trusting that God would still hear their prayers. After all, fervent prayers came even from the forges themselves, and certainly from the one where Moses toiled. Rhythmic, repetitive prayers of supplication. Wordless psalms beseeching the Lord for deliverance, for a crushing victory. Like this, like this, like this, let the Men of the Rock bash our enemies. Let them be consumed by fire, plunged to a watery death, trodden underfoot. Bash, bash, bash, oh Lord, bash, bash, bash!

Gawin sat reading and rereading the letter that had come from Emrys in Gwynedd some ten years earlier. News had reached Govan much more recently of the old man's death, so Emrys had been in Gawin's thoughts, and now the hammer beat of approaching war had drawn him back to the letter. Reading aloud, he found himself matching the words to the rhythm of the forges, such as it was. Emrys' bilingual letter was cacophonous enough in its own way to lend itself to the din. The roll call of Brittonic heroes jostled with biblical prophesy and cryptic aphorisms that Gawin would have stood no better chance of deciphering in pristine silence. If anything, the noise helped. By his sixth or seventh reading, he was no longer trying to understand the letter, but simply enjoying it like a piece of music accompanied by vigorous percussion. Gawin stopped reading when a particularly resounding crash came as he read the name Arthur, and he found himself closing his eyes to imagine the hero in his pomp: the once and future king, magnificently attired, looking now with disdain over his vanquished enemies and now with compassionate wisdom over his beloved people. And there, in the corner of Gawin's mind's eye, stood another figure watching his king from the shadows. Merlin the Wizard. Like all wizards, up to no good.

Gawin put the letter back in its place and said a prayer for the soul of its author before moving on to his routine private prayers, adding supplications for victory and peace. Then he called for his assistant Gethin, before remembering that the young man was away, accompanying Valentine on a visit to Pictland. He added another prayer for their safe conduct and for the success of what was, if not exactly a peace mission, an attempt on the part of the church to rise above worldly conflict, even as churchmen of each nation prayed for victory for their own worldly side.

The churchmen's prayers were no less pure-hearted for being complicated. The same could not be said for all international complications. At the shrine of Saint Mirin, conveniently situated between Govan and the Rock, a Pictish emissary awaited Valentine's late mother's widower, Rhodri, a man who would not have hesitated to put Merlin the Wizard on a retainer. The shrine's monks knew better than to ask the foreigner his business. They simply fed and watered him and left him to commune with Saint Mirin himself as they went about their business until their worldly patron arrived. When he did so, Rhodri spoke only briefly with the emissary before sending him on his way, following the White Water to the Great Western River, where he would no doubt hear the din of the forges carried downriver from Govan as he slipped across and continued his journey northwards. Rhodri continued his own westward journey from Govan to the Rock.

Back in Govan, Moses greeted Ieuan amiably when he appeared at the door of the forge. 'Are you here for Martha?' he asked. He suspected instead that Ieuan was here for his new helmet, but he felt the need to acknowledge his rival's ownership of Martha precisely because it pained him.

'Martha? No, no. Is she here?'

'No, she's not actually. Would you like to try that helmet then?'

'Indeed! Is it ready?

Moses fetched the helmet. It was not in fact new at all, but something of an antique. It had been badly damaged when Ieuan had acquired it. Rumour was it was Roman, though that seemed unlikely. The master blacksmith had said it was certainly not quite like anything he had seen before, so it was probably foreign. Saxon had been his guess, if not Northumbrian. But it had been Moses who had lovingly restored the helmet as best he could, using his imagination where necessary to complete some damaged ornamentation. Ieuan beamed when he saw it, taking a moment to admire it in the light before placing it proudly on his head. Moses placed his hands on the helmet's sides to gauge the fit, and then knocked it firmly with his knuckles at several points around Ieuan's head, just for fun, but with a deadly serious look on his face. 'Let me add a bit more padding,' he said at last. 'Your head's not as big as I thought.'

'Cheeky bastard,' Ieuan said. But for once the insult was not meant literally. He was pleased with the helmet, and happy to indulge Moses' sense of humour. 'Has the smith told you about the militia?' he asked.

'Indeed,' said Moses, shoving some extra shreds of material into the helmet's padding. 'I've already taken part in training.'

The militia was comprised of smithies and other tradesmen of Govan; not soldiers, but able-bodied men capable of defending the town from the enemy, if only by making it more trouble than it was worth for retreating enemy forces to plunder. Were the worst to happen and Alt Clut to fall, their task would be more desperate, perhaps hopeless, but it would be better to have some training than none.

'I'm glad to hear it,' said Ieuan as Moses handed him his helmet, 'We need all our men to be prepared. If not for this time, then for the next.'

Moses nodded, not exactly encouraged by this, and wondering what Ieuan knew that he did not.

'Well, thanks for this,' Ieuan said, patting his helmet like a puppy in the crook of his arm. 'You've done a magnificent job.'

'You're very welcome,' Moses said. 'May God grant that it survives the battle unscathed, and your head with it.'

Ieuan departed with a laugh, leaving Moses to his proper work. Soon he was immersed in it once more, weaving prayers into his toil and trying not to think too hard about what Ieuan had meant by 'next time'.

Suddenly the sky darkened and it began to rain heavily. Deep in the forge, Moses was confused for a split second by the sudden darkness, as if someone had blown out a candle though there had been no candle, before the sound of the rain solved the mystery. He took a deep breath of damp air and smiled. His mother had often told him the story of how it had rained like this immediately after his christening. She said he should always say a prayer when it rained like this, so he did just that, a prayer to the one father he knew beyond doubt was his. Then the rain began to fall even more heavily, in great sheets. Moses stood at the door and looked out in amazement. He had never seen rain quite like this, and his heart began to beat a little faster as it occurred to him to be afraid.

Then his eye was drawn to a figure rushing through the rain towards the forge, and a second later a very wet Martha was by his side.

'Holy Mother of Jesus, have you ever seen the like?' she said, wringing water from her hair and sleeves.

'I can't say I have, Martha,' he said, disoriented and delighted by this sudden intrusion of human warmth and familiarity into the apocalyptic scene. 'You'd better come and stand by the fire,' he added.

Martha did as Moses suggested. 'Will it work in our favour or not if it rains like this when they attack the Rock?' she asked.

Moses thought for a second. 'It would make it very hard to set fire to anything,' he observed. 'And…' As he made eye contact with Martha, they both realised he had no idea, and began to laugh.

'That's a question for your betrothed,' he said.

Martha scowled ever so slightly. 'Where's my father?' she asked.

'I think he's in the house,' Moses said, pointing rather unnecessarily in the direction of Martha's house, no more than a short dash away.

'Well, the rain's let up a little,' she said, and smiled politely before leaving.

Moses watched her go, and looked out at the rain, which had perhaps relented a little. Perhaps not. He returned to his work, his hammer blows given added aggression by something other than hopes of military victory for the Men of the Rock.

CHAPTER 53: PRITEN'S RETURN

Paul awoke in a state of agitation. He had not dreamt so vividly since his last visit to his native land nearly a decade before. Those dreams had been so intense, so real, they were not like dreams at all, more like memories, only memories of things that had never happened. And now he was to return and now the uncanny dreams had returned. It was surely no coincidence.

These past few years, he had rarely dreamt of Sister Brigid, and never quite as he had done back then on the mainland, with Brigid serving as a go-between, playing her part as Paul's wife in a fantastical other life before being transformed into someone else in a fantasy that was both less complete and less respectable; the former fantasy of a married life being respectable only in its own, quite imaginary terms, that is, with both Paul and Mary Brigid free from their holy orders. The someone else in the latter fantasy had always been Euphemia, Paul supposed, though he had not always known it at the time. Encountering his fantasy in the flesh had been a sobering experience, and returning to Iona, to the monastery that was his proper Earthly home, had consolidated his sobriety. He had been happy in his monk's life at last. Until now. If his state of agitation was anything to go by.

At least Sister Brigid had been left out of it this time, he reflected as he saw her later that morning, instructing a novice in the care of the stone crosses that stood in the grounds of the abbey. Not that the stones required much maintenance, but it was well known that Brigid had a special affection for the carvings, and she was no doubt keen to pass that affection on to her young charge.

The nuns were also responsible for tending to the graves of the abbey's dead. Paul was on his way to say a prayer over the grave of Brother Gregory. His old friend and countryman had joined the other saints less than a year ago, having died suddenly from a violent seizure, so he would not be joining Paul on his journey 'home'. Gregory was in his true home. Paul would miss him, and Brother Aidan too, who was alive and well but too important now to the scriptorium to be spared on a diplomatic mission. Paul would travel with Mark, a young monk and another fellow countryman who thus spoke the language and also had family connections in some noble house or other. Paul did not know him well, but he seemed bright and able. He knew he was expected to be something of a mentor to the youth, but it was not a role he relished. Watching Sister Brigid with her charge made him feel even more inadequate. Brigid exuded a natural warmth Paul knew he lacked, and it had little to do with their respective sexes. There were plenty of affable monks and icy nuns on Iona to disprove that hypothesis. Paul surmised uncomfortably that Brigid's warmth was more akin to a spiritual gift, and one he sorely lacked. He pitied young Mark.

Paul had not intended to speak to Mary Brigid, but she acknowledged him from a distance with a nod, and he found himself wandering over. 'Marvellous, aren't they?' he said to the novice.

'Yes, Brother,' agreed the novice shyly, grateful to be able to return her gaze from the intruding monk to the inert carvings.

'You're going back to the mainland, I hear?' said Brigid.

'That's right.'

'Well, God bless you.'

'Thank you, sister,' Paul said, nodding to excuse himself.

That night he dreamed once again of Brigid – the old dream set on the secluded island, but without the old transition to the someone else, Euphemia or otherwise. In the morning, it occurred to him that this had been a kind of farewell. He had a strange premonition that he would not return to Iona, but he did not allow himself to linger on that thought, any more than he allowed himself to recall the dream's more literally conjugal aspects. He thanked God for the monastic routine that filled his mind as it filled his hours.

It was only when Paul was finally at sea and, having exhausted idle conversation with young Mark and the boatmen, looked into the vast, silvery sky, that such thoughts came back to him. There were no birds to distract him, just great clouds heaving their way across the heavens and occasionally shimmering when caught by the otherwise invisible sun. The boatmen looked nervously at Mark when Paul began singing an old Pictish song, not as a man sings with other men, but as if to the sky itself, oblivious to his human audience. Mark made a reassuring gesture, but he too was unnerved. He did not know Paul well, but would surely have been warned if his mentor were someone who made a habit of this sort of thing. He recognised the tune from back home, but not the words, which were old, old words that made no sense even when he thought he knew their meaning. As for Paul, he had no idea he was singing. He was deep in his dreams.

Paul behaved strangely for the duration of the voyage. Even when he was not actually singing, he kept looking at the sky as if expecting a sign that never came. Mark said nothing, but silently prayed for his brother. He supposed Paul was unsettled by the prospect of returning home after so long. He did not seem excited – as Mark himself was, even having been away just three years – but he was clearly agitated in his very soul. Mark expected to see something of his family during their stay. He did not know if Paul still had family back home, or other ties, memories or associations that might explain his strange behaviour. Which is to say he did not know what we know.

What Mark did know was that the monastery they were to visit was the same that Paul and his brothers had visited ten years before, though he did not know, either, whether that had any particular significance for Paul. He did know that they were to meet brother monks there from other nations too, Britons and Northumbrians as well as Picts. For the purposes of this visit, Paul and Mark belonged not to the People of the Designs, but to Dalriada. They were Gaels, despite Mark's lamentable Gaelic. It was more useful to Iona for him to be fluent in Pictish. When Mark was not distracted by Paul's unworldly demeanour, then, his own thoughts were on the politics of the church, and her efforts to maintain brotherly love and doctrinal harmony even when her members were at war with one another.

◆ ◆ ◆

Bishop Boniface was not invited to the ecclesiastical summit. While he shared the organisers' international outlook and ambitions, he was not sufficiently esteemed among the churchmen of his own nation to be considered a suitable representative. Far from it, in fact. Not that it was a grand affair. The summit was not a gathering of princes of the church – of men whose names might be known in Rome – but rather a meeting of humble servants of the church who were known and trusted by those who exercised authority in God's name. Boniface certainly did not meet that description, and he knew it, just as he knew of the meeting. He had deliberately chosen to invest his time and energy on other priorities, however; there was always someone else who could act as his fly on the wall on such occasions, in this case King Brude's master stone carver, but more of that later. As Boniface's brother churchmen converged on the little monastery just a glen away from his own king's seat of power, the bishop was with his king and others converging on Alt Clut under King Onuist, even as King Eadberht's army marched from the south-east to help them subdue the Rock once and for all.

On their own journey south-west, a dozing lynx had been startled by the rumble of the approaching army, darted from its resting place and into the path of a pair of monks travelling in the other direction. All three creatures had halted in a panic, wide feline eyes meeting two pairs of nervous monastic eyes before the animal collected itself and bounded off, leaving the monks to look at one another and laugh at their scare. The monks were Valentine and his young assistant Gethin, and they soon discovered what had disturbed the lynx, as the sound of the approaching army rose from a murmur to a din before the soldiers appeared in the gap between two hills.

When the two parties passed, the monks yielded the rough track to the army and stood to wait, since the ground was too boggy to make progress off it. King Brude himself acknowledged their courtesy from his horse with a deep nod, while Boniface, also mounted, waved his right arm graciously. Most of the soldiers then trudged past without giving the monks a second look. It mattered not, even had it been apparent, that these monks were delegates from Govan, countrymen of the Men of the Rock, the enemy. Monks were monks, churchmen churchmen, most of the time. And for their part, while they knew very well where this Pictish army was headed, the monks harboured no animus. Well, they didn't know Boniface.

Boniface had of course been an ally of Valentine's mother's husband, Rhodri, though Valentine had not known anything about it. And Rhodri's successful strategy when the Picts had tried to take the Rock ten years earlier had perhaps had something to do with that alliance. If they were also up to something this time, Valentine knew nothing of that either.

He had seen less of Rhodri since his mother had died a few years ago, but they had never been close. Rhodri had used Valentine as a kind of political go-between, whose combined status as a not-quite-relative and a churchman meant he was never seen as Rhodri's pawn because he was indeed no such thing. He was more useful to Rhodri as a dutiful monk.

In being used this way, meanwhile, Valentine had advanced in influence within the church. Without the contacts and knowledge that had come from being used by Rhodri, it was unlikely that he would have been chosen as a delegate for the ecclesiastical summit. But those contacts and that knowledge were mostly limited to the church itself, albeit in its capacity as an informal powerbroker between various Brittonic noblemen like Rhodri. He knew who were Rhodri's allies and rivals among the Britons, but he knew nothing of Rhodri's dealings with foreigners, least of all Boniface. Their passing on the road like that barely counts as a coincidence.

When they arrived at the monastery for the summit, the monks from Govan did not even notice Pyrdie, tapping away at a large slab of stone on the hillside above them, though Gethin did admire the carved stone he saw standing by the gate. For his part, King Brude's master stone carver had little interest in the monks' more worldly business. Before sending him to the monastery this time, Boniface had made a show of asking him to keep his eyes and ears open so he could report back about anything he learned, but the little mole might as well have been deaf as well as blind for all the use he was as a spy. Pyrdie was only interested in his own craft. He was doing good work at the monastery on his regular stints there, and he liked it, regardless of whatever international intrigues might be going on. Some of the visitors were kind enough to remark on his carvings and he was happy to explain how he blended Northumbrian designs with those he had grown up with, those of the People of the Designs themselves, and how the difference between the two melted away as his work took shape, especially in the shape of the cross, however it might be adorned. The two nations shared a religion, after all, and like his grandfather before him, Pyrdie's appreciation of that religion had deepened over the years as he had sought to carve its truths in stone with his own two hands. For Pyrdie, working at the monastery was like standing with one foot in eternity. So, no, foreigners and politics held no fascination for him. As for women, well, that's another story.

CHAPTER 54: ALT CLUT

Cuthbert and his men braced themselves. They had waited until they had the tide in their favour before launching their boats and rowing furiously downstream on the Great Western River in an effort to slip past the defences of the Rock, but with the main assault already underway from the north, they did not have the element of surprise. They knew the Britons would anticipate further probes of their defences and be ready for them. Sure enough, as soon as the boats were in sight of the battlements, a barrage of missiles was launched at them. In each boat, three or four men ceased rowing to hold up shields against the onslaught, stones at first, which battered into the shields with terrifying thuds. Then arrows, less noisy but hardly less alarming as they thwacked deep into wood. Cuthbert hoped their allies in the main attack forces were grateful to them for having at least some of the archers diverted from the landward welcome.

In no time, though, the boats were past the Rock, and the new challenge was to turn and bring the boats against the tide into the smaller river that fed the Great Western River in the shadow of the Rock. The shieldmen put down their battered shields and took up oars again. After some struggle, though, Cuthbert ordered everyone out of their boats and into the shallows to wade ashore with the boats in tow. The shieldmen were soon required again, as while they were less exposed than when on the open river, they were still within range of the Rock's archers. Then the arrows stopped and after a short interval it was clear why. A body of men appeared as if from nowhere and charged at the invaders.

Cuthbert shouted words of encouragement to his men as he drew his seax and prepared for contact. Then he experienced a moment of serenity as his battle self began to take over and for a split second he felt utterly detached from the scene around him. The charging Britons did not roar their way into battle like many warriors, but simply rushed forward with deadly intent; Cuthbert admired that. The only sound would have been the quick stomping of their feet on the moist ground, except that the din of the main assault on the other side of the Rock washed over the whole scene. And then metal met metal on this side. Cuthbert parried, shuffled, thrust, kicked, swung, thrust, span, parried, thrust, all without thinking. To the extent that his conscious mind was engaged, it was scanning the bigger picture, assessing the balance of forces and looking out for his men. They were mostly young, but had tasted battle before. Several fell, but overall they were getting the better of the Britons, who seemed less experienced. And after some minutes, the Britons' captain – a tall young man in a splendid helmet – called the retreat. Cuthbert stopped his men from giving chase, a foolish move for a small diversionary force on the enemy's own stronghold. Instead he ordered his men to place their dead and wounded in the boats before continuing around the Rock. All being well, they would make further nuisance of themselves before joining the main attacking force.

Ieuan stood guard as the last of his men scrambled back up the steep, hidden path behind him to the relative safety of the fortress. The Picts were not following, more was the pity; they'd have been slaughtered in short order by men in an unassailable position in the fortress above. Ieuan had lost nearly a dozen of his own men, but he did not have time to dwell on that. He clambered onto a boulder for a better view of the enemy below before following his men back to the fortress to report their position. The senior commanders were deep in discussion in the strategy room deep in the fortress. When he got finally got their attention, Ieuan was ordered to have his men rest and stand by. The battle for the Rock was shaping up to be a siege.

Among those senior commanders were Ieuan's great uncle Rhodri, the mastermind of the Men of the Rock's victory over the Picts some ten years earlier, and Dumnagual, son of Teudebur, the nobleman – some had called him king – who had been credited with that victory, perhaps for no better reason than that some had called him king. Neither Rhodri nor Dumnagual was first to mention the possibility of seeking terms with the attackers. That contemptible task could only fall to a senior commander whose wits exceeded his ambition. Caradoc the Grey spoke up and was shouted down, but, once voiced, the idea continued to circulate wordlessly around the room. The Picts were attacking in greater numbers than anticipated, and were perhaps supported by Gaels as well as Northumbrians. The Rock was not about to fall, but neither would the enemy be easily dismissed. Perhaps Onuist would settle for something less than total conquest.

Cuthbert and his men joined the main attacking force just as the fighting was dying down and the attackers were setting up camp as a siege army. Freshly-assigned Pictish sentries panicked when they saw them coming, but Cuthbert and one of his men held aloft a banner to identify themselves and calm everyone down. They were expected, after all, and a translator was summoned so Cuthbert could brief a company of Picts now charged with going back the way the Northumbrians had come to blockade the Rock from the river. 'Keep out of arrow range and watch out for men appearing from nowhere.'

Spirits were high in the camp. It had been a bloody

day of fighting, but the combined forces of the attackers were formidable, and the Britons' defences did not look like holding out forever. King Onuist was in no hurry to lose more men than necessary in desperate fighting when the Men of the Rock could be starved into submission. His Northumbrian allies were similarly minded. And it was a beautiful summer's evening. Perfect conditions for an extended picnic.

After checking in with his superiors and supervising his men setting up camp, Cuthbert went for a wander. The camp as a whole was magnificent, spreading over the landscape with colourful flags fluttering in the wind. A number of tents stood out from the others. They were no bigger than the ordinary soldiers' tents, but while the latter accommodated scores of men, these special tents belonged to the kings of the Picts. None was more splendid than that of King Onuist himself, of course, but the tents of his underkings were still quite lavish, and one in particular did rival that of the overlord. Observers were surprised to learn that it belonged to King Brude, since while he was well known to all who followed Pictish military affairs, he was by no means the most powerful of Onuist's underkings. Cuthbert would not have known him if he'd bumped into him, but he did nod at or exchange pleasantries with those of his fellow captains he recognised, both Northumbrian and Pictish. And, as promised, there were also Gaels. As dusk approached, Cuthbert noticed a large group sitting around a fire next to which two men were standing and gesticulating wildly. Storytellers, he assumed, and as he approached he was delighted to recognise his old friends Domnall and Fergus. He sat and was soon absorbed by one of the old Irish tales, as tall as the giants that featured in it.

When the storytellers had finished and enjoyed their plaudits, Cuthbert approached them and called out an obscene Gaelic insult by way of a greeting. When they recognised their old friend, they roared with pleasure and embraced him as one. 'We've been hearing stories about you!' Domnall said.

'All lies,' Cuthbert insisted.

'Let's sort fact from fiction over a drink,' said Fergus.

After some time spent catching up on their own respective adventures, Domnall announced that he and Fergus had heard an intriguing story from someone in a previous camp, a couple of nights before the army had arrived at the Rock.

'And it's quite a story,' added Fergus.

Cuthbert was intrigued. 'A new story? Not one from the old country?'

'Not this one,' Domnall said, 'but funnily enough the old woman who told it came from Ireland a long time ago.'

'Is that so?'

Domnall told him how, having been regaling their Pictish comrades with a few Gaelic classics, he and Fergus had been asked to speak to an old woman who had been recruited as an interpreter. You see, she had fallen suddenly ill, and partially recovered only to find she had forgotten how to speak any tongue but that of her youth, which happened to be Gaelic, and with a distinct Leinster accent. She told them that she wanted to make a deathbed confession, and when they protested that they were soldiers, not priests, she replied that there was never a priest when you needed one, and if there had been one on hand twenty years ago, she would have no deathbed confession to make. 'All right,' they'd said, 'you've got us with that. Now, tell us your story. We mean confession.'

Fergus now took over to fill in the backstory, which they'd managed to procure after the confession itself. 'This old woman was taken by raiders when she was a girl. Nearly her whole little village in fact, was rounded up and herded onto a ship that took them she knew not where. At that time, such things were not unusual for coastal communities. After that she'd been separated from her family, and remembered little about what had happened to her, except that she'd been moved around a lot, and ended up here at Alt Clut, where she became a servant and learned the language. By the time she came of age, she was as much a Briton as a Gael, but her fate was to be even more confused. She married a half-Pictish soldier of the Rock, who came into some land on the plain of Coel and took her there to live as farmer and wife. There she learned Northumbrian from countrymen of yours who'd settled nearby, so she could speak every language there is bar Latin.'

'You're making me feel quite inadequate,' said the merely bilingual Cuthbert.

'Well, never mind that,' said Domnall, taking over. 'The important part of the story is all-Brittonic. It happened about twenty years ago, she said, when she'd been widowed a couple of years and was struggling to raise three little ones and manage the farm. No wonder she thought it was the hand of God that made a mysterious noblewoman burst through her door one night, begging for shelter. This noblewoman, a Briton herself, had a new-born baby with her, and explained that she and the child were being hunted by Northumbrian soldiers, for reasons she would not explain. She just begged the woman to take her baby and raise it as her own, since she was sure she would never escape the soldiers if she had to carry and tend to the baby too. Besides, the soldiers were looking for mother and baby, not one or the other. Well, our woman was shocked at the idea of a mother giving up her own baby like that, not to mention reluctant to take on the extra burden. But then it was clear that the noblewoman was terrified, and her plan made sense if the alternative was mother and child both being captured and killed as she claimed.

'And there was more. She had treasure: a sackful of silver, which she was willing to give up along with the child to pay for his upbringing and reward his saviour. And then there was the fact that our woman had been orphaned herself, and felt an affinity for this poor child at the mercy of the world. So she agreed. She took the baby and promised to swear he was her own should the soldiers come to the farm. The noblewoman cried with gratitude and announced that she would leave that very moment, even in the dead of night, both to put more distance between herself and the soldiers, and because she could not bear to linger in the presence of her baby. She told our woman that if she escaped she intended to make for Iona to become a nun, and that when the boy came of age – and not before – our woman was to tell him, so if he chose to do so, he could seek out his mother there and discover his true identity. Can you imagine?'

Cuthbert tried to imagine.

'But there's more,' Fergus said, taking up the story. 'She never did raise the child. You see, in the days that followed, there were indeed rumours of Northumbrian soldiers scouring the countryside in search of no one was quite sure what. Everyone was afraid. Well, perhaps driven by a combination of that and resentment at the imposition of a cuckoo child, our woman's oldest daughter took it upon herself to get rid of the baby, and rose before dawn one morning to take him to the little river that flowed by the family farm.'

'She drowned him?' Cuthbert asked, horrified.

'No, no,' Fergus said, 'she took him in the basket he'd come in, and put him on the water, trusting his fate to God, as our woman put it.'

'It's possible, of course,' said Domnall, 'that this part is a fabrication. It being the woman's daughter, that is, who disposed of the child. It might be that she did it herself, but felt unable to confess that much.'

'True,' said Fergus, 'but I believe her. I mean, this was where she said a priest would have made all the difference. If there had been a church or a monastery anywhere near their farm, she could have taken the child herself and placed him directly in the hands of the church.'

'And what about the silver?' Cuthbert asked.

Domnall and Fergus looked at one another wryly. 'There is that,' Fergus said, 'but she insisted the girl had put "most" of the treasure in the basket with its heir, glad to be rid of it. And she confessed her relief that she'd kept a number of coins about her person, just in case.'

Cuthbert produced a silver coin from the folds of his tunic and ran it between his fingers.

'You still have that!' Fergus gasped.

'Just the one, mind.'

'Ours are long gone.'

Of course, each of the friends had been given three coins from the hoard they had transported, also some twenty years before, but what of that? Cuthbert was thinking about something else, and asked tentatively, 'Are you sure it was a boy, not a girl? And just twenty years ago, not more?'

'Oh, she was quite clear,' Domnall confirmed. 'I suppose she could have been mistaken. After all, she had been very ill. But that's what she told us.'

Fergus nodded in agreement, but by now Cuthbert was resigned to the fact that this story differed in too many details to have anything to do with the story of the baby girl snatched from her family at another time and another place. God only knows how many stories there are about babies lost, abandoned or misplaced one way or another over the ages.

CHAPTER 55: ENTER THE DRAGON

The next day there was no fighting, except for a brief incident on the western side of the Rock, when Pictish soldiers there to seal off access from the river wandered within arrow range of the ramparts and drew fire. The mood in the main camp was one of resignation that they were going to be there for some time. A similar mood prevailed on the Rock itself, only with greater anxiety. The men in the strategy room knew it was their move. The men on the ramparts did too. Everyone knew it.

The sky was unusually overcast for a summer's day. There was a steady drizzle. Cuthbert watched his men play dice. He did not play. He thought of the stalemate on Lindisfarne some ten years before. The stalemate he had ended by murdering the pretender Offa. There would be no such simple resolution to this situation. He looked up at the Rock, where he and his Gaelic friends had spent a night some twenty years before. He wondered if Rhodri were in there now, weighing his side's options. If he had a trick up his sleeve, it had better be a good one. As far as Cuthbert could see, it would only be a matter of time until the Men of the Rock were forced to seek terms, and everyone knew King Onuist wanted nothing less than the Rock itself. Cuthbert's thoughts were interrupted by his men's squabbling. A disputed dice roll. That's how overcast it was now. Someone went to get a lamp.

Across the camp, Domnall and Fergus were reminiscing with a handful of their countrymen who, like them, had fought alongside the Men of the Rock ten years before. The fighting had taken place far from the Rock, of course, as the Britons and their allies had marched out to surprise the Pictish invaders, but the victory celebrations had been held on the very ground where this year's invaders were now camped, Picts, Northumbrians and Gaels alike. Back then, Domnall and Fergus had regaled their Brittonic comrades with the story of the combat of Cuhullin and Ferdiad. Friends reluctantly fighting to the death. Perhaps in a few days they would tell the same story to their Pictish comrades. But their reminiscences soon gave way to observations about how strangely dark it was.

Thunder struck and the sky darkened further. Throughout the camp, men began to mutter nervously. 'I've seen something like this before,' Cuthbert told his men. 'Worse, even. It was not the end of the world then, and I doubt it will be this time.'

Domnall and Fergus had experienced the same thing, of course, when fighting alongside Cuthbert and the Northumbrians against the Picts. 'But that was more sudden,' Fergus noted.

'And there was…' Domnall stopped himself. There was no need to speak of the unspeakable roar that had followed the darkness, unlike any kind of thunder. If it were coming, anticipation would only multiply the horror.

The leaders of the Men of the Rock were now on the ramparts, looking not at their mortal enemies below them but at the sky above. It was the worst of omens: none of them had ever seen a sky so dark in daytime. And worse, the darkness seemed to be closing in on the Rock from the north and east, as if summoned by the invaders themselves. Dumnagual son of Teudebur cursed his bad luck. Their bad luck, he meant.

Caradoc the Grey did not speak. He did not have to. The others muttered about what kind of terms they might expect if they surrendered the Rock now. Only Rhodri stood apart and looked not up but down, scanning the assembled host as if looking for someone in particular, a task that would have been made all the more difficult by the darkness. But it did mean he was the first to see a small delegation of Picts approach the Rock under a banner of peace: they wanted to talk.

The people of Govan were also looking at the sky with foreboding, as no doubt were their compatriots across the lands of the Britons. If the Rock fell to the enemy, no one was safe. Moses stood at the door of the forge and looked up at the unnaturally dark clouds, just as he had stood a week or so earlier, watching the unnaturally heavy rain, when... He glanced at the smith's house and there she was. Martha had also come out to look up at the sky, and was now looking at Moses. Immediately, they smiled at one another as if the sun were shining and all were well in the world. For an instant they were happy and in love. But then they remembered why they were standing where they were – the darkness, fear, dread – and looked up again, before returning their gazes to one another with very different expressions. Expressions of worry that the darkness was an ill portent. A sudden awareness of all that was not well with the world, including not only impending war, but also the fact that the two of them were not in fact happy and in love, that Martha was betrothed to someone else. Fleetingly, it occurred to Moses to wish for Ieuan's death on the Rock. Perhaps it occurred to Martha too. But it was a shameful thought for either of them to entertain. Moses for one refused to entertain it.

At the monastery, the monks broke with their normal routine and gathered to pray under the menacing heavens, but Gawin struggled to keep his thoughts from wandering to Emrys' letter, and the feeling it had given him, even after the Men of the Rock had seen off the Picts ten years before, that Alt Clut was doomed to be swept away like Gododdin before it. 'Not as I will, but as you will,' he prayed inwardly before forcing himself back to the brothers' collective supplications. Prayer was not like battle, after all. However hard they prayed, the brothers were not about to change anything, least of all the Almighty's mind.

'It is the Dragon!' was the whisper on the ramparts of the Rock as the darkness deepened still further. 'The Dragon descends, and we are doomed!'

In the camp of the besieging army, fear turned to a measure of hope as the flaming torches of their delegation were seen disappearing into the fortress of the Rock. 'Enter the Dragon,' said someone, and it was not clear whether this referred to the delegation entering the belly of the Brittonic beast or to the Pictish dragon entering the Rock. Perhaps it was both.

◆ ◆ ◆

Cuthbert awoke somewhere dark and smoky, with unfamiliar smells in the air. He did not know where he was or remember getting here. Nor, for now, did he remember where he had been before that. He was not even aware of not remembering. He was too disoriented to know he was disoriented. Gradually he became aware of a figure moving about quite close to him, and he began to make sense of the space they shared. It was a small hovel. The smoke that filled it was not static but rose to a little opening in the roof that also admitted a glimmer of light. There was also light from one side, a door or window. And more light from a fire that produced the smoke but was mostly obscured by the figure. A woman. Perhaps sensing his gaze, she turned to him. 'Are you awake, soldier?' she asked, but he did not understand her words. He knew only that she spoke the language of the Britons. He was in no condition to ponder further. He tried to smile, but in doing so realised that even if his mind was coming back to him, his body was not quite his own. The woman put a cup of water to his lips and his mouth drank thirstily without having to be told. Only then was Cuthbert conscious of feeling thirsty. ‘Cuthbert,’ he said when he was finished, as much to himself as to the woman.

‘Cuthbert,’ she repeated, and then pointed at him. ‘Cuthbert?’

He nodded painfully.

She pointed at herself: ‘Morgan.’

CHAPTER 56: A RECKONING

Paul and Mark had been walking on the mainland for nearly two whole days when a lone rider appeared on the horizon, heading towards them. They exchanged curious glances but continued unperturbed until, after several minutes of distance closed, Mark recognised the rider. 'That's my cousin Talorc,' he said, waving to his kinsman, who waved back before galloping up and dismounting.

'They said you were coming,' Talorc told Mark. 'I thought I'd ride out and see if I could catch you. It must have been God's will.'

'Indeed. But what are you doing in these parts?' Mark asked. 'I had hoped to take a day or two to come and see everyone during my visit, but hardly expected anyone to come so far from home.'

Talorc explained that he had married into a family whose land lay between here and the monastery Mark was to visit, so he had taken it upon himself to welcome him and offer him hospitality, along with his companion, of course. He offered his horse to Paul, who declined, protesting that he was not as old as he might look, so the three walked together with the horse at Talorc's side. Talorc was intrigued to find that Paul was a fellow countryman, and asked if the People of the Designs were well represented on Iona. Mark and Paul confirmed that there was a fair smattering from all the nations of the land.

'Britons too?' he added mischievously.

'One or two at least,' Mark said.

'Perhaps there will be more after the campaign,' Talorc said. 'There's talk of empire now, and Iona would be its natural spiritual centre, even if it is a little out of the way.'

'Out of the way suits us just fine,' Paul said. He had avoided showing his distaste at the worldliness of the word empire, and 'out of the way' gave him a suitable non-political way of expressing his feelings.

Mark did not pick up on this, however, as Talorc's comment had sent his thoughts in another direction. 'My brother?' he asked tentatively.

'It was Drust who brought word of your coming, on his way to join the little King Onuist for the campaign. So, yes, that's where he is now.'

'Little King Onuist?'

'The local underking. Everyone calls him Little Onuist to avoid confusion with the big man, though he hates it, of course.'

'I see. And Drust was well when you saw him?'

'Very well, and he assured me the rest of the family are flourishing too.'

Paul noticed a twinkle in Talorc's eye as he uttered this reassurance, and inwardly groaned. Sure enough, when they arrived at the homestead after a couple of hours, Mark was greeted not only by Talorc's in-laws, but by his own mother and sister, who had evidently undertaken to surprise their golden boy before he could be swallowed up in church business. But Paul could not help smiling when they burst into tears at the sight of him and smothered him with kisses. It was a moment or two before Mark's own emotional response to the reunion gave way to embarrassment, and he begged his womenfolk to show some decorum. Here was his mentor,

Brother Paul.

Paul was welcomed warmly and enjoyed the feast held in his and Mark's honour. The conversation was dominated by chatter about the campaign against Alt Clut. Both families had noble blood and consequently martial obligations, so not only Mark's brother Drust, but several other relatives were also with Little Onuist or another underking converging on the Rock. When the opportunity arose, however, Paul spoke privately to Mark, and told him it was fine for him to spend a day or two with his family. Paul would leave in the morning, though, and get to the summit in good time. Otherwise he would be distracted and mentally absent anyway. Mark had no doubt that was true, so having convinced himself that Paul really was content for him to stay a while, he agreed. In the morning, Paul accepted generous provisions, but again declined the offer of a horse and an escort – assuring his hosts that he had grown up not far from these parts and knew the country well – and set off alone for the monastery, perhaps just a day's walk away.

An eagle high above him might have seen the monk making his way through one glen, before it glided over the mountain to see two more human figures in the glen on the other side, a little wagon in tow. Fay and Tes were returning after performing at a wedding the previous night. Returning where though? This was a point of contention as they trudged through the glen.

'If we are no longer priestesses, then what are we?' Fay demanded.

'Bards! Like always. We are bards!' Tes replied.

'We have *never* been bards!' Fay spat. 'Or are we also men, since we perform as men?'

'Then we'll perform as women if it will make you happy.'

Fay spluttered in frustration. Stopped walking.

Tes also stopped and steadied the wagon, which she'd been pulling single-handedly, so she could lean on it as she looked Fay in the eye to show she was listening. 'What exactly do you want to do?'

'I don't know.'

Tes pushed her face forward, widened her eyes. What else could she say or do?

'Not this,' said Fay at last. 'I don't want to go back to the village,' she said. 'I don't want to keep doing this.'

'I know you don't want to go back to the village,' Tes said wearily, 'but we have nowhere else to go.'

Fay and Tes had spent the past few months living at a large village, in a hovel they'd been invited by a music-loving local farmer to use as a base, coming and going to perform at summer celebrations throughout the surrounding area. The villagers knew them as men, but occasionally noticed a woman – or was it two different women? – coming and going too, especially in the evenings. At least one widower had been discreetly enquiring whether anyone knew if this woman or women were married to the bards, or might be available.

'I just need,' Fay started, before correcting herself: '*We* need…' But that did not seem to be true: 'I need to know if this is it. I need to consult the gods one more time.'

Tes sighed. 'How? Where?'

Fay looked up at the mountain, perhaps noticing our eagle flying overhead. Perhaps not.

'Then go now,' Tes said, not bitterly, but only because she had stopped herself before it came out that way. 'You know where I am when you're ready.

'Can you manage the wagon on your own?' Fay asked, perhaps just to avoid showing her relief and excitement.

'I always have,' answered Tes. Now, that did come out a little bitterly. Tes had apparently been keeping count of their respective hours on wagon duty while Fay had not. But any guilt Fay felt on realising she had not been pulling her weight was outweighed by affectionate amusement at the spectacle of Tes holding a grudge, and she began to laugh. Tes was indeed not good at grudges, and immediately found herself laughing too. They embraced warmly, then, before parting. Tes continued towards the village with the wagon while Fay began her steady ascent up the mountainside. It began to rain.

Paul had been casting worried looks up at the sky for a while when he felt the first drops of rain on his tonsured head. He pulled his hood up and pressed on, muttering a prayer for safe passage before he began working methodically through his collection of memorised psalms. By the time he had finished, the rain had grown fierce, and he was already soaked through. The ground beneath him was mud. Ahead of him, he saw only yet more driving rain. It would still take hours to reach the monastery, if he could even find the way in these conditions. But he did know these glens, these mountains, these woods, more intimately than any monastery. And there was one place not so far away that he could find with his eyes closed if he had to. He would smell his way. Feel his way. As if by magic.

Fay was out of breath when she reached the mountain pass she had been thinking of when she'd set off up the mountain. In a narrow passage through to the next glen lay a secluded grove that had been sacred since ancient times. She had hoped to catch a grouse or a hare or something to sacrifice there in supplication – one life's blood for knowledge of another life's course – but now the chances seemed slim, and her thoughts turned instead to shelter. The rain had grown fierce, and she was already soaked through. The ground beneath her was mud. Ahead of her, she saw only yet more driving rain. She would never find her way back to the village even if she tried. Then she realised where else she was near. She set off with a renewed sense of purpose through the mountain pass and into the neighbouring glen, eastwards into the gathering gloom.

After some hours gradually descending in the rain, sheltered only intermittently by the thick wood that now surrounded her, it was nearly night. Fay almost slipped down the steep bank and into the gnarled roots of the old tree that partly hid the wooden door, round like a great battle shield, but with a metal ring to one side for a handle. She was about to pull the handle when something made her stop. A sound? A scent? The kind of feeling that could be either, and yet more primal than either. She pulled her hand back from the door, took a step back. Stopped breathing. Inside the cave something stirred. Fay leapt back now and hid herself to watch as the door shuddered to life and then opened wide. Out stepped a lone figure, just a dim shadow until a stroke of lightning flashed through the wood's canopy. Priten. Naked. Erect.

Paul looked vaguely around him before his ill-defined sense that someone had been outside the door coalesced in his mind and he looked up into the tree where Euphemia had sat twenty years earlier.

'Not this time,' said Fay, stepping out from behind a tree off to Priten's right.

He turned, saw her, covered himself with his hands. His mind raced.

'You came for shelter,' he said, having deduced that it was unlikely she had arrived in the middle of a storm just on the off-chance that he might be there after all those years away. 'Please,' he said, about to usher her in with a flourish of his arm before remembering. He darted inside and remerged in his still-soaking habit. 'Please,' he repeated, 'come inside'.

'There's no way I'm coming in there with you,' she said coldly.

'Then take it, please. I'll go away. I'll go. It's the least I can do.'

She just looked at him.

'Really, it's fine. I'm used to hardship.'

That made Fay angry. 'Unlike me?' she hissed. 'The delicate princess who must be protected from the world?'

Priten's gaze fell to the sodden ground.

Remembering herself as a vulnerable child-woman, Fay thought of something else: 'So once again, you've come back while the fighting men are away at war?'

'Church business,' Paul said, not defensively but

helplessly, not even lifting his gaze to meet Fay's.

'Of course,' Fay said. 'Has your God forgiven you yet?'

Paul took a moment to compose himself, not daring even to ask himself that question. 'I am truly sorry about what happened,' he said, looking up at her now.

'"What happened"?' Fay stared at him incredulously. 'You *sold* me!'

Once more, Paul's gazed dropped to the ground, and it seemed that he lost at least a foot in stature.

'You sold me,' Fay repeated more quietly.

He said nothing.

She pushed her face forward, widened her eyes. A flash of lightning illuminated her fierce, accusing face, and Paul shrank by another foot, then crumpled to the ground.

'We were supposed to be together,' Euphemia went on. 'You were supposed to love me like I loved you. Like I loved you! And you *sold* me to the Master, as if my *love* could be bought and sold.

Curled up in the mud, Paul began muttering now, as much to himself as to Euphemia, repeating words he had muttered many times before: 'The man was a heathen, but a sincere one, as was I. I knew he considered his so-called priestesses to be sacred, and none more so than the Sacred Virgin, so it was not as if... I would never have sold you as a mere slave, to be...' He broke off, realising how pathetic he sounded, as if congratulating himself for not having committed an even more heinous sin. Not only had he sold a fellow human being, a child of God, as if such a thing could ever be deemed permissible. He had betrayed someone who loved and trusted him. Someone he had loved. It was hard for Paul to imagine now what had motivated him to do what he had done. Every day, he thanked God for tearing out his heart of stone and replacing it with a heart of flesh. But his heart of flesh seared with pain when he remembered what he had done, and why. For magic. He looked up at the stars in a kind of daze.

Fay stood silently, shaking with emotion, her eyes fixed

on Priten.

'I never stopped loving you,' he said.

The furious Fay sprang forward and reached down to grab Paul by his habit, pulling him to his feet, still dazed, before pushing him towards the open door to the cave. He managed to stagger backwards for a few steps, in Fay's grip all the while, before falling backwards into the cave, Fay on top of him. Thunder struck violently as the door slammed hard behind them.

CHAPTER 57: MOSES' QUEST

After a week or so, Cuthbert and Morgan were able to communicate quite well in a combination of improvised sign language and Cuthbert's attempts at the Brittonic tongue, made up of odd words and phrases he'd picked up before or learned from Morgan, and bits of Gaelic, which was at least closer than Northumbrian and occasionally seemed to strike home when Cuthbert pronounced it in a funny accent.

Morgan explained that she had found Cuthbert in the woods. She had been gathering firewood when she heard someone or something tearing noisily through the undergrowth. She had hidden herself until the crashing stopped with a thud, then found the trail of disturbed foliage and broken branches and followed it to find Cuthbert passed out, bloodied and bruised. Then she had followed the trail backwards, at a distance, to satisfy herself that no one or nothing was in pursuit, before returning to check he was alive. Having ascertained that he was – and that he had an honest face – she had returned to the hovel to summon her son Moses to carry him home. His wounds had been dangerous, she told him, but she believed her remedies were proving effective. It had been lucky Moses had been there to help at the time and not at the forge in Govan, though it was not exactly by chance, since he had returned to check his mother was safe. Bands of armed men had been roaming the countryside foraging or worse in the aftermath of the siege at Alt Clut. Men like Cuthbert. Before returning to Govan, Moses had left a club by the hearth and made his mother promise to clobber her patient without hesitation if he showed signs of misbehaving. As long as he did behave, it mattered little to Morgan that Cuthbert was an enemy soldier. She knew nothing of politics, and cared less.

Cuthbert still remembered nothing after the darkness that had descended over the Rock, and Morgan was not able to tell him much about what had happened, save that she understood there had been another battle not far from here after whatever had happened at the Rock. It seemed likely that Cuthbert had been involved in that battle too, and perhaps not on the winning side. That at least was what Morgan and her son had decided as Cuthbert had been slipping fitfully between sleep and delirium. Moses would perhaps be able to tell him more about events beyond the woods when he returned from Govan.

On his previous visit home, Moses had in fact explained to his mother that the Rock had fallen to the Picts, but uninterested as she was in politics, this information had not stuck. The Rock had not literally fallen into the sea, after all, and it was not clear she had even understood what Moses was talking about. In any case, that news was out of date. At the forge, the smith was now explaining to Moses that while the commanders of Alt Clut had had indeed surrendered the Rock to King Onuist, he had subsequently been forced to withdraw and retreat. Apparently there had been a rift between the Picts and the Northumbrians, or factions within one or the other or both. The details were hazy, but Dumnagual son of Teudebur was now being blamed for surrendering prematurely – having panicked in the face of the ill portent in the sky – while Rhodri had credit for seizing the opportunity to recover the Rock.

The smith was delighted, since his soon-to-be son-in-law's fortunes would surely follow those of his great uncle. Ieuan was alive and also in good spirits, despite having been injured in a skirmish amid the confusion when the Men of the Rock had retaken their stronghold. Indeed, he was now back home being nursed by his betrothed. And, reading between the lines of the smith's report, it seemed that tending Ieuan's wounds these past few days had awoken Martha's sense of matrimonial piety, perhaps even love. Moses could not wait to get back to his mother. He had been working unusually hard these past few days, so the smith was happy to let him go for a week.

When Moses got home, he was relieved to find his mother safe and sound, and intrigued to learn about her patient. Northumbrian, then. But Cuthbert had as many questions for Moses as the other way round. With a rather impatient Morgan 'interpreting' when needed, Cuthbert explained the political situation as he understood it. As to the battle in which it was assumed Cuthbert had been wounded, there were many rumours, but Moses was not even sure who the belligerents had been. Perhaps Cuthbert would remember when he was feeling better.

'He has your eyes,' Cuthbert told Morgan when her son went outside to make some overdue repairs to the hovel's roof.

Morgan laughed, 'It's nice of you to say so, and I'd like to think it's true. But you know I didn't give birth to him myself.' She mimed a pregnant belly and then shook her finger to indicate her meaning. 'Moses came to me another way.' She pointed outside, and then mimed herself spying something and picking it up. 'I found him in a basket on the river,' she went on, holding the imaginary baby to her breast and smiling radiantly at the memory. For the first time, it struck Cuthbert that Morgan was very beautiful. But of course, as he processed the timing, that thought was overtaken by another. By a realisation, or at least a very definite and excited speculation.

'Moses is the missing baby!' he gasped.

Morgan cocked her head. 'Moses is what now?'

That evening, Cuthbert told Morgan and Moses the story he had learned from Domnall and Fergus. There were many 'aaah's and 'sooo's as the details dovetailed, and by the time Cuthbert had finished, no one was in any doubt that Moses was indeed the missing baby.

'How strange!' Morgan said. 'Who would ever have imagined that Moses had another mother before me? God never ceases to amaze with his mysterious ways.'

'Indeed,' said Cuthbert, glancing at Moses, who was looking into the fire thoughtfully.

Then Cuthbert produced his silver coin, prompting Morgan to produce one of the scraps of silver she'd taken from the hoard before it had been stolen. They were far from identical, but similar enough in size and hue to make you think.

'So where did yours come from?' Morgan asked.

'That's another story,' Cuthbert said, 'but I think you should take it. I owe you my life, after all.'

Morgan refused, but Cuthbert secretly resolved to give his coin to Moses before leaving.

The young man had not said anything since Cuthbert had finished the story, and now Morgan realised why not. 'You must go to Iona, of course,' she told him.

'She might be dead by now,' Moses pointed out. 'She might never even have got there.'

'Yes,' said Morgan, 'but you always wanted to go to Iona when you were a boy. Do you remember? And now you have another reason to go.' He said nothing, so she continued, 'I don't know how long it will take to get to Iona, or what kind of adventures you will have on the way, or on the way back, so let me say this here and now. If you ever have a daughter, you must bring her to me so I can talk to her about what to expect. But if you should have a daughter after I am gone, you must talk to her yourself. It's been known to skip a generation before, especially when men are involved. Do you understand?'

Moses nodded. 'I will come back,' he said.

'Of course you will, son.'

'With or without a granddaughter for you,' he added with a smile.

Cuthbert was silent, trying not to intrude as waves of emotion surged between mother and son. He had thoughts of his own to ponder. After all, Moses was not the only one who had always wanted to go to Iona. Cuthbert looked again at the silver coin in his hand and was transported back twenty years to when he was just a little younger than Moses was now and having his first adventure with his Gaelic friends. He had made up his mind then to visit Iona, only to have his plans thwarted, or to lose his nerve; he couldn't remember now. But perhaps it was not too late. He waited for what seemed like a suitable moment before chiming in, mostly to Morgan: 'I could go with him. Teach him a bit a Gaelic on the way.' Then to Moses, 'If you like?'

'Oh, yes,' said Morgan, before Moses could answer. 'I would like that very much.'

They both looked at Moses, who was looking at the fire again, thinking it over. 'Do you know the way?' he asked at last.

'I nearly went once before. I'm pretty sure I can find the way again,' said Cuthbert.

'Well, then. Let's go together.'

CHAPTER 58: OLD FRIENDS

The monk who arrived at Bamburgh on the heels of Ethel and Freia, and left with Wilfrid's war band, had led the men in prayer before the first day's assault on Alt Clut, but not of course taken part in the fighting. He was much more valuable the next day, as a source of spiritual succour and reassurance when the darkness descended. But after the Men of the Rock surrendered, he did not follow his Northumbrian countrymen on the journey home. So unlike Wilfrid – and unlike Cuthbert, though Cuthbert had forgotten it for now – he had not been with the supposedly triumphant Northumbrian army that was ambushed. That was because he had stayed in the camp of his original countrymen, the People of the Designs. The monk, of course, was Brother Martin, the historian from Wearmouth-Jarrow, and he was in the camp looking for the man who bore the name that had stirred him from his life there. King Brude.

When news of the ambush reached the slowly dispersing camp of the supposedly triumphant People of the Designs, there was chaos. Nobody was quite sure who had ambushed whom. Some said the defeated Men of the Rock had rallied to take revenge on the Northumbrians, others that the Northumbrians had traitorously attacked the People of the Designs themselves as they returned northeast in easily manageable numbers. Few comprehended the more surprising truth that while the ambushed army had indeed been that of the Northumbrians, the aggressors belonged to a renegade force of the People of Designs, led by – of course – King Brude.

Nevertheless, it was clear the peace had been short-lived, because whether by design or simply seizing an opportunity, the Men of the Rock were certainly rallying now, having launched several lightning raids on retreating Pictish troops (further confusing the rumours) before sending a delegation to demand the return of their stronghold. Having lost his allies and the shape of his own forces, King Onuist had barely made himself comfortable in the fortress of the Rock before being forced into a strategic withdrawal. Fresh from attacking the Northumbrians, King Brude and his forces then rejoined Onuist's forces as they withdrew, and added even more confusion by sowing conflicting accounts of what had happened and their part in it. (Indeed, many of the ordinary soldiers had no idea what the fight had been about.) When the retreating army made its first camp, a safe distance from Alt Clut, Brude's keeper Bishop Boniface was summoned to King Onuist's tent to provide an authoritative account for the court. Chaos indeed.

The unremarkable looking monk inveigled his way into that session of the court by telling the guards he was Boniface's secretary, but emerged none the wiser about what had actually happened. At least he knew King Brude was back with the main army, however, so he discretely shadowed Boniface until the bishop saw fit to visit his king's tent, which was more impressive than Brother Martin had expected. Then he circled the tent two or three times to gather his thoughts and avoid arriving on Boniface's heels, before slipping in more or less unnoticed, since King Brude evidently did not feel the need for guards.

It took Martin a few seconds to adjust to the darkness of the tent after broad daylight outside, and it was smoky too, but there was no mistaking the king, sitting at the back of the tent on a large stool that served as a throne, with the bishop perched on a smaller stool at his side, whispering intently in his ear. Perhaps a dozen retainers stood around the fire in the centre of the tent, while a few servants pottered about. Brother Martin watched for a couple of minutes before identifying the king's steward, and approached him to request an audience, causing a couple of retainers to turn and look the monk up and down. The steward told him to wait and then went about his business, but he was obviously alert to the matter, because as soon as the bishop had finished whispering, and the king seemed free, he approached him to announce the visitor. King Brude shrugged and looked up half-heartedly as his steward called the visitor forward, and suddenly all eyes were on the monk.

'My greetings to the man they call King Brude,' he began, causing some of the retainers to shift uncomfortably, but the man in question remained slouched in his throne and was barely paying attention. 'I stand before you a humble monk,' he went on, 'but though I have served the church in Northumbria for some twenty years, that is not why I am here. My fellow monks call me Brother Martin, but I wish to introduce myself to the king and his court by a different and older name.'

The monk's portentous manner caused some amused muttering among the retainers

'My name is Donuel,' he continued, 'They used to call be Donuel the Cunning, but that is of no account. What matters is that I am of noble blood, with a noble lineage on both sides. And as a noble, I challenge the right of this ill-bred upstart Brude to call himself king, and especially to claim kingship over my family's ancestral lands. I'd like to know who exactly the scoundrel thinks he is.'

There were gasps of – mostly amused – disbelief. King Brude himself sat bolt upright when he realised what the stranger was saying, and then craned his neck to get a better look at this monk in the smoky gloom of the tent. Then he began to laugh, uncertainly at first, but then the stranger also began laughing, even as he stood heroically with his legs apart and his hands on his hips, and Brude lost all control and began laughing uproariously, bent over in his throne. In an instant, the stranger too was bent double, heaving for breath between great guffaws. Half the court joined in, so infectious was the two men's laughter. The other half seemed immune, perhaps because they were looking at Bishop Boniface, who was not laughing at all.

King Brude managed to recover himself just long enough to utter the words: 'You, my good man, are not Donuel the Cunning!'

The monk drew himself up as solemnly as he could and demanded: 'How can you be so sure?'

'Because,' said the king, '*I* am Donuel the Cunning!'

Gasps of sheer astonishment this time.

'I am the one with noble blood,' continued Donuel the Cunning, 'and you, sir, are the ill-bred upstart!'

More hilarity, but this time just the nobleman and the upstart, whichever was which. Then the monk made a show of scratching his head to ponder this suggestion, before raising his finger suddenly and exclaiming, 'Come to think of it, I think you might be right! In which case, why am I not sitting where you are, in the upstart throne?'

Still laughing, the man on the throne stood up and theatrically offered his place to his usurper. Bishop Boniface also stood, but he was yielding nothing: he glared furiously at his misbehaving king. Anyway, the monk showed no interest in claiming the throne, so its former incumbent bounded over to him instead, and the two old friends embraced warmly, as the king's retainers looked at one another in bewilderment. Boniface summoned the king's steward with a furious gesture, and hissed, 'Find Constantine! And get him here now!' The steward duly made off in haste.

Meanwhile, King Brude, or Donuel the Cunning, or whoever he was now, gestured to his men that all was well, and they began reassuring one another that it was all a joke between friends, as those friends made for the exit. ‘We’re going for a walk!’

CHAPTER 59: THE RETURN OF THE LOST

During the journey to Iona, it became increasingly obvious that Cuthbert had not made as full a recovery as everyone had hoped. Often he seemed to struggle to walk because of the pain, but he brushed off Moses' concerns and refused to stop or even slow down. He insisted he felt better every day, but the wound in his side continued to weep. Every night when he thought Moses was asleep, he removed his bandage to inspect it, and it gave off a worrying smell. When they finally reached the sea after several days, he splashed the wound with salty water and grimaced with pain, not fleetingly but for several minutes after the water's impact, biting his knuckle when the pain did not quickly pass. 'That's better,' he told Moses, not very convincingly, when he regained his composure. Then, during the passage, Moses watched him take deep breaths of the briny air, as if still convinced that salt was his salvation. Once on the island, though, Cuthbert almost instantly abandoned the pretence that all was well, and Moses enlisted the help of a monk who had come over with them to half-lead and half-carry the patient to the monastery's tiny infirmary. As soon as he was able to lie flat, Cuthbert passed out, and the surgeon was summoned to examine him.

Moses left his friend in the elderly surgeon's care and said a prayer for him. What else could he do? He would have done whatever he could for Cuthbert, who might indeed have become something of a father figure to him, except that his mind was on his mother. His other mother. In a few prepared Gaelic phrases, supplemented with halting schoolboy Latin, he told the monk who had helped him why he had come to Iona, and asked where he should go.

The monk laughed, and then apologised. 'I know what to do with the sick and wounded,' he said, 'but the long-lost, grown-up son of one of our sisters? That's a new one on me. I'll take you to the Abbot's secretary.'

'That's quite a story,' said the Abbot's secretary, not exactly sceptically, but perhaps not completely convinced either. He bade the monk take Moses to the pilgrims' hostel. When monastic routine allowed, he would consult his counterpart, the Abbess' secretary, and find out if Moses' long-lost mother was indeed among the nuns.

It was late that evening, by monastic standards, that the Abbess' secretary herself came to the pilgrims' hostel to ask for Moses. He was directed to a bench just outside, where a lamp had been lit to compensate for the setting of the sun. The Abbess' secretary stood up from the bench as he approached, and drew back her hood.

Young Sister Lucky was sure there was something familiar about the patient she had been asked to tend, but equally sure she had never met him before. She had known very few men, of course. He did not look like anyone in the village she had once called home. Nor did he look anything like any of the monks she knew here on Iona, and with whom she very rarely interacted anyway. Looking at Cuthbert's naked, wounded side, she thought naturally enough of Jesus Christ himself, but that was not it either. Her life was a life lived among women, her sisters in Christ. But that was it. She looked again at Cuthbert's face. He was half-asleep, but there was something about the way his lips twitched and pursed unconsciously that made her think of her mentor, Sister Mary Brigid. Now she had seen it, the resemblance was remarkable.

If Moses had been introduced to the Abbess' secretary in any other context, he would have thought nothing of it. She had a familiar enough face – two eyes, a nose, a smiling mouth – but it was hardly like looking in a mirror. Would she have recognised her long-lost son? It would have been nice to think so, but it would not have seemed fair to insist on it, to judge her harshly for not seeing that this strange young man was the baby she had given up twenty years before. 'I do see your father in you,' she said after a while. 'Yes, the way your nose joins your brow, I see it now.'

She spoke to Moses in his own language, his mother tongue indeed. And yet, even before she began to unfold her story, his story, it struck Moses that her accent was not like his other mother's, or like that of anyone in Govan. He wondered if that were because she had been on Iona for so long now, but it turned out there was another reason. Moses' birth mother was not a native Briton but in fact Pictish. So Moses was half Pictish, by birth at least. But that was not the half of it.

'Your name is... was... Dyfnwal,' she told him by way of an opening. 'It would have been Prince Dyfnwal, indeed, since you are heir to the kingdom of Rheged.'

'Rheged? But Rheged was annexed by Northumbria a century ago.'

'Yes. I'm sorry I don't have a kingdom to bequeath you, son.'

Moses began laughing, and his mother joined in, before crossing herself in answer to some hidden instinct, glancing sadly at the setting sun, and continuing her story.

As Moses clearly knew, Rheged had been a Brittonic kingdom to the south of that ruled from Alt Clut (in what later became England). It transpired that Moses' father had been born and raised in Northumbria proper, the notional heir to the throne of its western province, or perhaps one of several notional heirs; it had been a moot point until Northumbria's King Ceolwulf had abdicated in favour of his cousin, the present king, in order to retire to Lindisfarne. This move had created a great deal of instability, as various rivals thought to make their own moves for the throne before Eadberht could consolidate his position. Everyone and anyone with a royal claim, however dubious or partial, was considered overnight to be in play, and Moses' father, though never a serious contender for the Northumbrian throne, was quickly murdered. That left his wife, a Pictish princess in her own right, holding a baby with a price on its head.

Moses barely had time to take in the fact that his father – the man who had given him his nose and his brow and now apparently a stillborn title – had been murdered, before his new-original mother went on. It had been natural enough for her to flee north: north to her late husband's countrymen, still further north to her own people, or perhaps north and west to Dalriada. Had not the infant Oswald's mother taken him from Northumbria to Iona for much the same reason? That had worked out quite well. But Dyfnwal's would-be assassins were in hot pursuit. His mother did not know any relatives in Alt Clut well enough to trust them, so when she found shelter with the widow, she hatched her awful plan. Set off for Iona alone. Moses knew the rest.

Indeed, Moses knew – as his mother did not – how quickly the plan had diverged from what she had imagined. 'My name is Moses,' he began. He told her the story he himself had heard only recently from Cuthbert, of how the widow's daughter had put him on the river. And then the story he had been told so often by his first-true mother, of how she had found him and raised him as her own. And finally his own story, of his life in the woods, his life in Govan, studying Latin and the scriptures with Gawin and learning his trade with the smith. He did not mention Martha, who now belonged to someone else's story. That part was not required to make the Abbess' secretary weep, and then try to smile, and then sob uncontrollably until her long-lost son put his arm around her and she could simply shake in silence.

The next morning, Moses woke before dawn and crept from the huddle of pilgrims with whom he had spent the night. Stepping outside, he took deep breaths of the cold, sea air, yawned and stretched his limbs. And seeing the vast, starry sky, he gazed up and span around in wonder. And noticing the swirling sound of the sea, he listened intently. This place surely could not have been more different from the hot, stuffy darkness of the forge. Even in the dead of night, Moses was surrounded by the cold light of the stars, and in the distance he could even see them reflected on the shimmering sea. The sounds that came to him were distant and ever-present, a world away from the close-up, deliberate din of the forge, much of which emanated from his own efforts, just as the very light from the fire and hot metal was bought with the sweat of his own face. In contrast, this world was indifferent to Moses. Infinite. Unsettling. He fell on his knees, which squelched into wet turf so he became aware of the damp, earthy smell as he prayed. He thanked God for preserving his birth mother, and for allowing him to know the story of his origins, and he asked for the wisdom to know what – if anything – to do about it. He imagined God laughing at that, as he himself had laughed when told he was heir to a kingdom that was no more. Then he asked for forgiveness for his presumption. God only knows what – if anything – makes God laugh. On that note, wisdom would never be enough, so Moses asked God to fill him with love. After all, he had two mothers to love now. Then he prayed for his first-true mother and his new-original mother, and while he was at it, he prayed for Cuthbert. And then, not at all sure he had said all the prayers he should, he ended as usual with the Lord's Prayer to cover the rest.

He stood up and brushed the moisture from his knees before looking around him to identify higher ground where he might have a better view of the sea. Then he strode purposefully up the slope to his vantage point and gazed out at the vastness of the sea, turning to see it shimmering all around him. To the east, the first glimmer of the sun was appearing over the isle of Mull, whence he and Cuthbert had come the day before. He would go and see his friend when the day had properly asserted itself, tell him the missing part of his story, perhaps make plans for what to do next. Then Moses noticed the island's graveyard, a solemn presence in the distance. He made his way there, trudging over unexpectedly boggy terrain, so by the time he reached it the sunrise was well underway. He was drawn to an impressive gravestone with a Latin inscription. Here lay (another) King Brude of the Picts, son of Beli of the Britons, who had been committed to the ground many decades before. His most famous achievement had been the defeat of the Northumbrians at the Battle of the Loch of the Herons, where King Ecgfrith himself had fallen and then been brought to this same hallowed ground to await his vanquisher. Now the two kings lay together, awaiting their resurrection not as enemies, nor even as kings of the nations, but as brothers in Christ. Moses smiled to himself. On that day, by the grace of God, the sometime heir to the lost kingdom of Rheged would join them. All the Earthly kingdoms would be lost kingdoms, all the nations dissolved into one.

When Moses got the infirmary, it was too late. Cuthbert's body lay in the embrace of a nun, whose tear-drenched face was strangely familiar. Because, of course, it was Cuthbert's face, albeit more feminine and much less world-weary. 'You must be Moses,' she gulped.

'I am,' he said.

'Well, apparently, I am Cwenburh,' she said, switching from Gaelic to Latin, 'or I was a long time ago. Did Cuthbert tell you he had a twin sister?'

'No, he didn't,' Moses said, confused and perhaps a little hurt.

'Oh, he didn't know I was here. Only God knew that, and sent him to die in... to die in...' She choked up and pressed her face against that of her long-lost twin.

Moses was also in tears by now. How could he not be, watching this poor woman stricken with grief? His own grief would come only later. 'Did you have long with him?' he asked.

'A few hours,' she said. 'Long enough for him to tell me the story of how I was lost and for me to tell him the story of how I was found. Then we spoke a little of our lives. He told me your story too. Did you find your mother?'

'Yes,' Moses said, 'she is the Abbess' secretary.'

'Really?' gasped Sister Mary Brigid, forgetting for a second that she was Cwenburh.

They were both silent for a moment as their thoughts returned to the unhappy matter at hand.

'What will you do next?' the bereaved sister said at last.

'I don't know,' Moses said sadly.

So Cuthbert was buried on Iona, where his long-lost, at-last-found sister could tend his grave. And probably Moses sojourned there for a while before doing whatever he did next. That too is another story.

◆ ◆ ◆

Back on the mainland, a pair of squirrels scurried for cover as two horsemen rode through a forest clearing, singing merrily but not quite in tune. They rode south. One was a monk, and had somewhere he belonged. Sooner or later, Brother Martin was expected back in Wearmouth-Jarrow. But there was no particular rush, no need to take the fastest route even. After all, the other man, who had no name, was only coming along for the ride. God only knew what adventures might befall them on the long journey, what new life might await the nameless man. More stories for another time, perhaps.

Far to the north, a third man rode with far more speed and far greater purpose. Having bidden farewell to his old friends, and diplomatically extricated himself – at least for now – from the machinations of a very unhappy bishop,

Constantine longed for home, and his home for him: Dyrael, the twins, the whole extended family and the farm that made them who they were.

Not all that far from their farm as the crow flies, the crow in question perhaps noticed some human figures below it, walking and talking in the grounds between a small cluster of buildings. Monks, Priten among them. It had been many days since he had awoken in the cave, haunted by the most vivid and disturbing dream he could remember ever having. An epic confrontation with his past, a kind of reckoning even. He had got up and staggered in a daze to the little stream to wash himself and then lain for some time on the bank, remembering the dream and wondering. Shaking his head. 'No. Impossible.' Then he had taken to his knees and prayed for perhaps three or four hours before hauling himself to his feet and continuing on his way to the monastery, where he and latterly his young assistant Mark had been wrapped up in church business ever since. There would have been little to detain our crow here, since monks are notoriously parsimonious with their food, so on it no doubt flew, perhaps flapping under the path of an eagle soaring far above and travelling some distance before observing another human gathering on the gentle slopes of a distant glen.

Fay, wild-haired and wandering without much purpose, as she had been for many days, noticed the crowd assembled on a hillside where she and her sister priestesses had often performed in their bardic pomp. This crowd had gathered to listen to someone address them as he stood on a wooden box at the bottom of the slope. She wandered over and sat down to listen at the edge of the crowd. It seemed the man was a Christian preacher, so she did not expect to be impressed. He did not even wear an impressive gold crucifix like the bishop she had once encountered at a royal wedding, the bishop who had once been her uncle, or Euphemia's uncle. The preacher wore a tattered robe more suited to a crippled old beggar. This man was nothing like Euphemia's uncle, nothing like a prince of the church as Euphemia had been brought up to understand it. He exuded neither power nor authority, not even charisma. He simply mumbled away, and that too with some kind of speech impediment, or perhaps the hint of a foreign accent. Fay let her guard down, laying back on her elbows to let the sun caress her face as the man's fables and ghost stories washed over her. There was a sense of calm and warmth among the people gathered on the slope, making it a comfortable place to be, to rest, to breathe. Some lay back casually like Fay; others gazed intensely at the preacher, eager not to miss a word. All, even Fay, shared the peculiar sense that the preacher was simultaneously addressing the whole crowd and him or her personally.

When the preacher had finished, the crowd slowly rose and dispersed, smiling warmly at one another as they parted, and at Fay, who remained lying on the grass, tired out. She acknowledged them with a smile of her own or a gentle nod, but she avoided looking at the preacher, who was in any case surrounded by people who wanted to greet him in person, to thank him, to touch him. Fay wanted to do none of those things. In time, the preacher was led away to be fed and rested in someone's home. Fay remained on the slope, her attention now drawn to the loch that lay in the distance, to the sky, the mountains.

Unaccountably, she knew two things suddenly and certainly. First, she was pregnant, carrying Priten's child. And secondly, she believed in Jesus Christ. She belonged to him in a way she had never belonged to her erstwhile, Earthly Master. She was a Christian, albeit a pregnant and unmarried Christian. How had that happened? And what could the erstwhile Sacred Virgin do but laugh out loud?

Far away, at the other end of the long, gently winding loch, one of the many young men who had once been infatuated with the Sacred Virgin sat on another hillside, gently tapping away at his latest creation. Pyrdie had recently returned home for a while from the monastery, which had become too frantic with activity for his liking since the summit had got underway. Now he was joined by his cousin Peter, who had just finished his day's farm work. Peter sat by Pyrdie and looked at the stone he was carving. 'Is that the old symbol for the return of the lost?' he asked.

'It is, or at least my version of it.'

'Do you have anyone in particular in mind?'

'Not really. But do you remember our grandfather's story about the boy on the loch?'

'Oh, the long-lost Prince Cargil, you mean? Riding his kelpie through the mist?'

Pyrdie smiled. 'Yes, Prince Cargil and his kelpie.' He looked thoughtfully out at the loch. The sun was beginning to set and its light played uncannily upon the surface of the water. 'I think the world is stranger and more wonderful than we know.'

'Yes, Pyrdie,' agreed Peter. 'You know, I think you're right. And the best part is that God only knows what will happen next.'

ABOUT THE AUTHOR

Dolan Cummings

Dolan is the author of two previous novels. A selection of his essays and other writing can be found at dolancummings.com.

BOOKS BY THIS AUTHOR

That Existential Leap: A Crime Story

Part bildungsroman and part psychological thriller, That Existential Leap is a novel of ideas about the struggle for self-realisation and belonging in the postmodern West.

Gehenna: A Novel Of Hell And Earth

Glasgow detective DCI Alexander is led on a journey through Hell... Dante's Hell seen through the prism of his own city, and populated by historical figures and characters from literature as well as those he knows from his own world.

Printed in Great Britain
by Amazon

22940691R00209